WEREGIRL: TYPHON

C. D. Bell

CHOOSECO

WAITSFIELD, VERMONT

Book design: Stacey Boyd, Big Eyedea Visual Design
Cover design: Dot Greene, Greene Dot Design

For information regarding permission, write to:

CHOOSECO
P.O. Box 46
Waitsfield, Vermont 05673
www.weregirl.com

ISBN 10 1-937133-60-5
ISBN 13 978-1-937133-60-3

Published simultaneously in the United States and Canada
Printed in the United States

10 9 8 7 6 5 4 3 2 1

To all courageous teens experimenting with new ways to define yourselves and shape the world—this book is for you.

"I have often thought that with any luck at all I could have been born a werewolf."

— Shirley Jackson,
We Have Always Lived in the Castle

CHAPTER ONE

*D*ressed for a run, Nessa set out at a jog, heading
down the blacktop in front of her father's house, past the carefully landscaped greenery and the turnoff for the airstrip.
It was high summer, the early morning cool and bright, the
birds filling the encroaching woods with shrieking songs, the
Chimera Corp. campus otherwise deserted.

Good, Nessa thought. She'd been putting off this trip for
weeks and didn't want anything to get in the way of her going

now.

Quickening her pace, she passed the pristine laboratory—the heart and soul of the company her father had founded. The building's simple appearance camouflaged a world-class research facility descending many stories into the earth, housing lab after lab dedicated to her father's experiments in genetic recombination.

As she turned left away from the lab, Nessa noted the change in the road surface—the blacktop gave way to gravel, and then to old dirt logging roads that headed north into the wilds of Daniel Host's forest preserve. She felt her shoulders relax as the stones crunched beneath her feet.

The air changed too. There was something cool and damp and piney that traveled over mountain streams and across loamy soil, picking up the tastes and smells of the ever-present, life-giving decay and carrying the cool, damp earth straight into Nessa's bloodstream.

Breathing in the musk of the forest, Nessa felt the familiar twitch. Without slowing, she became aware of her toes expanding into paws, her ears pricking with new sensitivity, her arms stretching at the elbow. She dropped to all fours. She lengthened her stride and arched her neck, shaking from the tip of her nose down through her paws and the base of her tail. She left the road and broke into the underbrush, keeping to the places where she knew there were blind spots in the Chimera Corp. security camera views of the forest floor.

Wolves can maintain speeds of twenty-five miles an hour

when moving at a full-on sprint, and Nessa was fast, even for a wolf. It wouldn't be long before she reached her destination. Running felt so good, she considered running right past the place she was heading. It was such a beautiful morning for a run ... why waste it?

She knew why. She had to do this. It had been her mother's dying wish. Reach this creature and protect her.

Nessa shuddered. Caged in a secret lab, the creature was her father's best-kept secret. His best kept chimera. His daughter.

Nessa's sister.

Vivian had made Nessa promise to look after her, but it had been three weeks, and Nessa had barely been able to stand looking *for* her.

She had been procrastinating, making up excuses. But now, Nessa was on her way.

To be clear, Nessa told herself as she ran, this new sister was not a sister the way Delphine was. She wasn't like Delphine, who Nessa had shared a room with, helped with homework, fought over bathroom access, managed sweater thefts. In the family Nessa had grown up in, Nate was the youngest and the most demanding of their mother's care. Delphine and Nessa were close. Nessa had been her protector. She'd been the one to tell Delphine it was cool to like computers even if girls in their school were pushed out of coding classes in eighth grade.

Once in elementary school, when a boy was teasing

Delphine about not having a father, Nessa had shoved the boy against a brick wall, and got a detention because she'd been in sixth grade then and should have known better. She remembered the look on Delphine's face after the boy had hit the wall and slid down onto his butt. Delphine had looked scared, like Nessa had shoved *her*. What would Delphine look like if she ever were to see this other sister—the one their mother had never mentioned, just as she'd never told them about their father?

This new sister was a monster, born in a lab, the result of a human-bat-pig-deer splice her father had created sixteen years before. Worse: she had been created using Delphine's genetic material. What was human of the monster could have been Delphine's twin. When Nessa had first seen the lab creation, she'd been sure the monster *was* Delphine.

Now, Nessa shook from the tip of her nose to the base of her tail, feeling her fur release dust and absorb the damp. She sniffed, searching for signs of the secret outpost lab she'd found when she'd been visiting her father the previous spring. This lab was unmarked on maps, buried under the cover of trees. Nessa had stumbled upon it while running.

She knew when she reached it again, though the smell was muted and different somehow. Almost buried.

Had the fence changed? Nessa didn't remember it being so high. Admittedly, her memory of the building wasn't great.

When she'd come before, the Delphine chimera had chased Nessa out in a jealous rage, after tearing down the metal bars that kept her confined. If Nessa hadn't transformed into a wolf, she had no idea what the Delphine chimera might have done to her.

"Good . . . kitty," Nessa said now, stopping to assess the new fence in all its glory—eight feet high, electrified, and topped with razor wire. And then, as she looked at it, the fence in her vision changed from thin, gray, crisscrossing chain to a shimmering miasma of silver and pewter and copper and yellow tones.

Ugh, Nessa thought. *Not now.*

She squeezed her eyes closed and willed the sensation away, leaning against a tree for a moment. She'd been having episodes like this often. She described them to herself as "color storms," where the colors in her vision separated, abstracted, splintered. It was crazy annoying—and sometimes—she thought she was *going* crazy, that the stress of the past few months was getting to her. Other times, she wondered if she was going blind. Now, thankfully, when she opened her eyes again, her vision was back to normal.

Nessa paced the perimeter of the fence, finding the gate she'd passed through before. The fence was new, but this gate looked just as Nessa remembered it. Hoping that the access code had not changed, Nessa transformed into human state and approached the keypad. There were some things humans could do better than wolves, and punching numbers on a keypad was one of them.

To her surprise, the gate whirred and clicked into motion, sliding open.

Not up to Chimera Corp. security snuff, Nessa thought, but that thought was interrupted as the colors of the gravel road started to shimmer. Nessa looked up into the trees and thought she saw a purple orb shimmering behind the green leaves. She took a deep breath to slow her heart rate. She looked again. The orb was gone.

Passing through the now-open gate, she headed for the lab, noting that the grass was high and the parking lot looked like it hadn't been driven across or walked on in months—weeds were growing up through the asphalt. Had it been like that when she was here before?

Maybe. But the door had not been unlocked that time and it was now.

Pushing through it, Nessa entered the kitchen. One of the creepier aspects of the Delphine chimera lab was that it had been set up to look like a suburban house. As if, at one point, someone had tried to make the Delphine chimera feel like she really was human.

Only the house was clearly unoccupied by a family, in a way that underscored the monster's loneliness more than even the most clinical of laboratory settings would have done.

And now, this "kitchen" was even more depressing than it had been originally. Then, it had been clear that it was a kitchen where no one cooked or ate, and no one talked on the phone.

It was a kitchen where no one had arguments or read the mail or opened the window to get rid of the smell of something that had burned. Nessa had seen that all the food the creature ate was brought by her caretakers who grumbled about having to spend even twenty minutes with her. But now the kitchen wasn't just unused—it had been stripped—all signs of even trying to pretend it was operational removed. It reminded Nessa of her old house back in Tether, which had been packed up and sold just a month before Nessa, Delphine, and Nate had moved out West.

Running a finger over the kitchen counter, she wondered how long this room had been abandoned. Her blood ran cold. Her mother had begged Nessa to protect the chimera version of Delphine, and Nessa had delayed.

She headed into the front hall, where there was a backlit digital photo of a yard through a fake "window" next to a fake front door. Those were still in place, though the light inside the window was out.

By the time Nessa reached the bedroom in the back, where she'd found the chimera behind bars, she was not surprised to find the room emptied as well. Even the bars in the doorway were gone.

Where had the chimera gone?

Was the chimera removed because someone knew Nessa had broken in and seen her?

Nessa looked for signs of the bars that had formerly blocked the room off. She remembered how scared she'd been when the chimera had shaken the bars free and come after her. They had fought: Nessa as a wolf, the chimera a hybrid of so many creatures.

Had that been caught on the surveillance cameras? Chimera Corp. used flat, disc-shaped interior cameras that lay flush with the wall. Once you knew how to spot them, you saw that they were everywhere.

Bingo. Nessa found a few cameras inside the room where the Delphine chimera had been caged. But these cameras looked different—larger, more obvious. Perhaps an earlier generation of technology?

Maybe when the Delphine chimera was younger, she'd been less dangerous? Maybe they'd given her full access to the house? And then, as she began to show more violent tendencies, they'd had to increase the security, adding bars, building up the fence? Nessa wondered if the older cameras were even recording now.

But if they weren't—if this particular cage had been abandoned when it became too insecure, and all the systems shut down—where had the creature gone?

Retracing her steps, returning to fresh air, Nessa winced with guilt at how relieved she was to be out of the house, not to have to confront the creature. Her mother had asked her to look after the chimera. Her mother had called the chimera Nessa's sister, elevating her from science experiment gone wrong to family.

And now, not only was Nessa failing in her attempt to check

in on the chimera, she was starting to wonder if her interference had caused the chimera's removal.

Pushing a hand into her hair, Nessa looked up at the sky and then out into the trees. The day was warming up—it was going to be hot. In fact, the air was already shimmering.

Except that wasn't the air that was shimmering, Nessa realized, dropping her hand, squinting into the woods. It was the trees. Like she had put on impressionist-painter goggles, she was seeing the trees not as trees but as tree-shaped objects, glowing with orbs of light. The orbs were pulsating, shifting, splitting into all colors of the rainbow, each one a puzzle of pieces that didn't so much fit together as bleed and flicker, like fish scales turned iridescent under water or a rainbow fading into wispy tendrils of color in a clearing sky.

Nessa squeezed her eyes closed. But still, she was seeing them. Colors that should not be there. Colors so intense her eyes hurt.

CHAPTER TWO

*B*ack when she was living in Tether, waiting out the end of the school year, Nessa had at first barely registered that colors had seemed brighter, more vibrant. It was stress, she'd assumed. After all, she'd been through a trauma.

Or traumas with an *s*. That's what her best friend Bree had called Nessa's losing her mom and her boyfriend, Luc, in the same week and getting ready to move in with her dad, whom she'd never even heard of until a few weeks before her mom passed away.

Whatever.

Back then, Nessa hadn't wanted to think about it. She hadn't wanted to waste energy griping about "trauma" and "stress." She knew she just had to get through. To look out for her younger brother and sister. To try to figure out what her mom had meant, encouraging them all to live with Daniel—Delphine and Nessa's dad—the man Vivian fled when they were still too young to remember.

It had all been a lot to take in. So the fact that the green in the newly leafed trees Nessa ran past every day during track practice were positively pulsing with greenness? That hadn't exactly been priority number one.

Except what she thought of as the "color storms" got worse. Soon, it wasn't just a brighter green tree. It was a tree so green Nessa could no longer make out its shape behind the green. In dappled sunshine, the tree became a migraine-inducing, moving kaleidoscope of yellows and chartreuses and shamrocks and seafoams; pickles, pines, olives, emeralds, and sages; daffodils, lemons, golds, bananas, dandelions, mustards, and squashes.

By the time June came and school ended, and Daniel had loaded the three kids onto an Amtrak Superliner sleeper car for a five-day cross-country train trip, Nessa was having color-enhanced episodes several times a day.

As Daniel and Nate explored the train, rode between the cars, and visited the engineer, Delphine glared into her phone, and Nessa stared through the glass-domed observation car, each new vista compounding her sense that something terrible was happening. Two things, actually: (1) She was probably going blind, and (2) this new version of her family was a disaster. "Are you enjoying this?" Daniel asked the kids every night at dinner—he'd planned the trip for Nate, a train obsessive, but had expected it to be a time of bonding for all four of them.

His question was routinely greeted by silence. Nate didn't like to talk about feelings—he couldn't, really. Delphine's only feeling seemed to be anger. She'd been talking about boredom in an aggrieved tone even before they'd come aboard. And Nessa didn't know how to explain what torture the train ride was for her without letting the panic she was feeling come through.

They ate, for the most part, in silence, and spent the days, for the most part, by themselves.

Nessa had seen how hard Daniel was trying. Before they'd left, he'd asked Delphine what she was looking at on her phone and when she showed him a slime-making video, he'd surprised her by having a slime-making station set up in the dining car, complete with two kinds of glue and a rainbow assortment of glitter. Delphine had only offered a weak, "Slime's over now," and not tried it out.

In the observation car, Nessa passed the hours alongside travelers who were gazing at the passing landscape, reading, knitting, sleeping, talking. Nessa began to see colors taking form *inside* the car—a cloud of color that seemed to hang in the room like cigarette smoke, shifting and seeping in and out of hair and skin, glowing orange then green, then blue, then gray.

The colors were occasionally useful. At the end of a day that two sixteen-year-old twins had spent playing cards and flirting with Delphine, a fight broke out over which one had cheated at hearts. Nessa had pointed to the twin with the annoying coral necklace and said, "It was you. Just be a man and say so." She didn't wonder for even a second if she was right. Every time coral necklace boy looked at his hand, a strong yellow light had pulsed around him, the way rain clouds look before a storm. Nessa just knew.

Nessa had hoped that the colors would abate in Oregon, but they'd only been getting worse. So had Delphine's moods. She'd been lashing out at Daniel and Nessa and sometimes even at Nate. She'd lost weight and dark circles had appeared under her eyes. Opening Delphine's closet door a few mornings ago to pull out her sister's hiking boots—Delphine kept disappearing into the woods, taking long solitary walks, and Nessa was trying to insist that she at least wear the right gear—Nessa had found a stash of food: rolls she recognized from dinner; a box of fancy crackers; apples from the kitchen; bizarrely, a lemon; and half a pie that James, the cook, had accusingly teased Daniel about midnight-snacking on when he'd noticed that it was gone. Was this hoarding connected to the nightmares Delphine was having? On the train west, they'd shared a sleeping compartment, and Delphine's cries had woken Nessa more than once. She'd been hearing Delphine crying out through the wall that separated their rooms in Daniel's house as well.

"What is all this?" Nessa said.

Delphine had had her head under the pillow when Nessa first opened the closet door, but she must have sensed Nessa's discovery. When Nessa turned, her sister was standing there in her tank top and pj shorts. She took a few quick strides into her en suite bathroom and slid the door closed behind her. If it had been anything but a pocket door, Nessa assumed Delphine would have slammed it. "Leave my closet alone."

"Jeez! Okay," said Nessa, then tried to break the tension with a joke. "But at least eat the pie if you're not going to let anyone else have some."

Delphine had not laughed. "I just want to get out of here," she said through the bathroom door. Nessa could hear that she was crying. "This place creeps me out. Daniel creeps me out. I want to go back to Aunt Jane's. I was okay there."

Nessa sat on the bed, feeling helpless. All spring, Delphine had been asking, "Why?" when Nessa insisted that going to live with Daniel would be good for them.

Nessa wanted to tell Delphine everything she knew—about the chimera, her promise to their mother to look out for her. For a year, Bree had been prodding Nessa to tell Delphine about Nessa's lupine transformation. Nate had seen Nessa turn into a wolf once, and never spoken of it again. It was time, Nessa knew, that Delphine found out as well.

She'd meant to tell her sister. She'd thought it would come up on the train. She'd thought it would come up once they got here. But now, Delphine was so angry, she wasn't sure she could even trust her with the secrets she had to share.

CHAPTER THREE

The run in the woods had taken longer than she thought it would. Returning to Daniel's house after searching for the Delphine chimera, Nessa was rushing, on the edge of becoming late for the shift she worked at the lab. She still took the time to FaceTime Bree. Nessa was itching to tell her about her visit to the Delphine chimera's empty lab, but this was Bree, so first things first: clothes.

Bree was about to start an internship with David Bergen,

the journalist who had most closely followed the Paravida case back in Tether, and she was trying on outfits. She had laid out a business suit with a short skirt (too corporate), a pair of jeans and an old sweater (what David Bergen generally wore), and something in between—slacks and a pretty silk blouse (the winner).

"He said I'm going to be spending a lot of time at the courthouse, the police precinct, and, if I'm *lucky*, the morgue," Bree said. She wrinkled her pleasingly round, freckled face at Nessa, bringing the phone so close to her nose that everything pixelated and blurred—one of her favorite tricks. "Do you think he was kidding?"

"No," said Nessa. "I don't." She knew Daniel Bergen. He was the one who persisted with the Paravida investigation when no one else was covering it. "He doesn't mess around."

Bree nodded, holding up a necklace against the blouse, then shaking her head.

"Have you heard anything from Isle Royale?" Nessa asked. She knew she asked Bree this every time they spoke, but she had to know. Trolling the internet, Nessa had learned that the scientists who studied the wolf population on this island in Lake Superior were pretty sure the new wolves moving in were the remainder of the packs of escaped, genetically altered Paravida wolves that had been mixing into the local wolf population around Tether. And it wasn't just the Paravida wolves. Scanning a picture taken from a helicopter and posted in a chat room, Nessa had identified a wolf who looked like Luc.

The question "Was it him?" still haunted her. Luc and Nessa had been separated trying to help the Paravida wolves escape, and she had not seen him since. She'd assumed he was dead, but still didn't want to believe it.

"Sorry, nothing new," Bree said. "But in other news, I looked on your dad's company website, and that guy Gabriel? He's adorable. You're saying he's the one who asked you to go hear some music last spring?"

"I knew I was going to regret telling you that story," Nessa said.

"You're blushing."

"Check your Wi-Fi signal," Nessa said. "I am so *not* blushing. I just got back from exercising. And Gabriel only asked me because I think my dad told him to or something."

"No!"

"Seriously," Nessa said. "I'm pretty sure that's true." She laughed, because it sounded even more pathetic out loud. One of the downsides of living in a remote laboratory in the woods? The only other people around were scientists. The closest kid her age, besides her siblings, was a nine-year-old. "But listen, I have to tell you, I finally went for that run we were talking about."

Bree knew enough about the surveillance systems at Chimera Corp. not to name names when talking about the Delphine chimera. But she nodded vigorously. "Did you, um . . . find . . . what you were looking for?" she asked.

"Sort of," Nessa said. She tried to think of a way to say what she needed to say next in code. And then gave up. It was too hard. "The building was there, but empty."

"For real?" Bree asked. She had her face up close to the phone again so all Nessa could see were the pixelated browns and pinks of her skin, but this time she wasn't doing it to be silly. "Where did ... everybody ... it? ... go?"

"She," Nessa corrected. "It almost feels like, I don't know, like Dad got rid of her."

"He wouldn't!" Bree said.

Nessa nodded. "I know," she said. "Maybe she had to go out for a bit and she'll be back?"

"Where would she go?" Bree asked. "Like, the dentist?"

The idea seemed so absurd that Nessa couldn't help but laugh.

CHAPTER FOUR

fter rushing off the call with Bree, Nessa hopped into the shower. She was *really* late now, but it was impossible not to stop and enjoy the shower's perfectly calibrated pressure and the steam coming from the base of the shower stall. With shampoo lathered into her hair, Nessa forgot the stress of the morning and caught herself staring out the floor-to-ceiling window, looking over the canopy of trees. She willed the greens and browns and grays to fragment themselves, for the world to

twist into a shapeless kaleidoscope. But there was nothing.

Wrenching at the faucet to get the water to stop flowing, Nessa pulled a tank top and a pair of clean shorts from her drawer, grabbed a sweater because of the air conditioning, snagged her lab ID from the dresser top, pulled the lanyard over her head, wrapped her wet blonde hair into a hastily constructed bun, and took the stairs up to the main level of the house two at a time, making for the golf cart Daniel had bought just for her to use.

After maxing out the top speed the little cart could manage on the downhill, she parked and jogged the few steps into the lab. She hadn't realized she was hungry until she passed by the employee kitchen, so she took the time to snag a protein smoothie from the fridge and a health muffin (Chimera Corp. employees had unlimited access to snacks, which was awesome, but they were all annoyingly healthy). Nessa reached the conference room with just enough time to slide into a seat against the back wall. The table was full, the leaders of the various research teams sitting in their usual spots.

As her father's assistant, Milton, called the meeting to order, Nessa leaned forward to see who else was in the room and spotted Delphine in the seat next to Gabriel.

Delphine. At a Chimera Corp. meeting? Whenever Daniel tried to talk to her about the lab, she'd acted like he was inviting her to drink battery acid. But here she was, attending the full company-wide meeting.

Nessa instinctively looked for Daniel, as if he might explain.

He was sitting at the table in the seat next to Milton's, and when Nessa caught his eye, he leaned back and nodded. He looked like he had something he wanted to say to her. *Was it about Delphine?* Nessa wondered.

"As I'm sure you are all by now aware," Milton began, "we are hosting a delegation of scientists from the Haken facility in Kyoto. Many of you have met them before and are, in fact, in communication with them and closely collaborating on projects. We're hoping this will be an opportunity to fast-track these collaborations that, from the beginning of our work, have been essential to our research.

"I'll let Daniel speak in a few moments to the importance and the long-term goals of this meeting," Milton said. "But first, we have a few logistical items to get out of the way, and we'll also hear about changes to security."

"Oh, great," Delphine said. "More security. As if this place wasn't a prison already."

Milton slid her eyes to Delphine, an impassive glance that was impossible to read. She clicked forward to a graphic that showed a week's calendar with different blocks of time worked out in different colors. "Green indicates a shared meal between our groups. Note that the visitors are on their own for breakfasts, which catering will be making separately. No marinated squid in the morning for you lot." There were some low laughs.

"Yellow: meetings. We will showcase certain projects most essential to our work together that we're hoping Haken will partner with us on. These meetings are crucial and your attendance is mandatory. We can't move forward on some of these without Haken's participation. The funding and the connections they have within the Japanese government are essential, so we need to put our best foot forward."

There were murmurs among the scientists. Nessa hadn't realized Chimera Corp. relied on anyone in the outside world—Daniel had always presented it as enormously successful and also fully independent from the financing woes or corporate entanglements that plagued most scientific researchers.

"The blue is time for informal connections," Milton went on. "To facilitate these connections, we are allowing ample time in the schedule for walks, outings, you name it. A fleet of bicycles arrives the day before the guests do. Of course, stay out of the preserve. Our guests know that it functions as a laboratory unto itself and understand there are experiments going on in real time. Safety and a positive attitude are critical to success."

Nessa looked down the row of seats to Delphine. Milton was too polite to direct a criticism directly at one of Daniel's daughters, but it did seem that both comments applied to Delphine. Delphine didn't seem to register the censure. She was staring intently at Milton's PowerPoint presentation.

"You'll note that Thursday we will spend all day on the final showcase, something Daniel will have to brief you on as I myself remain in the dark. We've planned a dinner—" Milton flashed a curt smile, "with very special live music. It should be quite elegant."

She flipped to a new slide—a map of the preserve. It showed

the campus map Nessa had seen many times before, but a new building appeared, well north of the campus but more easterly than the lab where the Delphine chimera had been housed. Nessa couldn't help but scan for the site of the lab she'd visited that morning. It wasn't marked, just as it had not been marked on all the other maps of the park she had seen.

"We're constructing a new lab that will showcase Daniel's project. Don't bother asking him what it is—this is the big reveal, and he intends to keep it a secret until the last moment."

A scientist on the other side of the table raised his hand. The researchers at Chimera tended to dress in business casual— no ruffled academics here—but his thinning hair was unruly and his blue oxford shirt was wrinkled. Nessa didn't know his name, which meant he wasn't on a team that Daniel had taken her to see on her first-day-of-work tour.

"Can you confirm whether my section will have an opportunity to meet with Takumi Okada?" the rumpled man asked. "I've been asking for information for months about his work with kelp and not getting answers."

The room went silent. The other researchers were looking anywhere but at the red-headed scientist. Or Daniel. Even Nessa knew that if you had to ask if you were being included, it probably meant you weren't. She could good as feel the heart rate among the scientists in the room spiking as Daniel's mouth turned down slightly. Something else unusual happened as well. At the man's aggressive question, the smog-like cloud hanging in the room was shot through with orange. There was something squid ink-like about the extrusion, both in the way the color bled into the cloud and the feeling of desperate self-defense that had surrounded it.

"I'll let Daniel address which teams will be involved in which showcases and which teams from Haken will be represented," Milton said, not missing a beat. "For now, just know that whatever is needed for your individual project has been considered."

But Daniel was already standing. "Look, Neil," he said, his voice calm but acerbic. He was using a tone Nessa had first heard when Daniel had discovered that the box carrying her mother's body back to Oregon to be used in scientific research had been discovered to be empty. This was his "keeping people who work for me in line" tone. "Your work on kelp is of long-term interest only at this point," Daniel said. "We've gone over that. The focus of this exchange is on mammals, and I'd like to keep it there. It's simply much sexier than kelp is ever going to be."

Neil raised his hand again, but Daniel dismissed him with a gesture of his extended finger that looked just like he was swiping right on a phone and began to talk about the history with the scientists from Japan, how they'd collaborated on projects together over the years, reviewed each other's research.

Daniel had lived in Japan for a year when he was younger, and many of these Haken scientists were colleagues he'd known then. "I know I've been keeping a lot of you in the dark about what I'm working on currently, but I want you to know that I'm hoping we'll all be able to take a look at it together when the visitors from Haken are here." Daniel looked on proudly. Nessa knew her father well enough at this point to be sure he wouldn't even hint at a reveal if his ability to deliver it was in any doubt.

What if Daniel's secret project had something to do with the missing chimera?

Oh, Dad, she thought, watching Daniel tapping a tablet with a stylus, exchanging a few words with Milton as the meeting was breaking up, *what have you done?*

CHAPTER FIVE

efore Nessa left the conference room, Daniel beckoned her over and led her to where Delphine was still sitting, one leg crossed over the other, her curly hair pushed back by a headband. Gabriel was standing. Delphine looked up at Daniel with half-closed eyes and eyebrows raised.

"Am I done?" she asked.

"Not quite," Daniel answered, and then he turned to Nessa, updating her. "I asked Delphine to join us this morning because

I think she should start working in the lab, like you. Gabriel developed a computer task for her, and I'm really glad she's agreed to take it on."

"She agreed?" Nessa said, trying to keep the surprised tone out of her voice. The computer part was not a surprise—Delphine had always been amazing with computers, taking their home machine apart and rebuilding it, making fashion apps in eighth grade. The surprise was that she had been willing to try anything Daniel suggested to her—since moving to Oregon she hadn't touched the laptop that had been waiting in her room when she arrived.

"It wasn't exactly presented as a choice," Delphine said.

"No," Daniel said, tightening the set to his mouth. "It wasn't." He crossed his arms over his chest. So far, he had yet to lose patience with Delphine. Vivian would have been screaming her head off—though of course, Delphine had never acted this way around their mother.

"It's cool you're here, though," Gabriel said. "I can show you the setup if you like." Delphine's sarcastic expression melted just a bit, and without giving Nessa as much as a glance, she followed Gabriel out of the conference room and toward the "Well"—the six-level column built into the ground. At each floor, balconies wrapped around the interior, while suites of laboratory facilities radiated out to the side.

Daniel looked at Nessa and raised his eyebrows. "I guess Gabriel has the magic touch," he said.

"I'm glad someone does," she answered, and then instantly

regretted it, seeing the pained expression on Daniel's face. Daniel had been trying so hard. When they first got to Oregon, Daniel had joined Delphine's obsessive Pilates workouts, dressed in his Stanford tracksuit, gamely attempting to invert his body into a V shape in imitation of the instructor on the video. Delphine had smiled a few times, but then had gone back to stone-faced withdrawal the moment the workouts ended.

"Sorry," Nessa said to Daniel. He smiled to let her know it was okay, and snarfing the rest of her health muffin, Nessa returned to the mice she was tending to two floors down.

She wasn't supposed to have named them, but she had, and now she used their names when telling them a story, letting the familiar routines of petting them and laying out nibbles of cheese in their maze calm her mind.

After her lab work was done, Nessa sat down at a computer to key in her notes about the mice's activities for the day.

Looking to either side to make sure no one was going to see what she was up to, she minimized the window of the program she used to enter the mouse data and went back to the landing page for Chimera's data storage. Everything at Chimera Corp. was stored in the cloud, and depending on your level of access, you could theoretically review and compare the data harvested from every project on campus, live. But only Daniel had access to every project. Nessa couldn't even see the "results" of her mouse study notes.

Chimera maintained a beautiful campus with the highest level of security, and the same went for their beautifully secure data cloud. Their firewall had been put in place by a company Delphine claimed was run by people who had started their careers at the NSA. And there was no such thing as a "download." The system did not support it. If researchers wanted to leave Chimera Corp., they took nothing with them.

There was one loophole, however, that everyone who worked at Chimera Corp. took advantage of—it was the only way to get anything done. When you searched for a keyword, you could see a list of every file that mentioned that word, if the file was coded mid-security or lower. This loophole allowed people to know whether files existed, and they could request access to files that would aid their research. Otherwise, Chimera would have been a tower of Babel, with researchers reinventing each other's wheels.

Nessa took advantage of that loophole now. She clicked Search. She typed in two words she knew would not help her.

Chimera. Delphine.

Practically every project created at Chimera Corp. included the word "chimera." So that search was a fail. "Delphine" was nowhere, except in a company-wide memo written by Milton to the staff three weeks before, introducing Daniel's children.

Nessa took another approach. She had access to the maps folder—everyone did. This was a private, interactive map of the corporate campus, showing what was open when and who to call about requesting access. Nessa had been here before, had zoomed in on the part of the map where she guessed the Delphine chimera to be. There was nothing changed about it.

The building—or the lack of building—remained unmarked. The roads did not even seem to go where they were supposed to.

Daniel, where is she? Nessa had to hold back from saying it out loud. She wished Bree were here. She had a way of asking leading questions that Nessa did not.

Nessa sat staring at the map a moment longer, separating out the places she had been from the places she had not. She located The Cliffs, a destination hike Daniel had taken them to on their first weekend here. The airstrip. The guest quarters, where the Haken researchers would stay. Nessa knew most of the buildings by now. But not the one labeled "camp." Was it new? She hadn't seen that before.

Could that be a secret code name for whatever new lab Daniel's using to house the chimera version of Delphine? Nessa wondered. The camp was close to the campus. Too close for comfort.

Nessa looked up at the ceiling, a maze of aluminum ventilation ducts, white water pipes, silver electricity conduits, a state-of-the-art sprinkler system studded with tiny flashing red lights. Instead of silver on white, Nessa saw bone-on-clamshell white, a ghostly glow-on-gray, a white that was tinted pink. The color attacks had been dizzying and disorienting before. This time they hurt. Colors and lighting in all the buildings Daniel had commissioned on the Chimera Corp. campus were muted, the palettes simple and neutral. The bland colors spiraling out of control were somehow unmanageable.

Nessa stood. She needed to get out of here. She needed to

get out into the forest, where at least there was darkness and shadow, rich shades of green and brown, every color backed by breath, by water, by life. She stumbled, aware of people looking at her as she pushed toward the doors. She caught a glimpse of Delphine in the employee kitchen with Gabriel. She was drinking a can of grapefruit soda through a straw, her cheeks puckered, her eyes big and staring. For a flash of a second, Nessa felt Delphine's sympathy, her own stumbles jarring her sister out of whatever pain she was in. For a half second, Nessa could feel Delphine's pain too.

She didn't want to think about Delphine right now. She wanted to get out. And then she had reached the door, and the moist forest air that rushed at her was the best thing she had felt since she'd stood up.

By the time her vision cleared, Nessa knew this color-seeing stuff was starting to feel scary. She had to talk to someone. An eye doctor? She was pretty sure that wouldn't help her. She had to speak to someone who understood wolves.

CHAPTER SIX

Nessa arrived for dinner that night and found Daniel alone at the table. He looked up from his phone, his eyebrows knitted together with worry. There were circles under his eyes, evidence of the long hours he'd been working. To his credit, he hadn't skipped a single one of the family dinners he'd told them would be part of their lives when they were living with him, every night at seven on the nose. But Nessa hadn't seen much of him otherwise.

"Can I ask for something?" Nessa said, heading to the side-board with its choices of water, milk, and juices always waiting. She kept her back to Daniel, hoping that if he couldn't see her face, he wouldn't pick up on the fact that she was lying.

"Of course."

"I'd like to meet with the cross-country coach the one you were talking about, at Stanford."

"That's great," Daniel said, as she knew he would. He'd mentioned several times that he thought the coach could weigh in on a summer training regimen for Nessa, something that would help her boost her times in preparation for the fall. "When do you want to go?"

"Soon," Nessa said. She lowered the carafe she'd been pouring milk from. "As soon as possible."

She turned. Daniel was looking at her, evaluating something, needing to see her eyes. She looked right back at him, forced herself to meet his gaze. She noticed, as she did, that the cloud of color from the morning meeting was back, gathered around Daniel like he was a mountain wreathed in a cloud of fog.

"You know," he said, "we never talked about what happened with your mom." He hesitated. "The way she died. Her . . . anomaly." His eyes darted to the kitchen, indicating that as much as it might feel like they were alone, James, the cook, could hear them.

"Yes," Nessa said, acknowledging both his statement about Vivian and the warning. "I know."

"One thing I've been wanting to ask," Daniel said. He lifted the glass of scotch he was drinking, swirling the copper-colored liquid in the light of the sepia chandelier that hung over the poured concrete table. "Did your mother ever have any communication with Dr. Raab? Nate and I have been talking about him. I hadn't realized what a force he was in Nate's life."

"Oh, yeah," Nessa said. "He saw him every three weeks. The clinic visits, they were a big deal. But I don't think Dr. Raab knew who Mom was or that she was a scientist."

"No?"

Nessa shook her head.

"Did he know she was a werewolf?"

Nessa felt herself bristle. This wasn't the first time Daniel had tried to raise the issue with her when they found themselves alone—but it was the first time he'd brought it up this directly.

"I don't think Dr. Raab knew anything about Mom except that she asked a lot of questions. He was always really nice about that. Everybody in Tether used the Paravida clinic—it was free healthcare. We were grateful. And here was Dr. Raab going above and beyond 'free.' He would call and talk personally about Nate's issues. He arranged a full neuro-psych evaluation for Nate when he was in first grade, and the doctor he told us to go to didn't even charge us. They usually cost thousands of dollars too."

"That was generous of him, then, wasn't it?"

Nessa felt herself blushing. "Well," she said, "now that I think about it, he was probably using everything for his research." Daniel realigned the position of his perfectly placed knife and spoon, then left his index finger on top of the knife, as if for good measure. "He was mostly drawing blood," Nessa said. "I think there were cheek swabs too. The study was funded by Paravida—they had to pay for it as part of the agreement when they bought the old Dutch Chemical plant. But no one knew they were sending all their samples to Paravida. And then this one kid, Billy Lark—"

"Before you get to that," Daniel said. "They were sending Nate's blood on to Paravida?"

"Yes," Nessa said, trying to remind herself that Daniel didn't know that Billy Lark had been the boy who was killed—he didn't realize how rude he sounded.

"But not yours or Delphine's? Only Nate's?" Daniel kept a relaxed attitude, a just-a-casual-conversation moment, but he must have moved his finger tip from the knife to the spoon, and he pushed down on it with so much force, it flipped over the side of the table like a Tiddley Wink.

"Yes," Nessa said. "Just Nate." She could see her father relax. As he bent down to pick up the spoon, Nessa wondered if he only worried about them because they were his biological children. As he returned to an upright position, Nessa added, "Except I guess they have mine? I had to get drug tested for cross-country and Paravida was the one processing the test, 'cause I guess they owned the clinic where I had it done."

"What?!" Daniel said, his expression of relief replaced by

one of irritation. "Are you sure?"

"Yes," she said, quietly. Out of the corner of her eye, she saw that Nate and his aide Micah were approaching from the other end of the very long living room.

Nessa saw that Daniel had seen them now too, which explained why he started talking loudly again, changing the subject so quickly, it took Nessa a moment to even remember what he was referring to.

"I can't get away right now to take you to Stanford," he said. "But you can fly down without me. I'll call tonight to make sure Coach DeBole can see you."

"Thanks," Nessa said, half standing as Nate and Micah joined them. They were laughing at something—Micah was a Taylor Swift fan (and a body builder), and Nate pretended to hate Taylor Swift and was always trash-talking about how he could beat Micah up. They could have that conversation fifteen times a day and not get sick of it.

"Hi Nate," Nessa said. Nate ducked his head and did not say hello. Nessa was used to this—Nate didn't mean anything by it.

But Micah said, "Hold on," pulled a sticker sheet out of one pocket and an index card out of the other. "Want to fill in a box?" he said to Nate.

Nate nodded, looked at Nessa, said, "Hi Nessie," while looking her in the eye, and then Micah peeled off a sticker and affixed it to the card.

Nessa could feel herself smiling. Micah really was good for Nate.

Nate looked so good these days. His dark hair was well trimmed, clean, and brushed. Aside from the one-on-one tutoring, Daniel had set up a kids' group in Stapleton—some of the participants in it were also on the spectrum, others were there for the basketball court and the model train set, which wasn't even half as cool as the one Nate and Daniel were building together in the house. No matter how busy Daniel had been in the lab, he made time for that every night after dinner.

"Hey, kid," Daniel said to Nate now. Nate raised his hand for a high five—no sticker prize required. He adored Daniel.

"Where's Delphine?" Nate asked, looking around like this was a puzzle with a missing piece—ever since Vivian had died, he'd been increasingly careful about keeping tabs on his sisters.

"Late as usual," they heard, and there Delphine was, crossing the long living room—really it was the size of three rooms, all facing a wall of glass looking out over the forest canopy. She must have just come up from downstairs.

She'd changed into a new outfit, with long, dangly earrings, a short, flared skirt, expensive-looking suede boots, a short-sleeved mock turtleneck sweater, and an elaborate necklace of some kind. Nessa was glad to see Delphine was making an effort.

Nessa watched Delphine pour herself a glass of water, giving Daniel a look as if daring him to make her drink milk the way Vivian always had. Then she slid into her seat next to Nessa.

The cloud around Daniel changed. Where it had been white

with gold flecks before, it was now run through with very dark indigo, close to black. Maybe it was just an effect of the light coming through the treated windows. The sunset would not come until later—it was high summer—but already the light was low and rich, and Nessa supposed anything was possible.

James brought out salads, sliding a small plate on top of the chargers the table had been set with. No matter what else they were eating, the meal always began with salad, and Nate— not a salad fan—was given sliced, peeled cucumbers, each with exactly five grains of sea salt on top.

Just as Nessa lifted her first forkful of greens to her mouth, there was a clatter. Nessa jumped at the sound. Everyone did. She saw what had made the noise—Nate's fist slamming into Micah's plate, rattling the salad plate on the charger. Now he was pointing.

"That's MOM!" he said. Nessa followed the direction of his finger. Nate seemed to be pointing at Delphine's necklace.

"What the—?" Nessa said, zeroing in on the oversize pendant. She'd thought it was just a complicated fashion-y thing of Delphine's, but now that she looked closely, she could see it was a picture of Vivian, framed in an ornate brass oval.

It was a picture Nessa knew well—it was Vivian at Delphine's middle school graduation. She looked uncharacter- istically made-up and dressed-up, and back in Tether, Delphine had hung it on her bulletin board.

Nessa felt a little surprised to see this image of her mother looking so familiar and normal—and then she felt a rush of anger at Delphine.

Delphine knew images of Vivian upset Nate. He didn't process feelings in the same way that Delphine and Nessa did, but Nessa thought she knew why he didn't like pictures. It was the incongruity. How could they be talking about normal stuff, like, "Do you want a bowl of cereal?" with Vivian's memory front and center, the image reminding him of his pain.

"Delphine, go take that off," Daniel ordered, his voice short and sharp, the way it had been when the researcher Neil was asking questions Daniel found irritating that morning in the lab.

Delphine narrowed her eyes and glared at Daniel. "I don't have to take it off," she said.

"Yes, you do!" Nate said, his voice rising, his words clipped. When he was upset, Nate tended to regress, his voice losing inflection, each word carrying as much stress as the one before. Certain forms of self-expression did not come naturally to him.

"She's my *mother*," Delphine said. "If you guys want to go around acting like she never existed, be my guest, but last time I checked, it was still a free country."

"Oh, please," Nessa said.

"Honestly, Delphine," Daniel began, and then he checked himself. He stabbed his salad and took a bite, chewing like it was leather.

Meanwhile, Nate was starting to shake. He was trying not to, holding on to the seat of his chair with both hands. Micah had the package of stickers out on the table, but Nate just pushed it away.

"Take it off, Delphy," he said, using Delphine's childhood nickname the way he always used Nessa's—not as a term of endearment but because, to him, those were simply Nessa's and Delphine's names.

Delphine glared at him. Her eyes were dark, her brows lowered. She looked . . . Nessa couldn't help but think this . . . sick.

Delphine stood up and pushed her untouched salad away. "Have a nice dinner," she said, and turned on her heel to head back downstairs.

It wasn't the first time she'd stormed off in anger. In fact, it was getting to be routine.

After watching her go, Daniel turned to Nate. "You okay?" he asked.

Nate nodded. Then he nodded again. He was nodding over and over. Nessa knew what he meant. He wasn't okay. He was glad the picture was gone, but didn't want to have had Delphine go with it.

"I'm sorry," Daniel said. "I'm running out of ideas. I thought working in the lab would help."

Nessa was the one who felt sorry. Here was this man who could buy anything he wanted. He was surrounded by prominent research scientists all looking to please him at every turn. And he could not crack the mood swings of an angry fifteen-year-old girl. Nessa looked at Nate: "Delphine will be okay," she said, though she had no idea whether that was true. To Daniel, she tried, "The computer project was a good idea." She wasn't good at this comforting stuff. She preferred problems she could wrestle to the ground.

As if just thinking of something, Daniel let out a little chuckle. "The thing about Delphine today," he said. "Gabriel set her up with a data entry project that should have taken her all day, but she wrote a quick program that did it for her, lifted all the hot chocolate packets from the kitchen, and then racked up five hundred dollars' worth of credit card damage at Sephora, sending lipsticks or some such to all of her new friends."

"Are you . . . mad?" Nate asked. This was a big inference for him to make, but Nessa didn't dwell on it as she watched Daniel for his answer.

"Well, I should be," Daniel said. "But mostly, I'm just impressed."

CHAPTER SEVEN

elphine was not in her room when Nessa checked after dinner, and she didn't look in on her before she rushed to the airstrip the next morning, meeting Daniel's pilot early for the quick flight down to Palo Alto, California.

Between the plane ride and the drive into campus in a town car, Nessa was walking on the Stanford campus by ten. She went straight to the meeting Daniel had arranged with the cross-country coach and then hurried toward the humanities building where Professor Halliday, a folklorist with a sideline in werewolves, had an office—the day before, Nessa had used her phone to look up Halliday. Fortunately, the timing was going to work.

Nessa had met the professor last spring while sitting in on one of her lectures. Halliday had recognized Nessa as a werewolf when Nessa was in human form in her classroom, and she'd been the one to tell Nessa about the existence of synthetic werewolves, mostly scientists who had transformed themselves into wolves through injection.

Professor Halliday's office was located on the fifth floor, far above the English and History departments. To get there, Nessa had had to take an elevator that was so old, it had a sliding gate like a cage. The hallway was wide and paneled in teak with a polished, institutional brown tile floor. Little light emanated from the simple yellow globes suspended from the ceiling, and the windows were few and far between, which was probably a good thing, given the dust and dirt that good lighting would have put on display. The paneling was pockmarked; the posters and flyers tacked to the walls advertising lectures, film series, and club meetings were months out of date.

Everything about the scene felt old and out of use. Nessa could hear her own footsteps—she'd worn flats with a hard sole and wished she'd opted for sneakers.

Professor Halliday's office was at the end of the hall. The door was forbidding, and there was no signage to confirm that she'd made it to the right place.

Nessa knocked forthrightly in spite of a feeling that maybe the smart thing to do would be to turn and retrace her steps—she was so used to holding on to her secrets. Was it really wise to share them now?

"Come in," she heard. "It's open." She turned the knob. The room was dark and small, with sloped ceilings and low shelves lining the walls that came right up into the eaves. There were books everywhere—not just in the shelving but in piles on the floor, on the tables, next to the two club chairs, and in stacks on the large wooden desk that appeared to be mostly ceremonial. The professor was working at a laptop on a small side table.

"Nessa," the professor said, her face displaying no sign of surprise. She nodded, as if answering a private question. "I'd assumed you'd be back sometime, and honestly, I thought it might be sooner." She stood and stepped around to the front of the big desk, rubbing her palms on the front of her leather skirt as if she were drying them. "I'm so sorry to hear about your mother."

She didn't offer Nessa a hug, and Nessa was glad. She wasn't sure what a hug from Professor Halliday would be like. Angular, likely. Some people were natural-born huggers and others were not. Nessa had not yet figured out which camp she fell into personally, but she figured Professor Halliday was pretty squarely lodged in the non-hugger category.

She was good with the eye contact, though. Maybe too good. Halliday blinked, slowly, like a cat. "I'm glad I have a chance to tell you. When I referred you to Daniel Host for the serum, I hadn't made the connection," she said. "I didn't know he was your father."

"Oh, uh, yeah," Nessa said, remembering how her heart had sunk when Professor Halliday had told her that the only person she knew who might be able to make the kind of serum Vivian would have needed to suppress her transformations, and possibly save her life, was Daniel. "I didn't expect you to know."

She felt herself take a step backward, stumble. She was aware that the professor was watching her in an impassive, but not uncaring manner. But now, the light in the room was starting to fracture, the blue of Halliday's eyes seeming to expand into the rest of the room. Nessa saw white. Shards of white, like the light had fractured into painful splinters of ecru and cream and silver, violent shards of crystallized, icy cold ice-blue and glacier white.

Taking her elbow, Professor Halliday led her to a chair and Nessa sank into it. The cushioning of the chair was thick, and it was upholstered in a soft, wool-like fabric, layered over with an even softer blanket—cashmere? All of it had the power to muffle sound and color.

Professor Halliday sat in the other chair. She continued to regard Nessa, not with worry, but with interest. She watched Nessa the way Nessa watched the Chimera Corp. mice in their feeding mazes.

"You think he might have hurt her?" Nessa asked.

"Do you?" Halliday asked.

"He wouldn't do that," Nessa said. "He's my father."

"Of course," Professor Halliday said. "But it didn't occur to you to wonder?"

Nessa shook her head. "It didn't," she said. She shook her head again. "And I'm not going to think about it now. I don't want to go there."

Professor Halliday shrugged. "You know him better than I do."

Nessa looked around the office to break away from the professor's gaze. She took in the embroideries, quilts, long-dull oil paintings in heavy frames, the leather-bound books, lamp-shades with fringes, patches of rugs on top of the tables. Judging by the dust, it looked like some of the books on the shelves had not been read—or touched—in years, but the glossy paper-backs stacked on the low table in front of Nessa looked current. One was open and a few others were closed over notepads with writing on the parts of the pages Nessa could see.

Nessa flipped the front cover over and scanned the title: *Shamainu: The Lost Wolf of Japan.* The illustration on the cover looked old: a black-and-white ink drawing of an unusual-looking wolf.

"They're small," Halliday said. "Or at least they were small. They've been extinct for over a century. At one time in Japan, they were so populous they were the basis of a significant folk-lore tradition. They were worshipped as gods."

"This doesn't look like a wolf," Nessa said. "What's with the tail?" It was short and bobbed. The wolf's legs looked short too.

She'd have thought the animal was a coyote or hyena before she'd have guessed wolf.

"They're a subspecies of gray wolf—like you—but some zoologists argue they should be characterized as their own species, separate from the gray wolf entirely."

"Does it matter?" Nessa said. "I mean, if they're extinct, who cares?"

"Some Japanese people care. Not as many as used to. For centuries, they worshipped these wolves. They believed their presence would keep wild boar and deer away from the crops the people needed to survive. They hung Honshu skulls and other bones in their homes. There are epic poems with these wolves as the heroes. A Japanese person living today may not know a Honshu immediately, but the stories have trickled down over the years. Even if they don't know them as 'wolf stories.' They are very powerful myths."

Nessa gave Halliday a skeptical look. Halliday raised her eyebrows in response. "It's not so simple, the relationship between people and animals. Your father asks this question from a scientific perspective, but don't discount culture. The way we use stories, the way we conceive of ourselves through them—it is part of the fabric of our brain. I'd argue it's more important to our fundamental biology than the decoding of the human genome. Animals are always at the heart of these old stories, because humans and animals used to have a much closer relationship."

"Some of us have a pretty close relationship to animals

right now," Nessa grumbled. Halliday didn't laugh, but she did consider Nessa's point.

"Well, you do. Your mother did. And for the rest of us, it's just Aesop's Fables. Stories etched into our hereditary memories. Fossilized evidence of old needs and old fears. Why do people keep pets in their homes? Why do young children run in delight toward a tank filled with swimming fish? Why do we hunt? Why do we photograph animals? Look at pictures and videos of them online? In Japan, there continue to be reports of Honshu sightings, but the Honshu haven't been culturally important for centuries—their extinction began with a plague-level rabies outbreak in seventeenth-century Japan. So why is there a small segment of the population there still searching for them? Why is newfound evidence of their existence cause for headline news?"

"Is that why *you're* reading about them?" Nessa asked. It occurred to her that Halliday was letting the conversation drift away from Nessa's own situation because she was intentionally giving Nessa a break from the intensity of her own problems. "Because they've proved they're back?"

"No," Halliday said, continuing her mini-lecture. "These Honshu sightings—I have a theory about them."

"You think people are seeing what they want to see because they're carrying around this deep love for these guys?"

Halliday laughed. "My work's not that straightforward, Nessa, but nice try. No." She looked up at the ceiling. "My question isn't why are the sightings happening, but why are they happening *now*? And I think it has to do with synthetic wolves."

"Like my mom?"

"Yes," Halliday said, her voice dropping in respect. "Your mom most likely chose to inject herself with the genetic material of a gray wolf, common to North America, particularly important to the ecosystem where you live. But what if she had been living in Japan? Wouldn't it have been tempting for her to experiment with transforming herself into a Honshu, the guardian of her ancestors?"

Nessa squeezed her eyes closed.

"My mom lived in Japan for a while," she said. This was something Aunt Jane had told Nessa, back when she felt Nessa had to know about her mother's past.

Nessa didn't want to imagine her mom injecting herself with wolf DNA, in Japan or anywhere else.

"Well, maybe she was a Honshu wolf after all. It's certainly more elegant to embody a species of wolf that otherwise would not be seen, wouldn't you think?"

"I suppose," Nessa said, thinking of the white wolf she had seen back in Tether. The one she'd been sure had Vivian's eyes. The one who had disappeared and not revealed herself to Nessa again after that one time. That wolf had been large. "But I don't think so. And didn't you say before that the synthetic wolves suppressed their transformations?"

"They do," Halliday said. "Most of them—it's the only way they can keep their secrets hidden. But perhaps there are some who do not."

Nessa nodded, considering this, feeling a little overwhelmed by the sheer size of the planet. When she was living in Tether, there had been the forest, the farms, the factory land, and the town. Moving to Oregon, she had the lab and the preserve, and it was hard enough acclimating to the change in environment. Everywhere she went, there would be more species, more plants, more ecosystems. Organisms going extinct before she'd had the chance to learn about them.

"So tell me why you're here," Halliday said. "How can I help you, Nessa Kurland?"

There were many ways to answer that question, but only one reason had compelled Nessa to Stanford, so she chose to be direct. "I'm seeing colors," Nessa blurted, "that shouldn't be there. Every color seems to have exploded. They're so vivid, they're blinding. And then sometimes I see clouds of color in a room. I don't know what they are."

For once the professor did not look smug, did not have that teacherly expression of someone who knows where your thinking is going to lead before you even have a chance to get there.

"You're telling me you're a tetrachromate?" Professor Halliday's stern face burst into a smile. "Nessa Kurland, you never do fail to surprise."

CHAPTER EIGHT

essa checked her skin for a rash. "What's a tetrachromate?" she said. "Do I have some kind of disease?"

At this, Halliday actually laughed. "No," she said. She stood and walked the length of one of her shelves, searching until she found a book on a high shelf. She pulled it down, blew the dust off the cover, then flipped through the pages, scanning until she found what she was looking for and passed it to Nessa. "Tetra-chromacy is a very rare condition that affects your vision."

Nessa looked down at the page in front of her, which had several diagrams of what looked like rainbows. Blocks of text had headlines that read Colorimetry, Spectrometry, Acromatic Colors. None of it made any sense.

"Most people have three types of cells in the eye that perceive color; tetrachromates have four. They are able to see color expressed in wavelengths of UV light, which most of us are not able to do."

"It's a . . . a . . . thing?" Nessa asked.

"A very rare one, but yes," Professor Halliday said. "It's believed about 12% of us carry the gene, and it's recessive, so the incidence is rare. On top of that, to express the trait, you must have some training in color perception. Artists, for instance—painters who spend time immersed in an under-standing of color—are best able to identify the phenomenon." She paused. "Now, there's really no delicate way for me to say this, but Nessa, my read on you is that you may in fact be one of the least artistic people I've met in some time."

"Gah," Nessa said, feeling the relief of being able to laugh out loud. It was true. From the early days of coloring pages and easel painting, she'd always been more interested in using the art materials to build towers and knock them down, or grab them and start running—forcing the more artistically inclined kids in the preschool to play tag. "Yeah," she said. "I'm not much of an artist."

"Have you always seen colors in this way?" Halliday asked.

"No," Nessa said. "It just started. Back in Tether. At first only when I was a . . . a wolf."

Professor Halliday nodded and for a second, Nessa breathed a silent sigh of relief. With Luc gone, there had been no one she could discuss being a wolf with. "When I transform, the way I see changes."

"Of course," Professor Halliday said. "Because wolves don't primarily see with their eyes."

"Right," said Nessa. "I feel like I'm seeing—"

"With your nose and ears? That's because your wolf brain is translating oral and olfactory sensation in the way your human brain translates visual information."

"I thought I was, I don't know, going to go blind or something—like my wolf vision wasn't shifting back. Like, there was something wrong."

Professor Halliday narrowed her eyes. "There's nothing wrong," she said. "This is quite a gift. I've never known a werewolf who had it."

"You don't think I'll go blind?"

"On the contrary. Nessa, you're going to see the unseen. You're going to see what others cannot."

The way Halliday was talking, the light in *her* eyes, Nessa felt that she was supposed to be excited. But also? She felt like someone had just made a big deal about a special dessert that turned out to be made of spinach and barley juice and wheat germ. "No offense," Nessa said, "but I don't really care about the colors. I just don't like the way all of it makes me feel."

"But don't you see?" Halliday said. "The way the color

makes you feel is exactly what you need to pay attention to." She must have been able to tell from the look on Nessa's face that she wasn't understanding. Halliday laughed. "Haven't you ever been moved by a painting?"

There were plenty of paintings at Daniel's house—generally abstract, geometric color washes in neutral browns and grays, chosen to complement the stunning views from the windows. But when Nessa thought "painting," she still imagined the picture of the country road and the barn surrounded by fall foliage hanging over the mantel of her house in Tether. It had been a paint by numbers done by her grandfather before he took up furniture refinishing as a retirement hobby.

"Paintings are nice, I guess."

"'Nice' is not what I'm talking about," Halliday said, pressing her fist into the arm of her chair. "I'm talking about paintings that are anything but nice. I'm talking about paintings that make you feel." Moving quickly now, she stood and started pacing her shelves again, pulling a book from the top corner, another from the bottom shelf near the office door, a third that she could only access after she had moved a whole stack that had been crammed in a double row. Once she had a stack she was evidently satisfied with, she beckoned Nessa to the window. "Come," she said. "The light is strongest here." Halliday put the books on a table and, pulling up a chair, commanded Nessa, "Sit."

Nessa sat.

"Now," she said. "Read." And for the next few hours, Nessa read. Fortunately most of the books were heavy on illustration, showing picture after picture of color diagrams. There was an explanation of light spectra, and of primary colors: good old red, blue, yellow. Another drawing showed how all the other colors were actually specific recipes for proportions of those three. Certain colors had the highest contrast with other colors: red against green, orange against blue, yellow against purple.

The book explained the branches of science based on understanding color and the crossover between the work of artists and scientists investigating color. Newton and Goethe had made early discoveries about color and light, and their understanding shaped inventions that changed humanity's trajectory; for example, color printing and the television.

Nessa read the sections on animals and color closely, though she was on familiar ground here, thinking about camouflage and the optical illusions some animals were able to pull off through disruptive patterning that caused their outlines to be difficult to detect. People returned to animals, as Halliday had described, not just for stories but for techniques, painting their airplanes and war machines to mimic the skillful disguises animals naturally employed.

Nessa read and read, her head starting to ache. She'd gotten up early, and now the only thing keeping her awake was hunger. Her stomach had been rumbling for half an hour when Halliday excused herself and came back in with sandwiches—a baguette with butter and ham, something Nessa would never have selected but which tasted delicious. "You can thank the French for the idea of buttering their ham," Halliday explained, and when Nessa opened her mouth to respond, Halliday gestured back to the books. "Read."

Nessa checked her watch. "I'm gonna have to take off at some point."

"When?"

Nessa figured it would take her twenty minutes to cross campus to the airport. And she had to be back early—she wanted to check in on Delphine. "Two thirty—it's going to take me ten minutes to get out of this building."

"Then stop reading," said Halliday. She put her hand down flat on the table. "But you have to promise me you'll come back. You know I can't contact you. That's not how this works. My work with wolves like you needs to be untraceable, understand? I can only function if no one can follow me."

Nessa thought about the sophisticated security systems in place not only at Chimera Corp. but also at the multinational Paravida, which had set up shop in Tether and likely played a role in the death of her mother. She nodded. Halliday's low-tech, no-tech approach made sense.

"I'll come back," Nessa promised.

"Now," the professor said, "let's connect what you've been reading about to what's in here." She pointed to the lapel on her blazer and Nessa knew what she was talking about. The heart.

For the next hour, Halliday called up images of paintings on the computer, and Nessa reported on how the colors made her feel. The muted browns and greens of *Mona Lisa*? Nessa found them restful and mysterious. The blue scarf in *Girl with a Pearl Earring?* Nessa felt hopeful. Matisse's *Harmony in Red?*

"Warm and cozy," Nessa replied. This went on and on, with Nessa finding that she *was* able to get more specific in her reactions to the colors.

The trick was to trust her first instinct and not overthink it. She found herself tapping into the wolf side of her brain—as a wolf, she trusted herself more. When every decision could mean life or death, you didn't have time for self-doubt. After a while, the color game they were playing became almost fun. Nessa felt like the colors were speaking to her, that they were an information code, another sense she could use to read a picture, a person, a room.

Then she looked at her phone and realized the time. "I gotta go!" she said, nearly choking on the words.

When Nessa stood, Professor Halliday did too. She silently handed Nessa the hoodie Nessa had left on the club chair and was about to forget, then closed the books while Nessa slipped her arms into the sleeves. "There was one more thing I have to tell you," she said, as Nessa headed for the door. "You're not ready for this yet, but you have to know. Once you build up your fluency with reading colors, you'll be able go further."

"Further how?" Nessa said. She hated to be rude, but time was running out. Was Halliday being purposefully evasive?

"You'll be able to move the colors. You'll be able to push color."

"Huh?" Nessa said.

For the first time, Halliday seemed flustered. "You really

must come back. Just—you see, you might stumble on this, and here's the thing. If you see black, you must stop. Because you see, this skill—it can turn into a weapon. And you need to be very, very careful with that when you don't know what you're doing."

"A *weapon?*" Nessa repeated. It was hard not to laugh. Right now, the colors felt like they were attacking her. "Is that what you mean by pushing color?"

"If you see black . . ." Professor Halliday's voice trailed off.

Nessa looked at her watch. She had to go. She really, really had to go.

Halliday took a deep breath. "I don't know how to explain this quickly," she said. "Except that if you see black, you should take that very seriously."

"Why?" Nessa asked.

"There's nuance, but basically a black—a true black—is irreversible, and it means someone is going to die."

Nessa reached the airport just in time for the scheduled return, but of course, they ended up waiting to take off. Nessa FaceTimed Bree.

"Hey you!" Bree said. "How's sunny California?" Nessa could tell Bree was in a car, but it wasn't Bree's car. Bree used the phone's camera to show Nessa the view from the window. Nessa saw green fields and a billboard moving so fast it was impossible to tell what was being advertised and what was being grown. "Look Nessa, it's a hot and humid July day here in Michigan!" Bree narrated, then, before Nessa could process the bolt of homesickness the totality of the image created, Bree swung the phone around to give a view of the driver. "Say hi to Dan Bergen! We're coming back from court. We're heading over to a town zoning meeting."

"Hi Nessa," said Dan, without taking his eyes off the road. "I told you, Bree, local reporting is not glamorous."

"What's not glamorous about a zoning meeting?" Bree said. She wasn't being sarcastic—this was just the kind of enthusiasm she was born with.

And it was catching. Nessa had hoped to fill Bree in on her newly discovered tetrachromacy, but instead, she just laughed while Bree talked about arcane zoning laws and Dan Bergen delivered occasional corrections, somehow managing to look both impressed by Bree's knowledge and focused on the road. By the time the plane was set to leave, Nessa felt slightly more normal. She might be a werewolf. She might be a tetrachromate. But she was also a teenager, and sometimes it felt good to stick with that.

As the plane lifted off, Nessa found herself staring into the pink light on the clouds, wishing she could feel as relaxed with Delphine as she did with Bree. Nessa resolved that whatever was going on with Delphine, she was going to come clean with her sister about her transformation and about their mom that very night.

CHAPTER NINE

*R*unning late, just an hour ok?

Nessa had texted Delphine from the airport and hadn't heard back. Was Delphine mad? She checked her watch when the plane landed. It was four.

At home, Nessa expected to find her sister sulking in her room, but when Nessa first gently knocked, then entered Delphine's room, it was empty. The bed was made, the shades turned one-third of the way, the clothes Delphine had dumped on the floor the night before folded neatly on the chair, as if no one had passed through since housekeeping had come by that morning.

Nessa checked with James, who was cooking dinner while listening to Earth, Wind & Fire, his sleeves rolled up to show his multiple tattoos. "She hasn't been in, which is weird," he said. "She usually drops by for a Nutella sandwich around now." He chuckled. "Sometimes, actually, she'll take a stack of them to go."

Nessa knew Delphine was supposed to have spent the first few hours of the day working her job in the lab. Maybe she'd gotten absorbed in her work and was still there?

Quickly changing into jeans and a sweatshirt—the temperature was dropping—Nessa headed to the lab. Delphine's desk on B level was empty, and when Nessa stopped at Milton's desk outside her father's office, Milton informed her that Delphine had not been in all day.

"But she was supposed to be working," Nessa said, hearing the fear in her voice. A thin wisp of ochre smoke entered the otherwise ice-blue aura hanging in the room, which Nessa surprised herself by recognizing it as the color of frustration.

She heard the low rumble of Daniel's voice through his office door. "Oh, he's in?" she said, heading for his office door. It was only a few steps, so she didn't have time to process Milton's rushed, "I think you might want to wait—" before she'd pushed her way into the room and heard Daniel saying sharply—there was no mistaking the displeasure in his voice—"I told you *not* to do that. I told you *twice*."

He was speaking to Gabriel, who was standing facing Daniel's desk, his back to Nessa.

It wasn't so much Daniel's angry, aggressive tone that registered with Nessa as it was something Daniel probably would not have wanted her to see. It was the look on his face. He was looking at Gabriel the way she would have expected him to look at someone who had broken into their house and was threatening them at gunpoint.

The colors in the room reflected his expression and tone, a cloud of battleship gray highlighted with crimson. That must be Gabriel's anger, she felt. *She* would certainly be mad if someone was talking to her in that way.

"Oh, Nessa, hello," Daniel said, his expression shifting instantly. Even the gray cloud dissipated to a certain extent, replaced with yellow. Which seemed to make the red even more pronounced—perhaps it was just easier to see that it was there with the gray gone?

"Have you seen Delphine?" Nessa asked, instinctively pretending she hadn't heard or seen the anger.

"No," Daniel said. "We were just discussing that, in fact. Apparently she never appeared at work at all."

"It's my fault," Gabriel said, his face earnest and regretful. *How could someone who is angry inside be so disarmingly humble?* Nessa thought. Just like Milton with her—frustrated on the inside, efficient and cheerful on the outside.

"It's no one's fault," Nessa said. "But the thing is, I can't find her."

"She's not at the house?" Daniel asked.

"No," Nessa said. She didn't volunteer the fact that it looked like Delphine hadn't been home all day. Nessa looked at her watch. It was almost five thirty. "Listen," she said. "I'm going to see if I can find her. Sometimes she goes out walking in the preserve. If I can catch up with her there, I'll give her a ride back in."

"Want me to ask James to hold dinner?" Daniel said.

"No," Nessa said. "Not yet. I'm sure I'll find her right away."

Daniel blinked his eyes, making a calculation, Nessa felt, before answering, "Sure thing."

"Do you want company out there?" Gabriel volunteered.

"Uh . . . no thanks," she said. She felt a little bad turning him down, especially since she would be leaving him alone to continue getting torn apart by Daniel. But she wanted to go alone. She might need to transform. Delphine would be easier to find if Nessa had access to her wolf-enhanced sense of smell.

"Yeah, uh, thanks," Gabriel said, and Nessa almost laughed. At least he had some perspective on the fact that he was getting harshed on. Poor guy. Nessa left him with what she hoped was a conspiratorial smile as Daniel said after her, "Just let us know if you think you'll be late for dinner."

Nessa took off, steering the golf cart up the hill to the left and into the preserve. It would be light until well after eight o'clock, and the only indication that the day was ending was the yellow mixing into the green of the leaves on the trees. Or maybe this was the tetrachromacy? Whatever, the trees were glowing with colors. It didn't hurt this time, though. It was just beautiful.

A few rabbits were out in the yellow-green grass by the side of the road. Well, she thought they were rabbits. The lab had done a lot of work on splicing DNA from cats with DNA from rabbits but stopped when the resulting population of "catbits" had made it abundantly clear they weren't vegetarians. They'd dug burrows across the preserve, not for self-protection but in order to hunt what had always been able to seek shelter under-ground. The chipmunk population had been devastated, and when that food source was gone, the catbits had gone after the natural rabbits.

Nessa remembered the redheaded researcher at the meeting mentioning the rumor of a cat on the prowl. It had sounded bigger than the catbits. She shook her head at the danger as she pushed the golf cart to its limit, heading up the hill. The golf cart was a high-end model, as golf carts went, but it wasn't designed for anything but the blacktop roads of the preserve—if she wanted to take some of the old logging roads that ran through the preserve, she would have needed to borrow Daniel's ATV, or take one of the trucks. But in general, the Chimera employees stayed on the pavement, never quite knowing what sort of experimental creatures they'd meet if they went too far into the woods. Nessa peered into the woods on either side of the road. *Delphine*, she thought. *Where are you?*

Then Nessa saw something that made her stop the cart. The trees—individual trees—were glowing. It looked as if they were lit internally by a glowing orb, pulsing with lavender and snow-white light, almost like they were breathing. Where had she seen this before?

She remembered. Right after she'd found the deserted and stripped Chimera lab. There had been about half a dozen trees, glowing just this way. Now it was happening again, though the glowing orbs were somewhat obscured this time—the trees that were glowing were set back into the woods.

It really isn't something wrong with my vision, Nessa thought. Because if it were, the trees at the edge of the roads would be the ones that looked strange. Maybe there was something in those trees that was glowing.

Maybe it was a new chimera—an owl laced with firefly capabilities, trained to glow from its perch on a tree limb?

As she tried to puzzle out the secret of the glowing trees, one of the glowing spots moved. And then another. She pulled the golf cart forward onto the side of the road, and headed into the woods to investigate. She knew she should be continuing her search for Delphine, but she wasn't sure when she'd see these orbs again. Maybe they had something to do with Delphine's disappearance?

There were parts of the forest preserve where the under-brush was thin, the mature trees having locked up all the available access from above so nothing else could grow. But here, the tree growth was relatively new and disorganized, and the underbrush was still heavy. Thorny branches slapped Nessa's lower legs. She was glad she'd changed into jeans. She considered transforming, but she was still holding out hope she'd stumble on her sister.

"Delphine?" she called out. "You there?" Up ahead, another orb of color shifted in a tree. From the sound it made—from the way the tree branch bounced back from its weight, Nessa could tell that whatever it was, it was heavy. Not an owl. Her wolf senses kicked in. Somewhere, distantly, she smelled a predator. The cat?

She thought about transforming again.

Movement in the branches caught her eye. She saw a gray shadow. Then something jumped.

Not a cat.

This was a dog. Standing in relative shadow, directly in front of her, its shoulders hunched, its head down, a low growl escaping its mouth, the dog had its tail between its legs. It was showing its teeth.

Oh, puh-lease, Nessa said to herself in Bree voice. The dog wasn't even large. Maybe 50 pounds tops. No collar, certainly no breed—its ears were way too small for its face, its legs too long for its body, and from what Nessa could see of its sandy coat and black markings, it had the matted fur of a dog that does not sleep inside.

She shook her head. "You poor thing, you have no idea

what you're dealing with."

The dog growled again, took a few steps toward her. This gave Nessa pause. No dog in its right mind should so aggressively approach a human, even a human who appeared defenseless and alone.

Then Nessa registered another pair of eyes looking at her from the left. *Okay, so,* she thought, *not rabid.* The reason for the dog's aggression was that he was not in fact alone. Still, there were only two of them. She could take them. Easily.

This new dog had short yellow fur and dark circles around her eyes. Nessa could smell that she was a female.

Thinking that she had better take a scan of the area, she turned right just in time to see two new dogs, stepping out from behind the trees. One was tiny, some kind of wire-haired terrier or schnauzer mix, and again she resisted the impulse to laugh. That impulse faded when she saw three more dogs behind the first one. They were all mutts and the biggest was not more than sixty pounds, but still, Nessa knew about the power of a pack. It wasn't the size of the individuals. It was how many, how well they communicated with each other, and how hungry they were.

These dogs looked hungry.

And unfortunately, she realized in that moment, she couldn't transform and run. They were too close. They would be on her before her thin human skin could coarsen and produce a protective layer of fur, before her claws could emerge, before her teeth would be ready to bite.

CHAPTER TEN

As the dogs continued to approach, Nessa heard a whistle. A definitively human-sounding whistle. She didn't take her eyes off the dogs, but she heard movement in the trees above and behind her and then heard a thump of a body landing on the ground. Then another. A voice said: "Tex, back off," and the lead dog took her eyes off Nessa for the first time. Nessa turned to see what the dog was looking at and blinked in surprise at what was there: a teenager in combat boots and baggy pants, who had dark skin and hair cut short and dyed blond at the tips.

Nessa couldn't tell if she was looking at a boy or a girl, only that the kid was tall and built like an athlete and with such balance and power and grace in the body—Nessa's first thought was, *I wish that was me.*

She didn't know where that thought came from any more than she knew where this kid had come from. The preserve was a closed ecosystem, with fences all around and only a few gates, all monitored 24/7. The kids of the scientists and lab workers— and there weren't many of them—were bused to Stapleton, the nearest town, for school. The oldest was twelve. She would have remembered if a gorgeous, athletic, androgynous person who would make a good running partner was on the premises.

Nessa forced herself to stop staring and checked in on the dogs. The leader, the one called Tex, had run to the teenager, who, on closer inspection, Nessa had decided was a girl. The girl bent down and scratched the dog behind its ears and it leaned against her leg. Clearly they were good friends.

Soon the other dogs were turning and running too, joining up with the other kids as they dropped from the trees behind their leader. The dogs look unwashed and skinny, and the kids didn't have much extra weight on them, either. They were all dressed in baggy pants, ripped shirts, jackets that looked several sizes too big. Some had bandanas wrapped around their heads, others were wearing baseball hats or sunglasses—they looked like a ragtag group of soldiers from the future, or people who had been camping out for a long time.

But they were good to their dogs, slipping them treats, petting them. The dogs sat with their owners. They must be well trained.

A dog-child army. Nessa let out a laugh of amazement. "Where did you all come from?"

Watching the leader kid's impassive expression turn into a slight smile, Nessa found herself smiling back, even though the scene looked like one from about the lost boys from the movie *Hook*. The dogs were under control, she reminded herself. These kids had not threatened her. But still, she was outnumbered by what looked like lost boys—and girls.

And also, she had started to notice wisps of acid green infiltrating the space between them. There was something menacing about the color forming up, expanding into a cloud. She needed to be careful.

A shorter kid stepped forward. He was pushing out his bottom lip and jutting his chest forward, his feet spread slightly to show exactly how ready he was to fight. "Same place you did, Blondie," he said. "Heaven."

There was nothing heavenly about the way he said it. The word had never before sounded quite so much like a threat.

"Right," Nessa said. "Copy that."

The leader held up a hand in a gesture that called off her lieutenant. "That's enough CJ," she said, and Nessa could hear a lot about her from her voice—she was calm, smart, experienced. Nessa noticed the cloud of color near the leader was shifting, from acid green to a shimmering aqua. Had she "moved" it? *Halliday would be proud.* "Sorry about the security system," the leader kid said. "Out here in these woods, you just never know who or what you're going to bump into."

Nessa wondered, *Does she mean the chimera?* And then Nessa had a chilling thought. *Are these* kids *chimeras?* She dismissed this idea quickly. One of the things she'd always been good at was keeping her head. These kids looked fully human. And what was that thing Vivian had always said? Don't hear hoofbeats and assume you're about to see a zebra. She couldn't go losing that ability now.

The leader girl took a few steps toward Nessa. She moved with grace and confidence, like she might have been a dancer. The younger one, CJ, followed. No dance associations there—he was all baseball-player swagger.

The other kids closed in too, emerging from the shadows where Nessa could see them only as orbs of light. Which made sense now. The light inside the trees—those had been people. Only their dogs stayed on the ground.

Nessa took a longer look at the kids, cataloging them in her mind the way a wolf would: there was one with the white bandana, the one with the shoulder strap, the one with the Camelback, the one with one leg ripped off her pants at the knee.

When the leader was standing an arm's length from Nessa, the girl looked Nessa in the eye, sizing Nessa up in the same way. The challenge reminded Nessa of Daniel's outburst over

Paravida the other night, a hairy eyeball running a brain scan, looking for secrets. Nessa saw that the girl's skin was tawny, her hair dark at the roots, almost black, and her eyes were honey-colored, flecked with green. Honest eyes. Angry eyes.

Nessa looked right back at her. She wanted this girl to trust her.

"You're one of the daughters, aren't you?" the girl said. "I've heard about you."

"Okay," said Nessa. "And who are you?"

"I'm Bo," she said, as if that should say it all. "And if you're looking for Delphine, I can take you to her."

Nessa felt her heart begin to race. In her mind, she'd imagined Delphine being lost. Not kidnapped. "You have Delphine?" Nessa asked.

"I don't have her," Bo said. "But I know where you can find her." She paused, looking Nessa up and down. Then she smiled, her face lighting up, and Nessa felt something relax inside her. It took her a second to identify the feeling. And then she got it. It was trust. She felt she could trust this girl. She wanted this girl to be her friend. "I can take you to her," she added. "If you want."

"Yeah, okay," Nessa said, catching herself smiling, holding herself back from asking questions, like, *How had this group of kids on Chimera Corp. land not been picked up by Chimera Corp. security?*

"You—uh—live near here?" Nessa said, hearing how over-eager she sounded.

Bo shook her head and laughed at Nessa, like Nessa was a puppy. "I'll tell you later," she said. "For now, let's go." She gave Nessa a smile, to let her know all was well, then turned before Nessa had indicated whether or not she would follow.

Nessa did. She hoped she didn't come to regret this. She hoped she was right in her reading of Bo. What if she was actually dangerous? Could she have lied about Delphine? Maybe this was a ruse to get Nessa further from safety and take her . . . wallet? Expensive running shoes? "One of the daughters," she'd said. She knew who Nessa was.

But then Nessa remembered the way Bo had been with Tex. The dogs were running alongside the group, sprinting ahead, then rushing back to check in with one kid or the other. Kids with dogs—they couldn't be all bad, could they?

Pulling out her cell phone, Nessa texted Daniel:

`Missing dinner. All is good with me. Let me`
`know if Delphine shows up.`

And then, knowing that her cell phone could be used to track her movements, she powered it off and slid it into her back pocket for safekeeping.

In spite of trusting her instinct that Bo was good, Nessa's heart was beating fast. What she was doing—running deep into the woods with a gang of kids who claimed to have Delphine—could reasonably be considered super dangerous. She tried not to think of what Bree would tell her to do. Bree was not here.

Bo was.

As Bo, CJ, and the others wove their way into the woods, it took Nessa a while to realize they were following a path. It barely qualified as one, at times disappearing altogether, then weaving back and forth in ways that were completely illogical until Nessa started looking for Chimera Corp. cameras and realized their route was designed to evade them.

The last in the group, a girl who looked to be about Delphine's age, who had dirt streaked on her face and dyed-pink braids, carried a long stick she used to stir up the leaves to cover their footsteps as they went.

"How will you know where the path is when you come back this way?" Nessa asked the boy directly behind her. He had white-blond hair and unhealthy-looking patches of eczema on his face.

"The trees tell you," he said.

Nessa sucked in air. *Okay, these kids are even crazier than they look.* "You mean, they *talk* to you?" she asked.

The boy frowned, looking at Nessa like she was stupid. "No," he said. "They're landmarks. Once you're out here long enough, you start to see that none of them looks the same."

"Oh," Nessa said, both relieved and chagrined. Add to that: curious. "How long have you all been out here exactly? Do you … live here?"

The boy just looked at her, pointedly not answering.

"Do you come from Stapleton?" Nessa asked, naming the town nearest to the entrance to the preserve.

"I'm from Portland," he said. "We come from all over. California, Chicago. Whatever. Except Bo. No one knows where she's from. She's always been here."

"You mean you guys didn't all come at the same time?"

"Nah," the kid said. "I heard about Bo when I was, uh, park-benching."

"In . . . in Portland?" Nessa said, to cover her surprise that this kid talked that way. Mentioned it so casually.

The kid shrugged. A slight tinge of neutral beige lifted into the air, and Nessa knew this kid was not lying to her. He picked up his pace and Nessa stopped asking questions. *Just as well,* she thought. The color thing was distracting. She had to get a better handle on it before she started using it to jump to conclusions. What if she couldn't trust this kid after all? What if a mellow beige tone actually meant *Run for cover, this is a live one!*

After they'd walked a bit longer, Bo left CJ at the front of the line and fell back with Nessa. "We're almost there," Bo said.

Nessa noticed again how quickly she was trusting this stranger. She wanted to—after all, the way the other kid had talked about Bo, it sounded like there was something special about her.

But still, Nessa was getting increasingly nervous. If this was a red herring, she was wasting precious time.

In her head, she'd been trying to track the path she believed they'd been following against her own mental map of the preserve. She'd probably left her golf cart a mile or so north of the lab. Now they'd probably covered another mile or so on foot. They were definitely keeping to the western side of the rectangular-shaped preserve, south of the stripped laboratory that had housed the Delphine chimera, and well west of the Cliffs. And now Bo was saying they were almost there.

"Like how almost?" Nessa said. "You're definitely taking me to Delphine, right?"

Bo put a hand on Nessa's arm. "Look," she said, leveling Nessa. "I know you're worried about your sister. I get it. I'm trying to help you."

Nessa swallowed.

She followed Bo down a ridge, into the dappled light of trees. She could hear running water and feel the water cooling the air.

"It's just here," Bo said, pointing in the direction from which Nessa could hear the water. Turning a corner, they came to the stream they'd been hearing, across which was a large, natural clearing. They crossed the stream on a series of stones that the kids ahead of her walked on with a confidence and sure-footedness that made Nessa realize they were used to this place—she looked down the streambed and saw that they were in a lowland. In one direction, the ground rose. In the other, it passed between a series of large boulders. She could hear what must have been a waterfall not too far downstream.

Bo stopped mid-crossing, letting the last of the kids pass around her—all of the dogs had shot forward already and were jumping on their companions, nipping and rolling. The light made the dogs' coats shine. It reflected off Bo's short, blonde-tipped hair. "Cute," Nessa said about the dogs.

"Yeah, but we can't count on cute out here," Bo said. "They're great therapy. And a built-in alarm system. Though mostly our security comes from not being seen." She pointed up, and Nessa followed her gaze to see a small village. In the trees. It was so well-camouflaged that Nessa would not have noticed it without having it pointed out to her. But now that she had seen it, she couldn't look away. She saw plywood, climbing ropes woven into webbing, ladders, platforms, roofs made of green and brown tarps. The more she looked, the more of the camp she spotted—a lot of the sleeping platforms were camouflaged by branches.

On the ground in front of the tree-camp, Nessa noticed a few fires burning, kids sitting on fallen tree trunks that must have been dragged into the clearing. On one of the fires—the largest one—Nessa saw a stew pot hanging over the flames. She smelled frying onions and a yeasty baked-bean odor over the cold damp air wafting up from the stream—then something tomato-y and cheese-y, like pizza. Nessa realized she hadn't eaten since Halliday's office. She was starving.

She turned to look at Bo. Bo flashed a smile that showed how proud she was of the camp, how much she loved it. For the first time, Nessa understood that Bo had built this place. She was sheltering kids who had been park-benching, dogs who likely had been strays. When Bo raised her eyebrows in a question, Nessa realized that Bo was asking her whether she liked it too. If she could see it. She hadn't lost the hardness Nessa had first seen in her—the set of her shoulders, the placement of her feet on the rocks spoke of someone on the defensive, waiting for a fight. Nessa didn't doubt Bo would throw down with her—with anyone—at even a minor provocation. But she also understood that Bo wanted something from her. Approval? Camaraderie? Maybe these were things Nessa wanted from Bo as well?

Breaking the moment, Bo turned, following the crew they'd traveled with, leaping the last few steps across the streambed. Nessa caught herself mimicking Bo's steps precisely, pushing herself to take the jumps with the same speed and assurance.

"What is this?" Nessa said, catching up to Bo ten steps before the camp. She wanted to ask her before there were others listening.

"This is our home," Bo said.

"But this is . . . uh . . . private property," Nessa said. She didn't finish that thought, explaining that the preserve was more than just private—it was heavily surveilled and guarded. Nessa knew how careful her father was—Chimera Corp. was—in monitoring the forest and everything in it. Given that it served as a natural laboratory of sorts for the research teams who worked in the lab, they had to. "It belongs to Chimera Corp."

"You see them using it?" Bo said, cavalier. "I don't."

As Bo strode into the clearing, greeting kids with fist bumps and handshakes, Nessa followed. She was looking for Delphine, but she was also looking out for herself. She felt all eyes looking at her. Surrounded by kids in clothes that looked like they hadn't been washed, in, well, ever, her sweatshirt and jeans were positively glowing with newness. She felt absurdly clean.

Dogs who hadn't been in their party ran to her, barking out an alarm, and Nessa held her hands down in front of her body to let them get a good sniff.

Looking up, she watched as two kids wearing dark jackets and carrying backpacks approached the camp from the outside. They shouldered off their packs while a third kid lifted a tarp off a platform hidden by tall grass. Underneath the tarp, Nessa saw what looked a bit like the distribution for a food pantry. Boxes of pancake mix, pasta, cans of soup, bags of beans. The kids with the packs tossed oranges and apples into a crate.

"That's how you get your food?" Nessa asked Bo, noticing that a tiny cloud of straw-colored yellow had been building between them. It was a comfortable color. Nessa didn't know what it meant, but it didn't make her anxious either. "You send out teams to buy the food?"

"In a sense," Bo said. She interlaced her fingers then pushed her hands inside out, her knuckles cracking. Nessa noticed that the cloud had suddenly been shot through with green streaks, spreading out now into the yellow. "Our philosophy is that we've paid for everything already."

"You mean you stole that food," Nessa said, immediately regretting her bluntness when Bo winced at the word. Bo shook off her discomfort, returning to the almost exaggerated casualness of her initial attitude.

Taking an orange from the bag, Bo led Nessa to a felled tree trunk and sat down. Peeling the orange, she passed half of it to Nessa. "Eat it," she said. "Food tastes better when you're actually hungry. Delphine is safe. She's fine."

Nessa separated a section and bit into it, and yes, Bo was right. She couldn't remember when the last time was she'd had an orange. It was delicious. Bo was watching her eat, smiling at Nessa's obvious enjoyment.

Nessa didn't explain that she was almost always ravenous, especially close to the new and full moons.

"Do you hunt?" Nessa asked.

Bo laughed again. "Sometimes. We're getting better. Although the animals on this land . . ."

Was Bo talking about the chimeras? Had Bo ever seen the chimera version of Delphine? "Some of the creatures out here are a little . . . experimental," Bo said.

Nessa laughed, careful not to give anything she knew away. "When you guys came out of the trees and your dogs surrounded me, I thought you all might be a little bit experimental yourselves."

Bo smiled. "Yeah, that's one way of putting it," she said.

Just then, a second group of kids with backpacks rolled into the clearing from the path Nessa had just taken. The dogs were barking and running to greet them. One kid looked a little bit cleaner than the others. Maybe a newbie? It was hard to tell with the watch cap and windbreaker and the aura that reminded Nessa of nothing more than the shade of bubblegum Barbie pink that Delphine had insisted on painting her half of their room in Tether. The kid nearest the pink kid reached out a hand to help, but the pink kid shrugged the offer away.

The unpackers were holding up portions of the haul in the light, and the new kid was stretching under the shapeless raincoat and identity-masking cap.

Then the kid pulled off the cap and Nessa was on her feet.

Nessa had seen the curly hair. Her mother's hair. And then the kid turned. It was Delphine.

Delphine, meanwhile, hadn't seen Nessa. Nessa could see her smile at one of the other kids who had been carrying a pack. The other girl was rubbing her shoulders—complaining about pain, it looked like. Delphine laughed at something she said, then pulled away from the little group, taking a few quick steps to reach another friend.

She looked . . . happy.

She looked like her regular self.

What the heck was she doing here?

CHAPTER ELEVEN

It took Delphine a few moments to notice Nessa, and during those first moments, Nessa just watched. Delphine was drinking from a water bottle and talking and laughing with one of the other kids. Throwing a stick to one of the dogs. Delphine's pink aura made every other kid's color glow a warmer shade of whatever they had been showing before.

Back in Tether, Delphine had always had a lot of friends and had been able to be friends with anyone—she had her fashion-y popular crowd friends, but she'd be in chat rooms with the kids in the computer club after school. Nessa wasn't surprised to see that Delphine was close with these outsider kids now—one of them threw an arm around her shoulder and another tossed her a can of something as they moved some of the food out from under the tarp to the food prep area. Nessa had been more surprised by what Delphine had been like all summer: antisocial, withdrawn, angry. This was Delphine restored.

"That's Topher," Bo said, pointing to the kid Delphine was helping open up cans now. "He was getting beat up in school for being gay and made the mistake of telling his dad."

"And he came here? To you?"

"Not for a long time," Bo said. "And even a short time for a kid living on the streets—it's pretty brutal. You're nobody's problem. You're everybody's punching bag. You steal to eat. You get caught, you get used. Topher's lucky he didn't end up dead."

"Does Delphine know about this?" Nessa asked. Nessa didn't quite know why she was worried about Delphine learning these stories. It wasn't like they hadn't heard stories about families going wrong in Tether. They'd known kids in foster care. Kids who dropped out of school.

"Of course she knows," Bo said.

Just then, the kid who had been working on the cooking pot started banging on an empty can with a stick, which must have been the signal for dinner because all the kids began heading in the direction of the kitchen area.

"You want to eat?" Bo said. She shrugged when she asked the question in a way that made Nessa understand—Bo wanted the answer to be yes.

"There's enough?"

"We always make enough," Bo said.

Nessa looked around. The light in the forest had turned golden yellow. The kids were settling in to eat along logs placed near the edge of the stream, watching the shifting yellows and greens of the trees on the opposite bank, hanging over the edge, the shifting sparkles of light on the water. The air felt cleaner, damp, and a little chilly out here. Some of the kids were building up a fire away from the water, and Nessa imagined that in a little while, it would be nice to have something warm in her belly. For a second, she thought about calling Daniel to let him know, but she didn't know what she'd say. She knew she couldn't tell him about these kids.

With Bo, Nessa got in the food line, grabbed one of the mismatched plastic bowls from the pile, and let the cook serve her. When Bo was pulled away to talk with a kid, Nessa stood alone for a moment with her meal, scanning for a place to sit. Just then, Delphine glanced up and their eyes met.

Nessa wasn't sure how this was going to go down. Delphine had been angry for just about a month solid. Ever since she'd left Aunt Jane's. What were the odds she'd become suddenly un-angry now?

Nessa might need to be able to run.

But though Delphine looked surprised to see Nessa, she

only tilted her head and smiled at her sister. She elbowed Topher and the kid on her other side, then put her own bowl down on the ground and stood.

"What are you doing here?" Delphine said as Nessa approached. She wasn't making an accusation. She was acting like she was delighted to have run into an old friend. Nessa felt herself smiling at her sister—it was just so nice to have Delphine sounding like her old self.

"I was looking for you," Nessa said. "I was going to tell you that dinner was ready, but I guess—" Nessa looked at her watch, then shrugged. "I guess that ship has sailed. Are you—are you okay?"

"Yeah, I guess so," said Delphine, her smile growing warmer and more welcoming with each passing minute. Nessa started to wonder how it was she and Delphine had ever stopped communicating.

Nessa bent her head down and lifted her spoon, taking a mouthful of soup. Which she immediately spat right back into the bowl. "What the heck is this?" she said, under her breath, to Delphine.

Delphine laughed. "It's stew," she said. "Come sit down. Eat it. They cook what they can find. Beans and canned soup and whatever. If you're hungry enough it tastes good." Delphine returned to her bench and slid over, making a spot between herself and Topher.

Nessa nodded at Topher, and then everyone tucked into the bowls of food, eating in silence. There was conversation among the kids who had already finished—small groups—but anyone actually eating was pretty much doing just that: eating, ravenously. Nessa wondered how much food they were getting. For all Bo's talk of having plenty, they looked like kids who were experiencing real hunger. The kids, after finishing their own portions of stew, refilled their bowls and offered stew to the dogs.

When almost everyone was finished, one of the kids grabbed a bucket, filled it with water from the stream, and brought it to the center of the circle. Every kid stood up with their bowl and brought it to the bucket, dumping it in.

"Someone will wash them all later," Delphine explained. "Everyone helps with the work."

Nodding, Nessa quickly scarfed the rest of her flavorless bean, tomato, and limp-canned-carrot medley before dumping the empty bowl into the bucket along with the other ones. She was wondering, "What now?" assuming that pretty soon she and Delphine would head home—it was getting dark, she didn't know how she was going to find her way to her golf cart through the woods—when a kid she could see said what Nessa thought was "anima."

Another kid joined the first and then a third and pretty soon the entire group was chanting "Anima! Anima!"

"What are they saying?" Nessa asked, feeling a little bit like she was an anthropologist studying the customs of villagers in Polynesia or something. "Is that some kind of special language?"

Delphine laughed. "It's English. They're saying 'animal.'"

"They are?" Nessa asked, looking around. "They aren't calling the animals out of the woods or something, are they?" She glanced around nervously, thinking about the unpredictable nature of their chimera neighbors.

"Don't be a cork," Delphine said. "It's a game."

"Oh," Nessa said.

"Bo thinks playing games keeps childhood alive," Topher said. "Whatever. They're kind of fun. And no one here has phones." Then he cupped his hands over his mouth and joined the "Anima! Anima!" cheer.

Before Nessa could ask any further questions, CJ jumped into the center of the group, like this was a dance circle and he had some moves to show off. He did have some moves too. Taking a few angular steps that somehow made Nessa feel light on her toes, CJ used his hands to draw a lion's mane around his face, traced a tail and shook the tip with his left hand, and then cupped his chin with his right as he let out a silent roar.

Nessa noticed that he was directing his performance mostly at a group of the smallest kids there. Nessa had noted them before but not paid particular attention. Now that she was looking at them, she realized they weren't older than twelve. "Lion, lion!" they shouted.

"What are they, eleven?" Nessa asked. "Someone kicked eleven-year-olds out of their house?" She had turned to Delphine as she said this, but unfortunately, at just that moment, the clapping and cheering stopped and Nessa's question— meant just for Delphine—was audible to everyone sitting close by. The little kids shot her a glance, big eyes, smiles frozen, and Nessa felt awful. She'd clearly broken the moment for them, and then Topher was staring at her too, and CJ, who had swiveled his head to see who the jerk was, was now shaking his head as if he should have known.

But then Nessa heard Bo's voice coming from behind her, clapping in a steady rhythm. The firelight cast deep shadows— her eyes shrouded, but the soft ovals of her forehead, cheeks, chin, and the tip of her nose glowing in the soft light. "Come on, guys," she said. "Animal! Let's go. Who's got one?"

Nessa knew about leadership—what makes a leader stand out, what makes the pack members respect that leader. Every wolf knows this, that leaders either have it or they don't. Now she saw that Bo had it. Her voice had the power to break the mood.

Topher stood. Shaking his head and hiking up his pants that were so baggy at the feet he looked a little bit like a clown, he took to the center of the circle. And in a way that Nessa couldn't quite trace or explain, he flattened his face until he looked exactly like a fish. But it wasn't just his face. His whole body turned fish-like as he bent his knees and swung his elbows behind him, making motions that looked like he could be swimming.

Hamming it up in the firelight, he puckered for the eleven-year-olds, then did the rounds of the circle. Kids were calling out guesses so wrong—"Skunk!" "Crawfish!" "Orangutan!"— that Nessa figured part of the game was delaying the moment when they got it right and Topher sat down.

Finally, one kid couldn't take it anymore. "It's a fish, a fish!"

And then Nessa felt a hand on her shoulder. It was Bo. She leaned down over Nessa's shoulder in a way that reminded Nessa of Coach Hoffman speaking words of encouragement just before race time. "You got something?" she said.

"Uh," Nessa said. Her first instinct was to say no. She was never good at this kind of game and in general she didn't like to stand up in front of a crowd. But then Bo looked at her. There was no expectation there. She wasn't pleading. Just noticing.

Nessa stood. She turned to face Bo. Only the felled tree Nessa had been sitting on came between them. The light was behind her, so her face would be unreadable in the shadow. She took the opportunity to really look at Bo—her bright eyes, her well-cut cheekbones. What was she asking of Nessa? Why had she brought her here, decided to bring her and Delphine back together? Nessa felt Bo had something on her. What could it be?

Bo stepped back, jamming her hands into her pockets.

And suddenly—Nessa didn't quite know how Bo had done this to her—Nessa was now turning with the intention of acting out an animal in front of a group of strangers. Strangers who were really good at acting out animals.

Nessa felt her breath growing shallow, sweat breaking out on her forehead. How was it that being a werewolf had done nothing to lessen her fear of standing up in front of a crowd? She didn't know how to pretend to be an animal. Which animal would she do? Delphine was watching her. This had to be good.

But it couldn't be too good. Nessa didn't want to actually transform.

Suddenly, thinking about transforming, she had an idea. When she transformed, she always felt hyperaware of her paws, and now she shook out her hands as if they were paws—large, mitten-type versions of her hands. She let her arms hang down from hunched shoulders, pretending her heavy hands were pulling them down by their sheer weight, the way it felt when she was a wolf. Locking elbows, raising first one shoulder then another, she imitated the gait of a wolf. She lifted up her head, pinched her eyebrows together, and let out a howl.

Something in the cloud of yellow light hanging over the gathering shifted as she realized she had the attention of the group. The youngest kids were focusing on her, but as she scanned the group, she saw lots of other eyes, red from the light of the fire, popping out of the yellow foggy light streaked with green. She sniffed, as she did when she was a wolf, inhaling in three sharp pulses of breath.

And then CJ howled back at her, and for a second, Nessa felt confused. Was this human or wolf communication? Because it felt real to her. It felt like real howling. And it felt sad. She hadn't communicated with wolves since Tether, and even then, there hadn't been any left since Luc had gone.

"Awoo, awoo!" the little ones joined in now, and then the rest of the kids were howling, their shoulders back, their faces raised to the night sky, sparks from a collapsing log rising along with their voices.

"Awoo! Awoo!" Nessa felt at home in a way she hadn't felt in a long while.

Then the howling stopped and Nessa heard—far in the distance—the answering cry of a wolf. An actual wolf.

There were wolves in the park. This was something Nessa knew. But she hadn't known how close they were. That they could hear her. She looked around at the Outsider Kids—the name they called themselves. She knew her hearing was more sensitive than theirs. It was possible they hadn't heard either? But she could see that at least a few of them had. Bo was looking up, her body tense and on edge.

"All right, all right," Bo said, stepping into the light of the fire, putting up her hands to show that it was time to shut the party down. "Nice job. Good wolf," she said to Nessa. "But that's enough, everyone. We rise with the sun. All Outsider Kids need to get into bed."

The kids dispersed, climbing ladders up to the platforms in the trees, pulling down tarps, lifting the dogs up the ladders, calling out to each other, tossing sleeping bag and quilts around. Nessa could see their flashlights sparking, like their movements were causing an inadvertent Morse code signal to be sent into the dark.

As Bo headed for the ladders, she said to Nessa and Delphine, "You guys can stay here while we get everyone into bed. The night patrol will be starting soon—they'll take you back. They've got flashlights and know the way."

"Thanks," Nessa said. She crossed her arms, trying to draw warmth toward her, wishing she had on more than just a thin sweatshirt. Wishing she had had longer to talk to Bo. She had questions for her. She wondered if they would see each other again.

Nessa was grateful, though, for the chance to talk to Delphine.

Now that they were alone, Nessa found herself watching Delphine's face. Her sister was looking right back at her. Not angry. Not afraid. Just relaxed and trusting.

Delphine laid an extra log on the fire and stirred the coals so it would catch, and as they watched the fire, Nessa realized that this might be the opening she'd been waiting for all summer.

"Hey Delphine?" Nessa said.

"Yeah."

"You know, I've always felt protective of you."

"Yeah."

"But watching you today. You're really doing something here. You're part of this. That's cool."

Delphine leaned forward, her elbows resting on her knees. "Thanks."

A moment passed where they just looked at the log catching flames in the fire.

"Nessa," Delphine said, speaking low. "There's something I've got to tell you."

"Okay," Nessa said.

"Ever since Mom died, I've had these dreams. I'm out on a

mountaintop somewhere. And I'm afraid—for some reason, I can tell that I'm in danger. And then out of the trees, I see something coming toward me. I don't know if I should be afraid or if it's something I'm expecting. Something I've been waiting for."

"Yes," Nessa said because she could feel Delphine's fear. Or maybe it was just the fact that she could see it—the bubblegum pink from before now turning a deep, unhealthy shade of purple, like a bruise.

"The feeling is with me all the time. I can't seem to understand how to shake it. It fills me up, and yet I feel so empty all the time."

Nessa nodded. She felt her heart literally hurting inside her chest, she was listening so hard.

"It's not as bad out here," Delphine said. "I found these kids when we got here and when I'm with them, I don't feel quite so afraid."

"Are you still having the dreams?" Nessa asked. "Are they still bad?"

Delphine nodded, biting her lip. She took a ragged breath. "They're getting worse," she said. "I feel like something is coming to get me." Delphine swallowed. "Something is coming. I see it."

"You do?" Nessa said.

"It's a wolf," Delphine said.

Nessa felt like she'd been punched. It was all she could do not to say, "Oof."

"It's this enormous wolf. A white wolf. And I'm not scared of it. I feel safe and happy, and like Mom is still here, and we never left Michigan, and I don't know."

Delphine's voice broke. She was crying.

Nessa still didn't know what to do or say. Tentatively she put a hand on Delphine's shoulder.

"I don't know if I want the dream to stop or to keep coming!" Delphine said, choking out the words. "I can't keep feeling this afraid all of the time. But I don't want to let the good parts of it go."

Delphine put her head in her hands. Nessa moved her hand from one shoulder to the other so she could bring Delphine close.

"It's okay," she said, over and over, feeling how empty those words were.

Finally, Delphine lifted her head. She collected herself. She fished an old napkin out of a pocket and blew her nose. "Delphine," Nessa said—whispered, actually. Delphine looked up, her big eyes open and trusting, not clouded by the anger she'd been feeling for so long. "There's something I have to tell you too."

Delphine pulled her sweatshirt sleeves over her hands and wrapped her hands under her armpits, like she was trying to straitjacket herself, trying to tie things down. Nessa almost didn't go on. Did she really want to be making things more complicated for her sister? But she had to tell her. Secrets in families were bad.

"That white wolf?" Nessa began. "It's no accident you're dreaming about her. That white wolf is Mom."

CHAPTER TWELVE

At first, Delphine did not understand. "You think the white wolf is standing in for Mom?" she said, her brow furrowed in confusion. "Why? And why is it always the same thing?"

"No," Nessa said. "You don't understand. The white wolf really is Mom."

Delphine stared. Using the gentlest voice possible, Nessa started to explain, hoping she could find the words. "I only figured it out last year," she began. "You know how at Chimera, they're combining DNA to make animals that have traits from more than one species?"

Delphine nodded. As if she knew this was only the beginning, she didn't say anything, just waited. And Nessa told her the story. She started with the parts Delphine had already learned about: How, in spite of the fact that all through their childhoods, Vivian had worked as a vet tech and had run a small under-the-radar veterinary practice out of her garage—mostly stitching up dogs and cats for friends and family who did not want to pay professional fees—she had started off as much more and hidden this past from her children. They'd believed her to have dropped out of college after two years, but in fact, she'd graduated within two years. With honors. And gone straight into a doctoral program in genetic research, quickly becoming a superstar in the field. She'd invented the technology at the heart of all the Chimera Corp. splicing of one species into another.

Delphine stared as Nessa reviewed this, her face lit by the glow of the fire, the sounds of the Outsider Kids receding into the night behind them.

Nessa continued on to the part of the story Delphine had not yet heard, explaining how, as a young scientist, before she'd invented the technology to create chimeras, Vivian had become fascinated by werewolf legends. "They were so consistent across so many cultures, she felt there might be some grounding in fact," Nessa said. "As Mom went deep into the literature, she started to hear rumors about underground experiments where scientists had injected themselves with wolf genetic material."

"That sounds so dangerous!" Delphine said, covering her mouth.

"Yeah," Nessa said. "It was. Crazy dangerous. Most of the people who tried it died. Mom said trying this was one of the stupidest decisions she'd ever made. But she was young."

"That's no excuse," Delphine said.

"I know," Nessa said. "But she did it anyway."

Delphine ran her hands up into her hair. "So you're saying Mom was a . . . a . . . werewolf?" she asked. "She was a werewolf all this time?"

"No," Nessa said, and explained how within the first year of transformations, Vivian began to inject herself with a serum that would suppress the transformations at the full and new moons. And then Nessa explained how Vivian never told anyone that she was doing this. Even Daniel. She continued to fabricate the serum after moving with Nessa and Delphine to Tether—she'd set up a lab at Dr. Morgan's.

Nessa paused before moving to the next part of the story. She didn't like to think about this part. But Delphine needed to know.

"When she got so sick last year," Nessa said, "it was because she couldn't get any more serum when she was in jail. That's why I called Dad in. He brought some at the end, but it was too late."

At this part of the story, Delphine's eyes filled with tears and her mouth contorted. But she rubbed the spasm away with a hand, almost like she was wiping her face. "Keep going," she said. "What else."

Nessa told her about the call she'd overheard Daniel taking a few days after Vivian's body had left for Oregon, via train. "There was some kind of break-in," she explained. "Except no one could see how that had happened. All they knew was that Mom's body was gone. And then I saw her. In Tether. Or at least I'm pretty sure it was her. She was a wolf. She was in good hands. She was safe. She was looking out for me."

"You weren't scared?" Delphine asked. "You ran into a wolf!"

"Nah," Nessa said. "I knew it was Mom. I can't say how exactly. Maybe it was the eyes, but I just knew."

Delphine was sitting on her hands now, pulling her arms straight by lifting her shoulders. "So the dream. It is Mom," Delphine said. Then she laughed.

"What's funny?"

"Nothing." Delphine looked down, then quickly up again to meet Nessa's gaze. "I guess that once you said the white wolf was a person, the first person I thought it would be was you."

Had the fire gotten stronger? Nessa was suddenly warm. She clapped her hands together in front of her a few times. Took a deep breath. "Okay, there might be a reason for that," she said.

And then, while Delphine was looking at her with exhausted eyes, Nessa forced herself to tell the rest of the story. About the night when she was running in the woods training for cross-country, trying to follow her competitive teammate Cynthia

Sinise.

"The night you got bit?" Delphine prompted. Before she'd even finished asking the question, she'd made the connection. "Oh God, Nessa, you too?"

Nessa nodded. She told Delphine about the changes she'd seen taking place in her body, the cravings for meat, her ability to run faster than she ever had before, the correction to her vision, the way dogs had reacted to her when she went to clean cages at the vet.

As she spoke, the cloud of color that hung between her and Delphine was pulsing. *Yes,* Nessa thought, *I suppose we will both be experiencing a whole jumble of feelings.* Who knew what the colors meant? One would barely settle into place before another took over.

Nessa could say for sure that the colors she was seeing were hot: oranges and yellow, pinks and reds, bright coils in the night sky that looked like they were sparking out of the fire itself. It was too much after a time, and the girls stopped talking and just stared into the flames or at the ground. Finally, Delphine asked, "So do you take the serum too?"

Nessa shook her head. "No." She knew what she had to do next. What she had to admit to. But somehow she could not force the words to form. She waited, breathing, slowing her breath purposefully, watching the way the colors calmed when she breathed this way. The cloud seemed to shrink, the oranges to fade to ochres, the reds to russets—cool, calming, shadowy colors slipping in with each inhale.

When the color cloud had calmed down to tolerable levels—and at this point, she didn't know whether the colors were reflecting her feelings or Delphine's—Nessa said what she needed to say.

"I don't take the serum," she said. "I never have. What happens to me is that—I—" The colors in the cloud started to heat up again, and she took a deep breath, cooling them. "I transform."

Delphine grabbed Nessa's hand. Her eyes were bright, her cheeks flushed, her curly hair seemed almost to be standing on end.

"Nessa!" she said.

Nessa had to plow on. If she stopped now, she'd lose her nerve. "There's something else you need to know," she said. "And this part has to do with you. When I came out here by myself last spring, I found something. Something Dad made."

"What did Dad make?" Delphine asked. Her voice sounded tight, like it was hard to ask that question.

"Mom wasn't the only one experimenting with human chimeras. Dad did it too. But instead of turning himself into one, he used the stem cells from when you were born and grew one from scratch."

"He . . . what?!" Delphine said. Her face contorted. All the fear and anger were back.

"Delphine, it was so bad that he did this. He kept it secret from Mom. When she found the baby version she left him."

"The baby version of what?"

"Well, you, I guess," Nessa said. She watched Delphine's face go dead, her cheeks seeming to slip lower on her face, the expression in her eyes freezing. "He made a clone. Sort of. It was a chimera. Part you, part stem cells that weren't you. Mom was really, really mad. She—this chimera—Mom didn't think it would survive. But it did. She. She grew up. I met her."

"I think I'm going to be sick," Delphine said.

Nessa felt the same way. Watching Delphine's face collapse into itself, all the light disappearing inside, Nessa felt like she was killing something. "She survived," Nessa said, barely getting the words out. "I saw her. She looks like you. Exactly like you." Delphine's face shrank at that. "Except for the parts of her that are from other . . . sources."

Delphine closed her eyes to form slits like she did during the scary parts of movies. "What sources?" she said.

"Certain animals are easier to blend than others," Nessa said. "It's nothing personal. He chose pig and bat and deer."

"And she doesn't transform?"

It took Nessa a second to understand this question. Why would Delphine ask this? Then Nessa made the connection. She had just told her about herself and Vivian, both of whom had lived with transformations.

Transformations suddenly struck Nessa as the most elegant possible solution to the chimera problem. She was looking for something to say to explain the lack of transformation to Delphine but before she could, Delphine shook her head, showing that her thinking had caught up to Nessa's. And then gone past it—moving in a different direction.

"Every time Dad looks at me he sees a science experiment?"

As soon as Delphine said this, Nessa realized how natural it would be that Delphine should think it. And how totally wrong it was. "He doesn't look at you that way," she said, hoping to reassure her.

"Yes, he does," Delphine insisted, her eyebrows drawn together, her mouth pursed as if she wanted to spit. "Every time he sees me there's this little moment. I can see it in his eyes. At first, I thought I must have done something wrong, but pretty soon I realized, he just hates me. It's funny, actually. I was worried, before we came out here, that maybe he wouldn't like Nate because Nate's not even his biological child. But no, it's me."

"No," Nessa said. "That's not true. All he does is try to connect with you."

As if she could read Nessa's mind, Delphine shook her head. "You can't see it," she said. "And maybe he can't either. But I can. And you know what else? The nightmares started the second he took over my life. I've known there was something wrong this whole time. At least now I know what it is."

"Delphine—" Nessa tried again. Delphine had always been better at reading people than Nessa, better at being with people in general. But this sounded paranoid.

"Maybe I should just join these kids. I feel like I belong more with them than I do anywhere else."

Nessa took a breath. She had to say something right away,

she knew, to counter Delphine's idea. Or at least question it. But as she struggled to find the right words, their conversation was interrupted by shouts. Looking up, Nessa saw lights appear in the trees on the other side of the stream. A few kids burst out of the woods, running, waving their arms, shouting.

"Bo! Bo!" they were shouting, barely getting the words out, they were breathing so hard. Nessa heard a commotion behind her as lights came on in the tree houses, flashlights shining into the clearing, lighting up the faces of the new kids, causing them to shield their eyes from the glare with their hands.

Bo was out of the trees, running for the three newcomers just as Nessa spotted a fourth kid, staggering in awkwardly.

"It's Rio!" the kid was shouting. Nessa heard panic in his voice. She saw it in the pulsating neon green light surrounding his body. And then, through the cloud of color, she saw what explained his staggering. He was carrying a dog. The dog lay limp in his arms, and for a second Nessa wondered if it was dead. Then she sprinted, grabbing a light from one of the kids, not caring that her shoes got soaked as she forded the stream in the dark. "Put him down! Put him down!" she shouted, then remembered that whenever her mother treated a sick animal, her first concern was always to keep her voice and body language calm.

Adjusting her tone, she went on: "Right here, that's good; now let me take a look, okay?" The kid said nothing. He appeared to be in shock. Nessa assumed that this dog was everything to him, the way she'd seen with the other kids and their dogs in the clearing earlier. Rubbing the dog from the chest to the throat to let him know she meant no harm, she found his jugular with her first two fingers.

Darn it. His pulse was slow.

Using the flashlight, she performed a quick exam. His eyes were unfocused, his pupils two different sizes—a sign of brain injury. There was a deep scrape on his left shoulder, but it wasn't deep and had already started to heal. Running the flashlight down to his hips, she saw the issue. There was a gash, a deep puncture wound, and some tearing of the flesh on the inside of his upper leg, near the abdomen. Nessa wasn't sure, but based on the bleeding, she could guess this had at least nicked the animal's femoral artery.

Ripping off her sweatshirt, she pressed it to the animal's wound.

"I need something to tie this off with," she said, looking up for the kid who had been carrying the dog. Delphine offered up her hair elastic. "We've got to get this dog to a vet," she said to Bo.

Bo bit her lip. "Town is fifteen miles away," she said. "And who knows if that vet's even there?"

"Take him to the lab," Delphine said. "They're scientists."

"We can get there fast if we take my golf cart," Nessa said. She scooped the animal into her arms. For a minute she debated transforming, but she would have had no way to carry the dog. Even in human form, she guessed she could run faster than anyone else here.

"Okay," Bo said, then shouted to the rest of the crew. "Tommy, Ian, CJ, you're in charge while I'm gone. Topher, Delphine, you come with me."

The boy whose dog it was stepped forward. "I won't leave him," the boy insisted.

It clearly wasn't what Bo thought was correct, but she gave in.

"Okay, Kai," she said. "Okay."

CHAPTER THIRTEEN

Nessa's arms burned as she rushed through the woods, carrying Rio. She could hear Delphine breathing heavily behind her. Delphine wasn't used to running like this, but she kept up, and they both followed Bo, who was in front, her flashlight leading the way. Somewhere in the dark behind the girls, Kai and Topher must have been running too. Colors were flashing for Nessa, highlights of blue and orange burning out against the dark of the night. She tried to ignore them. She didn't have time to analyze what they might mean.

Once the group reached the golf cart, they piled in, Kai holding Rio in the back, Topher helping him, Delphine and Bo sharing the front passenger seat next to Nessa. "I thought he was going after a squirrel when he took off into the woods," Kai said. "I'd been hearing rustling, and I was like, 'Go get 'em, boy.'" His voice cracked on the last few words. "I didn't know it would be dangerous."

"It's okay," Bo said, reaching back to touch Kai's hand, then gently resting a few fingers on Rio's head. Nessa felt an electric current pass through her body as she watched Bo being so kind to the kid. The current reminded her of the way she'd felt around Luc. "It wasn't your fault," Bo went on. "There's stuff out there we don't understand."

Nessa lowered her eyes. The "stuff" on the preserve was her own father's experiments. Experiments that might cause a dog to lose his life.

"I never saw it," said Kai, and Nessa could hear that he was crying—his voice soupy. "After Rio went into the brush, I heard bodies hitting the ground. I was trying to run to him. There was screeching. It sounded like a person laughing."

"That might have been a hyena," Bo said, "or a coyote."

"It was alone?" Nessa asked.

"I don't know," Kai said. "By the time I got there, whatever it was had gone. All I can remember is that Rio was crying so loud. The poor guy."

"Hey, we need some help here!" Delphine called when they stepped into the atrium of the Chimera Corp. lab. Clouds of bright green began to snake their way off her—Nessa guessed this color testified to her sister's fear. Nessa watched the tendrils of color drip down into the Well as, rushing toward the railing, Delphine leaned over it and shouted, "Anyone there?"

"Wow," Nessa heard Topher say as he, too, looked down into the Well.

Bo whistled. "I never knew this place was so big," she said. "That's where the scientists work?"

"Yeah," Nessa acknowledged, and said a silent prayer that at least one of the scientists working late had an expertise with mammals. A lot of the Chimera research involved reptiles, plants, flies, protozoa. . . . Meanwhile, Rio was growing heavy in her arms.

Nessa heard a voice from behind her: "Nessa? Delphine?" She turned to see a rumpled Daniel. He'd emerged from his office only two steps ahead of Milton. Gabriel was with them. Jonathan, Chimera Corp.'s head of security, brought up the rear of this unexpected procession. *What are they all doing here after hours . . . and together?* Nessa wondered. *Is something going on?*

"Where have you girls been?" Daniel demanded. "I've been worried sick. You didn't pick up your phones!"

For the first time since they'd met, Daniel sounded angry with his daughters. Nessa felt her insides tighten in response. She saw Delphine take a few steps backward, toward the door, a pink cloud rising. Nessa couldn't tell exactly who the cloud belonged to or what it meant, only that every other color in the lab—the beiges and browns—were now appearing pink-tinted, the colors blending and splitting so she could not see. She squeezed her eyes closed. "I texted you," Nessa said. "Did it not go through?"

"Oh, I got your text." Daniel spoke through gritted teeth. "Did you get mine?"

"I turned my phone off," Nessa confessed. "I wanted to be alone." She lowered her voice, "with Delphine."

Daniel's eyes darted to his younger daughter. Could he see how his angry tone was affecting her? "Well," he said. He sighed, and Nessa could tell he was reeling his anger back in. "You're safe now. But please don't do that again." He took a step closer to Nessa. "There was an unanticipated event out in the preserve. We were required to initiate a security protocol. I'm glad to see you're okay."

Before Nessa could ask what had caused the security protocol, Milton and Jonathan melted back into Daniel's office and Daniel gestured to Bo, Kai, and Topher. "Okay, now," he said. "Who are they?"

Nessa turned. "They're—" she started, and then stopped. How to explain them? Seeing Bo, Kai, and Topher in the bright light of the pristine lab, Nessa noticed that they seemed dirtier than they had in the woods.

Also younger. When Kai had come back from patrol, he'd been a veritable Han Solo with his flashlight and camo bandana wrapped around his forehead. Now, Nessa realized, she'd put him much more squarely into the Luke Skywalker category.

Delphine stepped forward. "They're my friends," she said. "And they need help." There was nothing supplicating or apologetic in her voice, and Nessa wished Delphine could be a little less aggressive—she sounded like she was daring Daniel to fail her.

"This is Rio," Nessa said, shifting to free up one hand and reveal the dog's face. Rio was barely breathing. His fur was matted with blood and one of his ears had been torn. "He belongs to these kids. They're—uh—hikers. Delphine got to know them today. Their dog got attacked in the woods."

Daniel sucked in his breath.

"Look at his leg," Nessa directed, and Daniel moved his examination down to the bleeding. "He ran into something in the woods that bit him."

As Daniel gingerly lifted the bandage, Gabriel leaned in too, using his thumb and forefinger to measure the gash. Under the powerful laboratory lights, Nessa could see evidence of tooth marks. She saw Daniel and Gabriel notice them too, then exchange meaningful looks.

"Can you tell what did this?" Nessa asked.

Gabriel looked at the floor. Daniel said, "Not specifically. You know, the animals in the preserve. They . . . *change* sometimes." He paused. "There's one we've been tracking, though it keeps slipping out of our grasp."

Daniel looked at Gabriel again—another meaningful

eyebrow raise. What was going on?

"This is why no one should be out in the woods," Daniel said. He looked at Nessa. "Especially not you, understand? When you're running, stay on the roads, and stay safely in the southern end of the preserve."

"Okay, fine," Delphine said, stepping forward. "But what matters now is helping this dog. Can you?"

Daniel looked at Delphine, narrowed his eyes, and said, "I can certainly try."

Moving with quick confidence, Daniel led the way into his lab, addressing the Outsider Kids over his shoulder, "There's tea and hot chocolate in the kitchen, if any of you want to have a hot drink while I look at him." None of the Outsider Kids took him up on the offer, choosing instead to follow Daniel, Gabriel, Nessa, and Delphine into the lab.

Gabriel quickly wiped down the surface of a stainless steel table with iodine. He then covered it over with surgical towels. Nessa laid Rio out on top of them. One of the techs rolled in a cart. "Bring it over here," Gabriel said. "Delphine, there should be bandages. Can you find them?"

Nessa shivered. Surgery. On animals. She knew this went on at Chimera—it had to—it was part of the investigation into how the genetic meddling they were doing manifested physiologically. Still, it creeped her out. Too many similarities to the work she had witnessed being done at the Paravida facility in

Tether, where wolves were being genetically as well as surgically altered.

She noticed Bo taking in the cabinets of supplies. Nessa now knew the names of the equipment after working in the lab: microplate washers and incubators, thermal cyclers, sonicators, spectrophotometers, centrifuges whose white boxy cases always reminded Nessa of her grandma's ancient sewing machine, custom-built DNA freezer facilities, pipettors, something called a polymerase chain reactor that Daniel generally referred to as "Hal."

What did Bo make of all of this? She was smart. She knew things in the forest weren't right. When Nessa caught her eye, Bo was looking at her. She felt as though Bo could see right through the lab. Through Nessa.

Topher raised himself up on his toes and then lowered back down to his heels, over and over again like he was pumping up to explode. Kai was standing beside Nessa, as close to Rio as he could get.

Rio's breaths were growing increasingly shallow and did not come often, but when they did, his ribs showed. Daniel readjusted Rio's bad leg, and Nessa saw that it was nearly separated from his body. Whatever had bitten him must have held on tight and for a good long time, thrashing mightily.

If this was a cat, as the bite suggested, it was a powerful one. Nessa saw yellow in the wound and squeezed her eyes closed. This was not a good moment for a color storm. She opened them again to see colors hanging in the room. Vermillion. A word Nessa had only learned from the books in Halliday's office. Was this maybe another indicator of fear?

What happened next went fast, like an explosion. Daniel lifted off the bandages he was pressing into the wound so Gabriel could irrigate the wound with saline. Then, ripping open a sterilized pouch, Gabriel stanched the blood with fresh gauze. "This was good work with the tourniquet and the field dressing," Daniel said. "But it's still bleeding freely."

Gabriel began pouring iodine on Rio's wound, as Daniel lifted a syringe and began injecting.

"This is an anesthetic," Daniel told Kai gently. "He won't feel the pain. Hold him while it sets in. I need to move his leg."

Kai grasped Rio by the shoulders to steady him, leaning forward to anchor the dog's body. Nessa—who had seen a lot of procedures like this back in Tether—didn't know how much strength Rio had left to fight.

But whatever he had, he brought. When Daniel pulled out Rio's leg, the dog's breathing became ragged and his leg started to kick. Daniel lost his grip and Rio kicked a tray of instruments to the floor, where they fell with a clatter Nessa felt in her teeth.

"Okay, buddy, okay," Daniel said, trying to get a firm grasp of him. But Rio was breathing raggedly and quickly now, his tongue out of his mouth.

His back leg kicked again. As Daniel finally got purchase on the leg and asked Gabriel for saline, Rio began to convulse, biting into his own tongue, releasing a trickle of blood down onto the side of the table, shaking the table, shaking—it felt—the room.

"Hold him!" Daniel shouted, reaching forward and wrestling a tongue depressor into Rio's clenched jaws, levering the mouth open and then wedging it in.

"More gauze," Gabriel said, his voice low and urgent. Delphine ripped open another pouch. Gabriel pushed against the wound with one hand, administering an injection with the other.

Nessa felt Rio's body relaxing as the convulsions slowed then stopped. Rio was still. A small cloud of color storm formed in the room. Black. Nessa looked straight at it with a gasp, remembering Halliday's warning. *Black indicates irreversible death. Do not intervene.* Bo narrowed her eyes and looked at the empty space that had Nessa transfixed, then looked at Nessa.

Daniel put an arm on Kai's shoulder. "He's still with us, but I don't think for much longer."

Kai reached his arms across Rio's body, as if he could block him from receiving this information. "This is my dog!"

"He's lost a lot of blood," Gabriel said. "His pulse is very weak. He's shutting down."

Nessa heard Daniel reciting details: Rio's artery had been severed; he'd lost a lot of blood; they didn't think they could keep him alive during the time it would take to stitch the artery back together. "That's a major surgery," Daniel explained. "It's more than we can do here. And honestly, even a vet with all the right equipment and blood supply probably couldn't do it now.

The convulsions. This dog's body is telling us it's time." He took a deep breath. "Can we take him out of this pain?"

Kai glared at Daniel. He actually growled. He wasn't letting go of Rio.

"Bo," Nessa said.

Bo looked back at Nessa. The look clearly said, "If you tell me to do this and you're wrong, I will end you," and Nessa—who a half second before had not been able to bear it—nodded to let Bo know that this was what she had to do.

"Kai," Bo said, covering the boy with her arms, enfolding him the way he was trying to enfold his dog. "This is going to be really hard, and I'm going to be right here with you the whole time."

Nessa turned. She could feel an old emptiness growing heavy inside her, like something in gaseous form was cooling, sinking, becoming a liquid she could not absorb.

Nessa felt a hand on her arm. It was Delphine. Delphine was crying silently, tears flowing down her cheeks. She said, "He can make it so Rio won't feel pain, right?" When Nessa nodded, Delphine leaned down to say to Kai, "Do you want that, Kai?"

Kai nodded. He raised himself, allowing access to the dog. Nessa saw a fat, wet tear land on the top of Rio's forehead. A gray-blue fog rose off Kai and descended over Rio's body like a blanket.

Gabriel removed the saline tubing again while Daniel readied a second injection. He wasn't making an announcement about what he was doing, but Nessa knew. She'd seen her mother put animals "to sleep" plenty of times.

Kai laid his cheek on the top of Rio's head. Bo was crying now too, wiping at each tear as it came. Topher turned away and coughed loudly. "Good boy," Kai whispered. "You're a very good boy and I'm so, so sorry." Then he lifted his head, wiped his nose on his sleeve, and said, "Okay."

It was perfectly silent in the room except for the consistent hum of the ventilation broken only by the inconsistent gasps of Kai weeping as they all watched Rio take his last few breaths. He trembled for one more minute as the medicine reached his heart, then he was still, frozen in what felt to Nessa to be midbreath.

Kai's blue haze lifted to hang above them, deepening in shade, dripping tentacles down into the room.

CHAPTER FOURTEEN

*D*aniel's cell phone buzzed. He pulled it out of his pocket, silenced it, exchanged a look with Gabriel. Gabriel nodded and, pulling off the surgical gloves he was still wearing, left the room.

Daniel looked at Nessa, then at Delphine. "I have to go," he said. As if apologizing to Delphine, he added, "There's a—uh—situation. I'm needed." Nessa had been so absorbed by the drama surrounding Rio, she'd forgotten about the security protocol Daniel had referred to when they'd arrived at the lab.

"Does the situation have anything to do with whatever went after Rio?" Nessa asked.

Daniel looked Nessa in the eye but didn't confirm. His face softened, and he put a hand on Kai's shoulder. "Take as much time in here as you need." To Delphine he added, "Your friends are welcome to spend the night. Arrange it with Milton. She should be in her office. I don't want any of you going back out into the preserve, do you understand?"

Delphine nodded, but she didn't look Daniel in the eye. "Nessa," he said. "I have to go."

"Wait!" Nessa said. Daniel stopped. "Can I—can I speak to you a moment?" He raised his eyebrows to let her know she could, but it should be quick.

Daniel spoke first as Nessa trailed him into his office.

"I'm putting you in charge," he said, pulling on a down jacket. "Keep those kids inside. Give them food. Wake up Scott, have him cook them a meal—they certainly look like they could use it." He fished a set of keys out of the top drawer of his desk—Nessa recognized them as the keys to the pickup he used for rough riding deep into the park.

"But Dad," Nessa said. "What's out there? What's going on? *Is* it a cat? Or something else?"

Daniel patted a pocket, like he was checking for his wallet. "It's very dangerous."

"Why would you let something dangerous like that out into the preserve?"

Daniel shook his head. "You know that's what the park is for. We use it to study nature, live and in action."

"I'm not sure I knew that dogs were going to die," Nessa said as he headed for the door. "How big is this thing? This was something big." Daniel sighed, then turned to leave the room. "Dad, what's going on?"

Daniel froze with his hand on the knob. The room went vermillion again, but Nessa didn't know if that was showing her fear or Daniel's. "Just stay put," he said. "I'll try to explain when I get back." He turned the knob and rushed through the atrium.

Nessa followed, in time to see him head outside with Jonathan, the security director. She watched them through the large plate glass windows. Jonathan turned and Nessa gasped, he was carrying a hunting rifle.

The two men disappeared from view, heading for the lot where the pickup was parked.

And then it registered. The atrium where Nessa was standing now was quiet. The Outsider Kids were supposed to have stayed in the lab, but she hadn't sensed that they were still there.

"Delphine!" she called, running for Daniel's lab. But her instinct was right. Her sister, the kids, the dog's body, the foil thermal blanket—they were gone.

Nessa put her hands on her face, forgetting that they were still stained with Rio's blood. She should have known. Delphine. Bo. They weren't going to wait, locked in the compound, while the rest of their group remained stuck out in the woods. These were kids who had decided that the dangers of their homes were more formidable than the dangers they'd experienced while homeless. They had lost faith in the families they came from but doubled down on a newly formed one.

Taking a deep breath, Nessa pushed through the doors after them, crossing the road in front of the lab and heading directly into the woods.

As she moved through the humid night, Nessa could feel the buzzing of nocturnal life. It was there, behind the bark of the trees and seeping into the soil, sniffing in the treetops and spying prey below. Swiveling heads, slithering bodies, growing, retracting, fighting, and flying. She joined in, her transformation the best way she knew to honor and acknowledge not just the life in the forest but the death she had just witnessed. As a human, she kept life and death separate in her mind, but in wolf form, they were simply two points in a single process. Nessa started to run.

She stuck close by the road, listening, smelling. She heard the pickup's roar and saw the headlights in the darkness. Daniel was heading north, she thought. Fine. That wasn't the area of the preserve she was worried about.

She ran west, silently, still tracking Delphine and the Outsider Kids. It was not long before she caught their olfactory trail. Perhaps they were safe in a group. Perhaps whatever had attacked Rio had picked him off because he was alone?

Nessa waited, perched on a small cliff behind the cover of

trees. Soon, she saw lights, and then the kids' shadowy forms appeared on the path below the cliff, moving quickly, in spite of the fact that they were carrying Rio's body, wrapped in a towel from the lab.

Nessa followed the kids, keeping to higher ground. As she got close to their camp, the dogs picked up her presence and began to wake each other with warning barks. She backed off, trotting a wide perimeter around the camp, doing what she could to protect the Outsider Kids by laying down scent.

She tried not to think about the scene Kai had described. The cackling laughter, the thumping bodies. The cat—or whatever attacked Rio—would not bother the kids once they were safely lodged in their trees. She hoped they'd haul Rio up with them if they weren't going to bury him until the morning.

Which gives me one night to track this chimera down, Nessa thought, charging through the underbrush, heading north toward the part of the park she'd explored the least. *You should stop hunting dogs, chimera. I am going to hunt you first.*

A few minutes later, Nessa caught the trail of a large animal and she tracked it. She was careful to stay off the park road, even if it would have been the easiest way to move north quickly. She didn't want to bump into Daniel. In wolf form, she'd be a stranger to her father. She hadn't forgotten about Jonathan's gun.

So she ran—to the Cliffs where they'd gone on their first

family tour of the preserve. They'd taken the pickup as far in as the logging road would go and then followed a trail that switched back and forth, climbing from a dried-up streambed upward through the forest. Nessa remembered how the thickly growing trees in the gully had quickly given way to sparser growth, the path underfoot clay-like, slippery, layered with shale.

As Nessa reached the summit, she could feel the openness. The wind puffed her fur. Sitting back on her haunches, she took a scan, the smells of the forest and its inhabitants rising with the moisture evaporating from below.

But it was not a smell that told her where she needed to go. It was lights. Floodlights. Glowing in the dark, brighter than anything on the Chimera Corp. campus. As she watched, she saw a smaller light approaching on the road that traveled through the park. Daniel's truck!

Nessa scrambled back down the path, forking off toward the facility as soon as the twisting path allowed. She headed north, led through the underbrush by the smell of diesel fuel and the sounds of boots pounding soft earth. Eventually she reached a tall, chain-link fence.

Before she could investigate further, she heard a hissing sound and turned to find herself face-to-face with an enormous cat, crouched in the low branch of a nearby tree as if it had been waiting for her.

Nessa froze, and the cat raised up, arching its back, hissing again, its fur standing on end. Then it seemed to relax, almost pursing its lips. It lifted a front paw and licked it.

Then the cat was gone, leaping to a higher branch in the tree and then another and another. It was fast. Nessa could barely track it as it leapt away.

Is this a chimera? she wondered. It seemed bigger and stronger than a bobcat should be.

Had she just met Rio's killer?

After waiting several long moments for the cat to return, Nessa pushed on toward the lights, moving past the fence, which turned out to be incomplete, and finding herself facing a construction site. Trees had been uprooted and the earth gouged by the tracks of heavy machinery, some of which were still parked in scattered positions on the outskirts of the buildings. She passed large coils of chain-link ready to be strung on poles already in place, bags of concrete mix and building materials under tarps.

Nessa hid in the shadows of the machines and the piles of dirt they'd dumped, darting from one to the next until she was close to the center of the new laboratory facility. There was a small shed, which looked like it housed utilities, and beyond it, there was a trailer beside a large, disc-shaped building that looked newly built. Nessa ducked behind the shed, finding shelter next to a pallet of concrete blocks.

And it was a good thing she waited. The trailer was occupied. She heard the clicking of keys on a computer keyboard, the hum of so many machines she could not tell how many or from where the sound came. Then she heard something that made her ears prick up. It was Jonathan, the security chief. He was talking animatedly. She kept hearing tantalizing tidbits but nothing that she could string together for meaning.

Hearing a door opening, Nessa crouched low and watched as a figure emerged from the shadows. It was Daniel.

The fur on her back stood on end, but Daniel was relaxed. He had his hands stuffed into the pockets of his khakis, as if this were an ordinary walk on an ordinary lawn, instead of what looked like a nighttime surveillance operation, beside a building, that looked like an alien spaceship.

Nessa darted forward, coming up right behind the trailer and looking inside its high windows. Inside, the trailer was outfitted with a row of video monitors, computer consoles built into the flimsy walls, sound boards. Two Chimera Corp. security officers were at the computers and Jonathan was standing behind them, his arms crossed, watching the monitors. There was a cloud of acid green, which compounded the tension she could see in the angle of the technicians' necks. One of them was rolling a pencil back and forth on the surface of the table in front of him, his eyes locked on Daniel's form as he entered the big Frisbee-shaped lab.

Nessa fixed her gaze on the monitors, each displaying the view of a room. There was a kitchen, a living room, but the screen Jonathan was focused on was a bedroom. It was dimly lit but Nessa could see the outlines of a bed, a dresser, a rug, lamps, paintings. "Okay, he's in," Jonathan said, just as Nessa saw the door in the bedroom open and Daniel appear on the screen. His presence caused the color cloud to shift, releasing a blue into the green. Daniel entering the room was making everyone in the surveillance van less afraid.

As if this were the opening scene in a play, the lights in the room Daniel had entered came up. Nessa saw that there was someone lying on the bed. Nessa connected the noise coming into the speakers in the room—a child crying.

Nessa heard a tech report, "There she is."

The crying figure in the bed lifted her head.

Nessa returned to the windows in the van as Jonathan noted, "She seems nice and calm. How much of the Proceptitor did you have to give her?"

The tech running the controls shook his head, consulted a tablet. "It took 20 cc in the end."

"Isn't that twice as much as last time?"

"Yep."

"At least we can be sure Daniel's safe in there."

"Is it true he wanted to go in there with nothing?"

The question was answered not by Jonathan, but by a voice Nessa recognized immediately—Gabriel's. She craned her neck to look for him in the trailer, but he must have been standing in a back corner of the room, and he remained out of Nessa's range of view. "Dr. Host believes the issues we're experiencing with this chimera are behavioral, not hardwired," he said.

"Shh," said the second tech. "I think he's talking to it."

"Her," Gabriel corrected and then the van went silent. Nessa located Daniel on the monitor. He was standing just inside the door to the bedroom, addressing the figure in the bed. "Sweetheart," he said, and for a moment, Nessa's own heart stood still. It wasn't that Daniel had ever called her that name. She wouldn't have expected him to. It was that that had been Vivian's word for Nessa. Vivian's name for both of them.

Nessa understood now. Daniel's visit to this place had nothing to do with the cat. The gun.

This was where Daniel must have been going on all those late nights, getting ready for the visit from the Haken lab. This was the chimera version of Delphine.

"Sweetheart," Daniel said again. "Are you awake still?" There was a noise from the bed. The crying had stopped when he'd first walked in. The noise was a grunt of sorts.

"Standby for Proceptitor gas at a 0.7 concentration," Gabriel said in a warning tone.

"Confirmed," the second tech replied. The acid color in the room intensified. *Is Daniel in danger?*

"I'm sorry you don't like your new house as much as I'd hoped," Daniel said.

There was another groan in reply. And then the creature mumbled, "Can't sleep here."

Daniel took a step forward. Nessa couldn't see his face on the screen, but she saw him hold out an arm toward the creature in the bed, and then let his arm fall to his side. Nessa had seen him be this careful choosing his gestures and words with the real Delphine too.

"Have you been having the dreams again?" Daniel asked

tentatively.

At his question, the creature in the bed was suddenly standing. She looked like she was in a fighter's ready position, her knees slightly bent, her arms loose. Everyone in the trailer jumped.

But Daniel did not move and neither did Nessa. She found herself transfixed by what she was seeing. Her sister. A chimera who stood over six feet tall.

"Should I gas her now?" the tech said.

"Not yet," was Gabriel's answer.

"He's flipping crazy, going in there," muttered the other tech, the one running the controls on the monitor.

"You said you could make them stop," the creature said, her voice as grating and screechy as it had been when Nessa first met her the previous spring. "You said that's what the shots were for."

Daniel was shaking his head slowly. Nessa could tell he was acting, slowing down his natural, businesslike demeanor in an effort to better communicate with the chimera. "I thought it would," he said. "I don't understand where the dreams are coming from."

"They're coming from just outside!" the chimera said, raising her voice. At the sound of it, Nessa felt herself stiffening. Inside the trailer, she saw Jonathan and the techs literally squirm. The tech who wanted to release the gas was jiggling his left leg.

"She's out there," the chimera said, pointing. "The white

wolf."

Nessa froze. Had the chimera seen her? How did she know Nessa was there?

And that's when she remembered: Delphine—the real Delphine—had been dreaming of a white wolf as well.

Daniel dragged a rocking chair around to face the bed and sat. "I'm glad they brought this old thing when they redecorated for you," he said. Nessa saw the chimera relax, and Nessa wondered if that was because Daniel seemed to be so relaxed. Maybe it was important to the chimera that people stop appearing to be so afraid of her? "We haven't had as many of our little chats these days. I'm sorry about that."

The chimera mumbled something Nessa couldn't understand. Nessa wished she could see the colors filling the room, but they weren't appearing in the monitor. It was funny how quickly she'd gotten used to the colors—how much she was starting to rely on her ability to read the emotions in a room.

Daniel started to rock. "I miss our talks," he said. The chimera took a step toward him. "I know you believe me. You can tell if I'm lying, can't you?"

The chimera took another step. "I usually can tell," she said, sounding both bashful and proud. The chimera lowered her head. "The dream is so scary, Daddy."

Daniel made a comforting, almost cooing sound. This seemed to draw the chimera the rest of the way toward him. As the chimera crossed the room, Nessa got the first real look at her that she'd had since the spring. Nessa was looking through a window, at a screen, which showed a camera located outside of yet another window. But still, the chimera looked so much like Delphine at this distance, Nessa would have sworn it was her sister. Same hair, same . . . posture. She swung her good arm in the same way Delphine did—a determined way of walking that Nessa associated with Delphine as far back as Nessa could remember.

But the rest of the walk was not the same. She was wearing shorts and a tank top, and from the bottom of her face to the top of one knee, Nessa could see the chimera was covered in a coat of fur. She had the ears of a bat. She hobbled on one leg that looked like it could belong to a deer and one leg that started that way but terminated in a human calf and bare foot. Now she lowered herself down at Daniel's feet and laid her head on his knee. "The white wolf wants to kill me," the chimera said, causing Nessa to look to either side of her. *Was* it possible the chimera knew she was here? She couldn't.

"There, there," said Daniel, a hand on the top of the Delphine chimera's head.

"Nessa," the chimera kept on. "Delphine. They want me to be dead also." Nessa felt a chill hearing her own name. It was almost worse to hear her sister's. "Your real daughters."

"They do not want you dead," Daniel said.

"Then why am I in this cage? You put me in a cage because you're afraid they'll see me and want me dead."

"Nonsense," Daniel said. "This is not a cage. This is your home. And you know as well as I the only reason we lock doors is because when I let you out you bite people. That was very naughty of you to gas that guard with his own gun."

The chimera laughed. "I didn't hurt him," she said. The chimera rubbed her cheek on Daniel's knee and he patted her again. She looked like a dog. A loyal, faithful dog. Dogs could bite, but their owners never believed it. They believed the dogs were their family.

As if confirming Nessa's suspicion, Jonathan, still watching the screen intently, chuckled. "You should have seen this thing when it was a baby. It bit everyone but Daniel. He'd go in there, and it would roll on its back to be scratched. He loved it like it was his own kid too."

Nessa thought about those years, after Vivian had taken Nessa and Delphine away from Daniel. Back then, this chimera must have seemed to Daniel all he had of family. The thought made her feel sorry for Daniel. Suddenly, she wanted to tell Jonathan to keep his thoughts to himself and was gratified when Gabriel did it for her. "She's human, you know," he said. "How'd you like to be locked up that way?"

"Look, I just keep the trains running around here," Jonathan said. "I don't have to have an opinion about the messed-up science experiments Dr. Host is running."

Over the speaker, Nessa heard Daniel singing. Leaning over the Delphine-like creature, he grasped her shoulders and helped her stand, walking her to the bed, humming all along, a song that cut Nessa to the core. Had he sung that to Nessa when she was a baby—so long ago that she'd forgotten it on all but the most subconscious level?

He drew back the covers and the Delphine chimera climbed in, like a little kid. Daniel sat on the mattress beside her, stroking her hair and continuing to hum. The tech at the monitor zoomed in on the chimera's face—her human eyes that she shared with Delphine, the string of drool descending from the mouth that could not quite close over mismatched teeth, the bat ears folding in as the eyes closed and she fell asleep. Daniel held up a hand, signaling. The tech pulled down on a switch that dimmed the lights back to low.

Daniel stood, walking silently out of the room, carefully closing the door so gently that even the microphones—which Nessa had noticed were extremely sensitive—did not pick up on any noise being made by the latch. He emerged moments later, heading for the trailer.

Nessa transformed behind the trailer before he could reach the door and found herself walking toward her father. There was something about the way he'd been with the chimera—sweet and caring—that had unlocked something inside Nessa.

"Dad," she said, registering the look of surprise on his face. Also registering that he was pleased to see her—as he always was. "This cage," she said, pointing to the new lab, which she could see head-on now—it was like an exhibit at a zoo. "You're keeping her here?"

The look on her father's face said it all. His guilt. How trapped he must feel. He didn't ask her any questions about how she'd followed him, what she'd seen and understood. It almost seemed he'd been expecting her, that he was happy to get caught. Daniel took in a deep breath and pulled the keys to his truck out of the pocket of his down coat. "Come Nessa," he said. "Let's drive."

CHAPTER FIFTEEN

She requires 24-hour surveillance now," Daniel said as he climbed into the truck after giving the team inside the trailer a nod of affirmation. He was carrying a strange shade of blue along with him that was more gray than the one she'd seen him emitting before—it reminded Nessa of the color that had lifted off Kai's body after Rio's death. Sadness? "But it didn't used to be like that. When she was a baby. Well, there was a fire in the lab. It was traumatic for her. For all of us, really."

Nessa knew about the fire. Her mother had set it.

Daniel looked at Nessa sideways. "Maybe you should tell me what you want to know. I have the feeling not all of this is news to you."

Nessa looked away from Daniel, studying her own reflection in the passenger window, thinking that the chimera looked like Delphine, but that she also looked like Nessa. Like Vivian. Like Daniel. Like family.

"I found the other lab when I was running," she admitted. "But you already know that?"

"I do," Daniel said. "CM told me."

"CM?" Nessa said.

"It's her name. What I call her. C for *chi-* and M for *-mera.*"

"Last spring, she told me she was Delphine. She called herself 'the other Delphine.'"

Daniel rolled his eyes. "CM can be dramatic."

Nessa laughed. There was something so unguarded about the way Daniel talked about the chimera. The chimera was family to him, Nessa saw. "Mom told me who she—CM—was." She tried to look Daniel in the eyes. She wanted to see his reaction. He glanced at her—she could see he was worried. "When Mom was in the hospital, she told me about that day when she found this human chimera baby. She told me how she tried to destroy her."

Now it was Daniel's turn to be silent. He closed his eyes for a second longer than a blink as the blue in the car shifted into a mauve-brown, a color that Nessa could not quite link to an emotion but made her uncomfortable.

"Nessa," he said, staring straight ahead. Nessa could see only what was illuminated by the lights of the truck—a contained area of flashing black and green, nothing you could focus on before it disappeared into the darkness the truck was cutting through.

Finally, Daniel cleared his throat. "Since I was young, curiosity about the body has been the driving force in my life. For years—well, after your mother left—I flew in a very good psychiatrist and unpacked all of this. . . ." He laughed, a short, bitter chuckle. "Not to bore you, but it goes back to my sister being sick my whole childhood and my mother sacrificing so much to care for her."

"You, Delphine, and Nate—what you three have is beautiful. I never felt like I had that kind of bond with my sister, or with any of my family. The equipment and care she needed, the way she could take a turn for the worse at a moment's notice, how there was never any time with my parents that I could be sure belonged to me. I was like Nate—I loved trains. The clear connections, the planning and design, the power of the engines, the simplicity of track. I found it infuriating when there was a break in the line. I found my sister's situation infuriating. That just a few scrambled elements of her genetic code upset everything."

"Yeah," Nessa said, feeling both sympathetic and like she wasn't sure where this was going. "That's messed up."

"My sister loved cats, so we always had them around. I

remember spending hours just watching the cats lie perfectly still, their beautiful twitching tails, their eyes that close via that interesting inner lid. Have you ever seen a cat jump? It's as if their joints are made of rubber."

"Cats are cool," Nessa agreed, although the one she'd encountered earlier that night hadn't exactly brought up this image of a friendly family pet.

"I remember thinking, 'How can they be so perfectly coordinated, their muscles so strong, everything working as it should, and my sister failing?' I thought, 'If humans were allowed to naturally select—if no one nursed the sick, allowed the unfit to reproduce themselves, we, as a species, might be better.' When I made CM, I was still thinking of that perfection animals achieve—of the beauty of these other life forms, their more stringently filtered genetic code."

"Stringently filtered?" Nessa said. "You mean 'cause animals don't live that long and the sick ones die right off the bat?"

"Ye-es," Daniel said. "But don't get me wrong—I quickly abandoned the idea that humans would be better if we eliminated our weaknesses. And not only for moral reasons, mind you." He smiled ruefully. "Weakness is hard to define as such. Beethoven was mad, but a genius. Einstein was a misfit as a child. I'm just saying, I wanted to put all that magnificent efficiency into the human body. I thought, 'Wouldn't it be wonderful to bring some animal-sourced strength into the human genome?'" He laughed. "You know, for me, there's always a lofty goal. But then there's the money. I was also thinking this could lead to cures for diseases worldwide."

Nessa was starting to have a hard time following Daniel's train of thought What did CM have to do with efficiency, magnificence, or curing disease? She could barely walk. The sound of her raspy voice made Nessa's skin crawl. "CM doesn't get sick?"

Daniel leveled Nessa with a meaningful gaze. "CM's immune system is remarkable," he said. "But don't get me wrong. CM is not the answer. She's not even a prototype. She's a . . . well, a failed experiment, if I'm going to be perfectly honest about it."

"Harsh!" Nessa said, feeling suddenly sad for the creature. "Isn't she, well, a person at this point?"

"Oh, yes, yes," Daniel said. "And that's the problem, isn't it? She is a person. A thinking person. And her contribution to science has gone beyond what I had hoped for. Her intelligence astounds me."

"Is she thinking as a human or an animal?" Nessa asked. She herself never knew how much her wolf mind was 100 percent wolf and how much she owed to its being human.

"Very good question," Daniel said. "The simple answer is we don't know, but CM is teaching us a lot about that very thing. I'm starting to see that animals use memory and instinctive reasoning in ways that make them possibly better at acquiring ultimate knowledge than we humans are."

Nessa already knew this to be true. In wolf form, she was able to think in different ways than she did as a human.

"We always celebrate our ability to use language," Daniel

went on. "But what if language is overrated? What if it actually prevents us from knowing—because we believe we only know what we can explain?" Daniel was tapping the steering wheel with his hands in his excitement. "Think about it—if there had been an easier way than language to transmit information about 'the bear heading in our direction,' would we humans have ever developed speech?"

This made Nessa laugh. Daniel smiled appreciatively. "CM has a way of almost absorbing knowledge from those around her—she knows things without being told. It's hard to keep a secret when she is around—she has a razor-sharp ability to read cues that, as a species, humans are essentially blind to, and then combine that information with what she has been told or knows through observation."

"What are you saying?" Nessa asked. "She reads minds?"

"Call it what you will," Daniel said. "She does it. And all of that—her language—that's just the first round of our study. She really doesn't get sick, so we're getting into her immune response now, and I have to tell you, what I'm finding is breathtaking."

"Breathtaking," Nessa repeated.

"Yes," Daniel said. "But still mysterious. Because our bodies are not machines. This is something I've learned—they're not trains. There are no springs, no drilled holes, no hinges or levers. We're not computers either—we're not made of chips or wires. Our brains are a collection of mysteriously animate tissue—bloodied, fat-sheathed, linked by a system of molecular microcommunications."

He swallowed, collecting himself. "All along, Nessa," he said, "I've pursued this research with CM without a long-term plan. I swear to you, I had no idea—ever—that we'd come as far as we have. First I wanted to see if an embryo could be created. Then I wanted to see how long it could go. I assumed at some point it would become unviable, but until it did, I just kept wondering, 'At what point . . . ?' And then I had a baby on my hands, a baby who was hooked up to ventilators, who I assumed had only days to live. Your mother sent her into the woods, and when I went to find her—I'd assumed she'd be dead—there she was, breathing on her own. She—" Daniel choked up here. "When I found her, I pulled off my jacket, wrapped her to keep her warm, and she held me. She held my finger."

"So you don't regret it?" Nessa asked. "That she lived?"

They'd reached the house now, and Daniel took a moment before answering, turning off the engine but making no move to get out of the cab. "I don't," he said. "And not just because the science has been rewarding beyond measure. Nessa, for so many years, I was a father without children. I was a family man whose family had disappeared. I sent money to you—that your mother never touched—but the hole in my life was filled, in some manner at least, by CM."

"Did you live in that house with her?" Nessa asked. "The one in the woods?"

Daniel sighed. "For the first few years, she lived with me. She slept in a crib in a room across the hall. One of the lab techs served as her nanny, but I was the primary caregiver. I taught her to read and to think. I devised games that revealed where her mind could go, and the limitations and extensions of her combined physical form."

"Then what happened?"

"She became too strong. She outsmarted her caretakers. She attacked them. She never hurt me, but she did make it . . . unsafe for the others."

Nessa nodded.

"I could never show her to the world. I was hard-pressed even to tell my colleague Dr. Ishikawa—who you'll meet in a few days—about her. This new lab we've built to house her—I'm hoping it can help us share the science while giving her more freedom and more security. CM's an asset to this lab as much as she is my daughter. Our investigation into her disease resistance has great potential. We're coming up with findings that might lead to some groundbreaking therapies. Dr. Ishikawa can connect us to funding and the support of the Japanese government—it's a precious opportunity to truly test what we're learning. I need to expand that relationship, get him on board, in order to see the work with CM through."

"But that lab. It's a giant cage. She says she doesn't like it."

"No, no," Daniel said. "She needs it. She has to come to terms with what she is. She was born of a lab. She exists for science. She and me together. There's some beauty there."

Nessa shook her head. "Before Mom died, she changed the way she felt about CM. She asked me to protect her."

Daniel's expression did not change, but the color in the cab did. The brown was joined by a warm, golden orange. "That should have been my job, protecting her," Daniel said. "It's what I've tried to do. I want you to know that I have tried."

"Dad," Nessa said, turning to face him. "You always say that we need to turn assumptions on their head. What if the assumption you're going with now—that you need to keep CM locked up at all—is wrong?"

Daniel shook his head. "She attacks her caregivers." He cleared his throat. "Routinely."

"What if she only is acting this way because she's being held as a prisoner?" Nessa said. "She loves you. She doesn't hurt you. She must know she's this big, shameful secret. Maybe she's like any of us. Maybe she couldn't control her aggression when she was little, but now, in the right environment, she'd be fine. Maybe if she feels included and comfortable, she wouldn't want to lash out." Nessa took a deep breath. "The human part of her belongs in a house with a family."

"What are you suggesting?" Daniel said.

Nessa thought of the time that she had first learned she was a werewolf. Half-transformed, her face, arms, legs covered in patches of unsightly fur, her hands half-morphed into paws, confused, scared for her life and her sanity, she had shown herself to Bree.

Bree could have run screaming, but she'd swallowed her initial shock, figured out how to get Nessa some help, and baked meat cookies.

Couldn't Nessa do that for the Delphine chimera? After all, Vivian had told her to take care of the chimera. She'd called the chimera Nessa's "other sister."

"I want to bring her home," Nessa said. "I want to try."

After that statement, they sat in silence looking into the lit-up windows of the house built into a cliff, the house with the views above the trees, the house that made Nessa feel light and easy and wise.

"Okay," Daniel said. The color in the truck was strange, and brilliant, like a kaleidoscope held to the sun. "We'll have to be careful about how we manage things with security, but I agree, especially if you want to, that it's worth a try."

CHAPTER SIXTEEN

The next morning, Nessa woke up early, transformed, and ran as a wolf to the Outsider Kids' camp, waiting patiently until she saw signs of life—kids throwing rope ladders down over the sides of the platforms, tarps moving, fires starting. Transforming back, Nessa located Delphine among the group of kids and jogged into their midst.

Delphine looked at her as she approached, and Nessa worried Delphine would harden her eyes and hunch her shoulders at the sight of her sister. But as Nessa got closer, she saw that Delphine's face was kind, and then, surprising Nessa, Delphine ran and threw her arms around Nessa's neck.

Wrapped up in the hug was everything they'd gone through together the night before—Nessa talking about the white wolf, watching Rio die. The hug made it clear: Things were different now.

"Look," Nessa said. "I don't want you walking around in the preserve alone, okay? There's a cat chimera on the prowl. I think it's what attacked Rio. Can you live with that?"

Delphine nodded.

"Will you come home with me now? Daniel's agreed to make a change that I think you'll want to be a part of."

Delphine nodded again.

They reached the house in time for breakfast. Scott had made bacon and eggs, and they dug in. Nessa was famished, and it looked like Delphine had worked up quite an appetite as well. Daniel kept looking over at her, trying to gauge, Nessa thought, her mood. But mostly he directed his attention to Nate, bringing up the train village they were constructing. Eventually, Delphine joined in the conversation and Nessa caught her smiling at Daniel.

Daniel seemed pleased. He seemed relaxed, enjoying the exchanges with Delphine and Nate. Then, after pouring himself a second cup of coffee, Daniel said, "There's something I have to tell you both, Nate and Delphine. There's someone I'd like you to meet."

Nessa watched Nate carefully as Daniel explained the situation. Nate didn't seem particularly fazed by the idea that he had a fourth sibling whom he was just finding out about now, that this sibling had some nonhuman parts to her. The colors above him—almost always a straightforward navy blue—did not shift. "Does she like trains?" he asked.

"I'm sure she does," Nessa promised, thinking, *She better.*

Delphine laughed at that with the rest of them. The colors above her were soft, mild pinks and mauves. When Nessa explained what she had seen the night before, how tender CM had been with Daniel, Delphine sounded like her old self when she said, "I think you're right, Ness. Anyone could go crazy being kept in a cage like that."

Nessa wondered if Delphine had felt caged herself. She didn't ask.

Over the course of the next few days, preparations were made for what Daniel and Milton referred to as "the visit."

They rigged CM's room with cameras. They installed locks on the doors to the bedrooms. There wasn't actually a lock (or a door) that would hold CM if she really wanted to break through it, but these locks were linked to the security system, so that if any of the doors were opened, it would alert the security team.

Nessa felt happy in a way she hadn't in a long time. The reality of CM was not breaking them apart as a family. If anything, it was bringing them together. It was setting things right.

But not everyone agreed. The next day, Nessa was out for a run after finishing her work at the lab, and she came across Bo, leaning against a tree alongside the road, whittling something that looked like a spear tip. Was this a stakeout?

Nessa could have run past her, but she stopped. The two girls said, "Hey," quietly, at the same time, and then there was a beat of silence.

It was a warm afternoon—how did Bo look so cool and comfortable in long pants and combat boots, her hair tucked up into her army cap? Nessa remembered how tough Bo had been on the night they took care of Rio. How clearly in charge. How careful she'd been with Kai's desperate sadness. Nessa respected Bo.

"How's Kai doing?" Nessa asked.

Bo's silence was tough to interpret, like she didn't have the words to explain. And then she took a step toward Nessa and put a hand on her shoulder.

Nessa didn't move. Bo's touch was soft, the pressure controlled. The gesture felt natural and expected, like it was a handshake. But also? Standing this close to Bo, Nessa could smell her. Bo had a smell she trusted. She smelled like a stream or a tree—clean, healthy, rich with earthiness.

There was also something familiar about it.

Nessa met Bo's eyes. "I think it's cool," Nessa said. "That you live out here. I wish—" She was trying to tell her something important, but she didn't know what she wanted to say. It might have been connected to the idea that Nessa sensed that

Bo loved the woods as much as Nessa did. That Bo could learn from them the way Nessa could. That they were alive to her.

Before Nessa could finish her sentence, Bo kissed her. On the lips.

The kiss was light, questioning, and took Nessa by surprise. Nessa stepped back away from Bo.

The kiss had deposited something electric deep inside her.

She hadn't realized this feeling was even possible.

Nessa pushed her hair off her forehead. She kept her feet planted firmly on the ground, watching Bo watch her, not taking her eyes off Bo.

In the kiss, Nessa had felt the sweetness buried beneath Bo's toughness, a need for connection that Nessa shared. Since Luc, Nessa had not wanted anyone's touch on her body. Nessa had felt as if her body had somehow been shrouded and now, suddenly, the shroud was being lifted.

Nessa took a step toward Bo and kissed her back. She could tell her kiss surprised Bo as much as Bo's kiss had surprised Nessa. But Bo did not pull away. Nessa pushed. The kiss went deeper. Nessa felt a tingling traveling down to her feet. Bo lifted a hand to Nessa's shoulder then pulled away. She smiled, mischievously, intoxicatingly, then turned and slipped into the woods, leaving Nessa breathless.

"What," Nessa said out loud as she leaned back and nearly fell onto the tree behind her, "was that?"

The plan for CM's day of arrival was carefully considered. CM would arrive in the afternoon. Daniel would be with her alone for the first few hours. Then they would all gather for dinner. If all went well, CM would sleep in the bedroom that had been set up next to Delphine's. (A member of Jonathan's security team would be sleeping in a storage closet off the kitchen that was hastily retrofitted as a security hub, complete with monitors into CM's room and anywhere else she was likely to go.)

"Are you sure this is a good idea?" Bree asked when she and Nessa were FaceTime-ing on the morning of CM's introduction—Nessa had told her the story of finding Delphine with the Outsider Kids, trying to save Rio. "Didn't she try to kill you last spring when you first met her?"

"She did," Nessa conceded. "But I just have a feeling about this." She repeated all the earlier justifications—how lonely and sad CM had seemed. How uncomfortable it felt to have someone who was your genetic sister housed in a cage, like an animal in a zoo.

"Maybe you should send her to Isle Royale," Bree said, changing the subject, explaining to Nessa how well the Paravida wolves who had repopulated the island were doing. Daniel Bergen had gotten permission to tag along on one of the scientists' helicopter surveillances, and Bree had been with him.

"Did you see Luc?" Nessa asked, holding herself back from sounding over eager. She hadn't told Bree about the kiss with Bo, even though she couldn't stop thinking about it. Every five minutes she considered running for the woods, tracking Bo down, asking her what it *meant*. But now, thinking about Luc with someone who had known him, the kiss was hard to re-imagine. And it felt wrong.

Bree lowered her eyes. "Maybe?" she said. "I can't say I could recognize him personally, but there's definitely a big gray wolf that's in charge of things up there."

"How does he seem?"

"Wolfy?" Bree said. She laughed. "You know I can't tell what the wolves are feeling the way you can. But Nessa, if it's really him, well, I guess it's not *him*. There just doesn't seem to be anything human about him left at all." Bree launched into an explanation of how the big gray lead wolf had had to fight off challenges to his alpha status, how fierce he had been. All the time she was talking, she used a sorrowful tone, as if trying to pad the landing of Nessa's inevitable disappointment.

Nessa started to laugh.

"Wait—what's—what's funny?" Bree asked.

"Luc," Nessa said. "Full wolf? No human residue? That's totally him."

Bree looked puzzled as Nessa continued to laugh at what felt like an inside joke.

"Nessa," she finally said, twirling one of her corkscrew curls around a finger. "You seem . . . happy."

Nessa could feel herself smiling. A big, wolfy grin. "Yeah," she said, "I guess I am."

Nessa and Bree spent the rest of the call talking about Bree's upcoming "vacation" with her dad. Ted was a long-haul truck driver. He and Bree had an annual tradition of her joining him for a week of travel, listening to audiobooks or the "Great Courses" Ted liked, stopping for ice cream cones on a daily basis. She was trying to convince him to switch routes with a buddy, so they could end up in Oregon.

"Seriously?" Nessa said. "That would be amazing. When?"

Bree explained the itinerary.

"That's so soon!" Nessa said. "It's the day after the Japanese scientists leave. That's perfect."

"Yeah, I was thinking of surprising you and just showing up, but do you know I Googled Chimera Corp. and the only publicly provided address is really the address of a law firm that represents them. It's not even in Oregon—it's in Seattle. I don't really know where you are."

"Ugh, security," Nessa said, but for once, she didn't want to dwell on it. She gave Bree the GPS coordinates. "Don't reveal this to anyone!"

"My lips are sealed," Bree promised.

That afternoon, after finishing up the work she was doing with a cute bunch of white rat-mole chimeras, Nessa distributed treats to them, then swung up to the floor above, where Delphine was reading something on the screen of a computer terminal, concentrating. "Hey, you," Nessa said, breaking her concentration.

They'd planned to travel back to the house in Nessa's golf cart together—CM would be waiting for them at the house.

"Hey," Delphine said, not looking away from the screen, the cloud of pink and acid green shimmering as she blinked her eyes.

"You, uh, doing something interesting?"

"Yeah," said Delphine, pulling out a lock of hair and stretching it behind her ear. A wisp of green smoke invaded the colors already playing all around her. "I'm trying to find out what happens to Chimera Corp. files when they get archived into the long-term storage." She began to describe various encryption methodologies and why Chimera Corp.'s was different. Nessa couldn't quite follow it, but she narrowed her eyes. There was something about the task at hand that sounded like it went beyond what a teenage intern was usually entrusted with. "Are you supposed to be looking into that?"

"Um . . . if I said no, would you be upset about that?"

Nessa laughed. She figured she probably didn't need to *actually* worry. Chimera's cyber security team were a few computer science degrees ahead of Delphine. "Forget I asked. My real question is this: I was wondering if you wanted a ride back to the house."

Delphine checked the time on her phone. "Isn't it early?" she said. "I thought we were supposed to give CM some adjustment time?"

"We are," said Nessa. The truth was, she'd been getting so anxious about the move that she wasn't able to concentrate. "I just need to see the sky a bit. Come with me? I'll drive slow."

"Fine," Delphine said, shutting down the computer and stowing the keyboard in a drawer.

They stopped by the employee kitchen to grab cans of seltzer for the ride home, then took the golf cart to a lookout spot on the company road. For a few minutes, they sat in silence, drinking seltzer, taking in the view. Nessa never got sick of the sight of rolling forested mountains of the Chimera Corp. park, but found herself thinking not about mountains but about Bo. She wanted to tell Delphine about the kiss—to tell someone what it felt like to be pulled out of herself again, to feel wanted and to want someone. But would she destroy the memory by shining too much light on it?

"So, you okay with all of this CM business?" Nessa asked. "And this wolf business on top of that?"

Delphine shrugged. She looked at Nessa, and Nessa could see her sister's eyes had teared up a bit. "I think so?" Delphine said. "I know—" She paused. "I know things will never go back to the way they were. I know the way they were wasn't what I thought it was."

"Yep," Nessa said.

"I really miss Mom," Delphine added. Nessa saw the smoky-blue tones that had surrounded Kai's body after Rio died. "I miss the way I always felt safe with her."

Nessa nodded. She missed that too.

"You're really a wolf?"

"Yes," Nessa said. She kept her eyes forward, looking out

over the treetops, her feet propped up on the dashboard, the seltzer balanced between her knees. "You can, you know, ask me questions about it if you want."

And Delphine did. She wanted to know how it felt to transform, what Nessa liked to do as a wolf. Nessa told her the story of breaking into the Paravida plant back in Tether, about saving the Paravida wolves from the National Guard, about finding the chimera version of Delphine while running in Daniel Host's preserve the year before.

She told Delphine about Luc—how much he had taught her about being a wolf. She told her about the pack back in Tether.

"Do you miss them?" Delphine said. "The other wolves?"

Nessa nodded. "I do," she said.

"But Mom never had a pack," she said. "She wasn't really a wolf the way you are."

Nessa shrugged. "I guess not."

Delphine shook her head. Nessa wondered how she could possibly be taking all of this in.

"The Outsider Kids say that at the end of June and the beginning of July—when you live outside—you feel this weird energy all the time, and now that the light's fading a bit, the energy is going out of you too. Like humans are solar powered or something."

"Ha," said Nessa, thinking that it was true. Also, she was glad that Delphine had found a way to change the subject.

Then Delphine laughed. "They're really cool, but I think

they're turning themselves into something like animals. They have this whole ritual when the full moon comes. They go to this one hilltop to watch it rise. They sing special songs."

"They do?" Nessa said, laughing.

"Maybe we can go with them sometime. If you're, you know, not a wolf then?" Delphine laughed at this, like she couldn't quite believe it. Then she said, "They live outside even in the winter. They dig holes and sleep inside them. They say it's actually not that bad."

"It sounds freezing," Nessa said.

Delphine laughed. "It's weird to think it's still the middle of summer, but at some point, it will be fall here. We'll go to school. We'll have Halloween and Christmas and Mom will still be gone."

Nessa said nothing. She was thinking about Vivian too. About how one of the best things about Vivian was that when you told her something, she didn't always feel she had to have an instant opinion. Sometimes she would just give your words air to breathe.

When they got to the house, they heard Nate's voice coming from the living room. They couldn't hear every word he was saying, but they could tell he was explaining something complicated. *He must be talking to Micah,* Nessa thought. *CM must still be in her room.* Micah and Nate had both been extensively briefed on CM's "differences," but still, Nate couldn't possibly sound this comfortable in her presence . . . not yet.

But when they turned into the sprawling living room, they saw that Nate and CM were together, arranging the television remotes and a few things from around the room in size order and setting them up on the low coffee table.

This was a game Nessa sometimes played with Nate. He'd move one object that was bugging him. He would do it without thinking, but she would make the next move and he would notice that she was helping him and thinking about the way that he was thinking and then it would become a game. It was one of the comfortable ways they had of being together. But now he was doing that with CM?

She shot a glance in Delphine's direction. Was Delphine getting it? That this was a good sign?

Delphine looked back at Nessa, her eyes open wide. Because of course this was the first time she was seeing CM. This was the first time she was seeing the chimera who was also, on a genetic level, at least, her partial twin.

For a moment, she just stared at the creature and the creature stared back at her, their eyes—their identical eyes— locked. Instinctively, Nessa unlocked her knees, felt her hands at her sides open, ready to respond should the chimera attack Delphine.

She willed herself to breathe, to wipe the assumption from her mind. But she could see the tension in the chimera's shoulders and forehead. What was going on in her half-human brain? There was a cloud in the room of mixed colors—blues and mustardy yellows that Nessa could not read.

After what felt like minutes but was probably only seconds, Nate broke the silence. "Hi girls!" he said. "This is my new sister! She can see you! She has a deer leg, but she can talk!"

Then something happened. CM smiled. It was not an attractive smile. Her uneven teeth showed, the whorls of variegated colored fur on her squarish cheeks shifted in a way that felt muscular and forced. But still, Nessa understood that CM wanted to be friendly. She felt her own body relaxing. She knew from her time with wolves, that she had to take the lead. "I'm glad you're here," Nessa said, heading toward CM, leaning down for an incredibly awkward, one-sided hug.

Had CM never been hugged before?

"This is Delphine," Nessa said to CM, pointing. To Delphine, Nessa said, "This is our other sister, CM."

Delphine, giving Nessa a here-goes-nothing glance, took a deep breath of air, raised her eyebrows, and held out her arms. "Bring it in, CM," she said. CM lowered her head, leaning toward Delphine but forgetting to use her arms. (*Note to self,* Nessa thought. *Someone should explain that to her.*) "Wow," Delphine said, pulling away. "We really do look alike."

CM blushed.

Just then Nessa noticed Daniel watching them from the dining room. He must have been there all along.

Dinner went smoothly. It was a little surprising to see CM

pick up fistfuls of peas and cram them into her mouth. It was more surprising when she lifted the pork chop and bit straight through the bone. But she didn't do anything aggressive or dangerous.

She didn't talk much, but she seemed to follow the conversation, turning to watch whoever was speaking, nodding from time to time.

Nessa followed Daniel's lead, not peppering her with questions.

Delphine kept stealing glances at CM, Nessa noticed. Was this not working? Nessa worried, but then, when CM had trouble drinking from her glass of water, Delphine jumped up, ran into the kitchen, and came back with a straw.

After dinner, they sat in the living room like a real family, drinking milkshakes (which turned out to be very CM-friendly—something Daniel must have told Scott about in advance). They played Parcheesi, a game which Daniel introduced like it was the definition of family togetherness. Frankly, it was boring. The cloud of color in the room shifted to a brownish green and Nessa almost laughed. So this was the color of boredom? It exactly matched the color of her Algebra II textbook back in Tether.

Nessa was slightly relieved when CM—who apparently could not stand to lose—upended the Parcheesi board and tore it down the middle, ending the game once and for all.

Her outburst had no other good outcomes, however. Nate looked scared, Delphine looked like she was holding back outrage (she had been in the lead), and Nessa was holding her breath, forming a plan of action in her mind—if CM got violent, Nessa would transform, put her body between CM and Delphine and Nate, get them out . . . .

Daniel was the only one who did not look surprised. "Now, now," he muttered. "Was that your only option?"

Before she could finish the plan in her mind, CM bent forward, drawing her deer leg up to her forehead, allowing her Delphine-hair to tumble down and cover her face. "I don't belong here, do I?" she said in her screechy, otherworldly voice.

Nessa felt her pity trump her fear, but she was not as quick to act as Delphine, who immediately slid closer to CM on the couch and put a tentative hand on her shoulder.

"It's okay," she said.

Nessa looked at Daniel, who was looking at CM with focused concentration. This isn't science, she wanted to tell him. This is your family.

But just then CM looked Nessa's way, and Nessa put all her energy into reassuring the creature that everything was going to be okay.

"Maybe we should all think about heading to bed," Daniel suggested. Everyone was quick to agree.

Nessa did not stay in bed for long. After the lights were out in the house, she threw on some running shoes and slid out the front door. There was not much of a moon, so she transformed under the cover of darkness and ran, heading for the Outsider Kids' camp, staying far back enough so that the dogs would not take notice of her and bark.

She told herself she was here because she wanted to ask Bo about CM. Bo knew about working with kids who were damaged. She knew about getting someone to trust you when they'd learned to trust no one.

But really, Nessa was there because of the kiss. She wanted to know what it was. She felt pulled by it. She felt pulled to Bo's smooth skin, her physical confidence, her wise, no-bullshit eyes.

What am I doing? Nessa thought, standing alone among the trees. The Outsider Kids were probably all tucked into their platform beds, asleep. Bo would not be out here. There was no sign of anyone.

Nessa finally transformed back to head home, taking in a deep breath first. She smelled cat again—that big cat, she was almost certain—but the smell was lost in all the other smells of the forest. She couldn't pull any information out. Almost like the cat knew how to camouflage its scent, how to travel unde-tected through the preserve.

CHAPTER SEVENTEEN

Nessa rarely saw her father at breakfast, but he was there the next morning, beaming. "I just checked the cameras," he said in a low voice to Nessa. "CM slept straight through the night, something she wasn't doing much in the lab setting." He used the tongs on the breakfast buffet to help himself to a health muffin and spooned yogurt into a small bowl, topping it with fruit.

A few moments later, CM joined them, approached them

in the dining room, walking unsteadily, holding onto chair backs and tabletops for balance as she made her way. She could run fluidly, Nessa remembered, but there was something about balance and motion that made it difficult for her to walk at slower speeds—the same principle you could apply to bike riding.

Daniel approached her, helping her to the table, offering her a juice, getting her situated with yogurt and fruit. Delphine was not far behind, and then Micah and Nate came out of the kitchen, laughing. Part of Nate's therapy with Micah was learning how to bake bread, and they'd mixed up a no-knead dough recipe together.

CM turned her head toward the sound of their laughter. She looked a little dazed and sleepy still, Nessa noticed. "Whole wheat," she said, like she was reciting from memory, "is the healthy one."

"Yes," said Nate. "Whole wheat has to be mixed more too. You cannot do it the same every time." Nessa was proud to hear him saying that—she knew one of the reasons Micah had introduced bread making was to teach Nate about flexibility.

Then CM added, "You like bread, and you are not scared to make it even though you can never know what will happen."

Nessa was confused by the comment, but Daniel seemed to understand. "CM?" he said, using a warning voice. "Remember?"

"Oh, yes," CM repeated, looking chagrined. She recited what sounded like yet another rule. "Only talk about what I can see or what they say. Not about what I know."

"That's right," said Daniel, lifting his coffee cup, taking a sip. Nessa remembered what he'd explained about CM's powerful intuition.

"I think it's cool you know things," Nessa said.

CM looked at her. Quickly. Then looked away.

"Me too," said Delphine. "And you're right. It is scary when you don't know what's going to happen." She smiled at CM. CM looked at her, like she was waiting for someone to hit her. Delphine did not look away.

Then CM took a bite of a hardboiled egg, shell and all. Nessa couldn't help it. She flinched. Delphine too.

"What?" said CM, her mouth full. "What did I do?"

"It's the shell," Daniel explained quietly. "Remember? You peel?"

"But that's so much work," CM said. At that, Delphine and Nessa laughed and CM smiled, proud of herself for being funny, though also, clearly, a little mystified.

The doorbell rang, and Nessa heard Scott open it, greeting Gabriel and inviting him into the dining room.

Nessa noticed how big Gabriel's eyes were, checking out the scene of CM eating breakfast at the table with them. He hung back slightly, holding out some papers he'd brought. "Sorry to disturb you guys. Milton says she needs these signed for Haken. Something about customs? Has to be hard copy if you can believe it."

"Of course," Daniel said. Wiping his mouth with a napkin, Daniel beckoned Gabriel toward him while reaching into his pocket for a pen. After signing, he pushed the papers back toward Gabriel, but Gabriel didn't pick them up. He had gotten distracted by the sight of CM trying to spoon yogurt into her mouth. This was a challenge for her. Her fingers were frozen—stiff almost like finger-shaped hoofs. So there was yogurt smeared all over her leathery lips and into the fur on her face.

"Uh, Gabriel?" Daniel said, and Gabriel snapped back to attention. "These are all set."

"Right," said Gabriel. "Yeah, sure."

After breakfast, a colleague of Micah's who'd been willing to come to Chimera Corp. on short notice arrived at the house. After signing a series of nondisclosure agreements, she'd agreed to help CM get transitioned. They were planning a week long orientation to life without bars, as well as training in some of the soft skills that CM had never needed when she'd been monitored by the lab workers.

Brett was pretty, Nessa thought, and looked friendly with her long hair clipped back at the nape of her neck and her serious hazel eyes, but CM stuck out her chin when she saw her. "I don't like babysitters," she said. Nessa wondered if this was what Daniel had called the guards and lab techs who had brought in CM's food and helped care for her—the ones whom she had physically attacked.

"Not a babysitter," Daniel said. "She's like Micah."

CM looked toward the windows for a minute while Nessa

held her breath. Then her gaze shifted. She was looking at the expanse of the luxurious living room, filled with books and art and objects of curiosity. Her gaze tracked across the open door to the kitchen. Nessa wondered if CM was making a calculation, recognizing the differences in the amount of freedom she was being afforded here and the old system where "babysitter" might have meant "guard." CM lowered her head, accepting.

"See ya, CM!" Delphine said cheerily as she and Nessa headed for the golf cart.

"Yeah, see ya," Nessa said, smiling as she followed Delphine. Outside, the sky was bright and clear, the weather hot. Gabriel was sitting in a golf cart that was parked next to Nessa's and checking email from his phone. She waved cheerfully. *It feels amazing that this is happening for real,* she thought. She was making a family. She was fulfilling her promise to her mom. Delphine was doing better. Nate was doing better.

Nessa felt so good she challenged Gabriel to a drag race. He gunned his engine. Nessa grimaced. Gabriel held up a fist. Delphine screamed her head off. Gabriel was grinning, even though Nessa beat him off the line.

Once they reached the lab, fun and games were over. With the first of the Japanese visitors due to arrive the next morning, everyone was scrubbing down their countertops, double- and triple-checking their data tables, proofreading their Power-Point presentations. Nessa passed one of the botanists washing the leaves of every plant in the greenhouse.

Milton was busiest of all, rushing from one task to the next in her practical flats and pedal pushers. "Did you know Japanese guests require toothbrushes in their rooms?" she asked, wild-eyed, waving a fistful of wrapped toothbrushes at no one in particular. "Apparently traveling with one's own toothbrush is cultural."

Later, Milton looked up from her tablet, rolled her eyes to the heavens, and said to Nessa, "How is it possible that Dr. Taneda, who has known for precisely three months that I had arranged a chartered flight for her transport to the lab, determines just this morning that she'll arrive under her own steam, and can we be sure to have a BMW R nineT motorcycle waiting for her at Sea-Tac?"

Nessa assumed no response was required, and even if one had been, Milton wouldn't have heard her, because she'd already moved on to bemoaning the fact that someone had not wrung out the kitchen sink sponge after use. "How many times, people," she said, striding over to the Well, leaning down into it, and directing her voice downward. "You're scientists. Meticulous is part of the job description."

Nessa backed away from her.

Note to self: Milton has left the room.

As Milton wrung out the sponge and adjusted the headset in her ear, dialing into a call, Nessa slipped into the spare running shoes she kept in her locker and went for a midday run.

It was hot, but not too bad in the woods. As she kicked up

her heels, Nessa felt the tension of the last few days leaving her body and decided to do some trail running. Or at least, that's what she told herself. Without thinking about it much, she ended up close to where she knew the Outsider Kids were camping.

The camp appeared to be deserted until she got close. Then she saw that the kids were staying cool in the shadows of trees. Bo stepped out from under the tree cover as Nessa crossed the stream, hopping from rock to rock, noting the thumping in her chest, the thrumming in her ears. A wry smile spread across Bo's face as Nessa reached the other side, and Nessa felt something give inside her. For a second she wondered whether she was going to need to sit down.

"I came to see if everything was okay," she heard herself say, her voice oddly low and throaty. "With, uh, Kai, and everybody."

"Kai is okay," Bo said. "But are you? You look hot." She paused. "From running." Nessa felt her face grow even more warm.

Bo gestured to a rock by the river, the way you might offer someone a chair in a living room. "You want to get your feet wet?" Nessa shrugged her consent. The water would be refreshing.

Bo slipped out of her boots and put her feet in the water. Her feet shone bright under the water, like river stones. They belonged there.

Nessa stripped off her shoes and socks and let her feet cool in the mountain stream—they seemed impossibly pale compared with Bo's.

"It's nice here," Nessa said. She felt the sun on her head, melted snow on her feet. The contrast was making her feel dizzy. Or maybe that was Bo?

Bo laughed, like she could read Nessa's mind. "Why'd you come out here, Nessa?" she asked, her voice low so no one else could hear.

The way Bo looked at her. The way she cut right to the chase. Nessa felt a bit like she was a guitar and someone was playing her—drawing out all kinds of music she'd never known were there.

"I don't know," Nessa said, in answer to Bo's question. Wasn't it obvious why she had come? She lifted her feet out of the stream to let them dry. "I should probably get back," she said.

"I'll walk you a bit," Bo said.

"Okay," said Nessa, feeling stupid, feeling like Bo thought she was stupid, thought that she needed to be protected.

But then it turned out that protection wasn't what was on Bo's mind. As soon as they were out of sight of the camp, Bo took Nessa's hand and pulled. Nessa stumbled a bit toward Bo and Bo caught her. In seconds, they were pressed together.

"This was why I came," Nessa blurted out, the words awkward and rushed.

And then she pulled away from Bo and ran off into the trees.

She ran all the way back. She felt energy pouring into her. She felt hopeful and giddy. The woods, the light, the leaves, the heat—it was beautiful. The camp and the kids inside it, they were lucky to be living an experiment. They were making a family, and she, Delphine, and Nate were doing the same thing—making a new life, standing on shakier ground than they'd ever known, not quite sure who to trust and how far. Maybe the thing was to just trust, to trust completely, to free-fall, and let the world hold you up?

CHAPTER EIGHTEEN

The next morning, right after breakfast, Micah and Nate flew to Milwaukee to visit Aunt Jane. Daniel thought the changes to the routine during the conference would be too much for him, and Jane was hankering for a visit.

The scientists from Haken arrived a few hours later, just before lunch. Daniel and Milton greeted them at the airstrip and then they were ferried to the lab, where tables were set up in the atrium for a light lunch. Next up on the schedule would be rest—they'd been traveling for nearly twenty-four hours.

Nessa watched from the sidelines as the two groups of researchers mingled. After so many days of anticipation, it was amazing that they were really here.

The Haken researchers were younger than Nessa had expected, but even so, they were formal. There was a lot of bowing and exchanging of gifts. Milton stood next to and just behind Daniel, passing him wrapped boxes. Occasionally she would address one of the researchers.

In Japanese.

Nessa couldn't help but look at Delphine, who rolled her eyes and mouthed the words, "Of course." Nessa smiled. After losing it over the kitchen sponge, Nessa could see that Milton had returned to her regular two modes: perfect and annoyingly perfect.

While Daniel was speaking with a white-haired, slightly stooped man, he beckoned for Nessa and Delphine to join him, introducing them. The man was Dr. Ishikawa.

"You hosted my dad when he was young?" Delphine said, bowing slightly and then shaking his offered hand.

Dr. Ishikawa smiled, then laughed. He wore thick-lensed glasses with red frames, which, Nessa noticed, matched his red Hush Puppies. "Your father was not so sharp a dresser back then. He wore the same sweater every day."

"I only brought one sweater," Daniel protested good-naturedly. Nessa had never seen anyone tease him before. "I didn't realize Japan would be so cold."

Dr. Ishikawa leaned toward Nessa and Delphine conspir-atorially. "When Americans come to Japan, they think only of Tokyo. My lab is near the water in a university town. It was winter when your father came." He delivered this information as if it would strike them as funny. He laughed heartily, and out of politeness, the girls joined in.

The girls drifted away from Dr. Ishikawa and took refuge by the snack table. Gabriel joined them there. "You liked talking to Dr. Ishikawa?" he asked.

"He's sweet," Delphine said.

"Yeah," scoffed Gabriel. "He's also one of the most highly connected and well-published researchers in this field."

"He is?" said Nessa. Dr. Ishikawa had seemed so . . . dorky.

"Yeah, he was a mentor to both of your parents when they were getting started. Their work paid him back tenfold for his investment, of course. He's using some of the technologies they invented—it's revolutionized his lab."

"Oh wow," said Nessa.

"Don't let his whole 'cute little old man' routine fool you."

Nessa nearly spat out her seltzer, the notion striking her as that funny. "What, the lab's just a front for a money-laundering operation?"

"No, no," Gabriel said, laughing. "He's a scientist. That's real. And he's a good person and everything. You just might not understand when you first talk to him that he's got one of the sharpest minds on our planet."

"Sharper than yours?" Delphine added, making all three of

them smile.

"I'm sure there's plenty of people out there—" he started to protest, before realizing it was probably better not to get into a conversation about his own intelligence and Dr. Ishikawa's. "Put it this way," Gabriel concluded, stumbling over the words a bit, his voice cracking. "On the day Nobel Prizes are announced, no one ever says they're setting early alarms in case the committee calls, but there are probably a half dozen people in the world who should. Dr. Ishikawa is one of them."

Once Gabriel had explained Dr. Ishikawa's status, Nessa felt dumb for not having noticed it before. All during lunch— which was a mix of appetizer-sized typically American food: miniature pizzas, cheeseburger sliders, tiny cups of Caesar salad—the visiting scientists kept stealing glances in Dr. Ishikawa's direction. When he stood, the rest of them rose as well. Daniel did too.

"So," Dr. Ishikawa said, patting his belly, looking at Daniel, "shall we see some of your work?"

"Aren't you fatigued?" Daniel asked. "You've been traveling."

"I'll nap later. For now, take me to the lab." Instantly, the rest of his team gathered as a group, smartphones and tablets at the ready.

But then Dr. Ishikawa looked around, clearly distressed. Was something missing? Milton stepped forward and addressed him in Japanese. Then Dr. Ishikawa whispered something to the underling at his elbow. "Is everything okay?" Nessa asked Gabriel.

Gabriel looked at his watch. "Dr. Taneda's late," he said.

Just then, there was a commotion at the front doors. Nessa turned to see a little boy in a black astronaut helmet. For a second, she wondered if it could be one of the Outsider Kids.

Then the helmet was gone, and Nessa realized it was a woman she was seeing. She had short hair cropped close to her head and was wearing black biker boots, jeans, a leather jacket.

Nessa glanced back at Dr. Ishikawa and saw the smile on his face. He was beaming at this intruder.

"That's her?" Nessa asked. Gabriel nodded.

Dr. Taneda strode into the room, heading straight for Daniel, laying her helmet on a table so she could extend both arms to him. He approached her, and she grabbed him in a way that was more direct and enthusiastic than the formal greetings he'd exchanged with the other researchers.

"Daniel!" she said, holding on to the hug a beat longer than necessary, slapping his back several times. Then she pulled back, bowed to Dr. Ishikawa, and said with a mischievous smile, "I'm not late, am I?"

Dr. Ishikawa laughed, shaking his head. "You are always late," he said. "But then you are here, and we wish you were later." He laughed a throaty, booming laugh and Taneda laughed too. She didn't seem anything like what Milton had told them to expect in her lengthy "etiquette trainings."

"Oh, pizza!" Taneda said. She raised her eyebrows at Daniel, grabbed a mini pizza off the food table, and stuffed it into her mouth. Milton had advised that meals would be formal, eaten slowly. Nessa thought: *not Dr. Taneda's meals.* Dr. Taneda caught Nessa's eye, and Nessa felt herself held by the woman's warm gaze, the energy and sense of rightness she'd brought into the room.

Taneda swallowed the bite and approached. "You must be Nessa," she said. She grabbed Nessa at the shoulders with the same force she'd directed at Daniel and Dr. Ishikawa. She was short. Nessa found herself looking down to meet her gaze, but she felt this woman somehow took up more space than her size would suggest. "And Delphine," Dr. Taneda said, lifting one hand away from Nessa and drawing Delphine in. "You girls, I cannot believe I am lucky enough to see you again."

"Again?" said Nessa.

"You don't remember," said Taneda, "but when you were really young, your mother and I were working so closely you thought I was your aunt."

"Really?" Delphine said. "Dad said you knew Mom, but I didn't know—"

"Knew her?" Taneda said, interrupting. She put a fist on top of her heart, thumped it several times. "Your mother's the reason I made it as a scientist in our messed-up sexist culture." She turned to flash Ishikawa a Cheshire cat smile. "You know it, right?" she called over to him. "We live in a man's world and Ishikawa gets into a lot of trouble because he has a woman on the team."

"It's not because you're a woman," Ishikawa said. "It's because you're a monster." He laughed his booming laugh again. Taneda dismissed him with a wave of her hand and spoke to Nessa and Delphine in a low voice, keeping a hand on their shoulders.

"I'm sorry to hear about your mom," she said. "Even though it has been so long since I saw her, I felt the loss when she died. A light in the world has gone dark."

"Ahem," Dr. Ishikawa said. "Taneda! You have held us up long enough. The tour! We've been waiting two years to see this lab."

Taneda winked at the girls. "We'll talk more soon, promise?" She pointed at Delphine. Delphine nodded, blushing and smiling.

Dr. Taneda scooped up a second pizza and grabbed Daniel by the elbow as they headed for the elevators. Nessa heard her say, "And when will we see her?" as they stepped into the cab.

"Actually," Daniel said, but just then, the doors closed and Nessa could not hear over the noise of the elevator machinery. She took a few steps closer, trying to hear, but it was no good.

When Nessa turned back, she saw that Delphine was gathering the platters of leftover pizzas and sliding them into boxes. It didn't take Nessa long to guess where Delphine was taking them.

"You're not going into the woods alone, with a dangerous animal still on the prowl, are you?" Nessa asked.

Delphine's face brightened. "Not at all," she said. "Because you're coming with me."

CHAPTER NINETEEN

The pizza was still relatively warm when they reached the Outsider Kids' campsite, and its arrival instantly created a party. There was enough that each kid got their own small pie—and some even had two. Topher shoved one whole mini pizza into his mouth, and even Kai, who still looked pretty sad by Nessa's estimation, was smiling.

Nessa watched Bo take her first bite after she was done supervising the distribution. She closed her eyes and took a deep breath, clearly savoring the experience. When she opened her eyes again, she caught Nessa looking at her. Clouds of deep rich colors hung between them, above all of them, really. They settled like morning fog in the valleys, strung hazily between trees.

The colors made Nessa understand why Delphine liked bringing these kids food, but it also made Nessa feel guilty, thinking about the third pie she'd had at the lunch, and she hadn't even been all that hungry.

"So, the visitors. Did you meet them?" Bo asked.

"Yeah," Nessa said.

"One of them is really cool," added Delphine. "Dr. Taneda. She knew our mom."

"Well, don't get too close to them. Haken's probably doing sick and twisted stuff like Chimera Corp."

"Chimera Corp.'s not sick and twisted!" Nessa objected.

"Whatever," said Bo.

But Nessa felt the record needed to be corrected—if not for Bo's sake, for her own. "You know, you're living off Chimera," Nessa said. "The food you think you're liberating or whatever."

A tendril the color of Mountain Dew snaked into her cloud of deep-red pizza contentment.

"Look," said Bo, shoving the last bite of crust into her mouth. "You and I know your dad is messing with stuff he probably shouldn't be messing with. I've seen things out here in the woods that aren't right." She lowered her voice. "Have you heard anything more about what got Rio?"

"Yeah," said Nessa. "I think it was a cat. I saw one. Big." She held her hand three feet off the ground to show.

Bo rolled her eyes. "It was not," she said, "a cat."

Now Nessa was starting to get annoyed.

"You didn't see this cat," Nessa said. "I did."

Bo just laughed. "Your dad probably didn't want to talk about it, did he? Why don't you ask him what really got Rio?"

Nessa felt herself becoming short of breath. Her face was warm. She knew she shouldn't keep going on with this. She was angry and not thinking clearly, but she plowed ahead anyway. "It's his property," she spat out. "He can use it any way he likes. And being out here with kids when there's a cat big enough to take down a dog? That's dangerous."

"What's dangerous is that monster you've moved into your house. And property or no, your dad's messing with nature," Bo corrected. "He can't draw a line around it and say, 'This is going to be part of the environment here, but not over there.' Nature's got its own ways. You think some fence is going to keep those changes from leaking outside of this—?"

"Preserve," Nessa said.

"Petri dish is more like it." Bo looked at Nessa meaningfully then shook her head. *Is this turning into a fight?* Nessa lowered her head consciously, breaking the contact first. She didn't want to fight with Bo.

Bo seemed to recognize this as a gesture of conciliation. The Mountain Dew color explosion, which had started to pulse, now faded. "All I know," she finished, in a much less confrontational tone, "is that these kids didn't sign on to be part of some kind of whack experiment."

"That's not what I meant," Nessa said. She was trying to get back to where she'd been with Bo earlier. But Bo just wiped her mouth and stared beyond Nessa, into the forest.

The conversation continued to irk Nessa, and she replayed it in her mind all the way back to the house. When she got there, feeling the relief of the air conditioning, the return to clean floors, and the hum of the ventilation system, she headed for Daniel's office.

"So, are you introducing CM at dinner?" Nessa asked. She was leaning in the doorway of his office, where she'd found him tapping away at his computer.

Daniel raised his head to look at Nessa. "You think it's too much, too soon?" he asked.

Nessa took a breath. She reminded herself: Just because Bo suspected Daniel of the worst, Nessa didn't need to. Bo didn't know him the way Nessa did. For instance, here Daniel was asking her opinion. Being open.

"I'm worried about her," she said. "I'm worried about how all that attention will make her feel."

Daniel drummed his fingers on the desk, lining up all the tips and bringing them down onto the polished surface as one. There was a white cloud hanging above him, as if he'd figured out how to empty himself of revealing color auras. Had he? "Dr.

Ishikawa has flown here just to see her—and he was as excited as you are to hear she's moved in to our home."

That *did* make Nessa feel better.

"When I told you that story about staying with Ishikawa's family, I suppose I was trying to make a point." He paused to swallow. "I guess I was doing it rather ineptly. I just want you to know that these relationships—they go past collegial. We're family. And we have a bit of a family business going. For years, Haken has helped bring our discoveries to light. We need to stay ahead of the curve—give all of us something to work with. We make our money through patented applications of scientific discoveries, not manufacturing, and I'd like to keep it that way."

The thought crossed Nessa's mind: What did "family" mean to the father who had been absent from her life for fourteen years?

Daniel went on. "All of our work is intertwined. We share agreements around technology. If we're discredited, everything Ishikawa has built in his career will be tarnished as well. If they're discredited, we lose a chief source of resources: the Japanese government. We keep each other's secrets."

Nessa clapped a hand on the doorframe. She didn't roll her eyes at what Daniel was saying or call him on how evasive he was being—but she wondered if Bo would have. "I guess I'll go get changed," she said.

Daniel nodded.

"I'll check in on CM as well."

"Do that," said Daniel. He looked at his watch. "She and Brett should be getting back just about now, but Brett can't stay for the dinner. I'll keep an eye on CM myself."

Nessa found CM in her room, leaning toward the mirror above her dresser.

Nessa couldn't help but wonder what CM saw when she looked at herself. Did she understand the feelings of revulsion she caused in others? Was she wondering how to remove the fur and the leathery lips, the scaled patch of skin on her fore-head, the way Nessa might have wondered about clearing up a patch of pimples? The air above CM was a sickly shade of coral pink, marbled with yellow and white incursions. What did that color explain about the workings of CM's mind?

"Nessa," CM said, attempting her version of a smile. She lurched toward Nessa, and Nessa forced herself forward.

"Hey, CM," she said. "Need any help getting ready?" She was conscious of the fact that she had to look up at CM. "We should go to the dinner soon."

CM lowered her chin, drew in the shorter of her two arms, and cradled it with the other, rocking slightly. She looked down at Nessa through the lowered eyelids. For a second, Nessa felt her body tense. Was CM going to attack?

"I don't know what I should wear," CM said, and Nessa forced herself to relax. She had to remember: Whatever Bo might say, CM only wanted to be human. The more Nessa could treat her that way, the safer they would all be. CM included.

"I'm probably not the right person to ask," Nessa said, letting out a sigh. "My friend Bree—she's good with this kind of thing. Delphine too. I tend to panic."

"Please," CM said, her voice grating still but soft.

"I guess you can't go wrong with black?" Nessa tried. Then she laughed out loud. She was really bad at this. CM looked at her expectantly, like she was waiting to get the joke. "The thing about clothes is you don't want to look like you're trying too hard."

CM nodded sincerely, like Nessa was describing how to defuse a bomb and everything depended on how hard she was listening. "Look, Bree would probably say the opposite. She'd say you'd want people to know you were trying, that you care."

"Bree is your best friend?"

"That's right," Nessa said, opening a drawer, looking through CM's collection of boxy tee shirts. She was about to tell CM that Bree might come visit and that she could meet her, but she got distracted by how boring the tee shirt options in the drawer were. *Did Daniel pick these out? Or worse, Milton?*

CM leaned against the wall and lifted her deer leg casually, picking something out of the hoof. "You think Bree has too many boyfriends?"

"Definitely," Nessa said, her mind still on the shirts. "She's got this internship now, so maybe. . . ." She drew her chin back. "Wait, how did you know that? What the heck, CM!" She heard how harsh her tone was and knew that she was probably overreacting.

Well, fine, Nessa thought. Harsh was how she felt because (a) she didn't want to slag Bree behind her back. (b) How the heck did CM even know that she *might* have thought that? And (c) Bree was *her* friend. This wasn't CM's business. End of story.

But then she looked up and saw that CM was blushing. Hard. Just like Delphine did. And the colors around her had turned pink as well. They were almost starting to flash.

"I forgot," CM said simply, "to pretend."

Nessa took a deep breath and let it out. She watched the intensity of CM's color cloud fade as she did so, as if Nessa's breath had calmed them both down. "That's okay," she said. *Maybe CM can't help it,* she thought. It must be hard, getting thrown into a world where you're supposed to control what comes naturally to you. You couldn't change yourself in just one day. To change the subject, she said, "The clothes in your drawers are hopeless. Let's check out your closet."

CM ended up in a long beige sweater coat. Nessa selected a white tee shirt from a drawer, and a pair of navy blue pants. CM couldn't quite manage shoes on her deer leg, but Nessa found a black flat for her human one. Size twelve.

CM went into the bathroom to change, and when she reemerged she looked, Nessa had to admit, nicely put together. She joined her in front of the mirror, and the two of them looked at their reflections together.

"Can you tell that we are sisters?" CM asked. "I can tell when I see you with her."

"You mean Delphine?" Nessa said.

"The *real* Delphine."

"Don't say that," Nessa said. "You're real."

"But isn't that how you think of me?"

Nessa shook her head. "It's not," she said.

But then, when Delphine did come down to the bedroom floors, in from the woods, Nessa couldn't help but notice how natural she looked, how right-sized, how smooth-skinned.

CM must have been feeling the same way because she spun on Nessa at that moment, glaring at her as she tried to extract herself from the beige sweater.

"This sweater you picked out for me is too hot," she fumed.

CHAPTER TWENTY

inner was informal—just Daniel, Milton, the girls, and the visiting scientists. They'd gone straight from travel to the lab tour and were tired, even if they wouldn't admit it. Milton had set Scott the task of an easy meal, over which they could talk among themselves as much as to Daniel, and then an early bedtime. The work would begin in earnest the next day, with speakers flying up from Stanford and time for the project leaders from both teams to convene.

But even so, Nessa could feel that CM was nervous. She was spouting all kinds of colors—too many to get a read on. Delphine must have sensed CM's anxiety also. She stood close to CM's other side, the sisters loyally flanking the chimera, leaving no doubt of their position: *We are all three the daughters of Daniel Host. We are sisters, however it may seem.*

Once Dr. Ishikawa appeared, Daniel made a big deal out of reintroducing him to CM. Nessa was free to wander, and she ended up out on the deck, at the railing, looking out into the treetops. In a few moments, Dr. Taneda joined her. She was drinking a beer out of a bottle, even though Scott had brought in a bartender and everyone else with a beer was drinking from glasses.

"So, Nessa, you've lost all of your Japanese?" she said.

Nessa didn't know what she was talking about and Dr. Taneda smiled. "I taught you some Japanese words when you were just learning to talk," she said. "Your mother and I were working on projects together, and I came to the US for a month. She would bring you into the lab and you'd play with toys there. I taught you the words in Japanese for *cup, ball, more.* You don't remember?"

Nessa laughed. "I don't remember anything about it," she admitted. "Until last spring, I didn't know my mother had been a scientist."

Taneda whistled, looked out into the forest as if it could

help her understand this overwhelming fact.

"Well, she was," she said, taking a swig of her beer. "She was a great scientist. She was fierce. Disciplined. Creative. A role model for me. A friend."

"Was my mom older than you?" Nessa asked.

"Yep," Taneda said. "I was a postdoc when I met your mom—I was the first woman to have any kind of position in Dr. Ishikawa's lab, so it was a big deal to me to meet this tall, blonde, confident, brilliant *woman*. It went a long way to making me feel there was a path for me. Of course, I fell all over myself to get a collaboration going, and I'm so glad I did."

Nessa smiled, feeling sad underneath it. What if Vivian had stuck it out? What if she had made her mark?

"The way your mom worked—she figured out a position for everyone on the team, got us all to follow our interests, not hers. Everyone was invested 100 percent. We didn't think twice about pulling the all-nighters and pushing through the technology meltdowns. It didn't feel like we were following someone's instructions. It felt like we were following our own desires."

This sounded right to Nessa—Vivian had approached Nessa's cross-country training in the same way, giving her the space to make it her own.

"Was that when she was working on the gene virus thing?" Nessa asked. Daniel had explained the technology he and Vivian had invented, the one that the Chimera Corp. work was still founded on. It involved using viruses to enter a cell and alter the genes of living things.

"Yes," Taneda said. "But she was also working on some other projects." She paused to narrow her eyes and really look at Nessa. Strangely, she took a whiff, like there was a funny smell in the air. "How familiar with your mother's body of work are you?"

"We never talked about it until she was dying," Nessa admitted. "Then my dad told me about it, and my mom explained some parts herself. At the very end."

"Again, I am so sorry to hear of her passing," Taneda said. Nessa nodded, feeling a lump grow in her throat. "Your mom was pretty experimental, especially early on. I don't know if she got into the details about that."

Nessa tried to wrap her brain around Taneda's words. Was she talking about Vivian's werewolfism? If Taneda had been hinting any more broadly, she would have had to have been winking.

Just then they were called to dinner. Nessa was so busy taking care of CM—she and Delphine sat on either side of her—that she lost track of Dr. Taneda. Most of the scientists near them had lapsed into speaking Japanese anyway, which Milton and Daniel could follow. They spoke fast and with excitement, the colors above them twisting into each other, mixing then remixing, floating up into the subtle lighting that gave the room its careful, calm appearance.

Nessa and Delphine made a game of pretending to understand the conversation, giving each other significant looks and saying, "Did you hear that?" and "I can't believe she just said they liked to eat toadstools." CM didn't understand the game at first, but with some broad hints, she got the idea. She laughed a little too hard, but Delphine and Nessa didn't care. It was good to see her joining in.

At the end of dinner, Ishikawa stood, pushing his seat back from the table, and everyone else stood along with him. "Now," he said. "We sleep."

The conference started bright and early the next morning. Nessa had thought of running in the woods before, hopefully running into Bo, but there wasn't quite enough time.

Daniel was not at breakfast, and Nessa barely had time to swallow a few bites of yogurt and health muffin before running out the door, yelling goodbye to Brett, and saying, "Try the muffins, they're good!" to CM.

"Toadstools!" CM yelled to Nessa, pointing at the health muffins. Brett smiled in her sunshiny way, but Nessa laughed out loud. *Humor is the biggest surprise CM has up her sleeve,* Nessa thought.

Once she reached the lab, she saw that the scientists and the Chimera staff and researchers were already getting settled in the open atrium at the top of the building, which had been transformed into a conference room with a projection screen against a wall, chairs set up in rows, and tables for snacks by the big glass doors that led on to the tented patio where lunch would be served later if it wasn't too hot. Since she'd first stepped outside, she'd notice the air felt heavy.

Daniel said a few words of welcome, explaining again, his long relationship with Dr. Ishikawa. Dr. Ishikawa spoke about how much he valued his relationship with Daniel—how far their collaboration had allowed them to push the field. Above them, a play of color-mixing seemed to underscore this message— red and blue became purple, yellow and blue became green.

Next one of the researchers from Haken took the podium— giving a talk on using genetic intervention to cure certain forms of hearing loss. Not the most exciting topic, but Nessa felt herself catching the enthusiasm in the room. The image Taneda had planted in her head of Vivian in her twenties—the fearless leader, the motivator, the tactician—had Nessa fired up as well.

But then the talk went straight over her head. Nessa could see Gabriel leaning forward in his seat, her dad jotting down a few notes from time to time, but Nessa had no understanding of what they found so intriguing. When the researcher got into the specifics about the construction and plasticity of the ear, Nessa discreetly took a look at her phone, scanning Bree's Instagram for photos of Isle Royale. She looked at Luc's Instagram as well—his family hadn't taken it down—but it was still just the same pictures of his sneakers in various woodsy locations and a series of before-and-after shots when he was fixing up the cabin he'd come upon in the woods.

The question and answer portion began and went on . . .

and on. Nessa's seat began to feel uncomfortable.

After the talk, there was a fifteen-minute break for coffee and chocolate chip cookies. Most of the scientists seemed too preoccupied by what they'd been learning about to even eat, but Nessa ate four cookies and Delphine took two.

Delphine leaned against Nessa's arm heavily. "I'm soooooo bored," she said.

"Go play on the computer," Nessa suggested.

"Ooh," Delphine said, standing up straight now. "Good idea. See ya!"

When it became clear that the next speaker—a Chimera Corp. scientist—was planning to spend an hour and a half on frog eggs, Nessa found herself wishing she had escaped with Delphine. The scientist hoped to restore extinct species by editing the stem cells in early forming eggs—which sounded cool—but so far, he had only landed on a new way of tweaking agar gel plates. Nessa was halfway through a monster-sized yawn when Gabriel slid into the empty seat next to her and whispered, "You can only imagine the theme park licensing implications." He was one of those people who didn't quite know how to whisper, so a few heads turned when he landed the punch line. "Jurassic Frog."

Nessa snorted. She shushed him. "You're a total dork," she said, but she was grateful for the bit of distraction.

Milton took the podium next, to announce apologetically that the terrace had been deemed too hot for lunch, and that the morning's talks had extended longer than expected, so sandwiches would be passed to the crowd in their seats.

As she ate, feeling trapped between a conversation in Japanese she couldn't understand and another in English that was so technical, she was equally lost, Nessa saw Delphine emerge from the Well, make a beeline for the leftovers table, and fill a plastic bag to overflowing. Nessa shook her head and frowned. Delphine had agreed not to go in the woods alone, but in response to Nessa's forbidding frown, just waved and headed for the door.

As the next speaker launched into his topic, Nessa despaired on two levels: One, this guy promised to be the most boring yet, and two, Delphine, the only person who might have been interested, was missing it.

The subject was data security, one of Delphine's favorite topics. Nessa just closed her eyes. "Is this going to be as boring as the last one?" she said to Gabriel, who had moved into the seat next to hers.

She opened her eyes again to see that Gabriel was giving her a meaningful look. "Nah, Haruki's amazing. You're going to love him."

Nessa held up a finger. "Don't lie to me."

But Gabriel wasn't lying.

Haruki Tamamoto was tall, with spiky hair, and he was wearing a shirt with giant checks of red and blue squares. He had an excited way of waving his hands in the air when he wanted to make a point that looked disturbingly like "spirit fingers." But that wasn't why his talk was awesome. He was developing a technique to use DNA as a means of storing digital data. He cracked up the room by taking a sequence of nucleic GACT acids, putting it through a translator he'd written code for, and then having it spit out a data file, which, when he loaded it into a laptop, turned out to be music, and the room was suddenly filled with the most memorable thirty seconds of "Forever Young."

Everyone laughed except for Gabriel, who was so rapt in listening and taking extensive notes on his tablet that Nessa had to elbow him and say, "Stop being such a brown-noser, this was supposed to be a joke."

Gabriel smiled sheepishly. Then he actually almost collapsed his folding chair before recovering himself. "Your dad's been working on something like this for years," he said. "You don't see him sharing the technology behind it."

"I thought he shared everything with Ishikawa."

"Not everything," Gabriel said, in his not-whisper. Nessa shushed him. "He's smart not to," Gabriel finished, nervously pulling on one ear, a weird science-geek habit that Nessa thought someone should tell him he should drop.

The sessions continued late into the afternoon, with longer and longer breaks between them as the scientists rushed up to each other after their talks to share ideas and follow up with questions. Nessa had to admit, it was cool to see people who were so into their work. It was cool to see how respected Daniel was.

Dinner that night was served in a large tent set up right outside the lab. Daniel had decided to give CM the night off—she and Brett were going to eat in the dining room at the house. Delphine volunteered to join them, so Nessa, on her own with the scientists, scanned the crowd for Taneda.

Instead, her eyes landed on someone she had never expected to see here.

"Professor Halliday?!" Nessa said.

Maxine Halliday was dressed in strappy high-heeled sandals and a wrinkled linen shift dress, and instead of a severe bun, her stringy gray-blonde hair was falling over her shoulders, her long nose and hooded eyes giving her face an august, mysterious air. In heels, she stood about a head taller than most of the scientists. She was taller even than Daniel, who Nessa saw greeting her now, shaking her hand and then leaning forward to kiss her once on each cheek.

Nessa ducked behind a flower arrangement to watch as Taneda joined them, and Daniel engaged both women in conversation.

What's going on here? They all know each other?

After a few minutes, Milton appeared, placing a hand on Daniel's elbow. He leaned in toward Halliday, said a few words, nodded at Taneda, and then followed Milton out of the tent, giving Nessa an opportunity to approach.

Seeing Nessa, the professor held up her palms in a gesture of welcome that was both direct and not familiar, reminding Nessa that she probably shouldn't make a big deal of the fact that they knew each other.

Taneda greeted Nessa with more enthusiasm, a burst of canary yellow leaping up above her head. "Nessa!" she said. "I haven't seen you all day!" She slapped her on the back.

Nessa smiled at her, then turned a full-bore gaze on Halliday. "What are you doing here?"

"Your father invited me," Halliday said simply, as if that would answer Nessa's question.

"We're co-presenting," Taneda said, leaning in toward Halliday like they were posing for a picture. "Daniel introduced us over email last spring. Our work has so many connections."

Halliday smiled at Nessa. "Are you surprised?"

"A little," Nessa admitted.

"My work in folklore has many intersections with Dr. Taneda's work on ancient, extinct mammals that may—" She smiled coyly, in lecture mode now— "or may not have been the inspiration for mythical or iconic creatures that humans preserved in stories. And after I met your father last spring—through you, you'll recall—he's become interested in my work."

"We are *all* interested in Maxine's work," said Taneda. "Discoveries we've been able to make about creatures whose bones or fossils retain some original DNA are changing the way we think of these forgotten stories. There is truth behind them all. Some of these mythical creatures were real."

Halliday rolled her eyes. "Yes, Virginia, there is a Santa Claus," she said, chuckling to herself as she took a sip of wine.

Taneda took the opportunity to look at Nessa sharply. "But

how do you two know each other?" she asked.

"I—uh—met her when I was on a tour at Stanford."

"And you?" Halliday said, directing the question to Taneda.

"Her mother introduced us," Taneda said. "A long time ago." Just then, something across the room caught Taneda's eye. She excused herself, leaving Halliday and Nessa alone. Nessa couldn't help herself. She put a hand on Halliday's arm, nearly causing her to drop her wine glass. "I can't believe you're here," she said.

Halliday raised her eyebrows. "Part of the reason I accepted this invitation was to come see you. I was hoping you'd have come see me already. We didn't have enough time, and I imagine you're encountering some questions about your tetra-chromacy."

"That and a bunch of other things, actually," Nessa said. "I have so many questions for you."

"For me? Why not Dr. Taneda?" She looked at Nessa mean-ingfully, a tendril of brown and pink blending together above her head. Something was amusing her.

"Dr. Taneda?" Nessa said. "What does she know about tetrachromacy?"

"Nothing," Halliday said cryptically.

Just then a server came by offering puff pastry cheese bites. Nessa shook her head no thanks, but Halliday reached for one and popped it into her mouth. "I shouldn't think I'd have to tell you," she said in a voice that sounded amused. "Can't you recognize another wolf when you see one?"

"She's a wolf?" Nessa said, her voice rising higher than she meant it to. A few heads turned.

Halliday lowered her gaze. "Why don't you ask her? And in the meantime, I want to talk more about the colors you're seeing. I'm speaking tomorrow, then I fly back to campus, but I'll be here on the last night. For some sort of dinner."

"Oh, right," Nessa said, remembering Milton's recitation of the schedule—the last dinner was going to be a party in honor of the Japanese team. It was black tie, dancing, a band was coming in from Portland.

"Any luck moving the colors yet?"

"I can barely remember what the colors mean," Nessa admitted. "Sometimes I feel like I can guess it, but other times I'm completely in the dark."

"You'll get there," Halliday said.

"I wish there was a chart or something. I wish I could just know."

"Of course you do," said Halliday. "But this is not a science. It's—what can I say? Biology. It's beautiful and it's messy."

"You sound like my dad," Nessa said, and if dinner hadn't been announced, she might have considered telling Halliday about CM.

Nessa left the dinner early, feeling that she should check in on CM. She found her with Delphine. They were just finishing up a movie in CM's room.

"Where's Brett?" Nessa asked.

"She went home," Delphine said calmly, though Nessa could see from the sparkle in her eye that she saw this as an accomplishment. The goal was exactly what Nessa was seeing now: CM feeling loved. CM self-regulating.

Scott appeared with hot fudge sundaes. "Look," Delphine said, pointing to the tray of dinner food he was removing. "Macaroni and cheese and Caesar salad."

Nessa turned to Delphine. "How did he know that was your favorite meal?" Delphine requested this combination every time she was allowed a menu choice.

"He didn't," said CM calmly. "He sent it because it's mine."

No one commented on how strange—or totally normal—that was.

The movie was one Nessa had seen years before with Bree, but she stayed to watch the ending with CM and Delphine anyway, laughing at the funny parts. When the bad boyfriend told the girl main character she shouldn't be friends with the girl who wasn't as popular as she was, Delphine pointed her ice cream spoon at the screen and said, "He's going down."

"Yeah, and I bet he smells like seaweed," said CM.

"Seaweed?!" Delphine said. CM just shrugged and all three of them laughed.

For a moment, Nessa just savored the sense of peace and rightness.

Or at least she savored it until the credits began to roll and Delphine said to CM, "Can you really read people's minds?"

CM drew her gnarled hands in front of her belly demurely and said, "Yes, I can."

"Like . . . always?" asked Delphine. "Or do you have to work up to it?"

"It comes and goes. I see things. I know things."

"Secrets?"

CM smiled again, and this time Nessa was sure the mysteriousness of her smile was intentional.

Delphine's own smile was searching, curious, tentative. "Can you read mine?"

There were wisps of baby blue, pale pink, and baby-chick yellow hanging in the air above them, stirring gently in the air conditioner's breeze. Nessa wasn't sure what those colors meant, but they certainly seemed nonthreatening.

CM looked at Delphine. "You are afraid of me," she said.

Delphine said, "That's not true." But the way she swallowed hard after that made it pretty obvious she was just taking a stab at being polite.

CM shrugged. "Okay," she said. "Maybe you don't know you're afraid, but you are."

Delphine shifted back into the pillows on the bed and drew her knees into her chest. "Tell me another one," she said.

"Maybe we shouldn't do this," Nessa warned. She had the feeling this was like the moment just before a truth-or-dare slumber party went wrong.

CM smiled. Or half smiled. Sometimes with her it wasn't that easy to tell what facial expression she meant to use. She started to speak, her high, scratchy voice wavering with the effort to sound normal. "Here's one," she near-hissed, her eyes half closing like a cat stalking its prey. "You have secrets about things you did when you were little."

"I do?" said Delphine, smiling in fascination. "When?"

"You were a mean little girl."

"I was not mean!" Delphine said, adopting a look of mock outrage, laughing.

Nessa laughed too, shaking her head forcefully, relieved by how off-the-mark this was.

CM was not laughing. "Yes, you were," she said. "You used to hide Nate's trains because you were mad that he got all the love."

"Are you kidding?" Nessa said. She did remember when Nate's trains would go missing, of course. Nate used to have horrible tantrums when he lost his trains, even banging his head against the floor. But she knew Delphine would never have taken them. "There's no way anyone would have brought that kind of headache into their own life."

Nessa looked at Delphine, anticipating agreement, but Delphine's face had frozen in an expression of horror.

Nessa immediately regretted laughing. She regretted joining them to watch the movie. She regretted not shooing everyone off to bed the minute it was over. She regretted sending Brett away, even though she'd offered to stay while the movie was on.

"You did it more than just one time," CM said. "You wanted to stop but you were a little happy that he was sad."

Delphine had gone white as a sheet, as if she'd had the wind knocked out of her, as if everything that pumped and flowed and circulated in her body had come to a halt. There were tears filling her ears. The cloud of Easter colors in the room was now shot through with scarlet.

She stood up. She was shaking. She looked at Nessa. "I'm going to bed," she said. She looked at CM. "And you—" She narrowed her eyes. "You are the one who is mean."

CM returned Delphine's stare, her dead eyes making it impossible to know how she felt.

Nessa found Delphine in her room, crying hard. "No one ever knew I did that!" she said. "It's just so . . . so humiliating!"

"But you never do things like that now," Nessa said. "It was a long time ago."

Delphine kept spewing words as if Nessa had not spoken. "I knew it was wrong when I did it. I was old enough to know better. But you were always so strong and good, and Nate was always getting all the attention, and I was just this huge . . . blank—and now." She was crying so hard she had to stop to blow her nose. "I just thought, that wasn't me. That's what Mom said when I told her. She said, 'You don't let that be you. You forget all about it.'"

"You still can!" Nessa said.

"No," Delphine said. "I can't because now *she* knows."

"I don't think she understood how hurtful it would be," Nessa said. "I think she was just trying to figure out the way she could prove the point. Which is kind of amazing. I mean, it's weird that she can see into people's minds, right?"

"It's awful!" said Delphine. "She's sitting around knowing all this terrible stuff about people, and she can't even talk right, and half the time she can probably tell all the terrible things people are thinking about her, right?" Delphine's tears had slowed down.

"Are you thinking terrible things about her?" Nessa asked.

"I'm trying not to, but her *voice*, Nessa, and the way she looks at me."

"Delphine," Nessa said. "You're doing a great job with her. I didn't know it was so hard. Maybe because you guys are twins, the way she feels about you is more complicated."

"We're not twins."

Nessa looked at her watch. She wasn't getting anywhere. "It's late and we have to get to sleep. Tomorrow is another big day of incredibly boring speeches."

Delphine at least smiled at that. She headed into the bathroom to shower and change. Nessa waited for her to finish and then sat with Delphine while she got into bed, reminding them both of the old days when they shared a room and fell asleep together every night. When Delphine fell asleep, Nessa headed to her own room, passing CM's open door on the way. She couldn't see the chimera but could overhear CM murmuring something low and unintelligible.

Nessa stayed awake for a long while. The nearly full moon was bright through her window. She wondered what Bo was up to. All Nessa wanted to do was forget the night's disastrous end, sneak out, transform, and run.

CHAPTER TWENTY ONE

The next morning, CM was not at breakfast. Neither was Daniel. "Rehearsal," said Milton in her clear, straightforward voice. "Your dad and CM are getting ready for the big presentation this afternoon. She's the subject of your dad's talk. She's also his assistant. Isn't that cute?"

Nessa nodded like she thought this was as normal as Milton was making it seem, then headed with Delphine for the morning sessions. Only Delphine didn't head toward the lab after Nessa parked the golf cart in the lot. "I'm uh—" she said, gestured toward the woods.

"You're going to see the Kids?" said Nessa. "Alone again?"

Delphine nodded, her faced screwed up in anticipation of Nessa's calling her out on this.

Nessa knew she should go with Delphine—that cat was still out there. But the first presenter of the morning was Taneda, and Nessa wanted to attend. Also, it was *so* hot. Predators were nocturnal. If anyone was going to get attacked it would be one of the Kids, outside during the night.

"Be careful," Nessa said. "Keep an eye out for that cat, okay?"

Delphine nodded, scooped up a muffin, and headed for the door.

Taneda began her presentation standing in front of the room, her legs planted firmly in a wide stance, her hands clasped below her waist. She wore jeans with wide cuffs and a sleeveless white oxford with the collar popped. Nessa noted a simple leather necklace at her throat, strung through a glass medallion the color of thick smoke.

Nessa expected Taneda to open with a joke—but her face was as solemn as a security guard's. "What is science?" she said. "I don't know. I used to think I did, but the definition keeps expanding in my mind. Where I end up, most days, is this: A scientist is a person who asks questions. Will this work? Given x, will y fail? We add to knowledge. We add our drop to the pool. The rate of change is slow. Drip, drip, drip." Finally, Taneda smiled. "Every time one of us breaks through, we all find the waters in the pool are deeper. We can move differently than we could before."

She let the silence that followed hang for a moment, and then she pointed to the front row of seats. "And so, I introduce my colleague, Dr. Maxine Halliday. She studies folklore. Her title is 'folklorist.' But today I introduce her as a fellow scientist. A poser of questions."

Halliday stood, bowing slightly to thank Taneda, then turned to face the room. "Today Professor Halliday and I will describe our work together," Taneda said. "We have been matching the traces of DNA found in ancient, fossilized life forms to the DNA of language—we extract this language from the stories and legends Professor Halliday has unearthed."

"Thank you," Halliday said. "How truly poetic." She launched directly into a description of the work she and Taneda were exploring. As she talked, she flashed images up on the projection screen, alternating with Taneda's images of gene maps and fossilized fragments of bone. Their project was in the early stages, but Nessa felt she could see the appeal.

"So, will you corroborate the existence of a yeti?" the Jurassic Frog scientist asked, his question sounding half-sincere, half-mocking.

"If we could, you can just imagine the headlines," Professor Halliday offered. "But we are not after sensationalism. We are drawn to knowledge that is slightly more true to the record.

The Honshu wolf, for instance. Once worshipped as a god in Japan. Now extinct. Imagine what we might learn matching the ancient stories to the scientific record?"

The Jurassic Frog scientist nodded, backing off the question as Halliday moved on to an obscure recounting of a lost scroll in Transylvania. Nessa remembered the stack of books in her office. Was that what she and Taneda were investigating for real? The Honshu?

And was Taneda *really* a wolf?

After her talk, Halliday rushed off to catch the plane back to Palo Alto, saying a quick goodbye to Nessa and promising a longer talk when she returned for the final dinner at the end of the week.

True to her word, Delphine arrived in time for lunch at the lab. After eating, everyone loaded into a minibus for the drive up to the new lab in the northern section of the park.

It was a beautiful day, bright and sunny, and the visiting scientists were pointing into the woods and exclaiming at the overlooks along the way. Nessa heard one of the Haken researchers comparing the soft hills with a section of the countryside in Japan. Another asked about the fish in the streams.

Finally, they reached the parking area at the new lab. "This is the new facility Dad built for CM," Nessa explained to Delphine in a hushed voice. Nessa was looking around, trying to target what was different. It went beyond the fact that it was daytime now. "It didn't look this . . . nice . . . then."

It was true. The circular-shaped building looked much like itself, but the construction-site vibe of the rest of the facility was gone, the trucks and piles of materials moved or used, and rolls of sod laid out, alternating with paved paths and gravel walkways.

Now, Nessa could see how this building had been designed—for exhibitions. Outside each wedge-shaped room there were benches that had been set up in front of the glass, three-deep. Milton was leading the Haken researchers to a cluster of benches.

Nessa and Delphine stood in the back, behind the tent that had been set up to provide shade over the benches. The room they were standing outside of was not a bedroom, but a school-room of sorts. There were books on shelves, maps on the walls, balls and blocks in bins. Nessa watched through the window as Daniel entered and then CM behind him, looking awkward, embarrassed to be seen.

Daniel was attaching something to his lapel and pretty soon he tapped it, and Nessa could hear the sound. It was a micro-phone—the speakers were built into the building. "Can you hear me out there?" Daniel asked. He turned to CM, including her in the question, and then the two of them walked together toward the glass. Daniel took her hand and raised it in the air, like he was congratulating her on a race she'd run. "Welcome," Daniel said.

As an introduction, he explained CM's history—everything

he had told Nessa, some things he hadn't. All the while he was talking, Nessa kept checking CM's face—looking for signs of pain, of shyness, of sadness, of not wanting to be the object on display—the animal. CM showed nothing, her expression fixed as if there was not a crowd gathered before her.

Daniel used the session to show pictures of CM when she was a baby. He showed graphs of her change in blood composition. One slide showed highlights of some of the patterns in her DNA coding, which caused Taneda to gasp. Ishikawa was up front and Nessa could see him nodding.

There were pictures of CM in what would have been elementary school, if she had gone to school—perched on a swing. Another of her eating a picnic on a blanket. She was always alone, though Nessa assumed Daniel had been the one behind the camera.

Daniel explained the research he had done on animal brain function, comparing the insights he'd collected from CM and the research on behavior.

"But now," he said. "I will reveal some new, potentially game-changing revelations about CM and her chimeric assumption of immunity. We'll get more into the mechanics of it in session two, but I believe what's written in her genetic code, in every blood cell, in every stem cell, is the future for our work. I have created a patent-pending toolkit that will allow all of us to use CM's DNA in every aspect of genetic research. The funding opportunities are basically infinite. This, my colleagues, is game changing."

There was a spattering of applause from the researchers in the benches. Nessa peered at CM. It was her blood Daniel was describing. Her genes. Her immunity that would produce the magic, and yet not even a shade of recognition crossed her face.

Dinner was held outdoors that evening, despite a lingering, stagnant heat. The energy from the day's conversations was high. The cloud above the table was a series of rainbows, colors shifting and pouring into each other. Wine was poured readily through a salad and a cheese course. The lights in the room were dim.

The family sat together: Daniel, CM, Delphine, and Nessa, alongside the most prominent researchers from Haken, and the mood was joyous. Just as Daniel had hoped, his revelations about the capability of CM's immune response had given the gathering a lift, a feeling of mission, of possibility. He was smiling more often, talking faster. He looked—Nessa swore—an inch taller.

CM was muted, maintaining the inward-facing gaze from this afternoon. Nessa tried to watch her, but she was seated next to a Japanese researcher who had a daughter Nessa's age and peppered her with questions about American trends so he could return with the best gift. "Uh," Nessa said. "Trends aren't my strong suit; that's Delphine's territory."

The next time Nessa was able to check in, CM was robotically pushing French fries into her mouth, providing nothing but monosyllabic answers to questions posed by Dr. Ishikawa, who was sitting next to her.

When Nessa checked again, Dr. Ishikawa appeared to have given up trying to engage CM, and CM had given up on her fries, staring fixedly at something, which, when Nessa followed CM's gaze, she realized was Delphine. Sitting with Taneda at the other end of the table, Delphine was smiling, laughing, unaware of CM's glare.

"Do you know the store Urban Outfitters?" the Japanese researcher asked Nessa. "My daughter asked me to buy her a wallet with a Ouija board print. Is there an Urban Outfitters in this area?"

"I'm sorry?" Nessa said. She hadn't been listening.

Gabriel, who was sitting on Nessa's other side, came to her rescue, explaining that there weren't any malls nearby, but that he could probably find an Urban Outfitters in Seattle, then directing the scientist to a conversation about his work.

Another course arrived, and Nessa looked over at CM again. CM was no longer watching Delphine. She was staring down, at her plate. At another glance, later, Nessa saw that CM was looking up at the ceiling, scowling. *She must be so bored,* Nessa thought.

Then finally, as little cookies and vanilla ice cream soaked in espresso were served, there was a crashing, shattering sound. The table went silent. Nessa, with her superior hearing, was able to locate the source of the shattering sound immediately, her eyes focusing on the wine glass lying in shards on CM's dessert plate, the stem grasped in CM's right hand.

CM's Delphine-like eyes opened wide, her mouth formed into an "Oops."

"I'm sorry, I'm so sorry," CM shouted. Nessa could see the strained expressions on the visiting scientists' faces as they heard CM raise her raspy voice.

"I didn't know it would break. I was squeezing. It was so pretty."

No one responded for a half second. Daniel just watched and at that moment Nessa flashed back to Bo's assessment of him. Was he seeing the entire world—even their family—through the eyes of science? It was Dr. Ishikawa who took action, gently taking CM's hand, extracting the wine glass stem, lifting her still-folded thick white linen dinner napkin and wrapping it around the center of the palm, which Nessa could see now was bleeding.

CHAPTER TWENTY TWO

fter CM's hand was wrapped, Dr. Ishikawa stood, signaling that he was ready for bed. The guests were led out to the van that would take them to the Chimera Corp. guesthouse. Daniel took CM downstairs to bandage her hand properly, and Nessa and Delphine headed to their rooms.

Nessa showered and changed into pajamas and was thinking about checking in with Bree when there was a soft knock on her door. She opened to see Delphine in the hall, dressed in pajamas as well. She was clasping a bunched-up pink hoodie to her chest and she looked behind her, like she was worried about being watched. "Can I come in?" she whispered.

Nessa took a step back into the room and Delphine entered, shutting the door behind her. Delphine then held the hoodie up for Nessa to see. "This hoodie—" she said. "It was in my drawer when I went up to dinner, but when I got back to my room, it was laid out on the bed."

Delphine drew her head back and waited, as if Nessa should understand something. Nessa was lost. "So?" she said.

"Everything on top of my bureau was moved as well."

Nessa still didn't know where Delphine was going with this. "Your room gets cleaned. You know that."

"But the cleaners don't move the stuff on my bureau. They don't come during dinner. And they don't take stuff *out* of my drawers." Delphine looked like she wanted to say something more but was holding back.

"What?" Nessa said.

"Okay," Delphine started. She pulled a lock of hair out in front of her face, stretched out the curl, and anchored it behind her ear. This was a gesture Delphine always made when she was concentrating. Once she let go, the curl sprang back into place. "Do you think it's possible that CM was going through my things?"

"CM?" Nessa said, willing her voice to stay neutral. "What makes you think it was her?"

Delphine rolled her eyes and Nessa stared her down. "Just

because she's not exactly . . . all there . . . doesn't mean you can accuse her when one little thing goes wrong."

"I'm not doing that," Delphine insisted. "It's just—Nessa, she's starting to really creep me out." Nessa took note of the deep purple rising into a cloud in the room. There was something menacing about this color. She felt the threat of Delphine's anger. Also: Delphine was afraid.

"Have you been having the dreams still?" Nessa asked. "Are you sleeping?"

Delphine nodded. "I know what you said about Mom and all, but I can't stop feeling scared." Delphine hugged the hoodie to her chest and sat on Nessa's bed, all the indignant anger disappearing, as the purple faded to a dull lavender-gray.

"Look," Nessa said. "I know CM is . . . unusual. But can you put yourself in her shoes for a minute? Her whole life she's been some kind of lab rat. We can't expect her to acclimate 100 percent to regular human society with the snap of our fingers."

"I was trying to be nice," Delphine said. Nessa could see Delphine was sincere. There were tears in her eyes. "I want to, okay?" Her color flashed brighter suddenly, the red that lives inside purple reasserting itself. "But today, I saw her looking at me, and it was like, I could just tell, she hated me. She looks at me like she wants to hurt me." By now, Delphine had raised her voice. The walls weren't particularly thin, but if CM heard them, what would it do to her feelings?

"Ugh, Delphine," Nessa said. "Can you not see everything as a betrayal? Can you think for just one second that maybe you are wrong?"

"The wine glass," Delphine said. She was whispering now. "She smashed it. I saw her smash it."

"Oh, come on," Nessa said. "Why would she do that?"

"I don't know," Delphine said. "But I saw her do it. She—" Delphine flicked her wrist to show the motion. "Dr. Taneda was telling me all these stories about Mom that made me feel—I don't know, happy?—for the first time in months. And CM was staring at me like I had stolen something from her. Which, by the way, I haven't. And then I just happened to glance over and she caught my eye, and then she checked to make sure no one was watching, lifted the glass, and purposefully smashed it into the plate."

Delphine stopped talking and looked at Nessa, like now Nessa could have no excuse but to be on her side.

But Nessa needed to think. She had to consider Delphine's weeks of anger, the trauma she had experienced, the adjustments she was being asked to make, against CM's lifetime of maltreatment, and the even larger adjustment going on in her world.

"I can't take this all in," Nessa finally said. "It's been a long day. Let's sleep on it and see how things go in the morning, okay?"

Delphine did not look like that was okay, but she nodded her head and turned for the door, walking out without saying goodnight.

Again, Nessa could not sleep. This often happened as her time to transform approached, especially at Daniel's where the sounds of the woods were so close, she might as well have been sleeping outdoors.

Giving up on sleep, Nessa opened her sliding glass door, and stepped onto the deck. There was a built-in bench covered in cushions and pillows, but the idea of reclining or even sitting did not appeal. Instead, she leaned against the railing and looked into the trees, thinking about Bo, contemplating sneaking out of the house.

It wasn't *just* that she wanted to see Bo. She did. It wasn't *just* that it was nice, after so many months of missing Luc, to feel like another person had the capacity to make her come alive with connection. It was that *and* the need to transform that kept her awake.

She also had the feeling that Bo knew something and wasn't telling her. Something about Daniel.

As she stood at the rail, Nessa heard a rustling in the trees. Her balcony looked out into the very top of the understory. Only birds and small animals made it up there, but she could sometimes spot a larger animal below—raccoons, opossum, the occasional unidentifiable creature whose DNA had been altered in Daniel's lab. She leaned forward now, attempting to see. At first it was too dark, but then a cloud shifted, and the moonlight shone through the branches above so that Nessa could make out a shape she recognized. The huge cat.

It was stretched out languorously along a branch, its tail twitching, its eyes meeting Nessa's. After just a few seconds had passed, it leapt away, disappearing from view, only the shaking of branches betraying the animal's path.

So that's interesting, Nessa thought. This cat Bo insisted could never have been the one to kill Rio. It was willing to come this close to the house and the people inside it. *Not natural. Not a good sign.*

The next morning, Nessa promised herself, she was going to lay down the law with Delphine. No more solo trips into the woods.

CHAPTER TWENTY THREE

At breakfast the next morning, Nessa found Milton and Daniel in the dining room, talking about work, both clearly still riding the high of the success of the first CM exhibition.

Milton had poured herself a black coffee while Daniel was nibbling on a health muffin and sipping tea. They bent their heads over Milton's tablet, running through the plans for adding another CM demonstration. Some of the Haken guests had already asked questions that went beyond the scope of what they had planned to show, and Daniel wanted to accommodate them.

"I don't know," Milton mused. "I hate to compress the afternoon session. But I suppose we can push lunch by fifteen minutes." She entered the adjustment on her tablet. "And we'll put out a few snacks late morning in case anyone is peckish."

"We'll see you shortly," Daniel said to Nessa as he and Milton hustled off to the lab.

"Be sure Delphine is on time!" Milton added.

Nessa nodded, only half listening to them, gazing out the window. The weather had gotten even *hotter* overnight—Milton had been talking about a storm coming—and though the house was air conditioned, Nessa practically saw steam rising from the trees.

Running was not going to be pleasant, but she'd skipped her run the day before and slept through her morning window. She'd have to get out later.

And not only was she going to have to find time for a run, she was going to need to transform. The full moon would force it on her very soon. Nessa tried to imagine the best way to transform and yet avoid the guests, the cat, the Outsider Kids. When had the woods become so crowded?

The sound of CM's voice behind her shocked Nessa out of her reverie. "Hi Nessa," CM said, her voice dragging out the "hi."

Nessa jolted in her seat. CM's voice was still so very hard to listen to. "Oh, hi CM," she said. Nessa smiled at her as openly as she could and jumped up to get her some toast and OJ with a straw.

CM smiled as Nessa set the dishes down. "Thank you," she said. Her voice was almost sweet. Or at least, Nessa registered, she was *trying* to be sweet.

Did she feel bad about breaking the glass the night before?

Had she broken the glass?

Nessa noticed that CM was wearing lip gloss. Her lips were not her most human of features—the skin tough and leathery, the lips unarticulated and wide. The addition of lip gloss gave them a kind of grotesque shine. Nessa knew a big sister should be able to tell CM the best way to approach her beauty regimen, a task Nessa was just plain not up for.

"You don't like it?" CM said.

Without bothering to question how CM had read her thoughts, Nessa replied, "No, it's, um, pretty." Which was dumb, she realized as she spoke. CM could probably tell she was lying. She could probably tell everything Nessa was thinking about her.

Just as she was about to admit what she was thinking—go for an honest approach—she saw Delphine coming across the living room.

"Hey, Delphine," Nessa said, when she was close to the table. And then to CM: "Let's ask Delphine if she can help find a better shade." She turned to Delphine: "CM needs help with lip gloss. Think you can give some advice?"

But Delphine just stared at CM, and then, to Nessa's horror, Delphine narrowed her eyes and balled up her fists. "No, I can't," she said.

Nessa and CM stared at Delphine as she banged a plate onto the buffet, threw one miniature croissant onto it, and slammed it on the table.

"Are you okay?" CM said, leaning across the table toward Delphine, her voice scratching over these innocuous words.

"Give me the lip gloss back," Delphine said. "And stay out of my room."

CM giggled. "You don't—you don't like it?" she said, her voice rising.

Delphine gave Nessa a punishing glance. "I told you CM's been in my room," she said. She looked at CM. "You were going through the stuff on my bureau and you took that lip gloss, didn't you?"

CM's expression went blank.

"CM?" Nessa said. "Is this true?"

Now, CM opened her eyes wide. "I got this lip gloss from Milton," she said. "She gave me a set."

"Oh, she did?" Delphine said. She had gone red. Nessa could tell she didn't believe CM.

CM looked down at the table. "I'm sorry," she said. "I asked Milton for a color just like yours. It looks so pretty on you. But it does not look so pretty on me."

Nessa looked at Delphine. Surely, she would stop being mad at CM and start feeling sorry for her now? The poor thing.

"Let's be friends," CM said. She sounded like she was reading cue cards, but still, Nessa could see, she was trying. CM held out a hand as if Delphine would shake it. And then she smiled a grotesque toothy grin. A bit of toast was stuck in her teeth. *Please, Delphine,* Nessa thought. *Please do something to make this less painful.*

"You're lying," Delphine said, staring CM down. "And maybe everyone else here is dumb enough to believe you but I'm not." She stood up and stormed out of the room, leaving Nessa to put a hand on CM's shoulder as she cried.

"It's okay," Nessa said, absentmindedly.

Is it, though?

As Nessa was brushing her teeth after breakfast, her phone buzzed. It was Bree. She had never been so glad to see her friend's curly hair and big smile over FaceTime. Bree was heading out the door for her internship, putting on makeup in her bathroom, and she needed advice. "Do you think the red is too much?" she said, puckering her lips for the camera.

"I can't even *think* about makeup right now," Nessa replied, explaining Delphine and CM's argument.

Bree listened while she put on mascara. It was hard reading her expression as she stretched up her eyes and focused on a point in the distance.

"So, *was* it Delphine's lip gloss?" Bree asked at the end.

"I don't know!" said Nessa. "And even if it was, who cares? The poor thing is learning how to become a human. She's going to make mistakes."

"Yeah, but Delphine is not an exaggerator," Bree said. "If Delphine says CM smashed the glass and that something feels weird, you need to listen to her."

"I guess," Nessa said. Bree hadn't been there for the weeks of Delphine's anger. Nessa had.

"And Bree, there's something else . . ." Nessa began. "Well, someone else."

Immediately Bree was all ears, her makeup suddenly out of the frame. "You've met a guy?" Bree said. "In the middle of the *woods*. Jeez, Nessa, I'm impressed. Who is it? Wait, no, of course. Gabriel. I knew he was into you . . ."

"Gabriel?" Nessa said. "Um . . . ew? He's totally awkward. It's not a guy. It's this girl. Bo. I—um—kissed her. And it was really nice."

There was a pause while Bree ingested this development in Nessa's life. Or perhaps she didn't even miss a beat, and it was just a glitch in the video feed. In any case, it wasn't longer than a half second before Bree said, "Well of course it was nice. I could tell the way you were talking about her before that there might be something there."

Nessa breathed a sigh of relief. She loved Bree. "I think she's mad at me."

"I see the Nessa Kurland charm is working." Bree laughed. "Honestly Nessa, you have to let people know you like them. I know things were easy with Luc because you had the wolf-to-wolf thing going, but with us humans, a little communication goes a long way."

"It's not that," Nessa said. "It's kind of. I don't know. She's not a big fan of the whole Chimera Corp. operation."

Bree sighed. "Oh, I see," she said. "And you are?"

The question caught Nessa off guard. "Well, I mean, it's my dad," she said.

"Your mom didn't trust him."

"She did by the end," Nessa said. "She sent us here."

"Hold on," Bree said. "I'm gonna use the blow-dryer for a sec."

Nessa turned down the volume on the phone to protect her ears from the blow-dryer's whine. "—like with Paravida," Bree was saying, as Nessa punched the volume back up. "All of these companies, they feel like it's a frontier, you know? Manifest Destiny. They have to rush to claim the knowledge. Dan has a theory—it's not just knowledge, it's the technology for extracting that knowledge that's valuable. Whoever controls that sets the pace for this whole field."

As Bree went on, talking about how Paravida was participating in deals with the Russian and Chinese governments, possibly building biological weapons, Nessa told herself that whatever Bo thought she knew about Chimera Corp., it could not be as bad as what Nessa and Bree knew about Paravida.

"I should talk to Bo," Nessa said.

"You mean you *want* to talk to Bo," Bree teased. Nessa felt her face getting hot as she sputtered reasons: Bo understood the forest. She knew things about Chimera.

Bree ignored these rationalizations. "So, is it nice?" she said.

"To have feelings for someone finally? To get a break from feeling sad about Luc?"

Nessa laughed. She wanted to say "yes," to believe that having room in her life for something new—and something differently new—was a sign that she was over the loss of Luc.

But hearing Luc's name, Nessa felt the same familiar mix of hope and the sadness that always followed the dashing of that hope. "I'm still sad," she said. "I don't think I will ever not be sad."

"No," Bree said. "And you just lost your mom too. Nessa, if all you did for the next year was feel sad, I would understand."

"That's nice," said Nessa. "But being sad doesn't mean I can't do anything."

"Yes," said Bree. "Especially when you're doing it with this hot militia chick."

"It's not a militia!" Nessa said. "It's just a bunch of kids and their dogs."

"Whatever," said Bree. "It's hot. Am I going to get to meet them when I come visit? You remember we're coming, right?"

Nessa promised. She remembered. The day after the visitors left. She'd told Daniel and Milton, and hoped that they remembered too. With so much effort and preparation going in to Haken's visit, she had to wonder if they were thinking past the moment the Haken researchers finally left.

CHAPTER TWENTY FOUR

The energy of the day before was still high when the conference started up again at nine, but over the course of the morning, the heat and humidity took their toll, and exhaustion began to set in. By lunchtime, two of the visitors had departed to rest. One of the presenter's files had been lost and the presentation had to be delayed.

Delphine was missing too. She must have been sulking somewhere. Nessa didn't see her until the end of the morning, when she slipped into the lab building and headed toward the stairs leading down into the Well.

Nessa followed, catching up with her at the cubicle Delphine had been assigned.

"I'm sorry about this morning," Nessa said.

Delphine drew her eyebrows together. "I want to like her," she said. "But what if she's—I don't know—really angry at all of us?"

"Because of what Dad did to her?"

"How about what *Mom* did? She left her out in the woods to die. She thought her very existence was wrong."

"But she changed her mind."

"Fourteen years later."

"Look," Nessa said. "I think CM is trying. I don't know what happened with that wine glass, but the whole situation is complicated. I think we need to give her a chance."

"Okay," Delphine said, and sighed. "I'll try."

Stepping outside, into the humidity, Nessa felt like she'd walked into a wall. She peeled off the loose button-down shirt she'd been wearing over a tank top and tied it around her waist, moving into the shade and standing still, trying not to resist the heat.

She heard her name and turned to the sound of the voice but couldn't spot anyone. "Nessa," she heard again. It was coming from the woods, and she felt a smile playing on her face. She knew whose voice that was. "School done for the day?"

Nessa pulled her hair up into a high bun, knotting it loosely. Lifting her arms high, she was conscious of her body in the tank top, how languorous and stretchy she felt, how she was maybe even showing it off a bit for Bo. She thought of that cat she'd seen twice now. It moved in the way she was moving now, like every micro-adjustment of bone or muscle mattered.

Of course, she had never done that kind of thing with Luc, she thought, smiling a bit, recalling that most of their relationship, they'd been wearing parkas and track pants.

As she stepped into the underbrush, Bo showed herself, and Nessa realized how much she had missed her. Something about the way Bo looked at her made her dizzy.

There was no pretending they didn't want to be touching each other. Nessa's fingers found Bo's almost immediately, and then Bo had a hand on Nessa's waist, and then Nessa was thinking that they should talk before they started kissing, but then it was too late for that and Bo had her pressed up against a tree, and it felt so amazing that Nessa believed the scratching of the bark on the bare skin of her shoulders and neck felt good.

Finally, Nessa was able to say, "I thought you were mad at me."

Bo said, "Not mad, just worried."

"About the chimeras?"

"About everything."

At dinner that night, Nessa sought out Taneda during the cocktail hour.

"Does anything seem weird to you," Nessa said. "About CM?"

For once, Taneda did not crack a joke. "There's nothing about her that *doesn't* seem weird," she said. "But why do you ask? I hear you were the one who convinced your father to bring her into the family."

"What do you think of that?" Nessa said.

"I think you are a very warm-hearted person. I think it might work. I think, 'What is the cost if it does not?'"

"Moral cost?" Nessa said.

"Is she a human being or is she not a human being?" Taneda said. "How much hurt do we expect her to bear?"

Just then, they were interrupted by one of Taneda's colleagues. Nessa didn't have a chance to answer Taneda's question. Not that she could have anyway.

CHAPTER TWENTY FIVE

Nessa dreamt she was chasing Delphine through the Amtrak train they'd ridden out West. The train was rocking. It was hard to walk, and Nessa kept grabbing at the walls for support. She wanted to call Delphine by name, but she'd transformed into a wolf and could only howl.

The train lurched so that she was thrown forward, down the hall toward her sister. She was able to get a paw on her shoulder. Delphine turned. But when she turned, Nessa saw that it was CM's face she was looking into. She woke with a start to see that Delphine was the one who was shaking her. It was light out, but just barely.

"What?" Nessa said, shooting up into a seated position, her sense that they were in danger coming hot and hard. "What is it?"

"Oh my god," Delphine whispered. She turned her head toward the door as if to check whether they were being watched. "Nessa, I'm so scared."

Nessa scooted off the bed, threw her feet over its side, in full fight-or-flight mode. She could feel that her body was inches away from transformation. Whatever she needed to fight, she'd be better able to handle it in wolf form.

"It's okay," Delphine said, seeing the expression of alarm on Nessa's face. "We're safe right now."

Nessa's internal alarm was still ringing. "What's going on?"

"In the night, I woke up. I had this weird feeling and I opened my eyes and there was CM."

"In your room?" Nessa said.

"Yeah, she was standing right over my bed. I pretended I was still asleep because, Nessa, I was so scared."

"Maybe she just wanted to talk. Did you talk to her?"

"I thought if she knew I was awake she'd attack me or something. Like when someone breaks into your house and if they think they've been seen then they have to kill you."

"Kill you?" Nessa said. She took a deep breath. This whole situation was escalating in ways that felt out of control. Someone had to inject some rationality.

"Maybe you should just let her in your room once and for all," Nessa said. "Give her a tour. Let her try out your clothes and makeup. I mean, sisters do that for real. You're always swiping my stuff."

Delphine put her arms on her hips and lowered her voice. "I don't think you're hearing me. A six-foot-tall monster is going through my room, taking my stuff, giving me dirty looks. Then she watches me sleep. Oh, *and* she can read my mind. This isn't about making *her* feel safe. This is about making *me* feel safe."

Nessa rubbed her eyes. "Wait, didn't you lock your door last night? I remember hearing you."

"I *did* lock my door," said Delphine. "And when I got up this morning the bolt was still in place."

For the first time, Nessa felt herself relax, an understanding of what must have happened forming in her mind. She was stupid not to have thought of it before. "Du-uh," she said. "You were *dreaming*." She smiled, expecting Delphine to smile back. "The doors don't unlock from the outside. She couldn't have come in."

"But I saw her."

"Dreams feel real."

Delphine stood. "I can't believe you," she said. "I'm your sister. Your *real* sister, not some test tube science experiment gone wrong. I'm telling you what I saw. Check the security cameras."

"There aren't any in our rooms," Nessa said.

"Yes," Delphine said. "There are. I found them looking for some other files. Which figures, you know? Did you really think Dad wouldn't have this whole place under surveillance?"

"Delphine!" Nessa said. "You hacked the surveillance system?"

Delphine shrugged. "The point is," she said. "There's cameras everywhere. Which means I hope you're changing in the bathroom. I am."

Nessa slapped her knees, making a mental note to bring the whole privacy issue up with Daniel. "So, great," she said. "We'll ask Dad for the footage of your room last night. We'll see what was really going on. We can clear up the lip gloss issue at the same time."

Delphine crossed her arms in front of her chest. "And if we do see her coming in and out of this room—which we will—I want to be clear. One of us is going to have to go. I'm not living with a monster."

They found Daniel at breakfast, and since CM was not up yet, they presented their request to see the security footage from Delphine's room right then and there. Daniel grumbled a bit, but eventually acquiesced, wagging a finger at Delphine for hacking the system.

"I'm going to set you to some actually meaningful programming tasks from here on out," he said, wiping his mouth with his napkin and standing.

Daniel led them through the kitchen, opening a door leading off the back hall, and finally bringing them in to a tiny room they'd never been in before. The room looked much like the observation trailer set up outside the windows of CM's lab, but it was smaller. The three of them plus the guard at the terminal just about filled the space to capacity.

"Hi Brian," Daniel said, greeting the tech. "We're trying to resolve a bit of a family dispute, and I'm wondering if you'd mind queuing up some footage from last night's stream?"

Brian, who had curly red hair and freckled skin and was clearly a junior member of the team, not used to direct interactions with Daniel, nearly knocked over his coffee. He fumbled as he navigated the video storage architecture to find the footage they were looking for. "What time did you go to bed?" Daniel asked, and when Delphine explained that it was just after ten, Brian queued the video to 9:55 p.m.

Nessa saw a blurry, but full-color image of Delphine's room, seen from the corner by the window. The bed was in view. So was the area around the bed and the pocket door that led into the hall.

"This is what you want to be able to see?" Brian confirmed.

"Yes," Delphine said. "It will be much later though. After I went to sleep and had been sleeping for a while."

"We'll fast-forward through the night starting here," Brian said. He glanced up at Daniel. "Then we won't miss anything."

"Please," said Daniel. Brian keyed in a few commands, while Nessa, Delphine, and Daniel stared intently at the screen.

At first nothing changed. The room remained empty as the clock on the bottom right corner of the screen counted forward in time. Finally, when it reached 10:19:37, the door slid open and the tech froze the image.

"That's you?" Brian said, turning around while pointing to a shadowy figure in the doorway.

Delphine nodded, biting her lip. The tech started the clock again, and they watched as Delphine slipped into the bathroom and then emerged in pjs, got under the covers, checked her phone for a bit before laying it on the nightstand. A half hour in real time had passed in under a minute. They waited for more as the clock made it to 11 p.m. and then 11:30 and then midnight and beyond. The image did not change. Delphine remained sleeping in the same near-frozen position. From years of sharing a room, Nessa knew this was her sister's pattern—Delphine slept like the dead until close to waking, at which time she always tossed and turned and often talked a lot as well.

"What time are you looking for exactly?" the tech turned to ask Delphine.

"I don't know," Delphine said. "She was in the room for a while. I just lay there waiting for her to go, and then finally there was a rustling sound, and I heard her go through the door and lock it back into place."

"That's impossible," Daniel said. "The doors don't lock from the outside."

"That's what I said," Nessa added.

"I know what I saw," insisted Delphine.

The time on the clock on the screen was at 2 a.m. now.

"Could it have been a dream?" Daniel asked, his voice soft and nonthreatening.

"It was *not* a dream," Delphine said, her jaw locked. But already the clock was showing three in the morning and there was no change, then four. There was nothing at five, six, and then the sun was shining through the curtains. The tech continued to let the video run, but Delphine turned away in frustration. "That video is wrong," she said. "I know she was there. I saw her."

"But Delphine," Daniel said, pointing to the monitor. "She wasn't." He launched into a lecture about how he learned as a scientist to trust what he saw, not what he thought he saw, how she must do this too. Delphine made it obvious she wasn't listening. As soon as Daniel was done speaking, she said, "Can I go now?"

"Yes," Daniel said, his shoulders slumping in defeat, and Delphine just about ran from the room. Nessa jogged a few steps, passing through the kitchen, and then pushing through the swinging doors that led to the dining room.

There, at the breakfast table, Delphine had come face-to-face with CM. CM was frozen, looking up at Delphine. Delphine's back was to Nessa, so Nessa could only read the frustration and surprise in the way Delphine had stopped short and held her arms at her side, as if asking the question, "What am I supposed to do now?"

Nessa could see CM's face, providing no answer. CM was caught in the act of sucking orange juice through her straw. Her lips were pursed, and her eyes opened wide in an expression that almost seemed comic. That and the fact that the lower, bearded half of her face was hidden made her seem more human.

Delphine threw her hands up in the air and stormed from the room.

CM lifted her head from the straw, and looked at Daniel. "I don't understand why she is so angry all the time," CM said.

Daniel set his jaw, then stepped over to the sideboard, helping himself to a cup of coffee. He didn't answer CM until he was sitting down with the coffee lined up in the exact center of his place setting. He made micro-adjustments to the placement of the cup and then placed his hands perfectly symmetrically on either side of it. CM watched all of this with patient curiosity. When he was done, Daniel looked her in the eye. "I don't understand either, CM," he said, sounding puzzled. And then he repeated himself in a tone that Nessa interpreted as threatening, though she did not know who was being threatened. "I don't understand at all."

CM looked up at Nessa then, her eyes big and wide, her sadness broadcasting loud and clear. "Are you going to eat with me this morning?" she said.

Nessa knew she should. But she couldn't do it. "I've got to go," she muttered and nearly ran for the bedrooms on the lower floor.

Passing her own room, she slid open the door to Delphine's. The room was empty, her bureau stripped, Delphine's black backpack gone.

CHAPTER TWENTY SIX

All the researchers had a session up at CM's lab that day, but Nessa didn't have the heart to join them. Instead, she lay in bed, texting nonsense with Bree, scanning Isle Royale photos for any sign of Luc, thinking about Bo. She stepped out onto her balcony to get some air, but it was so hot she went right back inside. The air felt strange and thick. She missed Luc. She missed Tether. She missed her mother. She missed winter. She missed Bo.

The vans brought the researchers back in time for lunch, and Nessa joined them in the tents in the hope that Delphine would have come back. She wasn't there, and it was too hot to eat, even in the shade.

Nessa tried *not* to think about the moon, though that was difficult. Even hidden in the blue sky, she could feel it pulling the wolf to the surface of her skin. At least she was near enough to the preserve that she knew she could transform without being seen.

When Milton announced that they were moving the meal inside, into the air conditioning, Nessa knew she could not go back in. She could not sit still in a chair, her body twitching with the desire to run.

By instinct more than decision, Nessa slipped off the terrace and into the still-hot air of the woods, letting the oppressive humidity seep into her skin.

By the time she reached the Outsider Kids' campsite, she was sweating and itchy from mosquito bites. It was slightly cooler by the stream that ran through the campsite, but not much of a relief.

There wasn't much going on at the camp—probably because of the heat. Bo was supervising a conversation that looked like two kids reporting on a fight they were having. Nessa spotted Delphine leaning back against a tree trunk, her feet planted on the ground, her knees pulled to her chest. She was chewing on a stalk of wheat-like grass and laughing at something Topher was saying.

She's happy here, Nessa thought. *At Daniel's house, she isn't happy.* Nessa thought of CM—her look of blank acceptance when Delphine had called her a monster. No one is happy there.

"Hey!" said Bo, spotting Nessa and heading toward her.

She was smiling at Nessa and Nessa felt herself smiling at Bo. Bo slid her hands into her hip pockets. It went without saying that they would not kiss in front of the kids. "I'm about to lose my mind in this heat. Everyone is. We're heading for the swimming hole. Want to come?"

"There's a swimming hole?" said Nessa.

Bo flung her arm out casually, pointing north. Nessa didn't know any pools up that way, though she hadn't explored much there either.

"We're running," Bo said. "Hope you're good with that."

"Oh, yeah?" Nessa felt a prick of competition, the feeling that used to spur her to kick it in for the last 200 meters of a race. "I think I can handle it."

Nessa walked over to Delphine, kicked her boot with the toe of her own sneaker. "You mind if I come swimming?"

Delphine looked down at her knees, then back up into Nessa's face. Delphine was spending so much time outside, her freckles were mellowing into her tanned skin. "You can come," she said.

Bo turned to Nessa. "You'll be back in two hours, tops. If you can keep up."

If Nessa had known that keeping up meant thirty straight minutes of sprinting along a trail, she might not have nodded her head so confidently. But running, even in the heat, provided its usual release.

Eventually, Nessa heard the sounds of a falls ahead of them. She could smell it too, the plant matter stirred by the roiling waters, the minerals released into the air.

As they got closer to the water, the kids began to strip off the long pants and flannel shirts they wore, running into the water in undershirts and shorts. Nessa was jogging toward the back of the pack and heard the splashing sounds of bodies hitting water before she saw glimpses of water between the trees.

Once she reached the water herself, she didn't think, just jumped into the swimming hole and felt the immediate relief of the cool temperature, the buoyancy. She looked over her shoulder and saw that Delphine was swimming too. Everyone was splashing and shouting. A cascade of water washed over Nessa, and she turned to see Kai, just before he launched himself on top of her. She went under, then rose to the surface, throwing Kai a good five feet away from her—he was lighter than he looked. Resurfacing, his tough kid expression was gone, a smile of delight splitting his face.

After a bit, the splashing calmed down and Nessa saw that a handful of kids—Delphine included—were now sunning themselves on rocks. Others floated, built dams. Bo was still playing with the younger kids. Nessa remembered how the most powerful wolves in her pack in Tether made a point of playing with the pups.

The falls they could hear were somewhere out of sight of

the pool, and Nessa moved to the downstream edge to look for them. Stepping awkwardly on the rocks, she had to wave her arms for balance, but she didn't mind. She felt cooler and more relaxed than she had in days, as if all the tension and difficult decisions she'd been asked to make had floated off into the water.

Or at least, she felt that way until one of the three kids she was standing near reached the lip of the pool, stood at the edge, raised her hands over her head, and dove off the side.

Nessa got closer and saw. The falls were a sheer drop to a pool below—maybe twenty feet down. Nessa couldn't see how deep the pool was, but given that she counted three heads floating, it was deep enough that none of those kids had broken their necks.

Someone touched her on the shoulder from behind and Nessa flinched, but it was just Bo, passing her, heading for the edge. "You up for it?" Bo asked, looking at Nessa over her shoulder.

Nessa still hadn't shaken the fear that had gripped her when the first kid had slipped over the edge. "I don't know," she said.

"*I* am." Nessa heard and turned—surprised by the voice. She hadn't been aware that Delphine was so close behind her. With her hair dark from being wet and clinging to the sides of her face, Delphine looked not like herself. Skinnier. More athletic. More like CM.

Nessa felt off balance and found herself saying, in a voice that sounded so much like her mom it chilled her, "No, you're not."

Delphine drew her chin back, but before she could fully respond, Nessa did something she'd seen alpha wolves do. She puffed out her chest and cut off Delphine's response before she could figure out what she wanted it to be. "We're leaving," she said. "It's time to get back."

"But—" Delphine said.

Delphine looked . . . at Bo.

Really? Nessa thought. *You're looking to her for guidance? Not me, your sister you've known your whole life?*

"Nessa, let her," Bo said. "You can trust her. Delphine's a smart kid."

"Kids can break their necks!" Nessa said. She heard Vivian's cadence in her words. This bugged her. Bo bugged her. Delphine was bugging her. "Delphine!" Nessa barked out. "Come with me now."

Delphine put her hands on her hips. Nessa saw Bo looking from Delphine to Nessa, then back to Delphine. "Why should I?" said Delphine.

Nessa didn't exactly know why, but something came out of her mouth regardless. "Because you're my sister. I'm your family, not these people. And we're going to be late to Dad's dinner."

"I'm not going to Dad's dinner," Delphine said, her eyes flashing, defiant. "I'm not going back there ever. Not until you believe what I saw."

"Delphine," Nessa said. "There was *video*."

"I don't care," Delphine retorted. "You tell me things and I trust and believe you. I tell you things and you tell me I'm making it up? You want me to be a good sister to CM. What kind of a sister are you being to me? Why should I believe anything you ever say?"

Nessa could feel Bo watching her. She could feel what Bo was thinking. Or maybe she could just feel what she herself was thinking. She was thinking that she sounded rigid. She was remembering what Bree said about trusting Delphine. And suddenly, Nessa understood. How could Nessa accuse Delphine of not knowing who her family was if Nessa didn't? "Okay," Nessa said.

"Okay, what?"

"Okay, you're right."

Delphine cocked her head. "What was *that*?" she asked.

Nessa spoke slightly more softly this time, repeating herself. She thought about stealing a look at Bo. What would Bo think of her for being weak, for letting her younger sister win a fight? Nessa decided she didn't care. "Look, Delphine," she said. "I want to show you something."

"What?"

"Not here."

"I'm not going with you."

Nessa looked at her sister, begged her to come along with her eyes. Finally, Delphine relented.

And so, with Delphine following her into a thicket of trees, Nessa led the way back, glancing back at the Outsider Kids only once, just as Bo took the plunge over the edge of the waterfall.

Nessa wasn't thinking about Bo right now. She turned her eyes forward and walked with Delphine until they were out of sight of the others.

Now, she thought. Nessa let an awareness of the moon's being nearly full come over her. She could feel it, pulling at the earth, moving the waters, moving her. The woods were still, the air hanging heavily like they were inside a cloud. "Look," she said to Delphine. "Just watch." She took a few steps away from Delphine, started to run, lost her awareness of Delphine for a moment, and then regained it, returning at a trot, coming to stand before her sister, and then sit. Somewhere during the course of this process, she had transformed.

Maybe this was a bad idea, she thought, as she saw how pale Delphine became. Her sister took a step backward, tripped over a stick buried in the leaves, fell, scooted backward, her eyes round with fear.

Nessa did the only thing she knew how to do to let Delphine know she had nothing to fear. She pushed her two paws forward, bowing. Then she dropped her rear haunches to the ground. She was as low as she could get. Did Delphine know that this meant Nessa would do her no harm?

Delphine took a step forward. She laid a hand on Nessa's head. Nessa's wild side resisted this human touch at first, but then something very human inside her relaxed into it. This was how the dogs felt, she realized.

Delphine moved her hand to scratch behind Nessa's ear. Nessa raised her snout in appreciation. Then, keeping a hand on Nessa's neck, Delphine came around the side of Nessa's body and threw a leg over. She was climbing onto Nessa's back.

This had not been Nessa's idea, but it felt right. Slowly, carefully, not wanting to jostle Delphine, she rose. They had done this many times over the years—piggyback rides, chicken fights in one of their neighbor's pools. Delphine had always been small. Nessa had always been strong. Those experiences didn't translate exactly, but still this wasn't totally new. Delphine had good balance, and Nessa remembered a fact she'd learned long ago—that wolves' backs are flatter than dogs', and do not rock back and forth with the movement of their walking.

Nessa walked, then trotted, then ran. She could feel Delphine's fists gripping the fur on her shoulders, could feel the pressure of Delphine squeezing her sides with her legs. Then she heard Delphine's shouts of triumph. "Woooo-hooo!" she was shouting, sounding free.

Nessa ran hard and fast. She was surprised when she realized they were nearly back to the house. Surprised that the sun was low down in the sky. She'd lost track of the time.

Nessa came to a stop. Delphine climbed off. Nessa transformed back into human form. She still didn't know why this had been the way she chose to end the fight brewing between them. All that mattered was it had.

"Look," she said as they walked the last hundred feet out

of the woods together. "If you say CM was in your room last night, I believe you. If she's scaring you, that's not right. I'll talk to Dad. We'll figure out some other way."

Delphine cocked her head, waiting for the catch.

There was no catch. Delphine had been right back at the waterfall. There should never be a catch. "You're my sister," Nessa said, and as the words came out of her mouth, she knew them to be enough. "You're not like those other kids. You have a family. You have a home. You're wanted. I know you're telling me the truth, and I will make it right."

CHAPTER TWENTY SEVEN

essa and Delphine rushed into their rooms to change, laughing from sheer giddiness after their ride together and the relief of becoming allies once again. They couldn't really talk about what had passed between them, but it was deep. Something had changed.

They met up again in the hall and made their way upstairs, splitting up at the top of the stairs as Delphine said she wanted to check something on the computer before dinner.

It was just as well—CM was standing at the front of the party, as if she was waiting for them. Nessa didn't feel like talking to her, but CM blocked her way. "You saw the video footage this morning, didn't you?" she said, scowling. "I know you were going to look. I know Delphine doesn't believe anything I say."

Nessa stood still, trying to figure out how to respond to this. "CM," she said at last. "Did you go into her room?"

CM scowled. "How can you ask that? You saw the video!" Her voice rose in a shriek that made it even more overwhelming than usual.

"Look CM, maybe we can talk about this later. I've got to go—" But CM was still not letting Nessa pass. She said, "I keep seeing you in my dreams. You've been chasing me so many years."

"Huh?" Nessa said.

"You're the white wolf," she said. "I know you."

Nessa turned her back.

"I know your . . . secret!" CM said. "I dream about you. I see the white wolf and I know that means you."

"You don't know anything," Nessa spat out. With a few quick steps, she darted past the girl and threaded her way into the crowd, hoping no one was listening to CM's ravings.

The caterers had moved some of the furniture in the living room and set up round tables so both teams could eat together in air conditioned comfort. The researchers were moving toward the tables now, and Nessa scanned the place cards until she found hers. With a sense of relief, she noted that she would be sitting with Gabriel. She scanned the cards for Delphine's, who was with Taneda, and then CM, who was seated with Dr. Ishikawa for the second night in a row. She barely had time to pick up a seltzer from the bartender who was set up on the deck under an awning before it was time to sit down.

Gabriel was late, so Nessa was free, during the first course, to watch Dr. Ishikawa talking to CM. CM looked both like she was trying to answer him—to understand what he wanted from her—and like she was angry. But slowly, her mood shifted. Nessa wondered what Ishikawa was saying to her, what tone he was using to calm her. Nessa thought about how hard it must be for CM to sustain this communication, to know more than she could say, to understand nothing so much as the morbid interest these scientists took in her.

"So," Gabriel said, pulling out his chair and sliding in next to Nessa as the salad plates were being cleared. "I heard Delphine's not doing so well with the whole CM introduction thing."

"Yep," Nessa said as a server slid a plate of quail with duck sausage and beet greens in front of Nessa and then slid an identical one in front of Gabriel. She glanced nervously in CM's direction as she lifted her utensils, skewered the quail with a fork, and then started to saw off a bite-sized piece with her knife.

"I think CM has to go back," Nessa said. "At least until she gets over whatever her issue is with Delphine."

Gabriel shook his head slightly. "Do you think she might actually be a danger to Delphine?"

Nessa stared. Gabriel looked at Daniel, as if checking to make sure he wasn't watching, then continued, lowering his voice, speaking intently. "Loneliness is toxic," he said. "We know that, right? Part of the challenge of being a chimera is going to be the loneliness. When you're one of a kind, you're never going to have a group—a species. Look at those wolves Paravida was experimenting with—coming from Tether, I'm sure you know all about them."

"*You* know about Paravida's wolves?"

"Not directly," he said. He swallowed a sip of water, which gave Nessa just enough time to remember that as far as her father's company was from Paravida geographically, there were connections. Dr. Raab, the doctor who had run experiments on children back in Tether, had been a colleague of Daniel's. Dr. Raab was probably the architect of the genetic modifications Paravida made to the wolves. Horrible as it was to think about, Paravida and Chimera Corp. were in the same line of work.

"Most of what I know about the Paravida wolves is that the company wasn't too happy with the outcome," Gabriel said. "Of course, they don't have anything like the tools Daniel has at his disposal. The point is, I think this whole approach to trying to identify CM as a human in a family is misguided."

"You don't think CM can learn to live as a human?"

"I don't," he said. He smiled ruefully. "Though I will say she's doing better with humans than with other animals."

"What do you mean?" Nessa asked.

"You don't know?" Gabriel raised his eyebrows. "About the

time Daniel got her a dog?"

"He did?"

Gabriel glanced behind him again, checking Daniel, then continued. "Daniel picked an older dog, a gentle female lab who was trained as a therapy dog. This was when CM was ten years old or so. He thought the dog would help her develop empathy."

"When she was ten? But you weren't here then."

"No, I wasn't," Gabriel conceded. "I read about this in the file."

"There's a file?"

"Oh yeah, and it's a doozy," Gabriel said. "It's in the archive."

"The archive," Nessa said, rolling her eyes. "You sound like Delphine. Do you know she was able to hack into the security feed and figure out where the secret cameras in our rooms are?" The minute the words left her mouth, Nessa realized she might have thought better of them. She'd meant it as, "Isn't it cute how Delphine thinks she's a hacker?" but Gabriel had blanched.

"Shh," he said. "If we were talking about anyone but Delphine, they'd be taken off the premises immediately."

"Right, sorry," Nessa said. She couldn't help but glance back to make sure Daniel wasn't listening. "Okay, anyway—go on."

"Yeah," Gabriel said. "I got to see CM's file one time. It was a little bit on the terrifying side. A lot of the techs have stopped working here rather than be assigned to her."

Nessa nodded. "What happened with the dog?"

Gabriel raised his eyebrows, like this was going to be juicy, and Nessa kept perfectly still to keep him from remembering that he probably shouldn't be telling her any of this.

"Daniel introduced the dog gradually, right?" Gabriel was holding his fork in the air, and Nessa thought the gesture seemed a little menacing, but in a goofy, Gabriel way. For someone very intelligent, he never seemed exactly aware of what he was doing with his body, a quality he shared with many of the researchers.

"Anyway," Gabriel went on, "it took time for CM and the dog to get used to each other. I guess because of all the mixed-up animal smells, the dog wasn't sure CM was human. She growled at her. She seemed afraid of her. But eventually they bonded. According to the reports, CM would pet the dog and wanted the dog to lie down next to her. The dog would—she was a therapy dog, remember, and this was part of her training. CM wanted the dog to spend the nights with her, and finally your dad decided they were ready."

Gabriel paused. He finally put the fork down, then took a swallow of water, and Nessa watched the color cloud above them change—a deep, dark red seeping into the grays and blues and yellows mixing above the table.

Gabriel put his glass down carefully on the table. "The dog didn't make it through the night."

"Didn't make it?" Nessa repeated. "What happened?"

Gabriel lifted his eyes to meet Nessa's. "CM happened," he said. The color above him intensified, and then a white stripe showed through it. What did that mean?

"When the techs came in the morning to bring CM breakfast, they found what was left of the dog lying at the threshold to her room."

Nessa felt herself nearly gag. "She killed the dog?"

Gabriel looked her straight in the eye. "She didn't just kill her," he said. "She killed her . . . slowly. And then clearly spent much of the night eating her."

Nessa clapped a hand over her mouth. For a moment, she felt she was going to be sick.

"They were only able to reconstruct the events of that night through forensic evidence. In fact, it led to Daniel finally deciding to have the cameras installed."

Nessa imagined the blood. The dog fur, the trusting eyes. When you are a wolf, a dog—even an old one—appears to be a baby. They never unlearn the cluelessness that marks wolf pups as not ready for prime time. They remain perky-eared, full-faced, and ridiculously trusting even in maturity. Natural victims.

"Why did she do it?" Nessa said. "It sounds like she loved the dog."

"Who knows?" Gabriel said. "Maybe she was trying to make a point to Daniel. Her file says she said she was jealous of the way Daniel had seemed to love the dog." He lifted his shoulders in a gentle shrug. "Maybe she's just a killer."

Nessa glanced across the table. "Wow," she said, finding it hard to wrap her mind around this new picture of CM. "To me, she's just always seemed sad. Like—I don't know—like she knows that she's trapped between worlds. That it's just unnatural to be two things at one time. That—" Nessa stopped herself, realizing she was maybe speaking about herself. Luc had always complained about feeling this way—feeling like he wanted to commit to the one thing, to truly inhabit his wolf form, but to Nessa there was something beautiful about being able to go back and forth. She felt complete in each form. Maybe to be like CM—stuck between—would be the nightmare.

Gabriel smiled, and when it was clear Nessa was done speculating, he offered a possible solution. "Maybe she just doesn't like dogs," he said.

Nessa frowned, then laughed. "Like, you think she'd do better with cats?"

"Maybe," Gabriel said, mischievously. "And I will say that ever since that time, CM's had this thing about dogs." He paused. "Have you ever noticed that no one here has them?" Nessa hadn't realized it, but suddenly it occurred to her that yes, it was strange. Neither Daniel nor any of the other scientists or staff members kept dogs.

"The few times she's broken free, it seems that she's gone hunting."

"Hunting?" Nessa wasn't following. And then she got it. "She hunts . . . *dogs?*"

"There are wild dogs in the preserve. They live in packs. Like that one those hiker kids you met brought in."

"Oh," Nessa said, and then under her breath. "Rio." She remembered Gabriel measuring the bite, sharing a significant look with Daniel.

She felt her voice cracking, unable to keep it under control.

"But she was in her . . . cage. That lab. When Rio was killed."

Gabriel shook his head, mournfully. "No," he said. "That night, she'd gotten out. Remember the security lockdown?"

"I thought that was because there was a prowling animal on the preserve?" Nessa said. "I thought it was a big chimera cat."

Gabriel said nothing, leaving Nessa to reach a conclusion out loud. "Oh," she said, realization dawning. "So that was her. CM was the prowling animal."

Gabriel lowered his voice even further. "She'd gotten away from one of the guards," he said. "Slipped one of her own tranquilizers into his coffee and then used his keys to open the doors. This happens with her from time to time. By the time you came in, Jonathan's team had already located her and were bringing her back." Gabriel paused, giving Nessa a second to take this information in.

Nessa was reconstructing the events of that night in her head. "My dad said it was a cat."

"No, you did," said Gabriel. "But it was CM. The bite marks confirmed it. I measured them."

Nessa shuddered. She had a sudden vision of CM standing over Delphine's bed. She remembered the crunching of pork chop bones in CM's strong jaws. No, she thought. This would not stand. Gabriel was right. CM had to go.

Tonight.

CHAPTER TWENTY EIGHT

ust as the dinner was finishing and everyone was moving from the tables to the couches for tea and cookies, Delphine came rushing in, her cheeks flushed and her eyes bright.

"Where were you?" Nessa asked.

"I was digging around in the system where they store the security footage," she began. "I looked at the data packets a little more closely . . ." Delphine launched into a technical explanation of what she had been doing, the upshot of which was that the video file they'd watched that morning was a fake. "Someone tampered with the file."

"But who?" Nessa said. "You don't think CM did it? She can barely hold a knife and fork."

"I don't know," Delphine said, "but that security file we watched this morning was a fake."

Nessa and Delphine didn't say anything about the file to Daniel until the guests had been loaded into the van, back to the guesthouse. Then the sisters followed Daniel into his study.

On a tablet, Delphine explained the path she'd followed to find the video that had been deleted.

Daniel crossed his arms over his chest. Nessa worried he was going to say that the fact that the video had been *deleted* meant the situation was inconclusive, but he didn't. He just set his jaw. "Okay, she's got to go."

"Tonight," Nessa said.

Daniel gave her a look so filled with pain, she understood without his explaining how conflicted he must be. It didn't make it better, but she got it.

Finally, Daniel nodded. He closed his eyes. "All right," he said, opening them. "I'll take her back to the lab."

Just then, there was a noise in the hallway. They turned in time to see CM watching them. This was the first time Nessa had looked CM in the eye since learning what she's done, and it was shocking how her eyes remained Delphine's eyes. They were eyes Nessa trusted. Eyes Nessa loved.

"You want to get rid of me," CM said, her voice so calm that Nessa felt she couldn't possibly understand what she had heard. Or maybe she didn't care? Maybe she felt sympathetic to their dilemma?

"We'll talk about it more later," Daniel said. "Tonight I want you to sleep at the lab because I want to be ready for tomorrow. You've been doing such a good job, but tomorrow's the day we do the blood work. It's the big show." Daniel was using the same voice with her that he'd used when he was putting her to sleep that time. Nessa wondered if it was something he'd developed in his years of working with CM, if it was a way around her mind-reading skills. "Uncle Ishikawa very much wants to see your miracle blood. You'll show him, right?"

"Uncle Ishikawa is my friend," CM said, sounding like she was reciting something she'd memorized. "I will be the star of the show."

"That's right," Daniel said. "And I will be there the whole time."

CM looked at Nessa. She looked at Delphine. She narrowed her eyes. Nessa knew CM would be able to read their minds. She would know that they knew that the video was faked, that Nessa knew that it was CM who had attacked Rio.

The cloud above them deepened from clear streaks of pinky-blue to a purple the shade of a bruise. *An intense shade,* Nessa thought, *too much.* And then she noticed that her thoughts had caused the color to lighten somehow, to push the cloud back in CM's direction.

Her thoughts had moved the cloud.

CM put a hand up to her head.

"Ow, Nessa, stop that," she said, irritated. Could CM feel Nessa pushing the cloud toward her?

"Stop what?" Nessa said, pushing the cloud even closer now. Yes, pushing—she could feel herself doing it now.

Is this what Halliday had been talking about?

CM looked at Daniel in anger. "She's making it so I can't think!"

Nessa held up her hands in a show of innocence and let the cloud go as Daniel took CM by the elbow and led her back toward the living room. "Let's talk," Nessa heard him telling CM in the hall.

That night, as Nessa brushed her teeth, she heard the water turning on and off in Delphine's bathroom. Stepping out into the hallway in her pajamas, Nessa passed the open door to CM's room—it already looked as if no one had ever slept in it—and knocked on Delphine's.

Delphine greeted her in her shorts pajamas, her long curly hair heavy from the humidity that was seeping into even the air conditioned spaces. "Feel safer?" Nessa asked. Delphine nodded, padding over to the floor-to-ceiling window, which showed only her reflection against the dark glass.

"I feel sad for her too," she said. "I wish—" Her voice trailed away, but Nessa understood what she meant. And then

Delphine headed to her bedside table, opened the drawer, and showed Nessa a small rectangle of black plastic. "She left me this," she said. "I don't know why."

"What is it?" Nessa asked, and stepping closer, saw it was a thumb drive.

"More important," Delphine said, "is what's on it?" She turned to the desk set up next to her bed and opened the screen on her laptop—the powerful Mac Daniel had sent Delphine when she was still living with Aunt Jane in Milwaukee last spring. It had quickly become Delphine's prized possession.

The drive contained a single folder, labeled "Typhon." *Sounds familiar,* thought Nessa. Then she remembered the name she found when she was doing her own research on Chimera Corp.'s old files.

"Typhon?" Delphine said. "Isn't that part of the Percy Jackson universe?" Nate had been obsessed with those books for a time.

"Yeah," Nessa agreed. Delphine tapped a few keys, calling up a search on "Typhon" and read to Nessa: "'Typhon was a Titan. One of the monsters the Greek gods were descended from.'" She scanned, reading under her breath. "'Son of Gaea and Tartarus'—okay, a match of earth and hell. 'Father of Cerberus, Hydra'—okay, that's some scary stuff—and—oh, my gosh, Nessa!"

"What?" Nessa said, leaning in over the screen but not seeing what had shocked Delphine.

"Look," Delphine said, pointing. "Father of Chimera."

Nessa sat down on the bed, next to Delphine. "Okay," she said. "What's in this file."

"Hold on a sec," Delphine said. She ejected the thumb drive, shut down her computer.

"What are you doing?" Nessa asked, as Delphine pulled a screw driver from a unicorn-emblazoned pencil case in her drawer. She flipped the laptop over, removed the cover, and popped out a small plastic device about the size of a nickel.

"Is that a battery?" Nessa asked.

"No, duh," said Delphine. "It's the network card. I'm going offline. I don't want anyone at Chimera to know what we're looking at."

"Is that really necessary?" Nessa scoffed, but then when she began to page through file after file on the thumb drive CM had left them—reports, pictures, blood work, genetic analyses, all under the heading "Project Typhon" and in parentheses "Subject: CM"—Nessa knew the precaution was fully warranted.

They opened and closed files while the minutes ticked by, getting an understanding of just how exhaustive Daniel's study of CM had been. There were pictures of a baby version of CM wearing electric nodes, a toddler strapped to a table with an IV connected to her arm. When she should have been going off to kindergarten, it looked like she'd spent about a year in a heavy helmet with lasers monitoring her eye movements.

There were "Damage Reports"—clinically observed notations of tantrums lasting more than two hours, after which CM would develop a fever or begin spontaneously vomiting.

Her history of violence and aggression wasn't limited to dogs. One of the techs had developed a lifelong injury after CM slipped a teaspoon under her pillow, spent weeks sharpening it at night, and then used it to slice his wrist in the precise spot where he had so often bound hers.

"Good lord," said Delphine at last. "I can't look at this anymore."

"I know, me neither," Nessa agreed.

"We have to talk to Dad," Delphine said.

Nessa nodded. Maybe this was what her mom had wanted when she said to look out for CM. Maybe she wanted this to stop.

"But what's that other part?" Nessa asked as Delphine closed down the Project Typhon folder. Next to it was a single file. "I think it's a text file," Delphine said, hovering over it with the mouse.

"Maybe it's a note. Maybe CM explained why she left this for us."

But it wasn't a note. When Delphine opened the file, all that they saw were letters. Random letters, grouped in even pairings.

"Is that code?" Nessa asked Delphine.

"Like computer code?" Delphine asked. "That's not even close to what computer code looks like."

"How should I know?" Nessa asked.

"But wait," Delphine said. "There's definitely some kind of pattern. Look at the letters. There're only four. They keep repeating. See? G . . . C . . ." She traced the screen with the tip of a finger. "A and then T. There's nothing more."

"Huh," said Nessa. And then suddenly the letters came to life in her mind. "OMG, how did we miss this?" she said. "That's not computer code. It's genetic code!"

"Written down like that?" Delphine said. "What does it mean?"

Quickly, Nessa explained the presentation Delphine had skipped. The one where Haruki Tamamoto showed how he'd encrypted a thirty-second MP3 clip of "Forever Young" in mouse DNA. "So it's data?" Delphine said. "But what data?"

"We'd need a translator."

"Should we ask Haruki?"

"We should ask Dad," Nessa said. "Gabriel said he's been interested in this kind of genetic data storage. And generally, when Dad gets 'interested'—" Nessa used air quotes.

"Yep," said Delphine. "He's probably designed his own."

"One that's better."

"Exactly," Delphine added.

"So we can add that to the list of things we need to talk to Dad about," Nessa said. She let out a giant yawn. "Tomorrow. For now, we need to get some sleep."

CHAPTER TWENTY NINE

The next morning, Nessa woke early. The smart thing to do, she knew, was to go for a run and transform, get that out of the way. But she was so tired from staying up the night before with Delphine, she ended up rolling over, pulling the covers over her head, and drifting back to sleep.

When she finally did get up, she stepped out onto the deck outside her room and let the warm air soak into her body. The air conditioning had been turned up too high in the night and she was chilled, so for once the warmth felt good.

She remembered how still and sweet the night air had been when she'd seen the cat. Or rather, when the cat had seen her, staring from a hiding place in the trees.

That cat who turned out not to have been the one to attack Rio.

The cat who was not the reason for the warnings to the Chimera employees. Not the cause of the security lockdown on the night Rio had died.

Was it possible Nessa had simply imagined the whole thing?

I'll ask Bo, she thought. *Tomorrow. As soon as the visiting scientists are gone, and I will . . . ask.*

Nessa slipped into a reverie, remembering the feel of Bo, but then she forced herself out of it. Maybe she could ask Bo about CM as well. For all the hints Bo had dropped, Nessa had the feeling she knew more than she was letting on.

Nessa showered, then stopped by Delphine's room, and the two of them headed up to breakfast together, planning to confront Daniel with what they'd learned about CM. But Daniel wasn't there. Milton told Nessa and Delphine that he'd stayed at CM's lab overnight. Milton drove the girls to see the presentation there, following the road Nessa and Daniel had traveled together in his pickup truck back when they had first decided that CM should come to stay.

While they were driving, Daniel called. He and Milton

started arguing about the weather. Apparently the storm coming in behind the heat wave was arriving earlier than anyone had anticipated.

"It says winds gusting up to ninety miles per hour!" Milton protested. "That's hurricane levels. How did this come up out of nowhere?"

"It didn't just come out of nowhere," Daniel said back through the speaker. "It's been stalled over the South Pacific for days, gathering force. The only thing that's surprising is that it's heading our way."

"Well, yes," Milton allowed. "I know all about that. What I just don't understand is how the forecast has been so accelerated. We were expecting it after Haken's flight departs for Tokyo tomorrow—we were worried they'd get stuck, possibly overnight, in Seattle, but now it seems that it may delay them getting to Seattle at all."

"So, great!" Daniel said. "We're all so fired up, we can hole up for an extra day and map out the work. It'll save us a trip in the fall."

"Daniel, what will they eat?" Milton asked. "And what happens if the power fails? What if one of them becomes ill and there's no way to medevac or even drive them to a hospital? Please consider ushering them out to Seattle tonight. That will give them at least twelve hours before the storm."

"But the final event is important," Daniel said. "There are relationships forming here. Some of the young researchers . . . the connections they're making remind me of Ishikawa and me when we were young."

"Ishikawa was never young when you knew him, Daniel," Milton muttered. "And he's positively ancient now. I know it doesn't seem likely, but imagine a stroke, a heart attack and you're all cut off out here. . . ."

Daniel was silent. The girls were too. Milton pressed her advantage: "We won't cancel the party, okay? It will be fun and elegant, and then we'll send them off at 10 p.m. I'll get sparklers. We can light fireworks! And then they'll be on the plane, in the air, and we can rest easy knowing the conference was a remarkable success and we got them out before the storm. And this really was a success Daniel."

Daniel seemed satisfied by this, except for Milton's last words. "Don't say 'was,'" he corrected. "It's not over yet."

"We really might lose power?" Delphine asked, after Daniel was off the line.

"We always lose power," Milton said. "Not at the lab, of course. That's protected by generators four-deep. The house, the guesthouse, different parts of the preserve often go out in storms. We're so isolated here."

Nessa tried to imagine the size of a generator required to keep the 10,000 square feet of laboratory heating and cooling, the refrigerator and venting systems fully functional. As the truck's air conditioner struggled—and for the most part, failed—to suck moisture out of the air coming in through the vents, Milton rehearsed the events still to come. This morning would be Daniel's last demonstration with CM. Ishikawa would present his work in the afternoon.

"Then the party!" Milton said, slapping the truck's steering wheel with her palms. "The tent, the band, and *then* the joy of returning to normalcy." Milton sounded like she was looking forward to the last item on the list most of all.

Nessa didn't know whether it was Milton's predictability or the fact that she was squeezed in pretty tight in the front of the cab between Delphine and the window, but she was starting to get a little claustrophobic.

"You know, the storm that's coming," Milton went on. "Since it originated in the Pacific—by all rights, it should be called a typhoon."

Milton looked at the girls as if she was expecting them to be excited by this slice of trivia, and they dutifully nodded and said, "Wow." But when Milton went back to speaking, they exchanged a look. Project Typhon. Typhoon. Typhon had been the god of high winds. Maybe the storm . . . could it possibly be CM's revenge? She could read minds. Could she control the weather as well?

"I hope the Outsider Kids have enough tarps," Nessa whispered to Delphine as they climbed out of the truck.

The CM demonstration started off just like the other. The scientists from Haken were seated on the benches outside a room Nessa had not seen into before. A pop-up tent had been placed over the benches to protect them from the sun, but looking up at the sky as she sat down, Nessa imagined the tent was more likely going to be needed to protect them all from rain.

"Mind if I join you?" she heard.

Dr. Taneda slid onto the bench next to her. She smiled at Nessa, and then got distracted rifling in her backpack for a tablet and a stylus. Laying those on the bench, she again went into the bag, this time producing a roll of butterscotch candies, which she offered to Delphine and Nessa. Next she extracted a red handkerchief, blew her nose, and then shoved it back into the bottom of the bag, pinching the front of her shirt and pulling it out from her chest a few times, pumping in some air. "Whew, it's hot out here!" she said.

"Yeah," said Nessa. She didn't say what she was thinking, that Dr. Taneda's fidgeting was making her feel hotter. Or maybe more than just hot—Nessa's own body was agitated with the need to transform. Nessa found herself giving Taneda a hard look, remembering what Halliday had said about her. *Was* Taneda a wolf too?

Taneda started crunching her candy, and then grabbed at her jaw. "I'm nervous," she said. "This—" She gestured to the tall glass window in front of them. "This feels wrong."

Taneda popped a second candy into her mouth. She pushed her hair back behind her ears. Delphine gave Nessa a meaningful look.

A movie theater screen-sized curtain lifted to reveal not another room in a life-sized dollhouse, but a lab. In the center, in a chair that looked like something you'd see at the dentist's office, was CM.

She had the same dazed expression on her face Nessa had noticed during CM and Daniel's first demonstration. "Do you think Dad sedated her?" Nessa whispered to Delphine.

"Good lord," Delphine said, and Nessa could tell that seeing CM strapped into her seat as she was now—after those pictures—felt just plain wrong to Delphine the way it did to Nessa.

As the last researchers found their seats, a monitor off to the side of the glass lit up, giving everyone a close-up view of the presentation as Daniel began to speak.

"Ready to get started?" he intoned.

Milton responded with a thumbs-up, and Nessa realized Daniel could not hear anything coming from outside the building—the windows must be soundproof.

As the demonstration went forward, most of the audience were riveted to the split screen image projecting the view from the electron microscope Daniel was using to display slides of CM's blood. He removed a vial, injected it with a flu strain that, although contained and rare, was new, and had already killed thirteen people in China. He then described how CM's system had reversed the virus, an immune response that even Nessa could see was remarkable.

"Now I'll show this to you in action," he said, and Nessa heard gasps as he prepared to inject CM with the virus itself. Daniel proceeded without ceremony to puncture CM's skin, moving the needle deftly to locate the vein.

Nessa carefully watched CM's face while all of this was happening. She saw intensifying colors rise—pinks and deep purples. Nessa realized CM felt ashamed. She felt this was her fault.

There were yellows and browns coming off of Daniel, mustards, taupe, cinnamon. She saw CM flinch when she was poked with the needle, her purple shot through with a deep, dark gray that reminded Nessa of Halliday's warning about the color black and irreversible death. Nessa looked closely, grateful to see this was just a dark gray.

Speaking of death, she saw CM looking at Daniel in a way that could be interpreted as a death threat. CM said something to him that they could not hear. Was she asking him to stop?

How many experiments like this had Daniel done on CM over the years? The images from the Typhon file were still painfully fresh in Nessa's mind.

After he'd injected CM, Daniel stood back, looked at his watch, waited. Outside the circle, the scientists waited as well.

Daniel leaned down, put a hand on CM's shoulder. Through the speaker, Nessa could hear he was saying, "Good job. Not much longer now. You're helping a lot of people by doing this."

Nessa wondered whether CM believed him.

And then Daniel looked at his watch a second time. "Shall we see what's happening here now?" he said and injected a new substance into CM's veins. Turning his back, he began to prepare a new syringe for drawing blood out—Nessa supposed the injection had been some sort of dye or other tool to show what was happening when they put CM's blood under the microscope.

But while Daniel's back was turned, CM began to shake. At first, Nessa thought the shaking was purposeful, that CM was trying to scare the audience, but as it continued, Nessa was reminded of the convulsing she'd witnessed in the dog Rio. "Someone help her!" Nessa shouted, but of course Daniel couldn't hear her through the tempered glass and by that point, he was already aware of the problem. He saw her, his face breaking out in alarm. He held her by the shoulders. Nessa could hear his voice through the speaker, telling CM it would be all right, saying, "Calm down, now, calm down."

"Is this part of the demonstration?" one of the Japanese scientists asked Milton. Milton, her face white, her lips drawn together, did not answer, just stared at the glass.

Taneda shouted, "What was in that syringe? She's been poisoned!"

Delphine leaned forward to share a look of distress with Nessa. As Daniel leaned over CM, her banging and wails were picked up by Daniel's microphone, echoing through the forest around them.

Daniel turned his back on CM, preparing another hypodermic, but as he did, Nessa saw CM had gotten one of her restraints loose. Then another. "Dad!" she shouted, but by then, CM had burst all four straps. She was standing. On the monitor Nessa could see that sweat was pouring down her temples and wetting the fur on the bottom half of her face.

Daniel turned to her, needle in hand. But she was ready for him. She slid her hands under his armpits then lifted Daniel straight up and threw him down into the chair where she'd been restrained for the demonstration. CM smashed the stainless steel cart Daniel had been working from, scattering equipment and vials of blood. She walked through the lab, smashing other things, making her way to the door.

She won't get out, Nessa thought. The whole point of the new lab was for it to work as a containment facility.

But no. CM pulled the door off its hinges. She took a giant step through the doorway and vanished from view. Seconds later, she reappeared, exiting the building. CM charged the onlookers, who screamed and fled in chaotic terror.

CM froze in place, staring as if she was the one who was scared, then she turned on her heel, running for the woods. The fencing, Nessa saw, was still not completed, not that barbed wire and chain-link would have the power to keep CM contained when she didn't want to be.

"Lockdown, lockdown," Daniel rasped into the mic that was still attached to his collar. "Milton, get everyone into the buses. Go. Now!"

As they ran, tripping over each other, jostling to board,

Nessa felt a hand on her arm and saw Delphine. "Nessa, no," she said. "We can't go. We have to get to the Kids. We have to warn them."

Nessa looked out into the woods. "Not you," she said. "I'll go." Delphine shook her head. "I promise," Nessa said. "As soon as you get into the van, I'll go after them."

Delphine screwed up her face, not liking what she was hearing.

"Come girls!" Milton was shouting. Jonathan and some of the security team had streamed out of the observation building and were supervising, their guns drawn, looking out toward the woods CM had run into. Gabriel had rushed into the lab and was emerging, a limping Daniel on his arm. Nessa ran to them. "Is he okay?" She looked at Gabriel. He nodded.

"I'm fine," said Daniel. "She didn't hurt me. She wouldn't hurt me. But are you all right? Where's Delphine?"

Nessa turned, expecting to see Delphine right behind her, but she was not there.

"Delphine!" Nessa called out, scanning the perimeter of the woods as the first fat drops of rain began to fall.

But Delphine was gone.

CHAPTER THIRTY

The wind was picking up and the rain spitting down, each drop a slap. Nessa saw dark spots dotting Daniel's terra-cotta-colored shirt. Then she saw clouds of terra-cotta lift into the air around Daniel's head. She didn't quite know what that color meant, but it wasn't a color of fear. "Why aren't you more afraid?" she asked him.

"Because I know more than you," Daniel said. "But I've been here with CM before. She does this. She'll go off on her own. She won't go after Delphine."

"You're underestimating her," Nessa said. "You don't really believe she will hurt people."

"Nessa," he said. "I know her better than you do. Ultimately, helping us in our work—she'll come to see that this is best for her. She'll want to feel she has a purpose." Nessa rolled her eyes, and Daniel pushed back. "This week was a disappointment. She is angry. But she will come around. We all need to stay rational if we want to minimize the damage done."

Nessa could see her *own* colors flashing now, colliding with Daniel's. It wasn't so much of a color as it was light, pulsing and interrupting his earth-toned spectrum.

"I know you want to go after Delphine," Daniel went on. "But don't. Let Jonathan's team take care of this. They have training for this, and equipment. And they know every inch of the forest."

"But—" Nessa said. Her white-hot light flashed brighter. She couldn't explain to her father that she'd be better able to track Delphine with her nose than Jonathan with his camera-enhanced eyes.

"We've got to get the Haken scientists back to the lab," Daniel explained. "Jonathan's team will bring CM in. They've done it before. They know where she goes. We've got to—"

Suddenly, Daniel's face went gray and he wobbled just a bit on his feet. Nessa put a hand on his elbow, squinted as she tried to get a read on what was wrong.

She noted a line of red running down Daniel's neck, originating somewhere behind his ear, staining the top of his shirt collar. "You're bleeding," she said. She'd been so busy resenting him, she hadn't remembered the trauma he'd gone through. CM had attacked him in the middle of a presentation he'd spent months preparing for. He'd been thrown into the chair.

The wind picked up, ruffling Daniel's shirt, lifting Nessa's hair. She heard branches cracking and sticks hitting the ground in the woods nearby.

Daniel ran his finger through the blood on his neck, contemplating the stain on his fingertip as if he were having a hard time identifying what it was. Nessa wondered if on top of everything else, he might have a concussion.

"Should I call Milton over?" Nessa asked.

Daniel shook his head. "Please, Nessa, just get in the van." He tightened his lips. "I don't want you to create a situation where *you* need a rescue also."

Gabriel had his arms out, literally herding the researchers. "Come on, all!" He was shouting to make himself heard over the wind. Milton examined Daniel's neck, darting worried looks at the crowd. Nessa didn't know who looked more shell-shocked, the Haken team who had just experienced a great scientific reveal gone wrong—or the Chimera researchers, who had just seen their leader tossed to the side like a sack of flour.

The colors in the air, pale and indistinct to begin with, kept shifting, almost as if they were being blown by the wind of the storm.

Milton dug a packet of antiseptic gauze from a zippered

pouch in her bag and gave it to Daniel. "Let's load in. The sooner we get back to campus, the better."

Once the van door closed and the train of vehicles began to pull out of the parking lot, claustrophobia set in for Nessa. The van was like a compression chamber, a soundproof box. She could no longer hear the wind, just see it blowing the trees. The colors collected more readily here, but they were ugly, unthinking, staid: olive green, a sedentary mustard, a burnished taupe.

As the air conditioner struggled to filter the oven-like outside air, Nessa felt 100 percent certain she'd made the wrong call by agreeing not to pursue CM. She could—right now—be streaking through the forest. If Delphine was in trouble, Nessa could stand in front of her sister and growl at whatever was threatening. She could outrun the wind. Now, she was trapped inside a tin can, helpless.

It's only ten minutes, she told herself, imagining that she could head into the woods the moment the vans reached the lab.

But then the vans turned left where they should have turned right, away from the lab. Raindrops hit the window as Nessa glared through it. The vans turned again, and Nessa felt her insides twisting. *Is this a shortcut? Where are we going?*

The answer to that question became clear at the next turn: They were leaving the park entirely. They passed through the Chimera Corp. entrance and gatehouse, then came to a stop in a turnaround about a half mile from the entrance. When the engine went quiet, Nessa felt like her own heart had stopped beating.

She was overtaken by a color storm the likes of which she had not seen since Halliday had first encouraged her to seek them out and organize them in her mind. But now, in her panic, the colors raged in disordered fragmentation. The ceiling of the van—normally a soft gray—shimmered snow then slate then platinum then pearl, the writhing tones refracting light, stinging Nessa's eyes, threatening to swallow each other, drawing Nessa after them.

Nessa hauled herself out of her seat, half blind, struggling awkwardly down the van's center aisle, past Chimera employees who had their heads buried in their hands, Haken researchers staring fixedly forward. Nessa felt like she was about to rip a fistful of upholstery and foam padding off the top of the seat backs she was holding on to. Milton, Gabriel, and her father were conferring in whispers in the sudden quiet up front.

"You're saying this is a *typhoon?*" Daniel was asking Milton, peering through the window.

"Not yet," Milton said. "What we're getting now is a precursor. The typhoon's coming tomorrow. Hopefully it will blow past us. We'll know more in a few hours."

"Perfect," Daniel said, leaning back in his seat in defeat.

"Dad," Nessa said. "Delphine's out there still. What's going on?"

Daniel looked at her, as if he hadn't noticed she was there, his gaze steady but not unkind. "Jonathan told me the team's tracking her. They should have word soon. They insisted we follow the protocols. We have to let Jonathan do his job."

"The protocol is to just sit here?" Nessa hissed. She pinched some skin on the base of her wrist as the gray she was still seeing flashing before her eyes tinged yellow.

Daniel maintained the same, mournful yet restrained tone. "After what happened to the scientists at Paravida, we set a procedure to completely evacuate in a situation of unexpected violence."

Nessa shook her head, put a finger to her temple. The spitting rain had stopped again, she noted.

She forced herself to focus on what Daniel had said. She knew what he was talking about—back in Tether, a team of Paravida employees had been killed by a pack of enhanced, dangerously aggressive wolves. Later, however improbably, members of the same rogue pack had made their way to California and attacked and killed Dr. Raab.

"You think CM is like the Paravida wolves?"

"Shh!" Milton said.

"When are we going back?"

Daniel did not reply.

"Let me off this van," Nessa hissed.

Daniel shook his head. Nessa looked to Milton, but she was keeping her gaze fixed on her tablet—perhaps she was the source of the determined, battleship gray? Gabriel was looking out the window, as if the view of scrub trees and farm fields in the distance had become suddenly revealing. Nessa saw swirls of dust rising from the ground in the twisting winds. The land outside the park felt stripped and barren. Nessa imagined breaking a window with her elbow, leaping from the bus, landing in a crouch on the side of the road in wolf form, having transformed in the air.

"We'll go back when Jonathan's team gives us the directive to, and no one will go anywhere until then," Daniel said. From his tone Nessa could hear that this was final.

She returned to her seat and slammed herself into it, a gesture that barely made a ripple among the scientists who had started talking now, the isolation and hush of the van giving them permission, their voices whispers, their gestures contained, the mixture of English and Japanese making it difficult for Nessa to pull out words. "If Daniel's chimera is gone, this certainly throws a wrench into our plans . . ." she heard. "A monster." "Not the first time."

Nessa shuddered, thinking about CM strapped into that chair. Was this what the researchers wanted? "A monster" restrained and on display for study? What they were doing was no different from the experiments Dr. Raab and the rest of Paravida had performed on children in Tether. Her own father was now a part of that kind of work.

So this is what I've learned about him, Nessa thought. *Science matters more here than life. More than family.* Daniel had said he'd changed, but he hadn't.

Nessa was interrupted from her angry thoughts by Gabriel, who slipped into the empty seat next to her.

"Worried?" he said. He was sitting too close and his voice was too loud—overeager. She had to hold back from telling him to stop being such a brownnoser.

Gabriel kept pushing. "Well, I'd be worried if it was my sister," he said, smugly. "So I just checked the security team's digital updates. I guess there was some funky stuff going on with the cameras—the wind might have been interfering with the signals, but Jonathan's team got a read on CM. She's been picked up on the surveillance. She seems to be headed way north in the park."

Nessa squeezed her eyes closed. *Okay,* she thought. *I shouldn't have thought all those mean things about Gabriel.* She was actually grateful for that information. "Thanks," she said, forcing herself to smile. "Was there anything on the updates about Delphine? Is she anywhere near her?"

"She . . . was," Gabriel said. "For a tense minute, it seemed they might have even spotted each other."

"What happened?" Nessa said, trying to sound calmer than she felt.

"It was confusing," Gabriel continued. "There was some static, and they were standing out of range of the nearest cameras. Whatever it was, the next thing we saw was Delphine headed off back toward campus. That was when CM headed north."

This was such good news Nessa was tempted not to believe it. There had to be a catch. How could CM have come into contact with Delphine and then just walked away? "Are they going to go get her?"

"When she's like this, you can't. She's raging."

"This has happened before?"

Gabriel looked down, then met Nessa's eyes.

"These breakouts," he said. "The rage. It comes on a lot. I think actually it's one of the reasons Daniel bought this much land. CM needs to run."

"Run?" Nessa said skeptically. "Don't you mean, hunt?"

"That too," Gabriel said.

For a few minutes he sat with Nessa in silence. They could hear the wind whistling through the windows in the van, and then it seemed to go still.

"Can you check again?" Nessa said. "Do you mind?"

"Of course," he said and went back up front.

He came back smiling. "Good news," he said. "The distance between Delphine and CM is getting wider. We think. It's hard, actually, to know where Delphine is."

"They don't know where Delphine *is?*" Nessa repeated. "What about the cameras?"

"They were tracking her for a while, but they keep losing her. It's strange." Gabriel scratched his head. "There are 30,000 cameras installed out there, but she seems to be evading most of them. This should be impossible. It would take a ton of time and research to figure out where they all are, to map out routes around them ..." Gabriel sounded like he was starting to understand the possibilities for this even as he worked the problem out loud. "No one could have learned how to evade them ... not this quickly."

"Bo," Nessa breathed.

"What?" Gabriel asked.

"Never mind."

"What are you smiling about then?" Gabriel said.

"Nothing," Nessa said, feeling instantly bad for not telling him. She pulled her lips into a frown. "I'm just relieved, I guess."

Gabriel kept watching her, eventually returning to his seat.

A few minutes later, the bus engine rumbled to life, and Gabriel returned with a final update—CM was safely located in the northern part of the park. Men from Jonathan's team were posted in the forest, staking out a perimeter. As long as she kept to that general area, the lockdown was lifted, and the scientists could return to the lab.

The researchers were now chatting almost at full volume, and the colors in the van had stabilized, following the rain and the view of the woods through the windows—earthy leaf greens mixing in with the gray-blues.

CHAPTER THIRTY ONE

*O*nce the vans finally reached the lab, it felt like it took hours to disembark. The spitting drizzle had turned to a steady, driving rain. Milton was standing out in it, an umbrella balanced on one shoulder, checking each researcher off a list. Gabriel stood beside her, passing out umbrellas to the guests.

"Have you seen Dr. Taneda?" Milton asked Nessa, who was one of the last in the procession. "I checked her onto a van, but she's not here now."

"That's weird," Nessa said.

"You were sitting together during the presentation, weren't you?" Milton asked. "Did you get in a van together?"

"I . . . I didn't see her," Nessa said.

Milton's frown intensified. "Have you heard anything about Delphine?" Nessa asked. She had to speak loudly—the sound of the rain on the umbrella made it hard to hear.

Milton shook her head, the beige that had collected beneath it deepening to a darker brown as she shouted, "Ask Jonathan. I know he's tracking her. She's priority number one."

Then Nessa saw something behind Milton that caused her to touch Milton's sleeve. "Look." She pointed, and Milton followed the direction of her finger to see Taneda across the parking lot, huddled with one of her colleagues under an umbrella. "She's over there."

"How did that happen?" Milton said. She squinted at Taneda. "Why doesn't she have an umbrella? I was so careful to count one out for everyone."

"I'm sure you were," Nessa said, then she pushed away from Milton, muttering, "Excuse me," without meeting Milton's eye.

Before she could talk to Taneda—Nessa had a theory about where she had been and figured she might as well confirm it now—Nessa saw Delphine. She was heading up the blacktop road toward the lab, a long, somewhat bedraggled column of kids behind her. Wet kids. Outsider Kids. Nessa counted over a dozen of them—it had to be the entire group—she saw Topher and Kai in the front, Bo bringing up the rear protectively.

They were carrying packs—ragged packs—laden with rolled-up, half-shredded tarps, sleeping bags, blanket rolls, walking sticks. One kid was holding a box of cooking items in his arms—Nessa saw the handle of a frying pan and the base of an upside-down colander poking out of the top.

Their dogs were with them. Nessa had never been able to get a count before, but now that they were on leashes—improvised from twine and, in some cases, strips of a tarp they must have sacrificed for the purpose—she could see that there were nearly twenty of them. Skinny, dirty, afraid. They shook as if they expected to be able to rid themselves of the leads along with the water that had collected in their fur as they hurried through the downpour. None of these dogs was used to leashes. None of them was used to strangers. And none seemed particularly thrilled with being soaking wet.

They stopped at the edge of the parking lot, the greens and browns of the forest rising off them. Only Delphine continued on, her pink color trailing a line behind her like the train of an evening gown. She came to a stop in front of Daniel, and the pink settled around her in patches, like petals. Her clothes were soaked, dotted with burrs, plastered to her body, torn in some places, her hair slicked down alongside her face. Nessa noted a scratch across one cheek.

The researchers took in the scene, heads bobbing as they looked first at soaking-wet Delphine, whom they all knew, to the ragtag group of soaking-wet kids and dogs, whom they did not. Daniel held his umbrella out over Delphine as far as he could, but she did not step closer to join him underneath its protection.

Instead she planted her feet, put her hands on her hips, and looked Daniel square in the eye. As if she'd been gone for days, not hours.

"Dad," Delphine said. Nessa had been calling him that on and off since shortly after she had met him, but this was the first time Delphine had used that name when addressing him directly. "These are my friends," she said. "They live in the forest, but it's not safe for them there anymore. They need a place to stay, so I told them they could come here."

Daniel raised his eyebrows and did not say anything right away. If he was surprised or annoyed, he did not let on. "Very well then," he conceded after half a minute had passed. He turned to Milton. "You can find rooms for them?"

Milton lowered a gaze at Daniel the likes of which Nessa had never seen her lower before, her deep brown morphing into a color closer to orange. With Milton, it was always, "Yes," and "Of course," and "I'll make that happen right away." But this time, all she said was, "It's going to have to be your living room."

Daniel swallowed. Nessa thought of the controlled elegance of the living room, the low tables, natural tones, pale cream couches.

"Perhaps," he said. "We can offer them showers before they settle in? And a separate accommodation for their dogs."

"Showers are fine," Delphine said. "But I promised them they could keep the dogs with them at all times. Otherwise, they wouldn't have come." She didn't finish the logic she was presenting to Daniel, but it was implied. It was his fault that a dangerous chimera was making the Outsider Kids' home unsafe. He had to make it right.

"Very well," Daniel said again. "But the dogs will have to bathe as well."

Delphine smiled in a businesslike way and only then ran her hand over her face, wiping away the water that was running into her eyes. "I'll bring them over now then," she said.

Grabbing an umbrella, Nessa quickly added, "I'll come too."

The rain slowed during the walk to the house. Nessa, Delphine, and the Outsider Kids reached the side door that led into the kitchen, and the deep, sad purple hanging over the Outsider Kids' group lightened. Nessa had so many questions to ask Delphine, but none that she wanted to ask in front of the group. Nessa also felt a need to speak to Bo as soon as possible. She needed to apologize and tell Bo she'd been right about CM.

Bo kept close to the other kids who, now that they were collected inside, seemed dirtier and rougher than Nessa remembered. Bo met Nessa's eyes, but she did not smile.

It wasn't lost on Nessa that Bo might be mad at her. Their camp had to be broken up, their existence exposed because the woods were unsafe—and why was that? Because Nessa had convinced Daniel to move CM, disrupting the balance.

Everyone was talking to the dogs, trying to calm them, as

Nessa led the group to the outdoor shower on a back deck. She helped hose off the dogs (who were not happy about this) and used old towels to dry them. She hoped Bo could see her making an effort to have this work for the dogs and kids.

Milton produced raw chicken from the Chimera kitchens, and they fed all of the dogs, setting bowls down in the laundry room and watching the dogs snuffle and scramble to eat as much as they could.

Nessa hadn't gotten to know any of the dogs before, but now she could see there was one puppy who could not handle the tile floors—his legs kept coming out from under him. And there was another one with one brown eye and one blue (he was named Bowie, of course) who managed, after finishing his bowl of food, to sneak bites from the bowls of nearly every dog in the room, until Bo grabbed him by the scruff of the neck. "Come on, you," she said in a firm but good-natured tone.

Bo gave Nessa a half-smile then, followed by a warmer look. She half-closed her eyes and shook her head as if to say, "You, I'll deal with later." Nessa felt her mood lift.

After the dogs were clean and fed, the kids brought the pack of them into the spacious laundry room, taking turns comforting the dogs and showering in the extra bathroom in the hall and downstairs. (Nessa decided Nate's and Micah's rooms should be off-limits—Nate didn't like people moving his stuff, and Micah deserved the privacy. And something told her to keep them out of CM's room, even though the door was open and, when they passed it, it appeared to have been cleared out and cleaned by the staff.)

"Here," Nessa said, cornering Bo, standing just a few inches closer than she needed to, passing her a towel. "You can use my room."

"Oh, *yours?*" Bo said, using the same tone Nessa would have adopted before Daniel Host had entered her life. "Your *personal* shower? You didn't offer it to everyone else?"

Without answering, Nessa turned. She could feel Bo follow her. They moved down the stairs, and rounded the corner into the hushed downstairs hallway, lit only by spotlights recessed into the ceiling, the thick carpeting swallowing any noise. Nessa turned, surprising Bo, who nearly slammed into her before stopping, inches away.

Nessa knew she should probably have it out with Bo here and now, admit that she was wrong, that CM was everything Bo had warned her about.

But instead, she just looked Bo straight in the eye, feeling the current that always seemed to come up between them, pushing and pulling with precision.

"You know what?" Nessa said, speaking slowly, seeing by the expression on Bo's face that as weak and woozy and amazing as it felt for Nessa to be this close to Bo, Bo felt the same way. "I think—" Nessa paused again. "I think you're going to really like my shower." Bo smiled, laughed a little. "If you used my shower all the time," Nessa went on. "You wouldn't want to share it, either."

"Well then," said Bo. "I can't wait to check it out."

After tossing her a pair of shorts and a black tee shirt, Nessa stepped out onto her balcony. Looking out over the treetops, she could see that the drops of water that had collected on the leaves had not evaporated. The air remained intensely humid.

Eventually Bo joined her, wearing Nessa's clothes, a towel wrapped around her hair.

"Man," she said, sitting on the bench built into the deck, stretching her bare feet up in front of her to rest on the railing. "I forgot how good a real shower can feel."

"Yep," said Nessa, continuing to look straight out in front, partly because she felt a little shy—seeing Bo in Nessa's clothes was a little disorienting—and partially because she didn't want to get caught up in the stuff that happened between them when they were touching. She had something important to say.

"I was wrong," Nessa admitted. "You warned me about CM, and I didn't listen to you. I didn't want to listen to you." She swallowed. "You can go ahead and say 'I told you so' if you need to. I can take it."

Nessa still wasn't looking in Bo's direction, so it took her by surprise when Bo laughed.

"Seriously," Nessa said. "It's my fault she's out terrorizing dogs or whatever. It wasn't your problem and now it is. That's on me."

"Nah," Bo said. "It's on your dad. You were just trying to fix his mistake."

Nessa turned, leaning back against the railing now, facing Bo on the bench. "Seriously?" she said.

"Seriously," said Bo.

The door to Nessa's room slid open and Delphine poked her head in. "Nessa, there you are. Have you seen Bo?" Delphine stepped onto the deck and spotted Bo. "Oh, hey, you're here," she said, looking from Nessa to Bo and then back to Nessa, giving her a puzzled look.

"I better get upstairs," Bo said. "I heard a rumor there's gonna be spaghetti and meatballs."

"Okay yeah," Delphine said. "That's why I came down. Topher said he needed you."

Bo moved out of the room, and Delphine started to follow her. "Hold up a sec," Nessa said. Delphine stopped.

"Am I in trouble?" she said, as Bo slid the door to the bedroom closed behind her, leaving Nessa and Delphine fully alone. The wind was picking back up. Nessa could see dark, low clouds rolling in and a gust shook enough water off the trees to make it seem like it was raining again. Nessa felt glad the Outsider Kids were safe inside, but with CM still out in the preserve, Nessa did not feel safe.

"Delphine, what were you thinking?" she said. "You can't just keep heading into the woods all alone; and especially this last time, when you knew that CM was out there."

Delphine's forthright pink aura from earlier muted to a deep rose. But her eyes remained hardened. Nessa flinched at the lack of trust she saw there.

"Don't look at me like that," Nessa said. "What you just did. It was insane."

"I didn't think about it," Delphine finally conceded, the hard look cracking a bit. "I just knew—the kids—if they lost one more dog. I don't know if they could have handled it. I had to warn them."

"But you put yourself in danger!" Nessa said.

"I didn't think CM was going to actually come after me!"

"But she did, didn't she?" Nessa pressed. "Gabriel told me Jonathan tracked you guys on the cameras. You missed most of them, but he knew you and CM were together. What happened?"

Now Delphine's face cracked all the way. "Nessa, it was so scary. I kept hearing her in the woods. She was—" Delphine swallowed, hard.

"What?" Nessa prompted.

"She was . . . *laughing,* Nessa. In this deranged, creepy way." Delphine's color heated up to a red-pink glare.

"Kai heard laughing just before Rio was attacked," Nessa added. "I think it was CM who killed him. But Kai never saw her. Did you *see* CM?"

"Oh, I saw her, all right." Delphine had been looking down at the deck railing, but now she looked up to meet Nessa's gaze. "And she saw me. Nessa, it was that same look. This hating look. Like, whatever it is she wants for herself she can only get if I am gone."

"You think she wants to *be* you?"

"I think she wants to be fully human."

Nessa shook her head. "So how did you get away from her?"

Delphine lowered her head. "The minute I saw her, Nessa, I knew how stupid I'd been. I saw what she is. How dangerous she is." Delphine choked back a swallow. "I got very, very lucky. This little coyote came out of nowhere and just—went for her. Full out. Bit her, growled at her, nipped at her ankles, barked and barked until CM had no choice but to step backward. She swatted at it, but the coyote was faster than her."

"A coyote?" Nessa asked. Weird.

"I guess I don't really know what a coyote looks like. This looked smaller than a dog and definitely smaller than a wolf. Smaller than you." Delphine said this last part quietly, like she was still getting used to the idea of Nessa as a wolf.

"I think I know what that was," Nessa said slowly.

"The coyote?" Delphine asked.

"That wasn't a coyote." Nessa pulled up a browser on her phone and performed a quick search, showing Delphine a photo. "Is this what you saw?"

Delphine nodded. "That's it," she said.

"Okay," said Nessa. "Next time you see Dr. Taneda, you should thank her for saving your life."

Delphine looked less surprised than Nessa thought she should have. "Dr. Taneda . . . transforms?" she said. Nessa nodded.

"Into a species of wolf that everyone thinks is extinct," Nessa said. "An old Japanese Honshu wolf. You would have learned about it if you'd gone to the conference!"

Delphine rolled her eyes. "So who was the cat?" she said.

Now it was Nessa's turn to stare. "What cat? The cat was there?" This had been even more dangerous than she'd thought. . . . "Did it—" Nessa reached out to the scratch on Delphine's cheek. "Did it do this to you?" Even as she asked, she was thinking that the scratch was not all it should be. That cat was enormous.

"No," Delphine said, breathless. "The cat didn't go after me at all. The cat went after CM!"

Nessa stared, the world of the woods reorganizing itself in her mind. Was the cat CM's enemy? Did that mean the cat had never been a threat? "But the cat was always—" Nessa started to say, "around when bad things happened," but then she thought about this assumption, challenging it in a way that probably would have made Daniel proud.

What evidence *did* they have that this cat was a predator? None.

"What did the cat do?" Nessa repeated, feeling like the gears in her brain might need to turn a few more times before she understood what had happened out in the woods with Delphine.

"It protected me," Delphine said. "If it ever went for me, I would have been Tender Vittles in no time flat. That thing has claws, Ness. It can jump, like, twenty feet in the air. I don't think, all alone, that little wolf would have been able to beat back CM, but when the cat showed up, it hissed at her, like this—" Delphine made a hissing sound that was truly painful to hear. "CM bolted."

Nessa was so relieved, she laughed. Delphine laughed with her, revving up to make the hissing sound again. Nessa stopped her. "Please don't ever do that again."

How was it possible that an hour after Delphine had almost died, they were out on the deck laughing about it? They'd gotten lucky, like Delphine said. But luck had a funny habit of turning on you.

When Delphine went back upstairs, Nessa pulled on her running shoes. In the midst of everything happening, she had to remember she was going to need to transform. Already her skin was starting to itch. Soon she would feel her throat closing off. Maybe if she transformed now, she'd be able to find CM in the woods. Or maybe she could locate the cat. There were so many open questions.

Slipping out the front door, promising herself she wouldn't be long, Nessa headed for the woods. She leapt forward, preparing to take those few strides where she could transform while in the air, when . . .

Her phone rang. She let the call go. She took a deep breath, feeling the expected shimmer, the sense of power that she'd learned to recognize, and then . . .

Her phone rang again.

Whoever was calling must really need to speak to her. She checked the screen. It was Bree.

She swiped to accept the FaceTime request.

Her friend's face was backlit—mostly what Nessa could see was a triangle of sky behind her. Then Bree moved the phone and the backlighting was gone. Nessa could see the ceiling of Ted's truck cab. It was papered with pictures that Bree had drawn over the years—Nessa would have recognized it anywhere. "Hi Nessa, say hi to Dad!" Bree called out, turning the phone again to show Ted behind the wheel. He nodded, grunted, "Nessa," kept his eyes on the road.

When Nessa was living with Ted and Stephanie and Bree, while Vivian was in the hospital, Ted had looked out for Nessa like she was his own daughter. She felt a bit of homesickness seeing him now. But that was quickly washed away when Bree zipped the phone out to the view from the window: guardrail, mown grass in a roadside gully, scrubby woods beyond. Nessa felt her stomach lurch.

"Look at that. Can you believe it?" Bree said. "Can you believe where we are?"

"You're . . . on a highway?" said Nessa. "That could be anywhere?"

Bree moved the phone back to her face, showing that she was nodding, vigorously, her curly hair shaking. Sometimes it was just so good to hear from a friend, it didn't matter what they said, it would make you happy. "Are you at Mount Rushmore yet?" Nessa asked. Bree and Ted had left for their truck-driving vacation, and Nessa remembered that Mount Rushmore was the first stop.

"No," Bree said. She moved the phone to show Nessa the view again—unchanged—and then shook the phone for emphasis in a way that made Nessa's stomach lurch again, though truth be told, she was so close to transformation, anything could make her stomach feel off.

Suddenly Ted was on Nessa's screen again, and he glanced over just for a half second, then returned his eyes to the road. "It's Oregon, Nessa," he said. "We're about an hour away."

Bree clucked, clearly frustrated by Ted's lack of sparkle in his delivery. "Oregon already, baby! We're almost there! Did you hear that?" she said.

"Loud and clear," said Nessa because, in fact, Bree had shouted it and Nessa had needed to pull the phone away to preserve her eardrums. "We've been driving straight to beat the storm. We're going to ride it out with you."

"If there's room," she heard Ted intone sternly in the background. "I hear your dad has guests."

"Of course there's room!" Bree said. "It's a huge house!"

"There's room," Nessa said, quickly calculating that Bree could sleep with her and Ted could have Nate's room. She felt the excitement of the news slowly begin to eclipse the logistical complications. Was this really happening? It just felt like the best news she'd had in an age.

Nessa heard Ted mumble. "We're gonna need to park an eighteen-wheeler on your property. Is that okay? We can bring our own dinner, we just want to get there before the storm."

"The storm's not hitting until tomorrow morning," Nessa

said.

Nessa could hear the rumble of Ted's voice but not what he was saying.

Then Bree was looking back at Nessa again. "My dad says that you should check the weather again. The truckers my dad's talking to are saying tonight. High winds, flooding, a lot of rain. Cozy, right?"

Nessa laughed. Cozy. "Just get here, okay?" she said.

Bree squealed. Nessa sighed, feeling hot and gross, wearing running clothes but no longer able to run. Or transform. She headed back inside.

CHAPTER THIRTY TWO

As Nessa entered the dining room, Scott emerged from the kitchen, carrying platters of food out to the table: the promised spaghetti and meatballs Bo had mentioned, garlic bread, celery with cream cheese and raisins, macaroni and cheese, a pile of peanut butter and jelly sandwiches, Tater Tots.

"You can cook this way?" Nessa said, realizing how much living with Daniel had made her miss the good Midwestern comfort food she'd been raised on. Daniel's idea of a perfect dinner generally consisted of a four-ounce piece of fish cooked to perfection, every leaf of arugula plated intentionally. Maybe a drizzle of a reduction or a small clump of cheese if you were feeling crazy.

Scott waved a spatula at Nessa mock-threateningly. "These kids are starving," he said. "And with the storm coming, I want to use the electricity while we still have it."

"Wow," Nessa said, feeling her own hunger stirring as she watched the kids shoveling enormous bites into their mouths, slurping glasses of milk, pulling the bowls of spaghetti across the table, holding their forks in their fists. *They eat like their dogs,* Nessa thought, as fat clouds of contented yellows dripped from above like so much melted cheese.

With her wet hair combed back and her cheeks red from the shower, Bo's eyes appeared bigger and brighter, her chin more chiseled, her athletic shoulders cut square beneath her borrowed clothes. She looked up at Nessa, seeming to read Nessa's mind. Bo actually blushed.

Nessa wished she could stay and eat. With Bo. She wished she could eat like a dog. She wished she'd had a chance to transform. She was going to have to find a time . . . and soon. But first, she had something else she needed to do.

The atmosphere back at the lab was tense. The scientists had been served lunch in the atrium, but it didn't look like many of them had had much of an appetite—the sandwich platters were basically untouched. Nessa scanned them raven-ously, keeping quiet as Dr. Ishikawa finished up a speech. He spoke in Japanese, which Nessa couldn't understand, but she could tell that it must be serious because the room was silent. The Haken researchers were listening with great attention, and the Chimera researchers were leaning forward as if they could make sense of his strings of words.

Daniel took the podium next. Nessa leaned against a back wall, near the entrance to the employee kitchen, but Daniel saw her. He made eye contact and raised his eyebrows inquis-itively. Nessa nodded to let him know everything was fine. (As long as "fine" included a literal village of kids and dogs overtaking his perfectly curated home while his science-experiment-gone-wrong mutant offspring roamed the preserve in a fit of murderous rage, intent on harming her near-twin. *Yes, Dad. Everything's just peachy!*)

"Science can be messy," Daniel began. "It can be dangerous, and I apologize to any of you who felt yourself to be in personal danger this morning." He paused to let that idea sink in. "For what it's worth, I did not believe you were."

The blood had been cleaned from Daniel's face, his hair was neatly combed, his pants creases were still crisp, and he must have changed his shirt. "I know that Dr. Ishikawa has just informed you that it is his intention to stay through the end of the conference. I want you all to know that he made that decision based in part on my recommendation that he do so and assurance that we are taking all steps to isolate the chimera and to bring her in safely. I am concerned for her safety as well as all of ours. I remain optimistic that we will again be able to convince her to help us and that many of the investigations we had been eagerly discussing are still on the table. However, I want you to know that should any of you wish to terminate your stay with us, we will arrange a flight for you as early as this afternoon.

"We do hope you will stay through our final dinner together tonight." He smiled. "The musicians from Seattle are en route despite the storm, and our colleagues and guest speakers' flights have been cleared now that the winds are down. Scott will be revealing a special cocktail inspired by all of you.

"Now, let's put logistics aside, and talk about what brings us together. The science."

Nessa could tell from the dull colors hanging in the air over the seated scientists that his talk was having the calming effect Daniel had intended.

Except on Nessa—she couldn't stop thinking about the sandwich platters. She visualized bending down and picking up the roast beef from inside one of the sandwiches with her teeth.

Yup, Nessa thought. *I am going to have to find a time to transform.* Stepping over to the table, she settled for using her fingers, tossing the bread in the trash and stuffing her mouth. It was so delicious, she had another, then crossed the room to where Taneda was leaning back in her seat, sipping a Coke from the can.

"Nessa," Taneda whispered, pushing out a chair with her foot to indicate that Nessa should sit. Taneda, who had been so jumpy this morning, now looked relaxed and calm.

Nessa sat. She leaned forward, bracing her elbows on her spread knees. "I have a question for you," Nessa whispered. Her father was still talking but Taneda was sitting far enough away that they could not be heard. "Why weren't you on the bus?"

Taneda shook her head slowly, took another sip of her Coke. "Don't tell Milton," she said. "I have her believing I was there and she just missed me."

"So you were . . . with Delphine?" Nessa said. It was strange how hard it was to ask the question she needed to ask. She didn't know how to be tactful about this. Bree might have, but not Nessa.

Taneda looked at Nessa, not smiling, not moving a muscle in her face. Nessa recognized this impassivity as wolf-like. The art of not showing was a wolf trick. Luc had been a master at it. It came in especially handy when starting (or avoiding) fights, something you do a lot of when you live in a pack.

Another wolf skill? Circling. Like a boxer waiting for the perfect opportunity, you were always looking for a fight, always aware that the best course of action was to avoid one. "You know," Nessa said, "I was thinking about your research. You and Halliday are studying the Honshu wolf, right?" Taneda nodded. "The extinct one?"

"It's believed to be," Taneda said.

"There have been sightings, though?"

Taneda lowered her cup to the table, the movement slow and precise.

"Were those sightings . . . you?" Nessa said. She couldn't help it. She laughed. Out of embarrassment mostly, but to some extent she was laughing at the absurdity. Was she really accusing this woman of being a werewolf?

Taneda scooted her chair closer to Nessa, scanning the nearby tables. Nessa imagined she was checking out the other researchers—determining if they could hear their conversation. "*Some* of the reported sightings of the Honshu wolf," Taneda said, "were sightings of me."

She leaned back in her seat, seeming to savor the mic-drop moment.

But Nessa was still leaning forward. "Were you the wolf that saved Delphine this morning?"

Taneda nodded again, slowly. "That was me," she said. "And thus I assume it's now okay for me to ask you if you are the wolf whose scent I've been tracking since I got here."

Nessa nodded.

"So who is the cat?" they both said, at exactly the same moment. And though it was frustrating that neither had an answer, they both laughed lightly.

Then Nessa stopped laughing. "CM," she said. "My mom—before she died—she asked me to look after her."

Taneda drew her chin back, clearly interested. Possibly surprised. "I didn't know what she meant, but now maybe I do. I think my mom didn't want—" Nessa gestured at the room,

Daniel speaking about protocol and testing opportunities, basically, farming out access to CM like she was any other scientific resource, another mass spectrometer or particle separator. "I think she maybe wanted me to save CM from this."

Taneda looked at Nessa, impassive again. The same no-commitment wolf gaze. "You knew my mom," Nessa said. "You knew her as a scientist. Do you think that's what she wanted?"

Taneda shrugged. "Your mom is gone," she said. "It doesn't matter what she wanted. It matters what you want."

Nessa shook her head. "I want CM not to be a monster, that's what I want," she said. She thought for another minute. "And I don't want to become a monster myself."

"Some would say you already are."

Nessa rolled her eyes. "I didn't mean the wolf thing," she said.

Taneda blinked slowly. "You know," she said, and sighed. "That cat I saw today. It's like us. There was a smell to it. I think it came from this lab."

"A chimera?" Nessa said. "That's what I thought! It would have to be to get so large. But I never saw anything else mixed in."

"I smelled something human."

"Huh," said Nessa.

"That cat saved your sister's life."

Nessa squeezed her eyes closed. The colors in the air had just shifted to a shade that actually hurt her brain—a noxious, acid yellow. "Why can't CM be like that?" Nessa said. "Why does she have to hate Delphine so much? What will hurting Delphine get her?"

"She is angry, scared, lost. And likely to remain that way. Perhaps she believes that if she kills Delphine she will find peace. Who knows? She is trapped in a body no one can understand, including herself. And on top of that, there has been trauma. Things have been done to her." Dr. Taneda put a hand on Nessa's forearm. "Your mother—you know she was . . . like us? That she had the ability to transform into a wolf?" Nessa nodded.

"She told me," Nessa said. "But only just before she died. She suppressed her transformations."

"Yes," Taneda said. "She did not always suppress them. When she was with me—during your parents' first visit to Japan—we would run together."

Nessa had an instant image—the white wolf that she knew as her mother and a smaller companion. The image took her breath away—every time she heard something new about her mother it brought her back to life a little bit, a feeling instantly followed by the emptiness of remembering that she was gone.

"My mom said she never told my dad that she could change. He didn't know?"

Taneda shook her head. "Never, not even then. And I think you should know that when your mother disappeared, he called me. He asked if I knew anything about her that she might not have told him. I said no."

Taneda nodded like she was remembering. "She never felt

just one thing about your father," she said, speaking slowly, like she was working out a puzzle. "You should know that. She loved him. But she knew him too. She knew that his curiosity would drive him where he shouldn't go. Like today, just now. You heard what he said? The science is dangerous. And yet he puts his colleagues in harm's way. His children, Nessa."

"I can take care of myself."

"Can you?" she said. There was a silence that grew to become uncomfortable. Then Taneda broke it, changing the subject. "The point is, your mother chose you and Delphine. Her children. The children she gave birth to and knew. Daniel chose science."

For a second they took in that pronouncement. Then Taneda spoke again. "He's just a human being. He has to live with his actions. He loves you. All three of you."

"He's been amazing with Nate," Nessa said.

"He's been amazing with CM too," Taneda said. "I know he will help you. We cannot demand perfection of each other. We can only demand commitment."

That struck Nessa as a comment she would need to digest later. All of this did. In the meantime, her father was heading their way with Ishikawa. Joining them, Daniel put a hand on Nessa's shoulder.

"What secrets are you two telling?" Ishikawa said, his voice booming in a way that made Nessa's face go warm. "This is girl talk?"

"Girl talk," Taneda said, rolling her eyes at Nessa, then

saying to Daniel, "You see what I'm dealing with here?"

Nessa took the opportunity that Taneda and Ishikawa laughing together provided to ask Daniel in a low voice, "Have you heard from CM yet? Is she going to be okay?"

Daniel shook his head, almost imperceptibly. "Sometimes her tantrums last a few days."

"It's not her fault," Nessa said. "Dad, I saw the file." It took Daniel a moment to understand what Nessa meant. "I read about Project Typhon. I know what it was like for her."

"But how?" Daniel said. "Where did you get it?"

"That doesn't matter," Nessa said. "What matters is what was in it. You have to stop. This can't go on anymore."

Daniel shook his head and gave her a look. "This isn't the time and place for this," he said.

"Yes, it is," Nessa said. "You're pushing all of this too far. You have a daughter who is in danger—"

"No," he said. "Delphine is safe now. She came back."

"I'm talking about CM," Nessa said. "Dad, there's a storm coming and you're throwing a party," Nessa went on. "Please stop this."

Just then Ishikawa turned to face them.

"More whispering!" he said. "First, girl talk. Now, family secrets. When will it stop?"

Daniel laughed politely, but he didn't look Nessa in the eye. Finally, she gave up trying to get him to. "By the way," she said as a parting shot. "My friend Bree, her dad, and their eighteen-wheeler are going to be here in less than an hour. I hope that's okay."

Daniel raised a hand in the air that was both a gesture of resignation and a dismissal. He turned away from Nessa, throwing an arm over Ishikawa's shoulder. "Before we end, let's make sure we've got some of those data protocols in writing . . ."

Nessa shook her head as she headed for the house.

CHAPTER THIRTY THREE

Bree and Ted looked exhausted climbing down from the truck. "We just drove eleven straight hours," Bree explained, as Nessa led them into the house. In a lower voice, she whispered, "Sorry. My dad gets really anal about bad weather."

"No one expected it to come in this early and this hard," Ted said, pushing his hands into the back pockets of his jeans. They were standing in the foyer, and Nessa was happy hearing the flat tones of Ted's accent—the sound of the people she'd grown up with. Midwestern. No drama.

While Ted was talking, Bree darted into the living room to get a look and then darted back. "Nessa!" she said, putting a hand on Nessa's arm. "This house is full of . . . kids. Are those the—" She caught the look Nessa was giving her, glanced up at her dad, and corrected. "Are those the—uh—hikers?"

"That's right," Nessa said.

Together, they stepped into the living room, which was so crowded it was growing uncomfortably hot. There were people everywhere—sprawled all over the living room, leafing through Daniel's coffee-table books, handling his small tabletop sculptures. Two of them had managed to figure out how to open a hidden panel that pulled back to reveal a flat-screen and a video game console that Nessa didn't even realize Daniel owned—they were playing Madden. Topher was using the electric switch that controlled the gas flames in one of the smaller fireplaces—turning it on, turning it up, turning it off—over and over again.

There were glasses with a few inches of milk and plates of half-finished spaghetti on the floor. A few of the dogs had managed to make their way into the living room. One was eating spaghetti while two others were wrestling by the glass doors to the deck.

"Um . . . where's Delphine?" Nessa asked Topher.

"Dunno," he said. "Maybe downstairs? With Bo?"

The house was layered with noise-canceling materials so that people on one floor were not aware of what was happening on the next, and downstairs was quieter. Nessa realized how used to this kind of peace and quiet—wide halls, thick carpeting—she had become. Daniel had designed his life so that very little would disrupt his ability to think clearly. Vivian's life had been all about unpaid bills, unfinished conversations, and un-defrosted meats needing to be transformed into family dinners within the thirty minutes that followed her return from an exhausting workday. Nessa missed the warmth of that.

"Ladies, if you'll excuse me," Ted said. "I'm going to call my wife, and then take a long-overdue nap."

"Don't forget to shower," Bree reminded him as they headed out the door.

"Yeah, about that," Nessa said. "You should probably dress up too. This dinner tonight's kind of a celebration of the end of the conference." She checked her watch. "It starts in just a few hours."

"You didn't tell me that on the phone," Bree said, her voice rising with excitement. "We're going to be here in time for the party?"

"Yeah, you'll love it. It's going to be in a tent. There's a band."

"Tonight?" Ted said. Nessa noticed an acid green slick of color spoil the otherwise sleepy gray above Ted's head. *Of course,* Nessa thought. *Ted probably wants to attend a formal dinner full of strangers the way I want a hole in the head.* "You're having a tent party with a hurricane on the way?"

"Technically, it's a typhoon," Bree said. "Remember?"

"My dad thinks the storm will hit just after the party," Nessa said.

Ted shook his head, raising his eyebrows skeptically. "I think that's cutting it mighty close," he said. "The only thing staying consistent about this storm is that it keeps coming in faster and harder than anyone thought it could."

Bree was not listening. "Oh, Dad, I knew the denim shirt I packed for you would come in handy. You can wear it with that bolo tie I got you for Christmas. I packed that also."

"Oh . . . great," said Ted as Bree pulled Nessa by the arm out of the room, and Ted slid the pocket door closed behind them.

At 5:45, Delphine texted that she and Bo were coming down to Delphine's room to change. Bo was coming to the dance, but not the other kids.

Bree went and woke up her dad, then came back to Nessa's room and jumped into the shower. Nessa contemplated her closet. She was not much into formal wear to begin with, and even less so at the thought of getting into the tight, green satin dress that Milton had ordered for her, especially when it was hot and raining outside, and she was feeling bloated because all her body really wanted to do was transform into a wild animal.

She pulled something else from her closet and had just wiggled it on over her head when Delphine emerged from her room five minutes after entering it, in a pink lace dress and chunky black sandals that made her look vintage and cool. Bo had been changing in Micah's room and emerged with her hair slicked back. She was wearing a simple black tee shirt, black pants, and red shoes to match her lipstick. She looked—Nessa could think of no better word for it—beautiful. And hot.

Ted looked hot also, but "hot" as in uncomfortable, awkward, and embarrassed. In spite of that, he had cleaned up nicely with a fresh shave, the denim shirt and bolo tie looking sharp with his black jeans.

Bree was wearing a strapless yellow dress that showed off her summer tan. She kept hiking it up under her armpits, the only thing that kept her from looking impossibly beautiful. Thinking of Halliday, Nessa had picked from her closet a cream-colored linen sheath that fell to just below her knees. She had braided her hair. The only concession to dressy shoes she could make was a pair of suede ankle boots Delphine had insisted she buy earlier in the year. She looked in the mirror, hardly recognizing this taller, slicker version of herself.

"Wow," Bo said, taking in Nessa's appearance. "You look beautiful."

Nessa felt her heart move into her throat, the compliment drilling down straight into the part of her that wanted nothing more than to run into the wind, pick up a stick in her teeth, and bite it clean in half.

Just then, a wave of nausea came over Nessa, and for a second she wondered whether she was even going to be able to make it to the party. This was not the kind of night anyone should be going to a party. You shouldn't party when one of your sisters is on the run in the woods, after having violently attacked the other.

She took a deep breath and caught Bo's eye. She answered her "what's up with you?" expression with a nod. "Shall we?" Delphine said, her mouth grim in direct contrast to how pretty she looked, her hair tied back in a simple half-up, half-down style.

Bree threw one arm over Delphine's shoulders, the other over Bo's. "Let's do this, ladies." Nessa joined the line next to Delphine.

"Dad?" Bree said. "Can you take our picture?"

All four girls—for one moment at least—smiled.

CHAPTER THIRTY FOUR

The wind was blowing as Nessa, Bo, Delphine, Bree, and Ted traveled by golf cart to the tents set up outside the guest-house. By the time they arrived, the tempo of the spitting drops of rain they'd started to hear on the golf cart roof had picked up. "Run!" Bree shouted as soon as Nessa had activated the brake. They got wet as they rushed across the grass to the tents, but not disastrously so.

Ted walked slowly up to the girls, shaking his head,

muttering, "I can't believe they're doing this," as he approached.

Nessa put an arm on his shoulder and pointed to Milton with her other hand. "This woman will make it happen," she promised him. "If anyone can do it, she can."

Ted looked at Milton. Ted did not appear to be impressed.

But Milton—dressed like a fisherman in a yellow ankle-length, hooded slicker and knee-high black rubber rain boots—had enacted a characteristic miracle with the party setup. A crew of workers was just finishing the task of rein-forcing the poles with sandbags, and inside the tent, it was dry and cozy. The band was playing some soft jazz, and there were twinkling lights running along the sides of the tents and into the rooflines. The tables were decorated with arrangements featuring some of the unusual chimeric flora cultivated within the preserve and in the lab's greenhouses and suffused with more fairy lights and tastefully placed green and brown velvet ribbon.

Nessa saw Halliday across the room. She was wearing a long black dress with a high white collar—she was talking to Daniel. Taneda was dancing a slow-paced swing with Haruki, laughing. Some of the researchers were undoubtedly still talking about their work—leaning over tablet computers, making drawings on cocktail napkins—but others had caught the mood of the night and were dancing or just wandering around, drinks in hand, marveling at the intricacy of the chandeliers made from lights embedded into vines that appeared to be growing inside the tent, which reminded Nessa more of the phosphorescent algae she'd seen glowing in one of Chimera Corp.'s most subterranean labs than anything as human-made as LEDs.

Nessa looked at Delphine, at Bo, at Bree—they were all still breathing hard from running, rain drops resting on the surface of their clothes and hair. She could see the yellow, pink, and red energy pouring up and out of them. Their mood was infectious. She caught Bo's eye, and something boiled up inside her that she immediately had to quell.

"Go on," Ted said, nodding at the girls. "I'm going to get myself a drink. You go dance. You're only young once." A server passed with a tray of sparkling pink drinks, but Bree shook her head at them, spinning out onto the parquet floor instead with an energy that pulled the other girls with her, as if they were working on the same principles as the raindrops that were hitting the tent flaps individually, then quickly finding each other and running down the sides of the tent as one.

For an hour, they forgot about the storm, about CM raging in the woods to the north of the park, about where they had come from and where they were headed. Nessa forgot about needing to transform, about the fact that every time she even thought about meeting Bo's eyes she could just about feel her skin breaking out in fur. She forgot that less than a mile from this tent, there was a lab filled with life at its most elemental form, viruses replicating themselves, attacking and altering DNA, mitochondria processing nutrients, cells dividing, differentiating, building tissue and organ, bone, tooth, nail, hair, fur. Life changing life. Life locked in steamy incubators. Life frozen, suspended, waiting to find a way to step into the dance.

Nessa felt a hand on her elbow. It was Bo. For a second, they held hands, their fingers knitted together. Nessa pulled away. For another moment, her elbow was linked with Bree's. Delphine and Bree put their arms in the air, bumping hips.

As the song ended, Nessa saw Gabriel enter the tent from the back, where the caterers were starting to bring in trays of plated food. He was wearing a well-cut tuxedo. Bree grabbed Nessa with both hands. "Oh, my god, is that Gabriel? He looks like James Bond."

Nessa laughed. Delphine rolled her eyes. Bree giggled.

But maybe Gabriel is James Bond? Nessa thought. At least for one night? When he saw them, he strutted onto the dance floor and struck a pose that was so funny Nessa doubled over laughing. Delphine had the same reaction—she was grabbing Nessa's elbow and pointing. And then Gabriel was on the dance floor with them, moving in an athletic way, then grabbing Delphine, who couldn't stop laughing as he spun her one way then another, or just watching and clapping when Delphine tried out different moves.

Afterward, Nessa left the dance floor, standing in the opening of the tent to get some air. All night, guests had been popping to this spot to look out into the storm, then returning, squealing after getting sprayed by rain. The cool air came to Nessa as a relief. She couldn't tell whether dancing was helping her manage her need to transform or making it worse. It brought her so close to the edge of transforming, she felt dancing would either allow her to master the urge or give in to it.

Looking out into the darkened lawn at the edge of the woods, she could see that the rain was coming down heavily and the wind was blowing hard. Ted appeared at her side. "I'm not loving this," he said. He checked his watch. "I'm giving Bree twenty more minutes, then I'm getting her out of here." Nessa looked down and saw the tent pole shift a few inches to the right, in spite of the pile of sandbags supposedly anchoring it in place.

"Wow," Nessa said, hugging herself slightly—the wind had gone positively cold now. The temperature must have dropped fifteen degrees. Did her dad know? Nessa checked and saw that he was dancing a polite foxtrot with Professor Halliday.

"Do you think someone should tell him what's going on?" Ted asked.

Nessa shrugged, and seeing that Gabriel had joined them, turned to him. "What do you think? Should we tell my dad that this storm is looking extremely typhonic?"

Gabriel looked out into the night and then he looked at Nessa. He looked at her a second too long, and not like he was trying to think of an answer to her question. He looked like he was sizing her up. He really was a different guy when he was wearing a tux. Assertive. Commanding.

Or was this a food-in-your-teeth moment? *Uh-oh*, Nessa thought. Had she partially transformed? Was there fur on her shoulder or a whisker poking out of her cheek?

She glanced in confusion at Ted and then back to Gabriel.

What did Gabriel want from her? She didn't know. He could want to fight her or kiss her. And given her mood just then—the dancing, the need to transform, the storm, seeing Bo looking so sexy but not being able to grab on to her in front of people—Nessa realized that if Gabriel jumped her just now, she would take him down. The dam that was just barely staying closed would break open and more would come flooding out of her than she had the power to control.

Gabriel leaned over and whispered, "This isn't enough for me." He was breathing in her ear. "Someday, I'm going to make everything your dad has built here look like an anthill."

She pulled away from him. *Did he really just say that?*

That was not Gabriel's way. He was the perfect lab assistant, the brilliant student, the dance-with-your-little-sister, the up-and-coming do-everything-right guy. But now, he was looking fierce and arrogant. He wanted to be the alpha.

"You'll see," he said, and then turned, and Nessa stumbled after him, collapsing into a chair by one of the pillars.

"Who is that guy?" Ted said. "Was he bothering you?"

"No," Nessa said. "He's probably had a little too much to drink. And it's been a long day." Two seconds later, Bree was in a chair next to her. She'd noticed the interaction also, though she had a different take on the "bothering."

"Gabriel looked like he was about to lick you or something. I thought you were into Bo?"

Without moving so much as her shoulders, Nessa rotated her head to look at her friend, unable to form words, or even blink.

Bree patted her knee. "Are you doing that thing where you get really extra feels-y when you need to transform?"

Suddenly, Nessa remembered. She did do that. She laughed. Poor Gabriel. She'd probably just imagined a whole bunch of stuff about him. She shook her head.

Absentmindedly, she scanned the room and saw that Ted was talking to Daniel. Then Milton joined them. She led Daniel to the opening at the other end of the tent. They were watching the rain and the wind. A gust burst into the tent, and knocked down a centerpiece. Milton rushed to put it back into place. Daniel was on his phone. Nessa knew he subscribed to a specialized weather reporting service and assumed, from the furrowed brow, that the news was not good.

The caterers were moving swiftly through the room, picking up the salad course that Nessa and her friends had ignored. Nessa's eyes found Bo leaning against a pole on the opposite side of the tent. Bo. She was glaring. Had she seen Gabriel and Nessa? Was she mad?

Gabriel was alone now, sitting across the room, watching Nessa also. He looked at his watch, then down at the table in front of him. Nessa looked away—to Daniel, who was striding purposefully across the room toward the band leader. When she looked back, Gabriel's chair was empty.

Suddenly she felt a hand on her shoulder. It was Bo. Nessa looked up at her—her amber eyes, her smooth skin, her strong, narrow shoulders. Not thinking, Nessa blurted out, "There's something I have to tell you. I may be acting strange."

"Tell me about it," Bo said.

"I'm not exactly myself right now."

Bo cocked her head and gave Nessa a look. "What do you mean?" she said. Then she swallowed hard. "There's something about me you should know too."

Nessa stood up from her chair, facing Bo. Realizing in that one second how little she knew about her. Like: hometown? No idea. Last name? Couldn't even guess. She trusted Bo, though, she knew that much. She trusted the way she looked. She trusted her smell.

"Is there somewhere we can go to talk?" Bo said.

But just then, the music came to a stop. Nessa saw that Daniel was standing at the center microphone, where the band leader had been. In the absence of music, the sound of the storm invaded the tent, a ripping and a cracking and whistling.

"Okay, everybody," Daniel said, making his voice heard. "The weather seems not to be cooperating. This storm has moved up from what it was projected to be, and it appears to be bearing down on us right now. I'm afraid we're going to have to get you all out of this tent. The vans will be here momentarily, and we'll take this party into my house. In the meantime, the caterers will be packing up the meal and organizing it picnic style. I just want to say thanks to all of you for—"

But whatever Daniel's next words were going to have been, the sound of a giant crack interrupted him. As if in slow motion, he looked up at the ceiling along with everyone else in the tent.

It was easy to see where the sound had come from. One of the poles holding the structure in place must have cracked. You could see that a portion of the ceiling had collapsed, hanging down in a large dimple of loosened tent fabric, chandeliers swinging erratically, one collapsing onto a table, accompanied by the sound of shattering glass and china.

Nessa felt Bo pulling her toward the exit, starting to run. "Let's get out of here!" she said. But Nessa shook her head, pulled her hand away. Where was Delphine?

CHAPTER THIRTY FIVE

"Okay, okay," Daniel said, his voice as calm and smooth as ever. "This certainly adds a new wrinkle. I—uh—Milton—" He got no further. A sudden gust of wind that sounded like a shriek came up then, and the dimpled roofline fell lower, threatening to trap the bystanders who were not scurrying to the side of the tent that was only partially collapsed.

The lights flickered. Once, then a second time. She heard her father's voice but could not make out the words as the microphone was cutting in and out—the sound system must have been affected by the tent's partial collapse. The lights clicked back on and Nessa was just about to breathe a sigh of relief when the rest of the tent began to fall and then the lights went out for good.

The darkness was not total. The phosphorescent chandeliers were still glowing, though the illumination did not cast enough light to show anything but the fixtures themselves.

Nessa raised a hand and felt tent fabric just a few inches above her head, and her hand came away wet. Was the water seeping through? Crouching, she felt her way forward. Where was Bree? She'd been right next to Nessa, and now, when Nessa put out a hand to reach for her, she wasn't there. "Bree!" Nessa called, but there was nothing except the roar of the storm, the wind, the rain. "Delphine!"

Nessa was pretty sure Ted would have taken care of getting Bree out the moment the tent started to give, but the last time Nessa had seen Delphine, her sister had been standing near the dance floor, talking with Taneda. That was at least ten minutes ago.

Nessa headed in the direction of the exit. It should have been just behind her, easy to find. But Nessa walked straight into a wall of collapsed tent. She spun around, heading toward the lights on the tables.

She saw a light tracing through the darkness. Then another. Flashlights. As Nessa headed toward them, their number multiplied so that they now created a diffuse light by which she could make out shadowy shapes. She saw Haruki. Taneda. The flashlights were coming from Jonathan's security team. She could hear Jonathan's guys now, shouting, calling for the scientists to follow the lights, seeking out stragglers and gathering them up. "There are vans waiting outside," she kept hearing. "Please exit the tent and board the vans now."

Nessa spied Brian, the young security team member who had played through the video for them the morning before. "Have you seen my sister?"

He stared at her blankly for a second before he recognized her. "I'm sure she's headed to one of the vans," he said.

Nessa exited the tent through flaps that two of her father's researchers were straining to hold open and was immediately drenched by pelting sheets of rain, coming at her sideways, driven by the wind. It was a struggle to walk, and Nessa covered her face with an arm to protect her eyes from the leaves and small sticks the wind was lifting. She peered through the windows of the lit van—no sign of Bree or Delphine. She saw Milton in her yellow slicker, tablet in hand. When Nessa peered under Milton's sloped, wide-brimmed fisherman's hat and shouted, "Where's Delphine?" she saw that Milton's face was awash in panic. A cloud of caution-tape yellow to match her slicker was pulsating off the crown of her head.

"I don't know!" she said. "A van left already for the house. She must have been on it. I can't keep track. Have you seen Gabriel? I've been looking for him all over." She held up the tablet. "This is waterlogged! It's useless. We're on radios now." She passed the tablet to Nessa and fished a walkie talkie out of her pocket. "Take this one. Channel 7, if you need me."

"You think Gabriel might be trapped?" Nessa shouted back, understanding with horror how dangerous that could be. With rain collecting inside heavy pockets of folded tent fabric, it could crush someone. *Is Delphine in there?*

Nessa turned to go back into the tent. Milton grabbed her arm. "Nessa!" she shouted. "You can't!"

Just then, Nessa saw Daniel supporting Dr. Ishikawa, walking slowly across the slick lawn. Dr. Ishikawa looked like he'd been struck on the head and Daniel wasn't much better off, slipping on the wet grass, barely able to sustain Dr. Ishikawa's weight. She reached them just in time to stabilize them both. "Help me get him to the van!" Daniel shouted, and Nessa took Ishikawa by the elbow. He collapsed most of his weight onto her.

"Where's Delphine?" Nessa tried to shout to Daniel across Ishikawa's body as they pushed against the wind and rain toward the van, but Daniel couldn't hear her.

Finally, they pushed Ishikawa into a seat and he collapsed, wiping his brow. Nessa saw him look at Daniel, shaking his head. "What have we done?" he said. Daniel looked right back at him.

"The storm came early, that's all," he said. "We will get everyone to the house. We'll bring CM back in. We'll get back on track, I promise."

Dr. Ishikawa was shaking his head. Nessa couldn't tell whether he was saying no or just reacting to the storm in some way. Could he have water in his ear, like a swimmer?

"I think we may have gone too far."

"WHERE'S DELPHINE?!" Nessa shouted.

"You haven't seen her?" Daniel said, pulling himself back out of the van, standing in the wind where he could barely stand at all.

"I'm going to look for her," Nessa shouted, heading for the tent.

Daniel stopped her, put a hand on her arm. "Please Nessa!" he said. "Let Jonathan."

"No!" she shouted back at him. "She's my sister and I'm not leaving her behind!"

In the few steps she took, she felt her body aching to make a transformation. She wondered whether, given the chaos, anyone would even see.

But then she saw a flash that looked human disappearing around one edge of the tent. "Delphine!" she called, forcing herself not to transform, following her sister.

Only it wasn't her. When she got close, the figure turned, and Nessa saw it was one of the Chimera researchers, a woman named Heather who worked on reptiles.

"Have you seen my sister?" Nessa shouted at her.

"No!" the woman replied. She pointed. "Milton will know!"

Nessa headed for the opening to the collapsed tent—she didn't have a flashlight but still, she could try to smell Delphine, she figured—when she saw Bree and Ted. Ted's denim shirt was soaked, his bolo tie whipping in the high winds, but he had an arm around Bree, who was limping, holding an arm gingerly. Nessa rushed to them, or tried to rush, pushing against the wind, and reached them as Ted was helping Bree into the van, where Dr. Ishikawa was still sitting in the front seat.

"What happened to your arm?" Nessa shouted.

"A tent pole fell on it!" Ted shouted. "We're lucky it didn't hit her head! It was only inches away."

"Have you seen Delphine?" Nessa asked.

Milton came up behind them. "Nessa, she's likely already back at the house. As long as *everyone heads to the house,* that's where we'll all wind up! In safety."

"Yes, Nessa," Ted said. "Come."

Nessa got into the van. Without Delphine. At the last minute the door opened, and Bo appeared. She was soaked. "Nessa," she said when their eyes met. "I looked for your sister. I went back in the tent. She wasn't there."

Nessa shook her head. "I don't know what to do." Embarrassingly enough, she was crying. Bo crouched down in the aisle next to Nessa's seat. She put her arm around Nessa's shoulder and pulled her in tight. Nessa inhaled Bo's damp but familiar smell. The desire to transform was like a magnet, pushing something out of her body, pushing her toward Bo.

She closed her eyes, worrying for Delphine, worrying that she might throw up.

As the van pulled up in front of Daniel's house, Bo peered

through the rain-washed windows. It was impossible to see much, but still, when Bo said, "There's something wrong." Nessa felt it too. The house was dark, the solar-powered lights illuminating the outdoor pathways were shining, but every other light was off. It looked as if no one was there. The Outsider Kids hadn't gone anywhere, had they? And Scott? According to Milton, an entire van should have already unloaded.

Nessa felt her airways clogging. She rushed to the front of the van, so she could be one of the first ones off. Bo was right behind her. The van door opened, and Nessa was out like a shot, running for the house, pushing against the wind, so strong now that the rhododendron hedges were being flattened to the ground. The trees were bending so their tips touched the roof of the house, wood groaning audibly above the whine of the wind. Somewhere a branch cracked.

When Nessa got inside, she understood why the windows were dark. The power was out.

The house was far from unoccupied. In fact, it was packed. The Outsider Kids were in the living room, some spread out on couches, sitting on the floor, playing cards by candlelight, scratching the bellies of the dogs, almost all of whom had laid claim to the furniture (*Daniel is going to freak*, Nessa thought). A few of the kids were helpfully carrying piles of towels and distributing flashlights to soaked party guests. Nessa spotted Topher taping cardboard to windows. One of the young Japanese researchers was helping Dr. Ishikawa find a seat.

"Where's Delphine?" Nessa said, touching Scott on the

shoulder. He looked back at her with concern, lowering a heavy-looking tray of steaming mugs.

"I haven't seen her," he said, his eyebrows knitted together in concern. "She's not at the tents?"

"Maybe she's downstairs?" Bo asked.

Nessa ran to check, looking in each of the bedrooms. Was it really possible that just a few hours ago, she'd stood with Delphine in this hallway, seeing how grownup she'd become, the four girls feeling they were in a posse, that they could take a few hours off from the stress and the worry of never feeling safe?

When she returned, she found Ted waiting for her, his arms crossed in front of his chest. "Want me to go back and look for her?" he offered.

"No," Nessa said. Ted meant well, but if he didn't know the woods, he wouldn't be safe. "You should take care of Bree."

"Maybe she'll be in the next van," Bo suggested. Nessa clung to that idea. She tried getting on the walkie that Milton had handed her, but no one responded on the channel Milton had set for communication. Or any of the other channels. Nessa tried them all.

When the front door blew open, Nessa ran, helping to greet the last van's passengers, praying Delphine would be among them. She didn't see any sign of her as, one by one, the soaked and traumatized party guests filed into the house. Milton and Daniel were the last to come in. Delphine was not with them.

Nessa rushed Daniel and explained about Delphine. "I

haven't seen her since the tent collapsed."

Daniel put a hand to his forehead. "I've been trying to radio Jonathan. I'm not getting through."

He peered into the living room, as if he'd be able to spot her where no one else had.

"Why are the lights off?" he said. He sounded irritated—even angry. He looked at Milton accusingly and roared. "Did you know the lights were off?"

Milton swallowed. "I'm sorry she's missing," she said calmly. "I don't know why the lights are off. The generator should be running things. There's a backup system for the backup system. They can't both be affected."

"What about the lab's generator?" Daniel added.

"That system does not go down," Milton said. "It was designed by the people who create systems for nuclear power plant cooling—there are only three nonmilitary systems built this way in the world. But perhaps that's where Gabriel is—checking on it." She turned to Nessa. "You haven't seen Gabriel, have you?" she said. "We haven't."

"I need Jonathan!" Daniel shouted. Nessa felt her insides freeze as the room went silent, everyone watching as Daniel, the never-flustered leader, lost control. Daniel hissed at Milton, "I have some burning questions and I need answers."

Milton wiped away some of the water that had been dripping onto her face from her soaked hair. She looked as abject as a person could look. "I'll go down there personally, but I'm concerned for Dr. Ishikawa's health right now." She gestured to him. "He was struck when the tent collapsed."

Just then, the front door blew open again and Jonathan came through, nearly unrecognizable in his black rain jacket, slick with water and dirty with splatters of mud and clinging rain. Daniel nearly rushed him. "Where's Delphine?" he said, looking over his shoulder to make sure that no one was listening to him. "Where's Gabriel? Tell me you've found them."

"I have guys looking for them. There's no word. The more pressing concern right now is the power. I don't understand why the system's down. I sent a few guys to the lab to make sure those are still online. I'm waiting to hear right now," Jonathan said. He looked at his watch. "Two minutes."

Daniel set his jaw, and Nessa stepped forward. "What about Delphine?" she said. "Where is she?"

"I have guys looking for her. If she would stop running away every six hours it would make the rest of our work a bit easier," he added.

"What makes you think she ran away?" Nessa said. "She could still be under that tent!"

Jonathan looked unimpressed. "How many times is this going to happen?" he said. "At some point, keeping my guys out there in a *typhoon*, you're looking at some pretty giant liability. If someone gets hurt . . ."

"She didn't run off," Nessa interrupted. "She wouldn't do that this time."

Jonathan shifted his gaze to look at Nessa and she felt a distinct I-work-for-your-Dad-not-you vibe coming off him.

"Look," Jonathan said. "I just don't know how much good we're going to be out there, looking for her. The gusts are reaching 60 miles per hour."

"Could we at least look at the security footage?" Nessa asked, remembering how they'd used it before.

"Once we have the power back on."

"Then let's get the power on," Daniel said. "And I want a full report of what's happening at the lab."

Jonathan picked up his radio and turned away from them.

Daniel shook his head, his face grim. Nessa saw Bo look over—she was standing by the fireplace with Topher, drinking one of Scott's mugs of tea. Halliday and Taneda came over but could offer nothing but looks of concern and questions no one had answers for. "This storm came up way faster than anyone predicted," Daniel mused.

Nessa thought, but did not say, that he had ignored the forecasts that every trucker in Oregon seemed to have been aware of. He had pushed too hard. He had taken an unnecessary risk.

As they waited for news from Jonathan, Bo left Topher and came to stand beside Nessa.

Through one of the uncovered windows they watched the shadows of trees, their thrashing lit up by the occasional lightning strike. She could still hear the howling too, though the house was so well insulated that the sound was muffled, far off.

"I'm never scared when I'm out there," Bo said. "In here,

where you're protected, that's when fear sets in."

At the word *fear*, Nessa saw only one image in her mind: her sister.

What was Delphine thinking about right now? Where was she?

Delphine belonged inside, with everyone else. Nessa was sure she would not have run off again. Not with the Outsider Kids all accounted for. Not after their conversation that afternoon.

No. Something had happened to Delphine, and Nessa had to find her.

CHAPTER THIRTY SIX

onathan was in the hallway for what felt like an hour, communicating with his team by radio. When he reappeared, Nessa rushed to him.

"Well, the good news is we can reroute enough power to the house to get the video fully operational," he said.

"And the lab?" Daniel asked.

"We believe the power is on."

Daniel breathed a sigh of relief and Nessa rolled her eyes.

He had to ask, she thought. Even with Delphine missing, even though he knew there was no chance that the three backup generator systems in place in the lab would fail, taking down decades of frozen and refrigerated samples.

Daniel caught Nessa's eye roll and must have understood what she was thinking. "It's not like losing a freezer full of steak and ice cream," he said. "Everything depends on those systems."

Jonathan cleared his throat. "The bad news is that we can't get a guy down there right now. A tree fell across the road, blocking access. We're going to have to get out there with chainsaws to clear it."

"So get the chainsaws," Daniel said.

"We will, but it's going to be slow," Jonathan said, his voice remaining calm. "It's dangerous out there right now."

"But we can look at the video?" Nessa asked.

Jonathan nodded, and Daniel, who had been staring at the floor, thinking through his next move, roused himself. "Let's go," he said, leading the way through the kitchen to the back hall.

Jonathan sat at the terminal in the darkened room where the tech named Brian had sat before and turned on the computer, the video screens coming to life to show a half dozen of the thousands of views supplied by the cameras installed throughout the park. Nessa couldn't help but remember that Bo probably knew the location of every single one of them.

Jonathan keyed in a passcode, and then toggled through a few camera views—two inside the tent that must have been set up with the intention of monitoring the party, and another few outside.

It was surreal, given how the party had ended, to see it playing out again—the dancing, the smiles, the greetings. Watching it all unfold, Nessa was more aware of the shaking of the tent, the way it bucked in the wind and strained against the ropes holding it in place. "Get out!" she wanted to warn everyone she was seeing on the screen.

It was also mortifying to see her own self dancing. Ugh.

She saw Delphine—taking to the dance floor, talking to Taneda. So much had happened that Nessa had not noticed while it was going on. She hadn't realized how much time Delphine had been spending with Gabriel. He danced with her. He brought her a plate of food. He leaned against a pillar talking to her, a drink in his hand.

Her mind was caught between hoping that boded well for her. Maybe wherever she was, she was with him, and he was looking out for her.

The other part of her was ready to slam Gabriel against a wall. *She's fifteen!* she wanted to shout at him. *Don't treat her like some girl at a fraternity party.* It was hard not to believe that this was real time, that she wasn't watching Delphine in the here and now.

Then Gabriel was gone, and Nessa saw that Delphine was engrossed in a conversation with Daniel. They even danced together. Nessa looked at her dad, inquiringly. "We were talking about CM," he said. "I was—" For a second, it appeared that

Daniel was choked up. "I—I apologized. She told me she appreciated that."

Nessa saw Delphine dancing with Gabriel again. Delphine must have gotten hot because Gabriel left her side and came back with two glasses. Then he gestured toward the doorway of the tent where everyone had gone to watch the storm, and they walked right out of the camera's frame.

"There's a bit of a blind spot," Jonathan warned. "We don't have the doorway at all."

Jonathan pointed to another view. "This view shows just outside the door. If anyone left, we'll pick them up on their way out of the tent here." He pointed to what looked like an unbroken side of the tent. "They must have been standing in the doorway. A lot of people were doing that."

"Watching the rain," Nessa said. She remembered standing there with Gabriel herself.

Daniel was leaning forward, looking not at the monitor they were watching but a different one.

"Check this out," he said. "Right there." They followed his finger to see what looked like nothing remarkable—another view of the tent from the exterior, but only a small section. For the most part the camera showed only trees blowing chaotically, rain obscuring the image, like static or an Instagram filter.

Then Nessa saw light. A beam of horizontally focused light, showing the raindrops in its path, showing the green in a wide circle of trees. On. Off. On. Off. A flashlight's beam. It looked almost like a signal.

Before she'd had a second to digest what the light could mean, there was a flash of movement on the screen. What happened on the screen next happened so quickly, Nessa could not see what it was. But it was something. Jonathan stopped the feed, moved it backward, froze the image and Nessa saw: CM.

"CM was there?" Nessa said, feeling a wave of heat, a wave of nausea, a shiver pass through her body all at the same time.

There she was—large, lurching, wet, angry. Running from behind that flashlight, straight across the plane of sight, slightly hunched over as if she was protecting her face from the wind and rain or trying to keep low to avoid being seen.

Had CM run into the tent? How could that be? Nessa would have seen her. Everyone would have. Jonathan checked all the other feeds, which had synced with the one he had frozen. There was nothing in any of them. Gabriel and Delphine were still standing at the door to the tent, Nessa assumed. The cameras had not picked up on them moving. But then, when Jonathan switched the camera again, Nessa saw them. Or at least Delphine. CM had her and there was no ambiguity about what "had" meant. CM was dragging Delphine through the rain, one arm wrapped around Delphine's torso, another hand clasped over Delphine's mouth. The images were grainy and dark, but Nessa could see the flash of skin where Delphine's legs were dragging, the trailing pink of her dress. Delphine's and CM's heads were close together, their identical curly hair making them appear as one body dragging its unwanted extra appendages behind.

"She took Delphine!" Nessa heard her voice rising into something that sounded like a wolf whine. Nessa looked down at her hand clutching the back of a chair—it was now marked by a patch of fur the size of a quarter.

It made her dizzy, the thought that Delphine was out there. With CM. That CM was hurting her. That this had happened while Nessa was still under the tent, dancing.

And where is Gabriel? On the security footage, the last she'd seen of him he'd been walking with Delphine to the entrance to the tent. Had he been with her when CM came out of the woods? Nessa imagined him trying to defend Delphine. CM knocking him down. Had he lost consciousness? She imagined him crumpled to the ground, just outside the tent's entrance, the water collecting in the already saturated lawn. He could be in danger of drowning. . . . Was he still there?

"Gabriel!" she said out loud, looking to Daniel, wondering whether he was taking her meaning.

"I know," Daniel said.

Jonathan moved the footage forward a few frames, and then there Gabriel was. The camera had him returning from where he'd presumably been standing just inside the door. He was adjusting his cuffs, perfectly cool and collected. What had Bree said? *He looked like James Bond.*

Was it possible he hadn't seen CM steal Delphine? But how could that be? Had Delphine gone out into the storm alone? Had she turned a corner and been in a place where Gabriel couldn't see her at the moment that CM appeared? No. That wasn't possible. Delphine was dressed up. She wouldn't have gone out into the rain.

Then Nessa remembered the light shining into the trees, the pinprick of a single beam coming out of the woods. A signal. A wave of sudden distrust washed over Nessa until she felt nauseous.

Gabriel . . . no. He and CM had been signaling.

Nessa covered her face with her hands. She felt another wolf whine coming on. She suppressed it.

She turned to Jonathan. "Where is she now?"

"I'm looking," Jonathan said. "They're sticking to the blind spots, the way your sister did this morning—I didn't realize there were quite so many until now. Usually the cameras can pick up on motion and follow it, but with this storm, I don't know . . ."

Jonathan typed in a few more commands. "Let me see if they're coming up in any of the other facilities." He scanned through images that only appeared on the monitor he could see, then said, "Aha. Here's something," as one of the monitors filled with an interior image that appeared impossibly clear and bright compared with the dark, thrashing foliage outside. Nessa squinted. Was that Daniel's lab, the one just next to his office, less than a mile away?

"This one is current," Jonathan said, excitement in his voice. "This is live video. This is happening now."

Daniel leaned forward, his face close to the screen.

There was Delphine with CM and Gabriel. So they were all

together. Delphine was sitting in a chair, her hands behind her in a position so unnatural Nessa assumed her wrists were tied. "Delphine, are you okay?" Nessa said, even though her sister could not hear. CM was sitting next to her. Nessa had the same sensation of dread at her appearance. And Gabriel! Gabriel was leaning over CM's outstretched arm. Delphine's face was contorted. She was struggling.

"What's he doing to her?" Nessa said. "Has he lost his mind?"

No one answered her question. "You have a team out there?" Daniel asked.

Jonathan was already radioing. Daniel put a hand on Nessa's shoulder. "He's got a team out there. This will be over shortly."

"I'll clear the road also," Jonathan said. He looked up at Nessa. "We'll get your sister. My team, they're prepared for this. They have armor, tasers. They've been trained. They'll be there in under five minutes."

Nessa swallowed hard. She'd fought CM before. She knew that even in wolf form she was barely a match for her. Tasers sounded like a good idea.

CHAPTER THIRTY SEVEN

hile they waited for Jonathan's team to arrive, they watched Gabriel draw blood from CM. He turned away, making notes on the vials he had collected, and for a second, CM looked directly into the camera with a look on her face that made it clear she knew the camera was there and that someone was watching.

Gabriel filled a backpack with items from the cabinet. He passed into Daniel's office. Jonathan switched the view—and they saw Gabriel working a monitor, then packing even more vials into bags.

He's stealing? He's stealing . . . CM's blood?

As Gabriel left the office, they switched to a camera outside the lab, watching Gabriel run through the rain to a Chimera Corp. truck.

"Uh, Jonathan?" Daniel said.

"Yeah, I got him," said Jonathan. Nessa heard him radioing other members of his team, explaining that they should stop Gabriel at the gate.

"Stupid," Daniel concluded. "He's gone to all the trouble to rob me. Why would he do that when he knows there will be no way to get out? Jonathan, make sure to close the gates to the park."

"Already done," Jonathan said.

Nessa was only half-listening, her eyes glued to the monitor. "What's CM doing in there?" she asked. She saw Delphine struggle in her chair. She lifted her head and said something to CM that Nessa could not hear. But Nessa could see that Delphine was crying. Nessa felt angry at herself. Why had she listened to her father and Jonathan? If she'd transformed, she would be halfway to the lab by now.

"My guys are thirty seconds out," Jonathan reported, as if reading Nessa's mind. CM went to the computer. Delphine, tied to the chair, yelled something out to her. Nessa willed them both to stay put, to stay in place until this could all be ended.

Then the computer Nessa was looking at began buzzing.

So did Jonathan's phone. And Daniel's. At first Nessa thought it was one of the storm warnings that had been hitting everyone's cell phones all evening. But then Nessa saw Daniel's face. It was like he had just become a two-dimensional object, his features flattened, his cheeks hanging loose. "Oh no," he said. "No, CM, no, what are you doing?"

The video monitors went dark. Nessa felt the loss immediately, in her gut. She reached out a hand and touched the spot where Delphine's image had been.

"Where is she?" she heard someone screech and then realized it was her own voice.

"She shut off the generators!" Daniel roared. She'd never heard his voice sound so low and gravely before. "Jonathan, is the road out of here clear yet? Get me a Jeep!"

But Nessa didn't wait to hear the rest. She was already moving. She ran back through the kitchen, into the living room, and then out of the house. She heard someone call her name behind her, but she didn't flinch or look back.

It was the wind and the rain that stopped her. The storm hit her like a wall, making it impossible to run and hard even to walk. Still, she pressed forward, heading across the driveway, making for a line of trees, thinking she might find some shelter there. Before she reached them, a branch blew down in front of her, striking the ground. Not letting her brain contemplate the fact that the branch could just as easily have come down on her, she forged ahead.

"Nessa!" she heard again, and this time, she turned. She saw that the door to the house was open, framing Bree with Ted beside her. Daniel was there, running toward her.

"You can't go out there alone!" he shouted over the wind. "You'll just make things more complicated for Jonathan! I don't think you understand that."

"No!" Nessa shouted back. "*You* don't understand."

"What's going on?" Bree shouted.

"CM's got Delphine! They're in the lab! CM blew the generator!"

"Jonathan's team should be there by now," Daniel countered. "We need to let them resolve this and focus on getting the power restored to the lab."

"We need to focus on Delphine!" Nessa shouted back.

But Daniel was holding on to Nessa. "I've already put two daughters in danger. I'm not going to add one more."

Nessa shrugged him off. And without intending to—emotions were running far too high, and the moon must have been full for hours—she felt herself starting to transform. Her skin was burning. She couldn't see. There was a feeling of heat and stretching she had never felt before.

This is what it's like to fight the transformation, she thought. And that was the last thought she had in her human state. Once the burning stopped, she was running through the storm, almost grateful for the rain soaking her fur. She did not stop to think about what Ted and Daniel must have made of seeing her transform right there in the driveway. That didn't matter. Nothing mattered but the pace at which she leapt over downed trees, pushed through the thick underbrush heavy with the weight of water on the surface of every leaf. The sodden ground slowed her, and smells were watery and diffuse, less reliable as signposts along the way.

She reached the lab and saw the beams of flashlights tracing patterns in the windows on the first floor. Jonathan's team! They'd made it. She circled the building at a sprint, trying to pick up a scent. It was almost impossible to register anything— the smells of the mountains, the clouds, the wind and rain were scrubbing away messages written in earth and leaf.

Jumping up to look into the laboratory window just as a lightning strike illuminated the inside of the lab, Nessa was able to take in the destruction—drawers had been pulled out, their contents dumped on the floor, tables knocked over. Shattered glass caught the light of something burning in another room. And then Jonathan's team was nearly on top of Nessa, rushing past and around her, not even noticing her white form, they were so focused on the task at hand. She crouched just behind a bench, watching them, not caring if she was seen. The wind was so high, they were gathered against the wall, clutching their hats and jackets, turning their faces away from the stinging rain.

"Empty!" one of the members bellowed into his radio. He was communicating with Jonathan, Nessa knew, even as she felt her heart sink.

Just then, Nessa felt the roar of a diesel engine bearing down on her. She turned to see headlights, a mounted rack of yellow fog lights up above, floodlights below. In the wind and rain, Ted's truck gunning for the front of the lab looked like a ship coming out of the fog. The horn sounded a deep bellow.

Unhitched from the trailer, the cab was capable of meeting and exceeding the force of the storm. Now the doors on the cab were flung open, and Nessa watched with a mixture of relief and wonder as Bree, Bo, Taneda, and Daniel emerged from the cab, and finally, Ted. He was carrying the shotgun he kept there.

Bree spotted Nessa. "There!" she said, pointing. Nessa knew there was no point in hiding. She moved forward, coming to stand in front of the line of allies, sitting, knowing that if she was to find Delphine, she'd need their help just as much as they would need hers. "Nessa," Bree said, crouching down, shouting over the sound of the storm.

She looked up and watched Daniel's face as he recognized her in wolf form. He didn't look horrified or even that surprised. He looked . . . pleased. As if, in the midst of the danger and the destruction, a biological miracle retained its power over him. "That's Nessa?" he said, looking at Bree.

Bree nodded.

"She's, well, you're—" he was addressing Nessa directly now, "the most beautiful wolf I've ever seen."

Bree rolled her eyes. "Whatever," she said.

For her part, Bo didn't appear shocked seeing Nessa in wolf form. She didn't even seem surprised.

Has she known all along? Nessa wondered. *How?*

Then Bo put her hands on her hips, arched her back, drew her chin up, and sprang forward, a lithe, gray cat.

The one Nessa had seen in the woods.

That was you! Nessa thought, realizing now it made sense. The black and gold colors coming off Bo were cat colors. The smell—the familiarity of it. The lack of a story—no hometown, no parents, nothing.

Bounding toward the cat, Nessa landed like a puppy, legs splayed, tongue lolling. Bo looked at her, lifted her chin in an expression of dignified disgust.

Ugh, Nessa thought. *She's* really *a cat.*

But no, she was still Bo. Elegant, strong, smart. Nessa felt safer. She felt so much less alone.

Bree approached and spoke into Nessa's ear, "Delphine's not here. CM still has her. One of Jonathan's guys spotted them on a security camera. They're mostly keeping to the blind spots—apparently CM's as good at threading her way through them as Delphine, but from that one sighting, it looks like they're headed north."

Nessa lowered her head. North. That included the bulk of the park.

"My dad said he'd take the truck up through the park. We'll try to give you backup."

"Go!" Bree said, pointing into the woods. "We'll come after, in the truck!"

As they began to run, a third animal stepped out from behind some nearby trees and began to run alongside them. A small wolf. A Honshu wolf.

Of course, Nessa thought. *Taneda.*

Nessa started to sprint, Taneda just behind her, Bo up in the trees. For a second, even the wind stopped blowing, and she had a sense of what had been missing all summer: a pack.

A weird pack, maybe. The wolves of Tether might not have approved. The wolf up in Isle Royale who used to be Luc might not even recognize them for what they were.

But Nessa knew. She would be safe with them. They would find her sister.

She turned one last time. There was Daniel, caught between the truck and the lab—family and science. Was he going to go with Ted and Bree and assist in the search for his missing daughters? Or would he stay to save what he could in the lab? He'd faced this decision before. Vivian had forced it on him.

Now he was being asked to make it again.

He stood, frozen in place. Nessa didn't have time to wait to see which way he would turn.

CHAPTER THIRTY EIGHT

It wasn't long before Nessa was able to pick up a scent in a relatively dry patch under a pine plantation. It was Delphine for sure, the rubber of her sneaker bottom, the Lavender Mist body spray she wore. Up ahead, Taneda called out. Nessa could tell from her bark that she was directing the chase, and Nessa bounded after her. When she was in wolf form, she didn't do the kind of calculations humans would do—she didn't think about speeding up or slowing down; her brain just showed her in an instinctive way how to track her target.

As always when she was a wolf, Nessa was alive to the woods. She could feel the life inside every bead of moisture reaching her nose. She could hear the way she could taste when she was a human—the layering of sap and the increasingly tight spiral of the wood grain. She could smell the algae threads passing liquid information from one system of tree roots to another.

Even now, even desperate to save her sister, she felt the woods cushioning her consciousness, welcoming her, promising a plan and a system that passed beyond her understanding. Perhaps it was just that she was freed for a time, in wolf form, from this obligation of understanding, this eternal human seeking, grasping, clawing toward knowledge. Wolves only needed to be, to hunt, to mark, to play, to live in the balance of calories ingested and calories expended, to have and raise their young, to follow the rules and to know that however short their lives might be, immortality of any kind had never been the goal.

Nessa didn't know if it was because they were now deep into the woods, or if the storm was starting to abate—the wind definitely seemed gentler. The rain had lessened also, though it was hard to know if it had really been raining so much as blowing water. She could hear Bo rustling in the trees above her, though she had the feeling that if Bo hadn't wanted to be heard, she would not be.

They worked together efficiently—Bo with the advantage of height and vision, Taneda using her small size to dart into holes and under fallen trees. Nessa, meanwhile, knew Delphine. *We must be gaining on them,* she thought. She could smell her sister on a gust of wind.

She could smell other animals too. Old smells stirred up by the wind and rain but also new smells, the fear of animals hiding, the final pheromonal gasps of animals who were not making it through the storm.

The trail she was following began to descend, then they crossed over a stream, and Nessa realized she knew where they were. They were following the hike Daniel had taken Nessa and Delphine on when they had first arrived at the Chimera Corp. campus. This realization was accompanied by waves of both dread and hope. This could be dangerous. After the stream, the trail began to climb. Nessa knew where it was headed: the top of a cliff. Nessa would have CM backed against a sheer, rocky drop.

It would be dark and wet. High winds, slippery rock.

Nessa quickened her pace.

The wind died, and for a few seconds, she thought she could hear Delphine's voice. Not any words per se, just her exhalation of breath. And then she was vaulting over the last scramble of rocks—when she'd been in human form on the hike with Daniel, she'd had to climb this part using her hands, but as a wolf, she scrabbled over the tumbled rocks with ease. Taneda appeared on her left and Bo on her right at the summit, a bald patch of exposed hilltop. A vibe passed through the three of them. They were as motivated to reach the scene individually as they were together. *They* were hunting. Hunting CM.

The wind was still blowing, but the rain had slowed. They could see, standing closer to the cliff edge, the tall form of CM with Delphine in an unnatural position at her side. Delphine's hands must still be tied at the wrists, Nessa realized.

Relief, fear, expectation—these flashed through Nessa's mind at the view of her two sisters, seeming to cling to each other, facing the danger together.

Nessa moved forward, closing the distance, fully aware of the danger of getting too close to CM, of spooking her.

As she crept forward, Nessa took in the scene—the way that Delphine was struggling against CM, the force CM was using to keep her from moving. Nessa couldn't judge how long they'd been in this position but didn't think it could have been longer than a minute. She didn't think they could hold it for much longer.

Nessa could see from the way the scarlets and deep purples they were emitting changed tone that CM and Delphine knew she was there. CM took in Nessa's appearance on the scene with quick glances.

"Stop following me!" she shouted, and her voice actually carried over the wind. "You can't kill me!" CM shouted. "I'm too important. I'm important to Daniel. I'm more important than you!"

Her voice was as grating and high pitched as always. The cloud above her head shifted to a deep color, red like thick blood, nearly dry and getting old. Nessa had never seen that color before.

"Your mother sent me out in the woods to die, but I didn't die! Well, guess what, now it's Delphine's turn. Can she make it on her own? Can she survive a fall from this cliff?"

Nessa couldn't help it. She growled and lunged.

CM took a step back, dragging Delphine with her. Nessa was aware of Bo's tail swishing behind her in low arcs. Taneda crouched, baring her teeth. Nessa didn't know if CM could hear Taneda's growl, but Nessa could. She could smell Delphine's fear and see it too, a cloud of acid green slipping into the air above her head. She knew a word would have likely made a difference. The best she could offer was a barking call.

Delphine looked up, the cloud of green softening. Nessa had the feeling that Delphine understood. It was too far and too dark to see Delphine's eyes, but her face was still and her gaze appeared steady. Nessa felt grounded momentarily by her sister's strength.

But the cloud over CM's head was deepening. Nessa felt it pressing on her. She felt the cloud was smoke, with the power to stifle her own breathing. Fire that ate up oxygen, an asphyxiating force.

"Yes, fire," CM said, reading Nessa's mind. "Fire like Vivian used to burn the lab."

No, Nessa thought, *I have to block her out.*

Or better yet, let her see, she thought. Maybe it would help if CM saw the truth.

Nessa focused on the thought that her mother had sent CM

out of the lab before she burned it. Nessa tried to control her mind so that this was the only thought CM would find there. She focused on the image of Vivian passing a bundled baby CM into the arms of the chimp who had carried the pregnancy. *You were not in the lab when she burned it,* Nessa repeated in her mind.

"I might as well have been," said CM. "She sent me into the woods to die. She believed I would not live without the ventilator." The red cloud deepened to scarlet. CM must have tightened her grip on Delphine's arm. Delphine flinched.

"Do you know how it is to feel that your mother wanted you dead? To be a freak of nature? To be disgusting to people? To belong to no one?"

You could have belonged to us, Nessa thought.

CM's face contorted. The color began to pulse.

Trying not to think through the small feelings of relief that the color change offered, Nessa took a step closer to her.

"You're the white wolf!" CM shouted. "I've been dreaming about you! You're going to kill me!"

Nessa could almost feel CM in her head now, the memory flowing. She tried to shut it down, but the valve was already open.

These were the facts that flowed through the open channel—that Delphine had been dreaming of a white wolf also, having these dreams since Vivian had died. That the white wolf was coming for her.

Nessa saw the colors over CM and Delphine changing, a

calming yellow taming the deep purples and dried-blood reds.

"Don't come closer," CM shouted out into the wind. "Don't make it happen."

Nessa took another step, and she felt Taneda stiffen next to her when CM moved in response, and nearly lost her footing.

"You can't fix anything," CM shouted. "Only Vivian could have. She could have changed this, but she didn't. She left me to die!"

Nessa opened her mouth to protest.

"I remember the fire," CM said. "I remember what it felt like to have Vivian pull me away from the feeding tube. How it felt in that first moment Vivian removed the ventilator, how I could not breathe."

Nessa inched closer. She was nearly within range, where she could reach them if she lunged. Perhaps if she broke them apart, she could hold off CM long enough for Delphine to slip and slide back down the trail? Maybe by now Jonathan would have spotted them on the cameras? Perhaps Ted's truck could make it as far as the trailhead and a group could come up the hill?

Nessa pushed these thoughts out of her mind as quickly as they formed, dismissing each without hope.

"I thought it was your mother. I thought Vivian was the white wolf, but it is you," CM said.

In that moment, time seemed to stand still. Nessa heard Delphine scream—registered what Delphine was seeing now—the view over the edge of the cliff, the white wolf, Nessa, both her best dream and her worst nightmare, the source of fear and strength for both of them.

The cloud above them turned instantly an intense shade of orange and yellow that Nessa associated with the explosion of a bomb—the splitting of atoms—and then it went dark. Gray like ash and then the color darkened, and Nessa was seeing what could only be described as black.

Black, she thought. Irreversible death. Do not intervene. *Delphine's going to die.*

Begging the universe for help, Nessa did something she did not know she had the power to do. She moved the cloud. She pushed it with her mind. She was concentrating as hard as she had ever concentrated in her life, and she was pushing and pushing, feeling as intent as if she were leaning a shoulder against a door. While she was doing this, she saw, CM could feel the force. She appeared to have been immobilized, her face contorted in pain.

Was this what Halliday had described?

She didn't know what to do next, except to just hold on. So Nessa held. She held with everything she had.

CHAPTER THIRTY NINE

As she felt her strength begin to fade, she lost her sense of Bo and Taneda. No longer feeling them beside her. She was alone, with her two sisters, on this cliffside.

Memories began to seep through Nessa's mind. Some of them were memories that belonged to her: She remembered running in Tether, the first practice as a freshman when she'd thought, "Hey, maybe I'll go out for cross-country" and had had the best times of any freshman on the 1K course they ran through the woods behind their house. She remembered when she and other kids in the neighborhood had rescued an injured rabbit, determined to save it, and Vivian had explained to them that the rabbit was going to die.

She lived through memories she had not experienced as well—she believed they were coming from CM: the appearance of a beam of sunlight on the floor of a room in the old house where she had once lived. The smell of soup heating while she woke up from a nap in a crib. Daniel, the feeling of being cradled in a rocking chair, knowing he could make the bad feelings better. She saw the lab burning, the old one, the one Vivian had set fire to. She saw trays of surgical instruments. Bright lights above her. She felt the prick of needles, she saw the faces of the men asking questions, she felt the ache in her knees that came from a brace she was forced to wear for years, meant to correct the abnormalities in her human-animal knees.

She heard Daniel, his voice high with passion, say through CM's memories: "The monster isn't in the code. The code is *in the monster.*"

Nessa continued to hear her father's voice. "CM!" he was calling. Shouting with urgency. "CM!" *What memory is this?* she asked herself, before realizing that this was real. There in her peripheral vision, she saw them: Bo and Taneda, now in human form, leading her father, Bree, and Ted up over the rocks. She did not know how long she had been holding the colors at bay, but she felt as if her mind were trembling with fatigue.

Not releasing her hold on the color, Nessa registered Daniel running. For a half second she nearly felt sorry for him, thinking that he didn't know what he was walking into, the suspended anger and hatred liable to drop on his head at any minute. But then he began to speak, and what he said had such power to calm and comfort Nessa that she realized that by moving color, by taking hold of the colors she could see above CM, she had opened up a channel between CM and herself. Those memories had been CM's. The feelings Nessa experienced now were CM's as well.

"CM, my love," Daniel began, facing CM, his hands out at his sides as if to show her he meant no harm. "I can see that you are hurting. I can see that you are in pain."

He used these feeling words as if he were feeling them as he spoke. Nessa felt he must have in order to speak them this way. She felt warmed and comforted, knowing he shared her pain. Yes, of course, he understood. He knew.

But then she shook off that feeling. *Look at him*, she thought. Or CM thought, Nessa realized. Look at him with his real daughters. The ones he wanted as people, not sick experiments in science. The ones he did not have to lock in cages. The ones he sought out when their weak murderous excuse for a mother had finally abandoned them as she had abandoned CM.

"I destroyed your precious lab," CM said.

"Like Vivian," Daniel said.

"Yes, like her," CM said. "But it's gone forever now, and I helped your enemy."

"Gabriel," Daniel said. "What you both did was very wrong. I must have made you angry. That was my fault. And that will be complicated to correct. But it isn't everything. It's not the end."

"It is," said CM. "I'm ending what you should never have begun."

"CM, sweetheart, you have to let Delphine go," Daniel said. "Let her go now and I won't be mad, I promise."

As if they were her own, she felt CM's fingers tightening around Delphine's arm.

And there was something about that gesture—Nessa knew that no matter what anyone said, CM would not let her sister go.

This understanding was so total, so hopeless, so sad that Nessa lost her hold on the color cloud. She lost her belief in her strength. She lost her sense of herself as a wolf and found herself standing in human form, suddenly bereft. Powerless, while CM was free.

And that's when Nessa saw black. The feeling, the color, they came on her at once, and Nessa felt the cold, sucking dread of it, the color of irreversible death coming off CM.

"Argh!" CM shouted. Nessa and she were no longer connected, but still Nessa could hear in her voice that she was feeling a sudden rush of freedom, which tipped her off balance just enough that Daniel was able to rush toward CM, pull Delphine away, and push her behind him.

Nessa wished she had remained in wolf form. If only she

could have held out a little longer. Instead, she'd let herself become drained of energy and power.

Daniel didn't so much as look at Delphine as keep his attention on CM. His invention, his creation, his daughter. Nessa watched as the two of them confronted everything it meant to be connected. To be human in awareness and animal in body. To want, to need, to love, to understand. To have made mistakes and consider the possibility of forgiveness.

CM stepped toward Daniel as if pulled by an invisible force. Her head was lowered, her shoulders collapsed, and Nessa thought: *She is going to let him hug her. She is giving herself over to him.* She wondered how tired CM was of being a danger to herself and the world. She imagined the solace Daniel could offer.

Daniel stepped forward, held out his hands. Nessa believed CM could see that he loved her. CM was the child he had raised. He took one more step, and CM seemed almost to wilt, losing all her drive, her anger, her hatred, her fear. *Yes,* Nessa thought. This is right. Daniel will save her. He will choose her well-being over research. He will see that family, love, it all trumps his desire to control and to know.

Then CM rose up, drew Daniel toward her in what looked like a hug, bent down, and locked her strong jaws on Daniel's throat. The blood came instantly, flowing freely, staining his white shirt.

CM shook, and Nessa watched in horror as Daniel's body was tossed from left to right before CM released her jaws and sent Daniel careening to the cliff edge, bouncing once on a rock before catapulting forward into empty space.

CM turned to face them, her mouth bloodied, her eyes wild, her hands spread at her side. She looked at Delphine. Nessa saw the cloud of color above Delphine deepen from dark red to black. Delphine looked at CM, tears coursing down her cheeks. "No, please," she said.

CM was unmoved. "You have no one here to protect you."

That, Nessa thought, *is not true.*

Even as a human, Nessa could still fight. With first one step and then another, which led to a third, Nessa was running, putting on an adrenaline-fueled giant push of speed, her arms forward, her hands reaching, grabbing onto Delphine. She pulled her sister toward her, feeling how warm and small her body was.

"Run!" Nessa breathed into Delphine's ear.

"I can't!" Delphine cried. "My foot—it's hurt."

CM had turned by now, her bloodied mouth yawning open. Nessa could carry Delphine, but not far, and certainly not fast. CM lifted her arms, flailing, her hand a hammer, stepping inevitably toward Delphine and Nessa. Nessa could feel the air coming off the cliff edge behind her. She knew she could not avoid CM's blow. CM's rage had no limit, nothing could stop her or save her or save them. This wasn't CM's fault, or Nessa's. It just was.

And then, the clouds must have parted—Nessa had her back to the sky, but she saw the light change on the ground, blue-gray shadows snapping the rocks, gravel, and scrub grass on the ground into focus. The moon had emerged.

CM must have sensed the change as well. She stopped and looked behind her. And in that moment, Nessa felt a familiar course of electricity. It moved through her body as she had come to expect, but faster, as irresistible as a sneeze.

When CM turned, she was not facing two cowering girls. She was facing a warrior mounted on the back of a proud white wolf.

Nessa saw the terror on CM's face. Delphine must have seen it, too, because she said, "No, CM, no. You don't have to be afraid. We won't hurt you. We just want you to stop."

CM did not stop. She lunged at them. Nessa stepped to the side. CM lunged again. Nessa stepped again. She was so much lighter of foot in wolf form. She was trying to lead CM away from the edge. Perhaps if she led her toward the others, she could be contained? Ted had that shotgun. He could shoot CM in a way that would slow her down. If Jonathan's team arrived in time. They could use tasers. There would be hope . . . They could . . .

CM lunged. She lunged again. And then she reached just a bit too far forward. Balance was her weakest point.

As if in slow motion, Nessa saw CM's face register what was happening. Nessa saw the surprise CM must have felt when the rock under her left foot shifted, knocking her knee out so that all her weight traveled to her unstable right foot. There was gravel beneath it, and she skidded on it, pinwheeling her arms behind her, reaching for something to catch hold of. But like a ship listing, once the ballast had been transferred to the bow, there was no way to right her. She slipped, down, down, backward. Nessa saw her disappear over the edge, her eyes locked on Nessa's the entire time.

Nessa froze in place for what felt like hours, but in all likelihood, it was not more than a few seconds. The information of what had just happened began collecting, forming conclusions in her mind. Then she collapsed, not hearing her own sobs as much as feeling the convulsions in her body, the shuddering of her breathing, hating to think about standing, righting herself, contemplating not just what she had done, but the fact that CM was gone.

Delphine wrapped her human body around Nessa's wolf one, her tears landing on Nessa's fur.

Nessa had reached for CM. She had wanted to heal her family. She had failed. But Delphine was there. Bo was standing, behind her. Taneda had a hand on Bo's shoulder. Bree was there with her dad.

Slowly she stood to watch as members of Jonathan's crew hacked through the thick brambles at the base of the cliff, looking for the bodies. Dreading what they would find, Nessa moved her gaze to the sky, watching the storm clouds roll away in the night, the stars emerge, the moon pushing higher and higher, full and bright. She let herself rest beneath its cool, dispassionate, distant glow, not thinking about what would come next. Trying not to think at all.

EPILOGUE

elphine

As soon as they retrieved my father's and sister's bodies from the ravine below the cliff on the night of the storm, I was carried off the mountain and taken to the hospital in an ambulance. It wasn't until the medics examined me that I even realized CM had gashed my shoulder when she first grabbed me outside the tent. Her right hand, which was more like a claw, dug in as she dragged me, and cut through to my shoulder bone. I have to be honest. I never felt it happening. Even afterward, when I knew I was safe, I felt nothing. I should have—the tear was nine inches long, requiring 83 stitches. The doctors said it was lucky that no tendons were severed. I guess that's why they call it shock.

From there the next week was a blur. My shoulder became infected and started to hurt worse than anything I can describe. My temp hit 105 and I started to have crazy dreams: I saw my mom fighting CM on the mountain, first in human form, and then as a wolf. I saw Daniel trying to talk to me on a train ride that never ended: asking question after question without being able to understand that CM had sewed my mouth closed. I would half wake screaming, but I couldn't wake up fully because of the drugs the doctors were giving me, I guess. I do remember that Nessa, Bree or Bree's dad Ted were by my side 24/7—every time I surfaced I would see one of them. At some point, Aunt Jane appeared. She must have flown in from Wisconsin. I remember her cool hand on my forehead. I heard Nessa's voice in the background. A nurse put a straw between my lips and I drank some apple juice. I think that moment was when I knew I was going to be okay.

The fever broke later that day. I slept without dreaming and when I next opened my eyes, Nessa was right there.

"CM?" I asked. "Dad?" I knew what had happened to them. I had been there when the rescue team lifted out their bodies, but still, I needed to hear it.

Nessa shook her head.

I think it surprised her that I started to cry. That I could actually care about Daniel and CM. Well, here's the thing. I didn't care about CM. I was crying for Daniel. Even if the whole reason CM was alive was because of what Daniel took from me, in losing them, I'd lost my chance to have a father.

For CM, I felt nothing, except relief that she was gone.

Seeing me cry, Nessa started to cry also. And she didn't just cry. She lost it so totally. Which surprised me. Stopped my own tears. Throughout everything she'd always been so strong. So there for me. Now I could see that she'd barely been holding it together. We were the same.

Aunt Jane came in when she heard us. She didn't join the total sobfest, but I could see she was affected. Tears streamed down her cheeks silently. I don't know how much she knew about the specifics of what had happened to us, but she could read our feelings. Good old Aunt Jane.

I felt better afterward, like something had flushed out from my system. Nessa did too, I could tell. She rolled her shoulders back, lifted her chin, and announced that she was hungry. Nessa is always hungry.

We went back to Daniel's house the next day. It still did not feel like home to me—never had, never would. Now it was even less homey than usual. I remember looking around and thinking that everything was different. Even the clothes in my closet felt like they belonged to a stranger, as if there was something new between me and everything else.

The funerals had been delayed until I got out of the hospital, but now that I was home, Milton wanted to meet about them right away. Nessa insisted on one thing: that we would have one funeral for Daniel and CM together.

"Daniel made her. He chose her. They should be together," Nessa said. I shrugged. I guess I agreed.

And even if I hadn't, it wasn't the time to pick a fight. Since I'd come to in the hospital, I'd noticed changes in Nessa. Not necessarily big ones, but they added up. She didn't ever end her statements with question marks anymore. She looked people in the eye now. She ate slowly and took careful sips of water between bites, like our mom always said to do.

She was still Nessa—my strong, kind-of quiet big sister with zero fashion sense—but at the same time, she'd become someone else. Someone it was clear could not ever be messed with.

Some of the time, she seemed a little robotic, like she was going through the motions of life. But other times, she'd say something incredibly calm or smart that no one was expecting her to say, and I'd realize she had gotten . . . older.

Her heart had been broken I guess. But the funny thing about healing is that often, with all the time and energy devoted to recovery, you come back stronger than you were before.

Once we met about the funeral for Daniel and CM, Milton went into high gear, pulling everything together and the service took place just a few days later. I thought it would be small—just the four scientists from Haken who had stayed behind to pay their respects, including Taneda and Dr. Ishikawa, and some of the Chimera Corp. staff. It turned out that my father was more famous than I realized and his funeral was enormous. The president of Stanford came to the service, along with at least ten professors from various science departments and a few muckety-mucks from the business school. Even that folklore professor who was a friend of Nessa's, Dr. Halliday, came.

All the Chimera staff left the lab to attend the funeral, some even wearing lab coats. Gabriel wasn't there. Of course. Gabriel was a monster. Maybe even more of one than CM had been.

The look on his face—the smile, the cold glint in his eye—when he pushed me out of the tent into CM's arms, I'll never forget it. Nessa told me he had disappeared into thin air after the storm and they were still searching the park for him although they thought he had left that night. I hope they catch him. I hope he rots in jail.

At the funeral, I noticed Bo had made sure that all the Outsider Kids were cleaned up, although she could not get them to sit with the rest of us. They hung in the trees and on top of rocks at the edge of the clearing where the service was held. Bo's eyes were red from crying when she arrived. She came to stand next to Nessa during the burial and Nessa was glad to have her there, I could tell. She kept looking in her direction.

The service was simple. One of Daniel's students was master of ceremonies, and spoke of my father's "genius" and his "rigor." Whatever. A famous young cellist played Bach's Cello Suite No. 1, which actually got to me because it was beautiful music Daniel had loved, and I couldn't help but think maybe there were other things he loved that we would never know about. Milton read "Sonnet—To Science" by Edgar Allen Poe. She was the only one who said CM's name out loud, when she spoke of Daniel's devotion to his children. Weirdly, we finished up by splitting into two teams and playing a game of softball. It had been Daniel's one specific request, and I was like, softball, who knew? Maybe his love of the sport came from when he was a kid, and not so much of a scientist. I have to admit it was pretty funny watching the president of Stanford run around the bases in fancy loafers with grass stains on his pants.

Everyone left late that afternoon. Taneda came over to Nessa and me and told us the Japanese equivalent of *mi casa es su casa.*

"Thank you for everything," I told her. "I know you helped save my life."

She laughed bitterly when I said that. "Yes, our genetic work is at least good for some things. But not all, I'm afraid."

There were three men in black suits and dark ties who had been at the service but had hung in the back. I assumed they were some sort of security team. Or maybe even FBI. It turned out they were lawyers and were staying in the guest house for a meeting the next day. A meeting with Nessa and me.

"Your father has left the two of you very rich young women," the lawyer who seemed to be in charge began. "You inherit the bulk of Daniel's liquid assets—stocks, bonds, real estate investments—in the form of an irrevocable trust. The other major asset that you inherit are all his shares in Chimera Corp."

It was Nessa, me, Aunt Jane, and Milton on one side of the table, and the three lawyers on the other, and for a few seconds no one said anything.

Finally I broke the silence. "How much is that exactly?" I wanted to know.

The lawyers looked at each other nervously.

"These folders contain a summary of the Trust's investments," the in-charge guy said. The number two guy handed Aunt Jane, Nessa, and me heavy white folders labeled "Summary of Assets of the Estate of Daniel Host."

The third lawyer cleared his throat. "The Trust is worth approximately $700 million give or take a few million on any given day. The truly valuable assets though are the patents held by Chimera Corp. which throw off tens of millions of dollars in license fees annually."

Aunt Jane hooted and laughed. I was speechless. Nessa frowned.

"So we own Chimera Corp.?" Nessa demanded. "Me and Delphine?"

The three lawyers nodded together. Later, Aunt Jane called them "Wynken, Blynken, and Nod."

"Also, per the agreement Daniel signed upon your mother's death, you all three become the legal wards of your Aunt Jane until you reach the age of consent. Your residence will be with her, wherever she should make it. She will of course be reimbursed for your living expenses during that time," Mr. Wynken added helpfully.

"What about Gabriel?" Milton asked. "Has he surfaced yet?"

"Our sources have just located him. It appears that Mr. Morales was a double agent in the employ of Paravida Corporation from the beginning," Mr. Blynken stated. "A deep plant. Here to steal from Daniel Host, putting it bluntly."

"He took our sister's blood. CM's. I saw him," Nessa said. She stood, clearly agitated. "There's source code in that blood. It's where Daniel hid his most important finds."

Milton had gone pale and her hands started to shake.

"We know," Mr. Wynken replied. "And we stand ready to take all steps necessary to stop him, and Paravida, and bring the full weight of the law down upon their respective shoulders."

Nessa mumbled something and ran from the dining room. We could all hear the front door slam a few seconds later. "I guess Nessa's out for a run?" Milton said, vaguely.

I nodded. I had gotten used to my sister running. I was glad to finally know why. Whenever she became deeply upset or agitated, she took off like that. It must have helped to clear her head, to become a wolf for a while.

That afternoon, Aunt Jane told us she'd like us to come back to Wisconsin. Nate and I said "yes" instantly. It took Nessa somewhat longer to agree. At first she wanted badly to stay. I think it was hard for her to let go of the idea that she'd be able to change what happened by running through the forest and thinking through all the what ifs. I wondered if part of her reason for wanting to stay behind was Bo. They'd become very close, very fast. It might have been more than just friendship, I'm not sure. But in the end, even Nessa came around to the idea of leaving. Losing Mom, CM, Dad—she kept talking about how much family mattered. We packed up our things, shipped them ahead and jammed into a rented SUV for the trip back East—me, Nessa, Aunt Jane, Nate, and Micah. (I hope Micah stays with Nate for his whole life.)

Nessa's slow decision-making meant starting the school year a little late. That and Aunt Jane's insisting on stopping at Yellowstone and the Black Hills in South Dakota along the way. Nate was okay as long as he could stay in a Best Western every night. The rooms were exactly the same, regardless of city or state.

Nessa and I agreed to do several things with our money. We sponsored Bo and the Outsider Kids to attend a boarding school centered on wilderness learning in Wyoming. A donation of our August and September patent royalties were enough to pay tuition for four years for twenty kids, and help the school add another 10,000 acres of land to its campus. We also agreed to buy Aunt Jane a really nice new house and have it decorated. It's not a mansion exactly, but it does have a bedroom for each of us plus two guest rooms, one of which has been frequently occupied by Bree. And a jacuzzi. And a gym. And a computer room. Okay, it is a mansion.

Nessa wants to shut down Chimera Corp. but the lawyers say that until Gabriel and Paravida have been prosecuted, it's best to keep it open. She pointed out that CM's last words to

Daniel were: "I'm ending what you should never have begun."

I agree with Nessa that our sister was right. About Gabriel: I hope he invents a creature that turns on him the way CM turned on me. Nessa says that's what's most likely to happen.

But Nessa and I have to let our anger go. Around Thanksgiving, I told Nessa—and she heard me—that it's time to move on. It's been a crazy year. Nessa became a wolf and won States and discovered all that weird stuff about Paravida. Our mother got arrested and became sick and died. After the tumultuous summer with Daniel in Oregon we had the school year, and getting used to a 6,000-square-foot brick house overlooking Lake Michigan with Nate, Micah, and Aunt Jane. Okay, it didn't take that much getting used to—the jacuzzi helps.

But now, Nessa's taking "moving on" to a whole new level. She's getting ready to leave us and go to college. It seems weird that after all those transitions she even wants to go, but the fact is, she does. "It's time, Delphine," Nessa said, as she loaded her second duffel into a new-to-her used Subaru wagon, her new sense of sureness showing through once again. "Stanford needs me."

She smiled. That was a joke. It's Nessa who needs Stanford. Nessa has always wanted to go to college, to become a biologist. That's why she'd worked so hard at cross-country in the first place. But now she's doubly motivated. She told me her goal is to become a scientist like Mom and Dad, but to use her knowledge for good.

She turned to give me one last hug.

"How long do you think it will take to get there?" I asked. She looked up at the sky as if the answers were there and I followed her gaze. The sun was shining overhead, but you could already feel the whiff of fall in the air.

"Three days?"

I hugged her tighter. And handed her my going away gift, a playlist of all my favorite songs. A link was waiting for her via text, but I'd also loaded the songs onto a thumb drive so she'd have something to open.

Pulling off the paper, Nessa's eyes got shiny, like she was about to cry. And I felt a lump in my throat.

"Tunes for the road." I smiled. As I'd put the list together, I'd thought about the different moods she'd be in as she drove, about how awesome she was, how brave, how cool it was to watch her transform into a wolf that first time, how powerful I felt when I rode on her back.

"You know Nessa, that you've been the best big sister and wolf a girl could have. You've watched out for me and for Nate when our parents couldn't—or wouldn't—be, well, parents."

Nessa nodded, taking that in. I think she knows that she did the right thing, that she protected us—me.

Then she smiled, moving past the moment. She got in the car, and I leaned in the window to give her a last kiss on the cheek.

"Now it's your turn to sing."

Sonnet—To Science

Science! true daughter of Old Time thou art!
  Who alterest all things with thy peering eyes.
Why preyest thou thus upon the poet's heart,
  Vulture, whose wings are dull realities?
How should he love thee? or how deem thee wise,
  Who wouldst not leave him in his wandering
To seek for treasure in the jewelled skies,
  Albeit he soared with an undaunted wing?
Hast thou not dragged Diana from her car,
  And driven the Hamadryad from the wood
To seek a shelter in some happier star?
  Hast thou not torn the Naiad from her flood,
The Elfin from the green grass, and from me
The summer dream beneath the tamarind tree?

— Edgar Allan Poe

Acknowledgments

Weregirl: Typhon was a collaborative effort involving many on the Chooseco team: Shannon Gilligan, publisher, Melissa Bounty, editor, Elizabeth Middleman, Elisabeth Lauffer, and Beth O'Grady. After we created the story together, I could not have completed the writing without their support, encouragement, friendship and faith. Dot Greene created yet another show-stopping cover and many sales reps, bookstore owners and librarians were directly involved in placing the books into the hands of readers. Thank you.

As we conceived of the conclusion to the Weregirl trilogy, we were inspired by Greek mythology, the lupine history of Japan, color theory, weather patterns, Buffy, Key Largo, Amtrak. We learned a great deal about the heroic efforts made by teen runaways to survive and hold onto themselves in the process, and hope this story honors and brings light to their collective one.

My family helped me to find space and time to write, as always. Thank you, Mom, Rick, Max, Eliza, Sophie and all my siblings, siblings-in-law, nieces and nephews for reading and reminding me why this is fun.

C. D. Bell
November 2018

A Note on Fonts

The text of this book is Minion Pro, a typeface designed in the 1990s by Robert Slimbach and inspired by the typefaces developed in the late Renaissance era.

Weregirl's title font is True North, designed by Cindy Kinash and Charles Gibbons. Cindy creates fonts and designs from Vancouver, and Charles is the chief designer for the U.S. Copyright office. The other font used on the cover of this book is Ruskin, which was created by Michael Harvey and Andrs Benedek as a commission for signs for the Dean Gallery in Edinburgh.

Every chapter begins with the fanciful letters of Jellyka Castle's Queen, designed by Jellyka Nereven aka Jessica, who has been designing fonts for the past fifteen years, since she was 13 years old.

Jean Bourbon

About the Author

When she's not hanging out with her two children and husband in Brooklyn, NY, you can find Cathleen Davitt Bell writing in a decrepit RV clinging to the side of a hill in upstate New York, trying to teach herself to watercolor, or inventing her own recipes. She received her undergraduate degree from Barnard College and her MFA in Creative Writing from Columbia University, and is the author of the novels *Weregirl, Weregirl: Chimera, Slipping, Little Blog on the Prairie, I Remember You*, and a co-author of *The Amanda Project*.